The Last Legionary Q

On the legendary planet o
and most skilful fighters a
returning from a routine mission,
Moros destroyed. He dedicates his life to finding those
responsible before he succumbs to the effects of
radiation from the dying planet, and finds himself – *the
last Legionary of Moros* – up against the most powerful
forces in the Universe . . .

Douglas Hill is a Canadian who has lived in Britain for
several years. He became addicted to science fiction at
an early age – by reading comics like *Flash Gordon* –
and has remained a hopeless addict ever since. In the
sixties he began reviewing science fiction regularly for
Tribune, at a time when the national press barely
acknowledged the existence of sf. He was for several
years Literary Editor of the *Tribune*, has written many
short stories and has compiled several sf anthologies.

Douglas Hill

The Last Legionary Quartet

GALACTIC WARLORD
DEATHWING OVER VEYNAA
THE DAY OF THE STARWIND
THE PLANET OF THE WARLORD

Pan Books   London and Sydney

First published in paperback in four volumes
under the Piccolo imprint by Pan Books Ltd

Galactic Warlord published 1980

Deathwing over Veynaa published 1981

Day of the Starwind published 1982

The Planet of the Warlord published 1982

This omnibus edition published 1985 by Pan Books Ltd,
Cavaye Place, London SW10 9PG
9 8 7 6 5 4 3 2 1
© Douglas Hill 1979, 1980, 1980, 1981, 1985
ISBN 0 330 28954 3
Printed and bound in Great Britain by
Cox & Wyman Ltd, Reading

Contents

book one

Galactic Warlord

Death of a world
chapter one

He had been walking the dirty streets since twilight first began to gather. The pain streamed like liquid fire through every cell of his body – but he locked it away in a corner of his mind, ignored it, and walked.

There was little to please the eye in his surroundings, and he paid scant attention to them. He was on a small poor unimportant planet whose very name, Coranex, meant nothing to him. But around the spaceport clustered a drab, seedy town, which was a well-known stopover on the main space lanes. It attracted freightermen, traders, wandering technicians, space drifters of every sort. Those were the people he was looking for. Those were the people most likely to pick up the kind of information he desperately sought.

He threaded his way through the clatter and glitter of the streets, thronged with people idling past the tawdry attractions offered to space-weary visitors – everything from ordinary holoscreens to shadowy, semi-illicit drug dives. Methodically he worked his way from place to place, concentrating mainly on the attendants, doorkeepers, bartenders – those in a position to collect and distil the talk, the gossip, of their hundreds of customers.

But he also watched faces in the crowds. Many people turned towards him with a flicker of curiosity – their interest caught for a moment by his tall leanness, the controlled litheness of his movements, most of all by the grey-black uniform with the brilliant, sky-blue circlet on shoulder and upper chest. Sometimes a person would glance at him curiously and then look again, with a flicker of recognition in their eyes. And then the uniformed man would pause, and intercept, and ask his questions.

Always the answers were the same. A shrug, a shake of the head, a negative. Sometimes a shadow of sympathy – most often the blankness of indifference. The Inhabited Galaxy was a big place; everybody had problems of their own.

Undeterred, he kept moving, as he had on a dozen planets or more before Coranex – while the pain clamoured for his full attention, while twilight darkened into deep night. His head remained high and his shoulders square, for a lifetime of military training cannot be erased in a few months – not by pain, not by weariness, not by loneliness, not even by despair.

Despair was near enough, though, ready to overwhelm him. He knew how much time he had left to go on searching. It was a good deal less than the time he had already spent. Yet in those months he had picked up nothing except scattered hints, all of them vague, fragmentary. They were enough to keep him going – but they were never enough to give his search some point, some clear direction.

But he kept on. He had nothing else to do. And the fiery pain in his body was nothing compared to the grim, vengeful determination that fuelled his search.

He was Keill Randor, once the youngest and, some said, the finest Strike Group Leader in the 41st Legion of the planet Moros.

But now he was a soldier without an army, a wanderer without a home, a man without a people.

And he was dying.

The bar was dim, half-empty, squalid, stinking of stale spilled drink and unwashed bodies. The bartender was an off-worlder, from one of the 'altered worlds' – where, over the centuries, local conditions had caused changes, mutations, in the humans who inhabited them. He was dwarfish and stocky, orange-skinned and hairless. But his shrug, when Keill asked his question, was an exact replica of all the others Keill had met in his searching.

'Legionaries? I heard what happened to 'em. Nothin' else. Anyway, got no time to stand around jawin', pickin' up rumours. Got a business t' run.'

The orange-skinned dwarf moved as if to turn away, but glanced up at Keill and changed his mind. Keill's expression had not altered, but something in his eyes told the bartender that, if he moved, he might not enjoy what would happen next.

Keill took out a handful of the plastic wafers that were galactic credits, selected one, and laid it on the bar. 'Is there anyone,' he said evenly, 'who might have had time to listen to rumours?'

The bartender's hand covered the credit, and pondered for a long moment. 'Maybe,' he said at last. 'Freighter pilot named Crask, gets around a lot, has big ears and a big mouth. Might know somethin'.'

'Where do I find him?'

The orange dwarf sneered. 'Blind drunk in an alley somewhere. Unless he's got back to the port. That's where he sleeps – in his ship.'

Keill nodded and left the bar. He did not seem to see the bartender gesture quickly towards a group of heavy-set men slouching over drinks at a nearby table.

A yawning security guard pointed out the freighter owned by the man called Crask. It was a battered hulk of a ship, bulbous and ungainly like all freighters – and it was deserted. Keill settled down to wait. He did not allow himself to hope; he did not allow himself to think about the possibility that Crask might know something, or the stronger possibility that he might be just another dead end. He merely leaned against the ship – relaxed, controlled, infinitely patient – and waited.

The men came soon, as he had half-expected. Four bulky shadows in the dim lighting, which focused mainly on the low buildings across the spaceport's flat plasticrete surface.

They ranged themselves in front of Keill, looking him up and down slowly. Keill had taken in the details of the four in a glance. All of a type – heavy muscle running to fat, soiled one-piece coveralls, hard, empty eyes. Small-time space drifters, who would be more willing to operate on the criminal fringe of interworld trade than off it.

The biggest of the four, almost bald, stood slightly to the front of the others, as if to underline the fact that he was their leader. Keill straightened up slowly, away from the ship, still relaxed and calm.

'I'm Crask,' said the balding man. 'You the one lookin' to hear about legionaries ?'

Keill nodded.

'An' you're a legionary yourself ?'

'I am.'

'Yeah. Too bad about your planet.'

The words were spoken as if Crask were sympathizing over some minor affliction, like a head-cold.

Keill's expression did not change. 'I was told that you might be able to give me some information.'

'I might,' Crask said. 'What'd it be worth ?'

'It depends on what you tell me.'

The big man snorted. 'You want me to tell you what I know – and *then* you name your price ?'

'You won't be cheated,' Keill replied.

'Ain't that easy,' Crask said stubbornly. 'Name us some kind o' figure.'

Keill sighed. 'I've got about three thousand galacs. I can pay your price.' He recalled for an instant the day that he had ripped out of his one-man fighter every expendable item he could – second space suit, escape capsule, some of his hand weapons, spare parts – and sold them to help finance his search.

Crask licked his lips. 'You got that kind of money with you ?'

'Not here. In my ship.' Keill pointed out into the darkness

of the spaceport, towards the central pad where his ship waited, just as he had left it after landing.

Crask's grin was unpleasant. 'Then let's us walk out there just now, an' you can get y'r money.'

Keill shook his head. 'We'll stay here, you'll tell me what you know, then I'll go and get the money.'

Crask's laughter was even more unpleasant. 'You don't get the idea at all. You're a drifter, a nothin'. You don't know nobody here, nobody knows you. So nobody's gonna raise trouble if you're found face-down in a gutter. Happens all the time t' drifters. Get drugged up, get into trouble, get dead. Nobody cares.'

As he spoke, Crask slid a meaty hand into a pocket and dragged out a slim plastic cylinder. A needle-gun – more likely, Keill knew, to be armed with a killer poison than an anaesthetic.

The other three men also drew out weapons. Two had the knobbly metal clubs favoured by backstreet thugs on many worlds. The third, unusually, had a glowing therm-knife, its blade superheated so that it burned, rather than cut, through most materials – including human flesh.

Keill stood calmly, watching, seeming not to move. Yet his body was gathering itself, balanced, ready.

It was almost unfair.

The thugs were grinning. They saw themselves as four tough, well-armed men facing only one man, empty-handed, helpless.

But they were facing a legionary of Moros. A man whose people were trained – all of them, and from infancy – to the highest pitch in the arts and skills of battle. And a man who, in his own right, had been a leading medal-winner for each of the previous two years in his planet's annual Festival of Martial Games. Many of those medals had been for unarmed combat.

So Crask was still in the process of raising the needler when Keill moved.

He gave no hint or warning, did not tense or poise his body. He simply dropped, full-length, to one side.

His right hand met the plasticrete, the arm rigid to take his weight. On the pivot of that hand, his body swung in a horizontal arc, legs scything.

One boot swept the feet out from under a club-wielder. The point of the other boot struck precisely against the beefy wrist of the hand that held the needler.

The crack of bone breaking was nearly drowned by Crask's shriek of pain. As the needle-gun sailed away into darkness, Keill had already flexed his body like a spring and come to his feet.

Crask had staggered and half-fallen, clutching his shattered wrist and moaning. The club-wielder whom Keill had felled was struggling to his feet; the second one had just begun to bring up his club. Keill moved again with the same bewildering speed, slipping under the raised weapon. A rib crunched as Keill's elbow slammed into the thick chest, and the man screamed and collapsed. In the same motion Keill lashed out with his left foot, the blow perfectly timed, burying the point of his toe in the first club-wielder's bulging paunch, sending him hurtling back to collide with the knife-man, both sprawling.

The knife-man picked himself up, staring wide-eyed at Keill, who stood quietly, waiting. Then the therm-blade drew a glowing curve in the air as the man's hand swept back, and threw.

As the white-hot knife spun towards him Keill seemed to sway aside almost lazily. But the other man's eye was not quick enough to follow the movement of the legionary's hand as it flashed up and plucked the knife from the air by its insulated handle.

In a continuation of the same blurred movement, Keill pressed the stud that deactivated the blade, and with a snap of wrist and forearm hurled the knife back.

He had thrown to deliver the knife hilt-first, for he had no wish to kill. The heavy handle made a dull smack as it struck the knife's owner exactly between the eyes. He toppled backwards and lay still.

Keill stepped past the crumpled forms of the two club-wielders and took hold of the collar of Crask's coverall, effortlessly jerking the bulky form to a sitting position.

'I want what information you have,' he said quietly, 'and I want it now.'

'You bust m' arm!' Crask groaned, almost sobbing.

Keill tightened his grip, twisting so the collar bit into the thick neck. 'Your neck will break as easily.'

'Don't – wait!' Crask shouted, half-choking. 'I'll tell y'!'

'Go on.' The steely grip eased a fraction.

'Don't really know much,' Crask mumbled.

Keill's other hand came round, palm under Crask's heavy jaw, bending the neck back. 'After all this, you had better know something,' he said grimly.

'Wait! All right!' Again the grip eased, and Crask, gasping, began to spill out words. 'Just bar-talk, see? Weeks back. When everybody was talkin' about your planet, wonderin' how it happened, lots of rumours.'

'What kind of rumours?'

'Just space talk. You know. One figures a sun flare, another figures a collision with somethin' from space. Nobody knows. Then one fella, freighterman, he says he's seen some legionaries. Two, three of 'em. An' they're like you – lookin' for others.'

'What did this freighterman say about them?'

'Not much. He didn't talk to them. One of them was a real big son – dangerous lookin'. But this fella, the freighterman, he heard that these legionaries were aimin' to set up a base somewhere.'

Urgency made Keill's grip tighten again on the collar. 'Where?'

'Listen, go easy, will y'?' Crask pawed weakly at the fierce grip. 'Somewhere out near Saltrenius. That's all he said – truth. Don't know nothin' more.'

Without a word Keill flung the man aside and turned to move swiftly towards his ship. Despite his control, his pulse had quickened, his eyes were bright, tendrils of hope rose within him. He had heard tales of legionaries being seen, had followed them all down to their ultimate dead ends. But this was different. A fixed base, of course! It was the right thing to do – and then from it send out the word to be picked up by any other survivors from Moros, to gather them in.

Above him the blunt wedge-shape of his ship loomed. He sprang up the ramp and through the hatch of the airlock, sealing it behind him ready for space. Strapping himself into the padded slingseat, he swiftly activated the control panel, feeding details into his guidance computer. Around him the life-support system hummed sweetly into action, and in moments the ship rose howling into the night, on a towering pillar of almost invisible energy.

As he hurtled through the territorial space of Coranex, Keill brought himself under control, regaining his calm, his patience. His eyes and hands automatically monitored the precision of his departure orbit, while his mind just as automatically sorted through the details of the journey ahead. He knew his fuel core was getting near to needing replenishment, but it would probably last. His air renewal, food concentrates and the rest would also hold out. Thankfully, he would need no stopovers till he reached the planet Saltrenius.

Idly he wondered why the group of legionaries – two? three? – would choose such a place. A sparsely inhabited world, in a minor system, well off the major spaceways. What could it offer? And who, he wondered, was the big legionary whom Crask's freighterman had described as 'dangerous looking'?

But Keill had learned long before the futility of asking

questions that could not be answered. Answers would come when he reached Saltrenius.

He had reached deep space now, the planet he had just left receding into a small disc of brightness in the rear viewscreen. The other screens, forward and side, presented the familiar panorama – the unnumbered points of light that made up mankind's Inhabited Galaxy.

Keill's fingertips issued more instructions to his computer, which searched its prodigious memory for the position of the planet Saltrenius, found it, and set its course.

On the viewscreens the points of light shimmered, blurred. The computer was obediently taking the ship out of planetary drive and into 'Overlight' – in which a ship could cross the breadth of the galaxy in only days.

The viewscreens went blank. A formless void gathered round Keill and his ship. In Overlight, he no longer existed in the normal universe. Moving unfathomable times faster than the speed of light, the ship had entered a *non-place*, leaving space and time behind it. Only Keill's inner time sense remained, to note the computer's estimate of arrival at Saltrenius in about ten hours.

He settled back against the slingseat, letting his eyes close wearily. It had been a long and active night – and somewhere, behind his rigid control, the pain still flamed and seared throughout his body.

Yet he felt a fierce gladness as sleep began to close round him. At least there was a chance now that he would find others of his kind, before he died. And perhaps then he would also find answers to *all* his questions. Even, if fortune willed it, a chance to wreak the bitter, hate-filled vengeance that blazed within him more fiercely than any physical pain.

But that thought, all thought, faded as he drifted into sleep. And with sleep, as if from the grey emptiness that surrounded his speeding ship, came the dreams.

chapter two

The dreams were fragmentary at first, as they always were. Broken, fleeting visions of a landscape – of a bleak and inhospitable world, dominated by chill expanses of desert, by towering ranges of rock-fanged mountains.

It was Keill Randor's world – the planet Moros, in the system of a white star on the outer reaches of the Inhabited Galaxy. A harsh world it was, a harsh life it gave to the space colonists who had made it their home so long ago, during the centuries of the Scattering – the time when the human race had spread itself out through the many millions of planets in the galaxy, to seek those thousands that could support human life.

Moros was one of them, for at least it had breathable air, with water and thin vegetation grudgingly available in its central regions. It also had a variety of its own life forms – the venomous reptiles of many weird shapes, the deadly sand cats, the huge, horned mammoths of the mountains, the tangled vine growths that fed on flesh – all as dangerous and threatening as the desert itself.

Yet they had survived, those early spacefarers – survived and adapted to their new home. And its rigours made them and their offspring tough, resourceful, self-reliant people, who even so had learned the need for order, stability and discipline in their lives. There was room for little else, from the beginning, if humans were to survive on Moros.

Yet the discipline was not *imposed*, from above. It was *accepted*, as a religion is accepted, by every human inhabitant of that world. It was taught to the children before they were weaned. It became a basic reality of life.

In the same way, as they learned to order and discipline

themselves, so the humans of Moros learned to fight to protect themselves. Fighting, against the alien beasts, the cruel environment, was also a reality of life, was essential for life itself. The people of Moros taught themselves and their children everything they needed to know for survival, in every kind of deadly circumstance. And that included a strict schooling in forms of self-defence and combat, unarmed or with a wide array of weaponry.

So the people lived, their numbers grew, even finding a share of contentment and satisfaction in the relentless hardships of their rugged, austere lives. But Moros was a poor planet, with little to offer the rest of the galaxy in trade. For centuries it remained mostly alone, unvisited. And all that time its people developed and refined their special way of life, becoming more fiercely independent, self-sufficient, at one with themselves. They also became a planetful of the most skilled, most effective fighting men and women in the galaxy.

Yet the people of Moros never lost that earliest sense of total commitment. In their world, *communality* ruled – co-operation, sharing, mutual aid and support. The people of Moros did not fight among themselves. All competition was relegated to an annual festival, the Martial Games. In their way of life, private greed, destructive ambition, selfish indifference to the needs of others – such anti-social, anti-survival ways were almost unknown.

Slowly, other human-inhabited planets in that region of the galaxy became aware of the uniqueness of Moros. And others saw what the people of Moros had not realized – that theirs was not truly a poor planet, for it had a special and valuable natural resource.

It had the martial skills of its population.

Gradually, the people of Moros were invited to use that resource, to trade with it as if it were minerals or food products. They took their skills out into the galaxy, small groups of fighting men and women, hired – at substantial sums – to fight in small wars on this planet or that. They became what, in an ancient human language, had once been called *mercenaries*. But they felt no shame in doing so, nor was any put upon them.

They learned just how supremely skilled they were, compared to other soldiers in the Inhabited Worlds. And the rest of the galaxy learned as well. Soon more offers were coming in then could be accepted, and Moros began to know a measure of wealth.

With that income – held in common, like most property on the planet – the people of Moros acquired new, up-to-date equipment and weapons. They bought spaceships, from one-man fighters to vast battle cruisers, and created a formidable fleet. They visited other worlds, studied other advanced combat techniques and took them home for their people to master them. So they organized themselves into an armed force that could, if needed, include every adult on the planet. It was a force that became legendary throughout the galaxy.

The Legions of Moros.

Even then, even though any army needs carefully drawn lines and levels of command, the communal spirit of Moros was not impaired. Nor was the order and discipline: discord, slacking, disobedience were unknown, and would have been shocking notions to any legionary. In battle, some led and others followed, but they did so in order that every section and unit would operate like a finely tuned machine.

Otherwise the legionaries shared their lives as equals – working together, going into combat together, celebrating victories together.

And, in the end, dying together.

(Keill Randor's dream shifted, as it always did, and the broken, fleeting images gathered, held steady. From the depths of his sleeping darkness Keill moaned, as the dream-memory rose, clear and terrible – of the words he had heard from his ship's communicator that day . . .)

He had been sent, with the other one-person ships of his Strike Group, on a simple reconnaissance mission. But it was more than halfway across the galaxy, and in one of the most densely populated sectors, where human worlds and their stars clustered like – as the Morosian saying had it – sand fleas at an oasis.

Keill and his Group had come out of Overlight and were moving on ordinary planetary drive towards their objective – a small planet where a local war looked like expanding into a major conflict, and where the Legions had been offered a huge sum to join in on one side.

The Strike Group's mission was simply to gather data, to study the planet from orbit, to assess the war potential, to monitor broadcasts and so on. This data would help the Central Command of the Legions to decide whether to take up the offer.

For the Legions, by then, could pick and choose among contracts. And their ethic, born of their history, would not allow them to take the side of aggressors, or fanatics, or would-be exploiters.

Often they had fought, for less payment, on the side of those defending themselves against just such enemies. Often, indeed, the mere presence of the Legions on the side of the defenders had prevented an aggressor from ever launching a full-scale attack.

As the planet grew larger in their viewscreens, Keill and his group were checking their inter-ship communications link, preparing to slide into an orbit suitable for scanning the surface of this world. They were not advertising their presence, and hoped to go unnoticed – so Keill was mildly annoyed when he spotted a handful of silvery, tubular shapes rising towards his group through clouds beneath them. A subdued ripple of voices on the communicator showed that the rest of the group had also seen the other ships.

'Maybe they're friendly, maybe not,' Keill said to his group. 'We'll ease away on a new course and be ready for evasive action.'

His fingers moved over the controls, programming in the

new course that his group would pick up and follow. He kept his eyes firmly on the approaching ships, waiting for some sign of their intention, some communication from them.

As he watched, twin points of light glimmered from the tapering noses of each of the oncoming ships. Keill clenched his teeth angrily. It was all the sign he needed: he knew an ion-energy beam-gun when he saw one.

'They're firing,' he snapped into his communicator. 'Amateurs – they're way out of range still. Begin new course for evasive action.'

'Do we return fire?' The voice from the communicator was that of young Oni Wolda, Keill's next-in-command and his closest friend in the Strike Group. Her voice was calm, but with a faint note of eagerness that made Keill smile.

'No,' he said quickly. 'We're not here to fight. Evasive action will take us far enough out for Overlight – that'll lose them. Then we'll report back.'

Again he made his course corrections on the control panel. Then he added, 'I'll drop back into rear position and find out who this gun-happy bunch belongs to.'

But before any of his group could acknowledge, his communicator hummed for an instant and then spoke, not in the voices of his friends but in the abrasive, metallic tone of a long-range communication.

URGENT MESSAGE FROM HOME PLANET – MESSAGE FROM HOME PLANET.

Keill sat up, startled. Messages seldom came from Moros to legionaries on a mission, unless the legionaries themselves first made contact, to report or to call for reinforcements in an emergency.

The communicator seemed to have plucked the word from his thoughts.

EMERGENCY MESSAGE ALL LEGIONARIES – EMERGENCY ALL LEGIONARIES

PLANET UNDER ATTACK BY UNKNOWN FORCES

ALL LEGIONARIES RETURN TO MOROS AT ONCE – REPEAT

Shock turned Keill's blood to ice. Moros under attack? It had never happened – not in all the centuries. Who would be foolhardy enough to attack the home world of the galaxy's most renowned fighting force?

But the words had been spoken, and had to be true.

'Emergency procedure!' he shouted. 'Prepare for Overlight at my signal!'

It was risky, entering Overlight that close to a planet's gravitational pull, but there was no choice. *At once*, the terrible order had said – and Keill had no intention of arriving too late, if only by seconds, to be of use.

His fingers flowed over the controls, making his ship ready for Overlight. His hand was hovering over the activator, his mouth beginning to form the order to his group, when his ship jerked and leaped beneath him like a startled animal.

Furious, he glanced at his rear viewscreen. He had nearly forgotten the other ships, in the shock of the message from Moros. And because he had dropped back into the rear position of his group, he had come within range of the others' beam-guns. One of them had got lucky: he had been hit.

It would take time before his computer could produce a damage report – but he could feel his ship slowing, juddering slightly. Behind him the attacking ships were closing the gap, still firing wildly.

All he could do was to take his group into safety – and hope desperately that it was not his Overlight drive that had been damaged.

'Ready to enter Overlight,' he snapped, '*now*!'

His hand punched the activator – and the formless void gathered him in.

Though in Overlight, a ship seemed to be at rest, motionless, while leaping across the unimaginable distances, there were many special stresses and pressures within the void. It was a place from which a damaged ship might very well never emerge.

So Keill sweated and waited for the computer's damage report. It came in seconds, but they seemed like hours.

Damage recorded from energy beam contact   Hull sector eight-A

Keill's heart sank. It was a forward sector of the ship's hull, holding some of the weaponry and much of the navigational equipment. The computer went on, confirming his fears:

Hull buckled but unbroken and holding   One forward beam-gun inoperable   Navigation system planetary drive inoperable

Keill reached for the computer keys. *Report status of Overlight drive*, he ordered, *and other systems*.

The obedient computer replied at once. *Overlight drive undamaged   Other weapons systems undamaged   Life support systems undamaged   Communications system undamaged*

Relief left Keill sagging back into his slingseat. The Overlight was intact. The emptiness beyond space would not claim him.

He touched the keys again. *Estimate repair time for planetary drive and damaged weapons*, he ordered.

E R T for damaged beam-gun nil   Weapon not repairable   Full replacement required   E R T for navigation system six hours

He cursed softly. Six hours! He begrudged every moment that he was in Overlight – yet now he would need to work for six hours before his planetary drive could take him to his planet's aid. And even then he would arrive with part of his armament out of action.

But there was nothing he could do. No one went outside a ship in Overlight. No repairs could be begun until he emerged into normal space, many hours from then.

Gritting his teeth, he fingered the keys again. At least he could occupy himself usefully during the agonising wait – as legionaries were trained to do. *Begin full check of all equipment and systems*, he ordered, *other than damaged sector*.

And he turned his full, disciplined concentration on to the laborious routine check, while his crippled ship plunged ahead through an emptiness as unknowable as the future.

chapter three

(The dream-memories were gathering pace now, and Keill writhed in his sleep, powerless to stop his unconscious mind from forming the images that he had re-lived so often before, in horror and despair . . .)

The time of waiting had ground finally to its end, and the ships of Keill's Strike Group came out of Overlight. They had re-entered normal space at a maximal orbital distance: legionaries did not plunge blindly into confrontations without knowing what they were confronting.

But, as Keill studied the face of the planet Moros looming and filling his viewscreen, all seemed puzzlingly calm and normal. There was a faint, hazy aura round the image of the planet, but Keill discounted that as a possible minor malfunction of the screen, to do with the damage his ship had suffered. Certainly his ship sensors reported no other ships of any sort within the planet's range, and no form of attack going on.

At least, then, his Group seemed to be in no visible danger. So he sent the other ships curving away in their approach path to the planet's surface. And he dragged on a spacesuit, trudged out on to the ship's exterior, and began with desperate speed to work on his damaged navigation system.

The computer's estimate was accurate: more than two hours later, the work was only half done. Keill sweated and fumed as he laboured – yet his hands remained deft, controlled, and his concentration remained complete.

Until it was broken by the warning, from the computer in his helmet communicator, that the sensors had picked up a lone ship, approaching fast from the planet's surface.

Keill was back at his controls in seconds, readying his undamaged weapons, examining in his screen the glinting speck of metal that was sweeping towards him.

Then it was close enough for him to recognize the blue circlet embossed on its side, and his battle-readiness relaxed. It was one of the ships from his own Strike Group – the ship of Oni Wolda.

Keill waited tensely while the other ship slid into parallel orbit. Then, as he expected, the communicator came to life. It did so with a cracking buzz that indicated strong interference – which might have puzzled Keill, had not the words themselves driven all other thoughts from his mind.

'Oni Wolda to Keill Randor Oni to Keill The planet is dead The whole planet Every person Every living thing Nothing left alive on the surface'

The horror took hold of Keill, stopping his breathing, seeming to squeeze his heart in its icy grip. Even the communicator paused, as if Oni herself could not find words to follow the enormity of that statement.

'Attack came with no warning Unknown radiation released over entire planet Central Command set up a beacon, before they died, to warn groups like ours But too much interference Too weak We did not pick up the warning till too late'

Too late? The words echoed in Keill's shocked mind as Oni went on.

'Keill Pain began in us almost at once Knew what it meant Nothing to be done Rest of Group went on to land To die on Moros with the others I came to stop you Don't know if you're safe even this far out'

Keill's face twisted, his body hunched, aching, torn with a grief that was inconsolable, a fury that was beyond bearing. Oni's voice went on, though Keill had already anticipated the rest of the terrible message.

'This is a recording Keill I am dying too Will be dead when you hear this Go Overlight and get away Do not approach planet Nothing to be seen or done Save yourself if you still can Warn other legionaries if there are any alive

'And if you live try to find who did this evil   Avenge us Keill Avenge the murder of Moros'

For a long time – too long – Keill sat motionless, while grief and horror and savage rage tore at his sanity. But in the end some of the strength of his mind and will returned. He forced his numb fingers to the controls, and sent his ship into Overlight.

Only moments later he re-emerged into normal space, far beyond the outer reaches of the solar system that contained his now dead and deadly world. There he set up a beacon of his own, instructing his computer to broadcast a message on a wide and regular sweep, which would be picked up by any other late-coming legionaries and save them from the death-trap that awaited them on Moros.

Then he went doggedly, automatically, back to the labour of finishing the repairs to his planetary drive.

The work was completed quickly. But even then Keill did not move away. Blank and unmoving, he sat and stared out at space, unaware of the passage of time, trying to come to terms with the monstrous reality that had so nearly unhinged his mind. Several times he toyed with the thought that Oni might have been wrong – or that it had not been Oni at all, but some enemy's trick – and that he should after all return and descend to Moros to see for himself.

But he always managed to resist the impulse. It had been Oni's ship, and there had been no time for an enemy to use it for an elaborate deception. And he knew by instinct somehow that her dying message had been real, and true.

Meanwhile his communicator tirelessly broadcast his warning – but received no reply. And a fearful thought began to grow in him – that there might never be a reply.

What if his Strike Group had been the farthest from home of any unit of the Legions? What if they had been the very last to arrive, and last to descend into the fatal aura of the radiation? That would make him . . .

The last legionary.

But as the hours passed, something else – not intuition but physical sensation, from within his body – told him that, even if it were true, that he was the only one left, it was not likely to matter to him for very long.

It seemed to emanate from his very bones – faint, but tangible and definite.

A deep-lying sensation of burning pain.

Oni's gallant attempt to save him had not worked. Even as far from the planet as he had been, some radiation must have reached him. A weaker dose, though, which would let him live a while yet.

How long he would have was not the most important question in his mind. Far more urgent were the questions that bore with them the full power of his sorrow and his rage: *who* and *why*?

But the fact that he would have only a limited time to seek the answers restored him to himself, a legionary again, and galvanized him into action.

He turned his ship away from the solar system of Moros, and began the slow, frustrating process of his search.

From world to world he moved, watching, listening, asking his careful questions. Whenever he was in space, his communicator kept up its patient broadcast. And the weeks, the months, passed uselessly.

Whoever had attacked Moros had covered their tracks well. The news of the planet's destruction spread round the Inhabited Worlds quickly, as such news always did – but Keill could find not one grain of fact or hope within the quantities of speculation and rumour. So he had come to Coranex, just one more stop in his random, desperate planet-hopping – knowing with bitter rage how rapidly his time was running out.

The pain within him had grown steadily more fierce, though

in the legionary's way he had kept it firmly under control, so that no one would have guessed that he was not in perfect health. But at last, on one of his earlier planetary stops, he had spent a few galacs to consult a space medic.

The medic made exhaustive tests. And the gloom that settled on his brow was enough to tell Keill the results.

The radiation – from some altered isotope unrecognized by either Keill or the medic – had settled in Keill's bones. There it was creating cellular changes and breakdowns that were surely, inevitably, killing him.

A month more, the medic had said. Two at the most.

More than half of that month had passed by the time he made planetfall on Coranex. Keill had almost begun looking forward to the end – not only as a release from the pain. It would also release him from the dreams that came to torment his nights, in which he re-lived the terrible day when he thought he was rushing to his planet's aid and found he had come to join it only in death.

And it would release him from the despair which came with the growing realization that his search for other legionary survivors seemed more and more hopeless.

But now . . . hope had revived. If the man called Crask had been speaking the truth, he was only hours from a meeting with other survivors, and perhaps some answers to the questions that plagued him as fiercely as the pain.

(The flavour of that anticipation reached into the dream, filled it, changed its nature. The tense movements of his closed eyes dwindled as the dream images fragmented again and scattered. For the first time in weeks, Keill sank deeper into a peaceful, undisturbed sleep. And his ship plunged on through nothingness, towards a planet called Saltrenius.)

The spaceport at Saltrenius might have been the port at Coranex – the same plasticrete surface, scarred and crumbled here and there from shoddy maintenance and the batterings of a thousand ships – the same low, shabby buildings where bored officials scanned identification, took details, yawningly accepted landing fees.

Even the town clustered near the port might have been transplanted from Coranex and all the other small, unimportant worlds like it. Of course there were differences: the shape of the buildings, the appearance and dress of the people. Saltrenius was grimier than most worlds, for much of the planet was devoted to gathering and processing a dusty residue from the bark of a native plant, used on many worlds in medical compounds. The dust, Keill found, was everywhere – especially, it seemed, on the usual assortment of dingy buildings devoted to the less choosy pleasure-seekers among space travellers.

This time, though, Keill avoided those streets. He was looking for a different source of information – local facts, this time, rather than space talk. Every world naturally had its own forms of communications media – holo-screen or the more out-dated ultravid. The media people were the ones most likely to know what he needed to know.

A few questions, and he located the building he wanted, which housed the local office of the communications network. Squat, grey and dull the building was, and Keill spared it hardly a glance. A few more questions, a few galacs changing hands, and a secretary was going in search of a network newsman. 'Just the man you want,' Keill had been told. 'Knows everything going on in Saltrenius.'

Only minutes later Keill was sitting in a noisy, crowded reception area, with a beaker of some unidentifiable fluid before him, while across the table a grey old man who said his name was Xann Exur was gulping a similar beakerful with every sign of deep enjoyment.

At last the beaker was set down, empty. Keill, his own still untasted, signalled a bartender for another, then looked hopefully at the old man.

Exur wiped his lips, loose grey flesh wobbling at jowl and

throat. 'Sure I can help you, boy. Glad to. Always thought well of the Legions – terrible thing that happened.'

Keill nodded, waiting.

The old man leaned forward. In his eyes shone the eternal hope of a professional newsman scenting a story. 'Any ideas yourself how it happened?'

Keill shook his head. 'If you can tell me what I want to know, I might be on the way to some ideas. But I haven't much time.'

Exur looked disappointed. 'Ah well, imagine it'll all come out someday.' His second drink came, and he was about to gulp it in the wake of the first when Keill leaned forward and took hold of the skinny wrist. The grip was light, but the old man did not fail to sense the steely strength within those fingers.

'I said I haven't much time,' Keill said quietly.

'Oh, right, sure,' Exur said rapidly. 'Like I said, glad to help. What's happened is this . . .'

Keill released his grip and listened patiently as the old man told his rambling tale. Three men in legionary uniform had come to Saltrenius, a month or so earlier. They had picked up supplies, and had spent some time in the town, where Exur had heard of their presence and had spoken to them.

The three had confirmed that Moros was destroyed, and that they might be the last living members of the Legions. But in case they weren't, they had been spreading the word round the spaceways. They were planning to set up a base, so that if there were other survivors they too could make their way to Saltrenius and join their fellows.

'Did they say why they had chosen this place?' Keill asked.

'Nope. And I didn't press them. They didn't mind talking to me, telling me their story, but they didn't like too many questions. Especially the big fella.'

'But did you find out where this base is?'

'Sure.' The old man grinned, pleased with himself. 'On Creffa.'

'Creffa?'

Exur waved a skinny hand in the air. 'One of our moons. Saltrenius's got two.'

Keill looked baffled. Why a moon? Why Saltrenius at all? And the old man read his expression correctly.

'Yep, I wondered why Creffa too. Didn't like to ask, by then, but they told me. There's an old space-dome out there, built when we were exploring the moons, years back. They're fixing it up to be their base. Guess they like to keep themselves to themselves.'

Keill was still slightly puzzled, but at least that part made sense. Moros had, after all, been *attacked*. The attacker, whoever it might be, was still around somewhere. A handful of legionaries would think first of setting up a base that was at once remote and defensible. A dome on an airless moon might do very well.

'Then they're still there?' he asked.

'Sure,' Exur said. 'Been seen just recently, down here. They come down now and then to pick up stuff they need.'

'And there's no doubt in your mind that they're legionaries?'

'Well, they said they were, that's all I can say. And they were wearing uniforms like yours, with that blue circle thing.' The old man paused. 'All except that big fella . . .'

'What about him?'

Exur chortled. 'He didn't seem to like clothes too much. Oh, he had on the pants and boots like yours – but he always went round stripped to the waist. Still, reckon if I had muscles like him I'd show 'em off too.'

Keill frowned, then reached up to undo the top fasteners of his tunic. From round his neck he drew a light metal chain, from which dangled a disc of hard plastic. He held out the disc in the palm of his hand.

'Was the big man wearing one of these?' he asked.

Exur studied the disc with interest. Around its edge was the brilliant blue circlet that was the Legion insignia. Within it, embedded deep in the plastic, were coded shapes – which, to other legionraies, would reveal Keill's place of origin on Moros and his rank in the Legions. There was also a tiny but perfectly clear three-dimensional colour image of Keill's face.

'Now I never saw one of those before,' Exur said. 'Identification, is it?'

Keill nodded. 'Every legionary has one. And each disc is chemically tuned to the physical make-up of its owner. No one can wear anyone else's, and they're hard to forge. Here.'

He placed the disc in the old man's hand. At once the sky-blue circlet began to alter – darkening, shifting, until in seconds it glowed a deep, almost angry red.

Exur stared, fascinated. 'Nice bit of work, that. Interesting.' He handed back the disc – which returned to its normal blue as Keill took it and slipped the chain round his neck again. 'Anyway,' the old man went on, 'the big fella definitely didn't have one of them.'

'Are you sure?'

'Course. Man's got a chest like a wall. Didn't have any decorations on it.' Again a pause. 'Except for the markings.'

'Markings?'

'Yep – like tattoos, maybe, or like scars, except they were too neat and even. Raised ridges of skin, like – one round his neck, one round his belly.' A skinny finger demonstrated. 'Legionaries have them, too?'

'No,' Keill said thoughtfully. 'Nothing like that.'

The old man's eyes sparkled with curiosity. 'Are you thinking that these fellas aren't real legionaries?'

'I don't know what I'm thinking. But this big man *did* say he was . . . ?'

'Yep. He did most of the talking. Lot of laughing, too. Not very pleasant. Made me downright nervous – I was glad to get away, I can tell you.'

Keill nodded, and stood up. 'I'm grateful for your help, Xann Exur – more than I can say. I wish I'd met you sooner.

33

I'm deeply in your debt, and I doubt if I'll be able to repay it.'
As if to echo his words, the pain stabbed through him more savagely than ever.

But the old man noticed nothing. 'My pleasure, son, and my job. I'm a newsman, and you could be news. If you find out those fellas are fakes, let me know, will you?'

Keill smiled grimly. 'If they really *are* legionaries, I'll let you know. If they're not – then I'll probably be too busy, for a while.'

chapter four

Keill went back to the spaceport as rapidly as he could, fighting to keep his inner calm and control despite the puzzlement and urgency that chafed at him. Questions upon questions, mysteries upon mysteries heaped themselves up in his mind, with one especially looming largest and most disturbing.

Were the three men legionaries?

If they were, a huge range of possibilities – and other questions – would open up, mainly to do with the murder of Moros and the unknown destroyer.

But if they were *not* . . . then what were they up to?

And what could he do about it?

He knew it would be a journey of less than an hour from lift-off to landing on the moon Creffa, where some at least of these questions would be answered. But he knew also that he would resent the passage of each one of those minutes.

Time was now his most precious possession. Every minute gone was another step towards the day – soon now, as the medic had said – when the pain would grow strong enough to batter down his iron control, when the radiation within him would overwhelm and quench his life.

Every delay, however brief, was a robbery – making it even less likely that he would find the answers he needed before that final moment came.

So another man – a man without the inner discipline of a legionary – might have gone wholly berserk with fury and frustration if he had found what Keill found at the spaceport.

He could not enter his ship.

Someone had fixed an electromolecular seal across the hatch

of the airlock – a plain metal band, but as secure and unopenable a fastening as could be found in the galaxy.

Someone did not want Keill Randor to leave.

The senior security officer of the spaceport was not inclined to be helpful.

'Can't tell you any more.' The official was a grey-faced Saltrenian with a permanently sour expression, made sourer by the visible anger behind Keill's questions. 'Like I said, official orders came – for me to seal your ship and give you that.'

He pointed to the paper Keill held. What it contained had only served to deepen the mystery. The paper had announced, unnecessarily, the official sealing of his ship. And it had 'requested' Keill to take a room at a spacer hostel near the port, and wait there to be contacted on 'a matter of some urgency'.

The paper did not say who would make the contact. But it was signed by the Deputy Co-ordinator of the Saltrenian Civil Control.

'I've broken no laws on this planet,' Keill said fiercely. 'I've been here barely a day – now I simply want to leave. Peacefully. Your people have no right to stop me.'

'I've got my orders,' said the officer, 'and that's all there is.' He let one hand stray meaningfully near the weapon at his side – another needle-gun, Keill had seen. 'If you want to argue, and talk about rights, take it up with the CC. Your ship stays sealed till they say otherwise.'

'I will.' Keill turned away, then looked back and said almost casually, 'But you have the key here?'

'No concern of yours where it is,' the official growled. 'Not till the CC says otherwise.'

Keill nodded and left the room, hiding his grim satisfaction. Before the officer had replied, his eyes had briefly flicked sideways, towards a locked metal cabinet against one wall. The man had probably not even realized that he had made the movement. But it was all Keill needed.

Leaving the spaceport building, he glanced for a moment across the empty plasticrete towards where his ship stood. The distance was considerable, for the main pads were well away from the buildings. But Keill's eyes could make out enough details – and what he saw made him stop abruptly and stare.

Four men had gathered around his ship. One of the men was a uniformed spaceport security guard. Two of the others wore different uniforms, which Keill recognized at once despite their abundant covering of Saltrenian dust. Legion uniforms.

And the fourth man . . .

At least a head taller than the others, massively built. And naked to the waist.

The three men seemed to be examining Keill's ship, while chatting with the security guard. And the big man was laughing.

Keill had taken three running strides across the plasticrete before a sharp voice behind him brought him up short.

'Randor!'

He turned and saw the senior security officer in the doorway.

'My orders say you're to be kept away from that ship,' he growled. 'I've put a man on it. Don't get any ideas.'

Anger swelled within Keill, but his voice was cool. 'There are some men out there,' he said, pointing, 'who I must talk to.'

The officer narrowed his eyes and peered.

'Do you know them?' Keill asked quickly.

'Yes – think so.' The officer nodded. 'Those're the legionaries who've set up on Creffa.' He looked down at Keill, some of the sourness leaving his eyes. 'Guess I can understand you wanting to see them. Go on, then – just stay away from the ship.'

Keill whirled and ran. But in that moment – whether by some instinct or accident – the half-naked giant in the distance turned, and caught sight of the figure sprinting towards them.

Immediately the huge man spoke to his companions – who turned, looked, and began to walk away. They did not seem to hurry, but they did not stroll. And it was only a short distance to the bulky cylinder of the space cruiser that stood waiting on the next pad.

Despite his desperate speed, Keill had covered only half the distance when the three men vanished through the airlock of their ship. But not before the big man had paused for one more look back at Keill.

Keill was able to see him more closely then. He could see the vast muscles swelling beneath bronze skin. And, faintly, the peculiar markings that the newsman had mentioned – the narrow, raised bands encircling the thick throat, the ridged belly.

He could also see the mockery behind the big man's laughter.

Then the hatch closed, and Keill was left to watch helplessly as, in seconds, the cruiser lifted away.

He might have screamed with rage and desperation. He might have rushed to his own ship to tear with crazed hopelessness at the unbreakable seal.

Instead, he turned on his heel and walked calmly away to find the offices of the Civil Control.

The afternoon was beginning to wane by the time he had found his way. And there, too, he met frustration. The uniformed Civil Control officer in the front office was less sour than the man at the spaceport, but no more helpful. He knew nothing about the seal on Keill's ship, or the reasons for it. The Deputy Co-ordinator was not available. No one else would be able to tell Keill anything.

'Why don't you just do what the letter says?' the officer suggested. 'Go to the hostel and wait. The Deputy will be along. It's all you can do.'

Again the helplessness swept over Keill. Again deep anger

throbbed within him. Again he was icily impassive as he turned and left the offices.

Through the gathering dusk he located the spacer hostel that the official letter had named, and took a room – indifferent to its drab, functional, none-too-clean interior. And there he waited.

It was all he could do.

He was standing at the open window of his second-floor room, ignoring the dust-laden breeze, staring out at the two moons that had risen into the night sky of Saltrenius, when the knock came. He flung open the door before the startled man who had knocked had even begun to lower his hand.

The Deputy Co-ordinator was a civil servant through and through. His name was Shenn, and he was small, grey as any Saltrenian, precise in movements and speech. Less small and less neat were the two large uniformed men behind him, with the metallic 'CC' gleaming on cap and collar. But the Deputy left them outside, at the door, and even managed a precise little smile as he greeted Keill.

The smile faded somewhat when Keill told him, in terms all the more unnerving for the frozen, knife-edged tone of voice, what he thought of his situation, the CC, and Saltrenius in general.

'I fear I can explain very little to you,' Shenn said at last. 'Orders came to me that you were not to leave the planet.'

'Orders from whom?' Keill demanded.

'Higher authority. In the government.'

'And why,' Keill wanted to know, 'should your government want to keep me here against my will?'

'It seems that they received a request.' Shenn quickly lifted a small hand before Keill could interrupt. 'I do not know its origin – it is not for me to know. But someone of, apparently, great importance, off-world, is sending a message to Saltrenius for you. On a matter of grave urgency. We were requested to ensure that you remained, till this message arrives.'

'Nothing more?'

'Nothing.'

'No idea what this mysterious message is about, or who sent it?'

'None.'

'Then,' Keill said, 'you are wasting my time.'

He took hold of the Deputy before the little man could even draw breath to shout. One hand over the mouth to silence him, one hand clamped on his neck, thumb pressing the carotid artery that feeds blood to the brain. In seconds Deputy Shenn crumpled into unconsciousness, with not a sound to alert the waiting guards outside.

Keill dumped the man on the bed, knowing that he would awaken, unharmed, almost as quickly as he had collapsed. But for a second he paused, curiosity tugging at him. He wanted very much to know what lay behind the sealing of his ship, and who was the mystery person with so much influence, who was sending an unknown message. Yet he wanted even more to get off-planet, to find the three men who said they were legionaries.

The lack of time demanded that a choice must be made. And Keill's choice was obvious.

Perhaps he would try, afterwards, to contact Saltrenius and learn more about this mystery. If there was time. If he was still alive to contact anyone.

Meanwhile . . .

He eased himself out of the window, and glanced down. A gloomy passageway ran behind the hostel, filled with stenches and shadows. He moved out on to the sill – then halted.

An odd sound above him, like a rustle of cloth.

He glanced up quickly. Nothing but the blank edge of the roof, the night sky above it.

A legionary's training covers a great many physical skills, including knowing how to fall – even two storeys. He took the impact with legs well bent – rolled, and bounced to his feet again, casually rubbing one slightly bruised hip. Then he slid into a shadow, and was gone.

*

Spaceport security guards on minor planets do not have a difficult job. The owners of spaceships pay a small fee for the use of the port – a larger fee if passengers or freight handling are involved. But shipowners are responsible for protecting their own ships, usually managed with little more than some advanced technology in the locking mechanisms on both entrances and control panels. Few spaceships were stolen, in Keill's day: they were too easy to trace, to difficult to re-sell. Saltrenius had not had a spaceship theft in living memory.

So the guard on the perimeter of the central port buildings might have been forgiven for being half asleep, lulled by the unbroken silence and darkness around him. He might not even have felt the blow that deepened his doze into unconsciousness.

Keill lowered the guard's body to the ground, listening carefully to the man's breathing. He had struck with precision at the base of the skull, using only the tips of stiffened fingers, for he was not there to kill. Even so, some people have thinner skulls than others – and he was glad to hear the guard begin softly snoring.

He slipped the guard's pistol from its holster – a needle-gun, as he had hoped – and snapped it open, sniffing at the points of the tiny projectiles within it. Also as he had hoped, the guards used anaesthetic in their needlers. They, too, were not there to kill.

Like a shadow himself he moved through shadow towards his goal – the office of the senior security man, he with the sour expression. A dimly lit window drew him. Peering carefully in, he saw one guard, seated at the central desk with his back to the door, chewing at a handful of some nameless Saltrenian confection.

Keill ghosted to the door, opened it without a sound. Even the needle-gun seemed to whisper as he fired it. The guard, mouth still full, sagged forward onto the desk.

The metal cabinet – at which the senior officer had taken his giveaway look – was securely shut, with some form of electronic combination lock. The cabinet was sheet metal, a sturdy alloy. Keill stepped a pace away, took a deep breath, another.

Then he leaped, and drove a booted foot at full stretch into the centre of the cabinet door.

The blow had every gram of his weight perfectly poised and delivered behind it. It also had all the pent-up frustration, anger, desperation and urgency that had accompanied Keill throughout the whole of his day on Saltrenius.

The metal cabinet boomed hollowly. And the door seemed to fold inwards, as if it had developed new hinges down its centre.

Keill stood silent for a moment, listening. But the sound, loud enough in the enclosed room, would not have carried far outside. And more than one guard must have been feeling sleepy that night. No voices were raised, no footsteps began, no alarm sounded.

He turned back to the cabinet. On one side of the door, the electronic lock had held. On the other side, the door had been completely ripped off its hinges. In a moment Keill had pulled aside the crumpled metal and was rummaging through the shelves. In another moment a thin strip of light metal lay in his hand.

The key to the seal that held his ship prisoner.

Then he was outside again, circling, more silent than the dust that swirled softly in the air. He approached his ship from the rear, rounded it cautiously. The lone guard was at least wakeful, but when he saw Keill he could not decide for an instant whether to shout or to reach for his pistol. Keill shot him before he could make up his mind.

While he was dragging the unconscious man to safety, well away from the energy blast of his lift-off, Keill heard a sound, on the threshold of audibility. Like the sound he had heard at the hostel – a soft rustle, as if of cloth. He spun round, pistol ready – but saw nothing, except his waiting ship and swirls of soft dust. Carefully, warily, he circled his ship. Nothing. The plasticrete was bare, deserted, as far as he could see in the darkness.

Quickly he returned to the seal, slipping in the key, catching the band of heavy metal as it fell away, opening the airlock hatch, moving swiftly in . . .

The sound again. Behind him. Not a rustle this time – more like a cloth flapping in the wind.

He was quick enough to turn, quick enough to glimpse the shape that hovered outside – like a wide sheet, like a sail, blackly silhouetted against the star-filled sky.

Then the needle bit into his neck, and it seemed that all the shadows in the world rose to engulf him in darkness.

The hidden asteroid
chapter five

He opened his eyes slowly, his mind sluggish, resisting wake-fulness. The messages from his senses were coming to him slowly, as if from a great distance, with difficulty.

The first message they sent was frightening. He was totally immobilized. He could not move a single muscle in his body except those around his eyes and mouth.

The second message was reassuring. He still had feeling in his body – he was not paralysed. Instead, something was constraining him, something that clung to every centimetre of his skin except his face, preventing even the smallest movement.

The third message was unbelievable. Though he could not move, though his mind was far from clear, though he felt an immense weariness throughout his entire being, so that even moistening his lips with his tongue was an effort – despite all this, he felt wonderful.

The pain had gone.

The lancing fire that had seared every cell in the depths of his body, through every waking minute of the months past . . . Gone.

Unless, of course, he was dreaming again. Or perhaps delirious, in the final stages of the death that the pain had been a prelude to.

He rolled his eyes, up, down, sideways, to the limits of his peripheral vision. He saw the plain walls and ceiling of an unremarkable room, with cheerful diffuse lighting. He noted that he was not lying flat on his back but propped up, half-reclining, on some padded surface contoured to fit his body perfectly.

He saw all that, but it was overridden by the shock of having seen himself.

He was entirely covered by a garment that clung like a second skin, which was certainly what held him immobile. It was silvery, shiny, and apparently without a seam. From many points on the garment – and so, presumably, from Keill's body, though he felt no discomfort – sprouted a huge array of tubes and wires, like the tendrils of some wild alien growth. The tubes and wires led on each side to a variety of complicated machinery, none of which seemed familiar to Keill in any way.

It was no dream, he decided. And it was an odd, unlikely scene for a delirium to shape. But then – *what was it*?

At that moment a voice spoke in the room. A firm male voice, with a note of friendliness, even kindliness, that seemed to come from everywhere.

'Are you awake, Keill Randor?'

Keill struggled in his throat to find his voice, found only a whisper. 'Who are you?'

The voice did not return at once. When it did, it seemed slightly muffled, as if the speaker had turned aside, addressing someone other than Keill.

'Amazing powers of recuperation . . . He shouldn't have wakened for days yet.'

'Days?' Keill whispered.

The voice replied at full volume again, but with an extra firmness. 'It is too soon, Keill Randor, for you to ask questions or receive answers. You will sleep again now, and we will speak later when you are entirely restored.'

Keill fought his voice into a desperate croak. 'Who are you? What are you? *What are you doing to me*?'

There was a pause. 'Very well, I see that those questions deserve some answer.' The voice grew even kindlier. 'My name is Talis, though that will mean little to you. I am a man, much as yourself, if a good deal older.' A chuckle. 'And what we are doing, Keill Randor, is saving your life.'

Keill wanted to cry out, wanted to scream questions, but his mind was a darkening jumble, unable to focus on words or their meanings, and he knew that one of the tubes in his eerie garment had slid a drug into his veins. He struggled with numbing lips, with the spreading blankness in his mind, and mumbled the only question he could manage.

'*Why*?'

He was not sure he had heard the answer, as he drifted into sleep. But it had sounded like—

'Because you are needed.'

He opened his eyes slowly, as before. But sensation flooded in upon him. His mind was not dulled this time, but alert, functioning, with a strange extra feeling of being marvellously refreshed.

And there was still no pain.

Yet his body was behaving in a disturbing way. He still could not move his head or limbs, still felt himself gripped and held in the half-lifted position – but every muscle was quivering, uncontrollably.

He glanced round, and down at himself, the memory of his previous awakening complete. He was no longer wearing the silvery garment. Instead, a light covering had been drawn over him, up to his neck. Beneath it, he knew he was naked. And he was still lying on the same padded bed, deeply contoured to fit the shape of his body exactly.

It was the contours of the bed that gripped him, and that were trembling – vibrating over the whole surface of his body. Relaxing with relief, he saw that it was an advanced form of massage unit, designed to maintain muscle tone and circulation in an immobilized patient.

He remembered the mysterious voice that had spoken to him. It had made clear that he would sleep for days. So he must have lain on that bed for a long time in the restrictions of the strange garment. The massage unit would have kept his muscles from weakening and deteriorating too much.

How weak he might be remained to be seen. It was not the

most important of the questions that clamoured in his mind. But it was probably the only one that he could answer for himself.

He inhaled deeply, aware that his body was relaxed, but testing the relaxation, letting it spread through every muscle, out of the centre of his being. Then he concentrated on his right arm, gathering his energies, focusing them, channelling them to that arm, building the power within it to a higher and higher peak . . .

Then, with a fierce exhalation, he released that power.

His arm ripped free of the constriction.

It was a small triumph, but an important first step – to regaining control over his own person, to putting an end to his time of lying trapped like a swaddled baby, while unknown people and strange machines did whatever they wished with him.

Yet he found that he was bathed in sweat after the exertion, and his free arm was oddly heavy. He let it fall on the outside of the covering, reaching again for the inner relaxation, knowing that he would need to rest awhile before trying to summon the power to free his other arm.

At that point a human figure appeared – materialized, from empty air – before him.

And the voice that Keill had heard before spoke again, still from no specific point within the room.

'Quite astonishing,' it said. 'You should not be at all strong enough, yet, to break free of the unit.'

Keill said nothing. Around him the massage unit's vibrations dwindled and stopped, and its grip on his body eased. It became merely a comfortably contoured bed, and Keill could move again. He began making small, minimal movements, stretching and twisting, testing the state of his body, while warily studying the figure that had appeared so suddenly.

An unadorned robe covered all of the figure's body, and extended into a heavy cowl, or hood, that was pulled forward so that the face was obscured in shadow. But from the posture of the figure, which was seated on a tall, plain chair, and the size and shape of the hands, Keill could see that he was in the presence of someone thin, elderly and probably male.

But then he saw that he was not actually in the *presence* of the figure. The angles of the shadowings and the faint haziness of outline told him that he was looking at a holo-image. Which explained the sudden materialization, and the apparently disembodied voice.

'Do not be alarmed, Keill Randor. You are not among enemies.'

'Who are you?' Keil said sharply, glad to find that his voice was working normally. 'What am I doing here?'

'You asked those questions before – do you remember?' said the voice. 'I am Talis, who spoke to you when you awoke prematurely . . .'

'I remember,' Keill replied. 'But you told me little, and explained nothing. Now I want explanations.'

'That is why I am here,' said the kindly voice. 'But tell me first how you feel.'

'I feel weak, as you must surely know,' Keill said brusquely. 'But everything seems to be functional. And the pain is gone.'

'Yes – we have removed the radiation from your body. Soon you will be fully restored to your normal state of health – which, it seems, is quite remarkable.'

'If that is so,' Keill said slowly, 'then I will owe you a debt that I can never repay. And I will want to know all the more who you are, and why this is happening.'

'Just so,' said the figure. 'There is much to tell you. There is much also that you cannot be told. But I will explain what I can.'

The figure settled back in its chair, folding its long hands, and continued.

'I am one of a group of people, mostly old dodderers like myself—' the warm voice chuckled as before—'who can immodestly call themselves some of the leading intellects of the Inhabited Worlds. Most of us are scientists of one sort or another. You would doubtless recognize many of our names, if you were ever to know them.'

'You told me your name,' Keill interjected.

'Talis is the name I use now. It is not my true name – and that I cannot tell you.'

Keill shrugged and remained silent, while the image of the old man called Talis went on. He told Keill how most of the individuals in the group had known each other for a long time, had often worked together, conferring over problems of far-reaching importance round the galaxy. More and more they had been invited to work on specific problems by governments of different planets, here and there – because they were able to bring a vast range of knowledge, and a special kind of *overview*, to the solution of such problems.

And it was just that overview, Talis said, that gave them an early warning of a new problem within the human worlds. A threat, a danger, that might well in the end affect the future of the entire galaxy.

Keill might have interrupted again, but the old man, not to be hurried, held up a hand to stop him.

'When we saw the magnitude of this danger,' Talis continued, 'we made up our minds that we must pool all our resources, all our knowledge and abilities, to oppose it. We also knew that if we opposed it, we ourselves would be in immediate danger. So we abandoned the lives we were then leading, and came here.'

'Where is *here*?' Keill asked.

'We are on – more correctly, within – an asteroid,' Talis said. 'A wandering piece of space debris, which appears on no star maps or charts of the spaceways.'

And he explained how he and the nameless others had constructed a secret base for themselves within the asteroid – with the most advanced laboratories, communications equipment and special protective devices that they could contrive. It had been a long, slow process, for secrecy had to be absolute. During the process, Talis said, all of his companions had disappeared from their home worlds, as undramatically as possible. They had made sure that official records would show, if anyone inquired, that many of them had died, as old people will. The rest of them would have seemed to have retired, fading away into obscurity and senility.

'We know that we cannot be traced here, or located,' Talis said. 'And we know that here we must stay, within our asteroid, and do everything in our power to counter the growing threat – that may one day soon endanger the very existence of the galaxy as we know it.'

Keill frowned dubiously. 'You'll pardon me if I find all this hard to take in. What is this terrible threat? And what is it all to do with me being here?'

'Do not take it too lightly, Keill Randor.' The old voice was sombre. 'We are confronting an enemy of frightening power, and even more frightening intentions. He is all humanity's enemy – but he is even more particularly your enemy. For he is the one who murdered your world.'

chapter six

Shock jolted Keill into a sitting position – but the movement drenched him with sweat again, and dizziness swept over him, blurring his vision. He sagged back against the cushioned bed, and the hooded figure in the holo-image leaned forward anxiously.

'You must not over-tax yourself,' Talis said. 'I have spoken for too long, and I fear I have distressed you. Now you must rest, and we will speak again when you are stronger.'

'No – wait . . .' Keill said weakly. 'I must know . . .'

But the holo-image vanished as abruptly as it had appeared, and the room was silent once more.

Keill lay back, limp with the emotions that boiled within him, the desperate need to know more. He might have tried to shout, even to get up, though his limbs felt as if they were made of water. But a sound from one side diverted him.

Twisting his head around, he saw a section of the wall swing silently inwards, though there had been no sign of a door-seam. Through the opening rolled a wheeled, upright cylindrical shape – a robot servitor, bearing a beaker upon its level upper surface.

It came to a stop beside the bed. The beaker held a milky liquid, fragrant, steaming slightly. Keill found that he was desperately thirsty. He picked up the beaker, grimly forbidding his hand to shake, and drained the contents. When the empty beaker was replaced, the servitor rolled away, and the wall closed as blank and seamless as before.

The drink had been bland, but flavoursome and warm. It also seemed soothing, relaxing – and then Keill knew that it was certainly drugged, that again the numbness was invading his mind, quietening its turmoil, and he was drifting into sleep.

When he awoke again he felt as refreshed as before, and more of his strength seemed to have returned. He was able to sit up without effort – though when he swung his legs off the bed and tried to stand, he found himself shaky, and was glad to sink back down on to the contoured padding.

But the room remained empty. Keill tried shouting, calling Talis's name, demanding his return – but no image formed, no voice came.

Instead the robot servitor appeared, as before. It bore another drink – a clear, cool liquid this time – and a bowl containing a gruel-like substance. Keill tasted them suspiciously at first, but growing thirst and hunger drove him to empty the containers. And this time there was no drug, only refreshment, pleasant tastes, and the restorative feeling of food in the stomach.

The robot's entrance had also coincided with the opening of another panel in the wall behind Keill, revealing a small shower-and-lavatory unit, as compact as the same facility on a spaceship. He needed the support of the robot to make use of it, and fell back exhausted when he returned to the bed. But it was another step ahead, another step towards the time when his strength would be returned and he could become his own master again – and begin to find out what was really happening.

From then on, the undisturbed days continued – if they were days, for Keill had no way of measuring the passage of time within the blank-walled room. He slept and woke, ate and drank, rested and thought – sorting through the questions and the doubts that swarmed within him.

He could not bring himself to accept what he had been told by the old man called Talis – because it seemed too improbable, and because too much had been left unexplained. A group of aged scientists hiding themselves away so as to fight some nameless enemy? The same enemy being the destroyer who had wiped out the Legions of Moros?

The questions of 'who' and 'why' bulked too large, too unanswerable. And he had been offered no evidence of any of it, save one holo-image of an old man keeping his face hidden.

He assembled what facts he had, testing their solidity. He had just entered his ship, on Saltrenius, when someone – or something – had come behind him and felled him with a needler. He was now in an empty room somewhere, tended by a robot. He had gone through some prolonged physical ordeal, which had left him weakened – and which had seemed to require some highly sophisticated technology. And he was free of pain.

Or was he? Was even that a true fact? Certainly there were drugs that could blot out even that much pain. But he did not feel drugged – he was alert and clear-headed, despite his body's shakiness.

Then perhaps, as he had thought before, he was lying in a hospital somewhere, in the terminal stages of his illness, finishing out his life in delirium.

Did the hallucinations of delirium go on as long as these past events seemed to have? He did not know. Would they be so detailed, in such an ordered routine, as his days now were in this room? He did not know.

The questions pursued themselves round in circles within his mind till he was weary of them. In the end, he knew very little. In time, perhaps, if Talis returned, or if other developments came along, he would learn more.

Meanwhile, his legionary discipline reasserted itself. A man did not fret over situations he could not hope to alter. A man did not waste energy gnawing at questions for which there seemed, as yet, no answers. If it was necessary to wait, then a man must wait – calm, controlled, patient.

And he must keep himself ready at all times to act, instantly, when action became possible.

So Keill readied himself. He began a programme of light exercises at regular intervals – routine ones that he had known from childhood. As he grew stronger, he extended the workouts, regaining more and more of his normal suppleness, agility and strength. And he was aware that Talis, or someone, was keeping his progress under observation – for his meals grew larger and more substantial as his output of energy increased.

Then one day, as if to underline how far he had come from being weak and bed-ridden, the robot brought not only his usual meal but also his clothing.

His full uniform was there – cleaned, fresh, showing no signs of wear. As if it were a new one made exactly to the specifications of the old.

He dressed quickly, delighting in the familiarity of the garments, feeling even more fully himself. And his delight increased when he slipped a hand into a tunic pocket and drew out the light chain with, dangling from it, his identity disc. Its angry red glow faded, shifted to the sky-blue of normality as he took it in his hand, then quickly put the chain round his neck.

Now, he thought, I am a legionary again.

Even so, the routine went on, and still no contact came from Talis. Keill persisted in his self-directed programme of exercise, testing himself ever more strenuously. Until the time came at last when he could put himself through the complete routine of gruelling physical stresses that had formed his basic training scheme for the Festival of Martial Games, on Moros.

When he emerged from that routine sweating only lightly, his breathing even, his body still resilient, with a reserve of energy left, he knew he was ready.

The time of waiting was over.

When the robot next came, Keill did not hesitate. As the wall panel swung open, he simply hurdled the small wheeled cylinder, and was out – to seek his freedom.

*

He found himself in a narrow passageway, dimly lit, with metallic floor, walls and ceiling. Closed doors, like the hatchways of spaceships, interrupted the smoothness of one wall here and there along its length.

The doors were tightly secured, and Keill did not waste energy trying to break through them. They were made of the special quaternium alloy used for the hulls of fighting ships, well able to resist heavier assaults than even he could manage bare-handed.

He raced along the passage. It took an L-turn to the right, and offered him two gangways, downwards and upwards. Without pausing he chose the downward steps – and came to a sizeable chamber containing an array of complex machinery, in separated compartments.

Most of this equipment he recognized – the air and water recyclers especially. It all seemed to be larger and more intricate forms of the standard life-support systems for spacecraft. And the bulkiest device, in the central position, was surely a very advanced form of gravitational unit.

So he *was* on some form of space station or artificial satellite, he realized. Perhaps Talis's story of a secret, hollowed-out asteroid was true.

But he would not know unless he could get outside it. And for that he would need at least a space suit, preferably with a weapon, and – if luck were really with him – a ship of some sort.

He retraced his steps, racing up to the upper level. More passageways, but often now with doors that opened. They revealed a series of chambers that were clearly laboratories – crammed, one and all, with collections of equipment that Keill, who thought of himself as fairly knowledgeable about technology, could not begin to fathom.

Another gangway led upwards, and he sprinted along it. It took him up to a chamber heaped, floor to ceiling, with book tapes and information tapes of every kind, and a number of viewers scattered among them. Beyond that room was an observation chamber, with a broad viewscreen offering a panoramic segment of star-filled space. Abundant star-maps, charts of the space lanes, computer outlets were available around the room.

It was a welcome sight, for Keill knew that if he was able to escape, he might need the information within that room to get his bearings, and his direction.

But he did not linger there just yet. He had heard no sound of an alarm being raised, nor had there been any sign of pursuit. But he did not doubt that his disappearance from the room had been noted – and Talis, or someone, would surely be working out how to put an end to his wild flight.

Another passageway, and more closed doors. Another gangway, leading again to a higher level. Another chamber . . .

He came to an abrupt halt, barely able to contain the yell of exultation that rose in his chest.

The broad chamber before him – with a high, curved ceiling that had to be the outer hull of whatever space structure he was in – contained his own ship.

It gleamed and shone as it had not done since it had first come out of production on Moros. Old battle scars and stains had been removed, the blue Legion insignia re-embossed, the blunt snouts of the weapons polished. It looked as newly remade as his uniform had. And it was the most heartening sight Keill had seen for a long time.

His first instinct was simply to climb in and blast his way out through the ceiling. But as he began to move round the ship towards the entrance, he hesitated.

It might be more sensible, he thought, to arm himself from the store of weapons in his ship, and go in search of Talis. Even if he had to burn his way through some of those closed doors.

Then he would be able to demand answers to all those crucial questions that the old man had left hanging in the air. About why he was keeping Keill there. And what Talis knew of the destruction of Moros.

It was possible that his store of weapons had been removed from the ship. But at least the airlock hatch was invitingly open, the ramp down. And there was no one in the way.

But as he approached the ramp, he heard a weirdly out-of-place sound. One he had heard before – the night he had tried to steal his own ship, on Saltrenius.

Like a cloth, flapping in the wind . . .

He glanced up, and froze.

A winged creature, like nothing he had ever seen, was hovering above his ship.

The wings – broad, veined membranes that looked flimsy, almost translucent – flapped again as the creature settled upon the ship's hatchway. There it perched, folding its wings, regarding Keill through two large, colourless, perfectly circular eyes.

Its body was less than a metre high, and narrow, covered with what looked like overlapping plates of soft skin, purplish-grey. Its head seemed too large for the little body, rounded and dome-like, with a small tapering snout beneath the great eyes. And it was a biped – though each of the two small feet seemed in fact more like hands, having three sturdy, jointed toes like fingers, and a fourth one opposing, like a thumb.

But it was not perched on both feet. It was balanced on one.

The other one was, incredibly, gripping a needle-gun – and aiming it unwaveringly at Keill.

Keill's astonishment deepened even further in the next instant – when he heard a voice.

Not the voice, as before, of the old man called Talis. Not any kind of voice that Keill could hear externally, in his ears.

This voice formed itself within Keill's mind.

And it said:

Is it not comical, human-called-Randor, that I must once again use a weapon to keep you from your own ship?

chapter seven

At gun-point, with the winged creature fluttering behind and above him – out of reach even if Keill had been tempted to attack it – he was herded out of the domed chamber that held his spaceship. Down another passage they went, the creature's wing-tips brushing the walls, and finally through a door that, Keill remembered, had been solidly locked when he had come that way before.

Now it swung silently open, revealing a long, low, abundantly furnished room that was clearly designed for comfort and relaxation. Low, cushioned seats were scattered around on the soft floor-covering, the lighting was quiet and mellow, tables here and there were piled with book tapes.

Keill took it all in with a glance, reserving his full attention for the figure seated in the centre of the room. It was Talis, robed and cowled as before – but there was no doubt that this time it was not a holo-image. He was there in the flesh.

The old man gestured towards a chair opposite him, inviting Keill to sit. Keill did so slowly, turning to watch the winged creature – which settled on the back of another chair, folding its delicate wings, still well out of reach. And still aiming the needle-gun at Keill, while gazing at him unblinkingly with its round, luminous eyes.

'I very much regret . . .' Talis's kindly voice began.

Keill interrupted. 'Is this,' he asked, gesturing at the creature, 'the thing that attacked me on Saltrenius?'

Talis sighed. 'Yes, but attacked is not really the right word . . .'

'What is it?' Keill demanded.

'An alien,' said Talis, 'of a race that calls itself the Ehrlil. From another galaxy.'

Keill was startled, but his face remained impassive. 'And telepathic?'

Before Talis could reply, words again formed soundlessly in the depths of Keill's mind.

I project with ease, human. But I receive with difficulty from the mudheads of this galaxy.

Keill frowned, feeling slightly unnerved. 'I think, old man, that you are setting up some kind of elaborate hoax, for reasons that I cannot guess.'

'It is no hoax,' Talis said quietly. 'I have told you only the truth.'

'But an alien? A mind-reading alien?'

It was not impossible, Keill knew. Just highly unlikely. Intergalactic travel had been tried many times by human explorers – but it presented its own special problems and rigours, and few had returned. Those that did come back had mostly had their minds unhinged by loneliness, unknown dangers and the long-term effects of Overlight, and their babbled accounts made little sense. But recent history included some tales of alien beings making the intergalactic journey in the other direction – and making brief, uneventful contact with humans on the Inhabited Worlds, before going on their unguessable ways.

Keill had never seen such an alien, though, nor had he ever met anyone who had.

Yet there were no such beings native to his own galaxy. When man first went out among the stars, during the Scattering, the planets that were to become the Inhabited Worlds held many kinds of strange life forms. But it had been a grave disappointment for the early colonists (though, for some, a relief) that none of the life forms had been intelligent. Mankind found himself to be the only intelligent species in his galaxy.

As for telepathy, again Keill knew that it probably existed

in some form. He had heard of a few humans – some of the altered ones, whose planets had produced mutations in their human populations – who could reach into other minds. But always in a limited, erratic way.

He brought his attention back to Talis, who was expounding on the subject. '. . . an intrepid race of explorers, it seems, who think nothing of the awesome emptiness between galaxies. They are very long-lived, of course, and are always in mental contact with one another . . .'

'Why is it here?' Keill demanded.

'Not *it*,' Talis said with a chuckle, '*she*. Glr is a female of her species.'

'All right,' Keill said patiently, 'why is *she* here?'

'Her ship developed a malfunction,' Talis replied, 'and she was forced to land on a human world. In time a leading scientist met her and befriended her. And she has stayed, finding humanity a source of considerable interest . . .'

And amusement, said the voice in Keill's mind, with soundless laughter behind it.

'When we began the process of setting up our base,' Talis went on, 'Glr came as well.'

'I find this no easier to believe than anything else you tell me,' Keill said gruffly. 'Surely the arrival of such an alien would have been widely reported throughout the Worlds. But I have heard nothing of this . . . Glr.'

'I told you the Ehrlil are long-lived,' said Talis. 'Her arrival was reported – but it was some sixty years ago. The scientist who befriended her was my father.'

Keill leaned back against the cushions of his chair, feeling slightly dazed. And the alien's voice formed in his mind again, still bubbling with laughter.

I am in fact quite young – about four of your centuries. The Ehrlil elders think of me as a wayward, foolish child whose curiosity will get her into trouble.

*

Keill shook his head as if to clear it. Again he wondered if he was in the grip of some nightmare from a terminal delirium – or if Talis was merely a crazed old space hermit with an odd taste in pets. Pets with guns.

'Isn't it time,' he said at last, 'that you told me what I'm doing here, being held at gunpoint by an alien?'

'I regret the gun,' Talis said quickly. 'But the others felt that, because you are given to rash and hasty action, I ought not meet you in person without some protection.'

'Fearing I might attack you?' Keill said. 'If I wanted to do so, old man, your flying alien would not stop me.' Behind him the creature's wings flared, but he ignored it. 'And I might do so yet – if you don't start *now* to give me some explanations.'

'Of course,' Talis said soothingly. 'That is why we are here. But there is so much to tell . . .'

'I know,' Keill said, 'and so much you can't tell me. You said as much, earlier. But you *will* tell me, old man. You'll tell me why I am here – and what you know about this person, this enemy, who you say destroyed Moros.'

'The enemy,' Talis replied sombrely, 'is why you are here. Just as he is why my group and myself are here.'

'So you also have said,' Keill interrupted. 'But I have seen only yourself, and your alien.'

'The others are nearby, and are listening. You may see them if you wish – though I fear you will learn little from it.'

He moved one hand to the side of his chair, and a portion of the wall nearest them grew hazy – changing, as Keill watched, from a solid surface into what seemed to be a window, but was in fact an enlarged viewscreen.

It revealed a group of people, sitting quietly together. Like Talis, most of them seemed elderly – as far as Keill could tell. For, also like Talis, each of them wore a voluminous robe, with a cowl that kept the face in darkness.

Keill smiled sardonically. 'More mystery. What do you call yourselves – the Hooded Brethren of Secrecy?'

Talis moved his hand again, and the silent group faded from view, the wall resuming its smooth solidity. 'You will come to understand our need for secrecy,' he said quietly. 'And we have no name for ourselves – though Glr has given us one.'

I call them the 'Overseers', said the alien's voice in Keill's mind, *because they alone among you mudheads seem able to see the wholeness of events in this galaxy. You would do well, Randor, to show them some respect.*

'I will show respect,' Keill replied aloud, 'when I have been given proof that respect is due.'

'Just so,' said Talis. 'I wish to provide such proof. I want you to understand what we began to see, more than two years ago.'

The group, Talis went on, made regular, wide-ranging studies of major happenings in the Inhabited Worlds. They analysed and investigated, and often they also made projections – trying to foresee problems before they occurred, so they could aid and advise planetary leaders whose worlds might be affected.

In the course of their work, they began to see a strange and unsettling pattern in many of the events – no matter how widely scattered these events might be in the Galaxy. They made more studies, more analyses – and reached their conclusion.

'The fact was inescapable,' Talis said. 'It was that many more *wars* were happening, everywhere, than should have been happening.'

Keill frowned. 'There are always wars.'

'Of course. But mostly local wars, growing out of local conditions – and happening at random, with no connections among them.' The old man leaned forward intently. 'But the wars we studied had too much in common, for mere coincidence. Too much of a pattern.'

What a violent species you are, said the amused alien voice.

Talis went on, unaware of the interruption. 'I will give you tapes to study, which are summaries of our findings. You will see for yourself that the pattern had to be *contrived*. Someone was setting out with the conscious, murderous intention of *starting* wars, around the galaxy.'

'And this someone is the enemy you speak of?'

'Just so.'

'Who is he? And where?'

Talis sighed. 'That I cannot tell you, because we do not yet know. We know only that such a being must exist. We know his ruthless and evil purpose, and we know something of his methods. No more. Except that for convenience we have given him something of a code name. We call him the Warlord.'

Keill's frown deepened. 'You'll show me evidence that this . . . Warlord . . . exists?'

'We will. But you already possess one proof of his reality.'

Keill tensed, suspecting what was coming. 'What proof?'

'The murder of the Legions.'

'Go on,' Keill said fiercely.

'Consider,' Talis said. 'Everyone knew the reputation of the Legions – that they would fight only on the side of people who were defending themselves, whose cause contained some right and justice in it. But words like right and justice are not in the vocabulary of the Warlord. He would surely have foreseen a time when a war he sought might be prevented by the Legions. And he might have foreseen a time when the Legions themselves would guess at his existence, and move against him directly. It may be that your Central Command had already guessed. So – he moved first, with power we had not imagined, to erase that threat.'

'A pre-emptive strike,' Keill said through gritted teeth.

'Just so.'

'If any of this is true,' Keill said bitterly, 'such a war-maker would have to be insane.'

'It is all true,' Talis replied, 'and he may well be insane – with the kind of madness that keeps company with a hunger for ultimate power. For we believe it is his aim to set the Inhabited Worlds at each other's throats, in war upon war that gradually spread to more and more planets – ultimately to the entire galaxy. And out of that evil, that terrible destruction, he would hope to emerge as the sole and supreme ruler over what remains of all humanity.'

chapter eight

The information tapes provided by Talis, summarizing long months of investigation by the Overseers, were voluminous and thorough. Hour upon hour Keill sat at the viewer, his patient concentration never wavering – hardly aware of consuming the food and drink brought to him at one point by the robot servitor.

He saw, on the tapes, human societies upon world after world torn apart by war. On one distant planet, far-flung tribes of nomads who had roamed their grasslands for peaceful generations came together, over a few brief years, for no understandable reason, to launch a vicious attack on the scattered cities of that planet. On another world, where the people of its one populated continent lived in wealth and plenty because of their supplies of a valuable mineral, a ferocious civil war broke out between two political groups – each side wrongly believing that the other was seeking total control over the mineral.

He saw entire solar systems erupt with violence. In one, a large, industrialized planet moved suddenly and inexplicably to attack a smaller, under-developed neighbour. Elsewhere, two small planets came together to invade – without clear cause – a third, and then after their victory fell out and fought between themselves.

He saw such wars arise, time and again, without warning and almost without reason. An irrational growth of racial prejudice between two planets that had once been wholly friendly – an eruption of a new religious cult that led its followers into holy war – an unexplained political assassination – an outburst of space piracy – a senseless breakdown of simple trade negotiations . . .

And much more. As the hours passed and the facts accumulated, the tapes made the crucial points clear. In each case there had been no likelihood or prospect of war – until something had begun stirring up the worst elements of the human character. Greed and self-interest; the urge to power; suspicion, prejudice and fear. And these stirrings were fed by unexpected events – and by deception, lying propaganda, treachery and murder.

Further, Keill saw, on every one of the planets there were one or two people who had seemed to come out of nowhere, but who rose swiftly to positions of power and influence. These individuals were always at the heart of the events that led to the catastrophe of war.

Finally, his mind swimming with the terrible images that had been revealed to him, Keill returned to the relaxation room in search of Talis. The old man had preceded him, and was waiting, still shadowed within his cowl.

'Now you have seen the summaries of our findings,' the old voice said, 'do you believe what I have told you?'

Keill looked at him impassively for a long moment. 'I have seen the stories of a great many wars,' he said at last. 'None of them pleasant – but wars never are.'

'Did you not perceive the pattern?' Talis insisted.

Keill shrugged. 'I saw resemblances. But the essence of war is usually much the same, wherever it happens. I saw no final proof of *connections*. And I still find it hard to believe that all those wars were caused by one . . . Warlord. Surely others would have guessed at the existence of such a being.'

'The galaxy is large,' Talis said, 'and there is not enough information-sharing among planets. Aside from trade and short-range travelling, there are hardly any galaxy-wide links.

So no one would assemble all the data, to see what is happening on the overall, galactic scale.'

'Except yourselves.'

'Just so.'

'Yet for all your *overview*,' Keill said bluntly, 'you seem to know very little. What of these individuals that the tapes singled out – the ones who rose so quickly to positions of power?'

'They are of course servants of the Warlord,' Talis replied, 'sent as emissaries to worm their way into positions where they can spread the infection that leads to war.'

'Could you not have these people investigated,' Keill asked, 'to see if there are connections among them that might lead back to your Warlord?'

'It has been tried,' said Talis glumly. 'But on most worlds where they have appeared, they have quickly become too powerful to be investigated. In the few cases, though, where a planet has resisted the infection, and has stopped the Warlord's servants before they gained power, we have learned some things. We have learned that the Warlord is hidden even to his emissaries, who receive their orders indirectly. And we have learned that a *failed* emissary, like those of whom I speak, does not remain alive for long.'

'It is not much,' Keill said.

'True – but we dare not press too hard. As far as we know the Warlord has not guessed our existence. And he must not, as yet, for we know too little to oppose him properly. That is why we, too, are so secretive – even with you, Keill Randor. If you were ever to fall into the hands of the Warlord or his servants, they would not be able to wrest knowledge from you that you do not have – of who we are, where we are.'

Keill smiled dryly. 'You must hide, so he won't know of you – yet while you're hiding, you can't learn more of him. This is foolishness!'

'No,' said Talis quietly, 'it is the reason why we, too, need an emissary.'

'By which,' Keill said, 'you mean me.'

'Just so. We cannot go out among the Worlds ourselves. We have devices that can monitor events on nearly any planet of our choosing – but we need someone to be our eyes and ears at close range. Someone who can go on to worlds threatened by the Warlord – and survive.'

'One man against this . . . emperor of wars?'

'Not just a man. A legionary. No one in the galaxy would have a higher potential for survival.'

But as Talis spoke, another voice was also speaking – in Keill's mind.

In the midst of all your doubts, Randor, you would do well to remember that you survive now only because of the Overseers' skills, which they gave to you at considerable risk.

Keill turned swiftly. The alien, Glr, was floating across the room on her translucent wings, to settle on a perch near the door, her great eyes fixed as before on Keill.

'I haven't forgotten,' he said slowly, 'the unpayable debt I owe, for my healing. If I *am* healed.'

Glr fluttered her wings as if echoing the exasperation in Talis's voice. 'Do you doubt even that?'

'The medic told me,' Keill said stubbornly, 'that the effects of the radiation couldn't be reversed.'

'True,' Talis replied. 'It had settled in your bones, irreversibly. So – we replaced them.'

'Replaced . . . ?'

'A process of my own invention, if I may say so,' Talis went on. 'Your skeletal structure is now composed of an organic alloy.'

Keill stared at him speechlessly.

'It was an interesting operation. The replacement had to be done molecule by molecule, taking care to match your original skeleton exactly in shape and weight, and to ensure that your bone marrow adapted. But—' he gestured expansively at Keill —'it all seems entirely successful.'

Keill did not see the gesture. He was looking down at himself, at his arms and legs, his ribs, his knuckles . . .

'There is an interesting side effect,' Talis continued chattily. 'The alloy has quite surprising resilience and strength. Our tests have shown that it is almost completely infrangible.'

'Infrangible? What . . .'

It means, mudhead, laughed Glr in his mind, *that your bones cannot be broken.*

Keill's head jerked up, eyes wide with disbelief. Then a smile began to form on his lips – a smile of scornful irony, but tinged with disappointment.

'Now you have gone too far,' he said. 'If you thought you could ease my doubts with a wild tale like that . . .'

I would gladly arrange a test for you, Glr put in, *but your flesh would suffer painful bruising in the process.*

Keill stood up abruptly. 'Talis, if that is your name, I can swallow no more absurdity. You may cling to your fantasies of Warlords and galactic empires – and bone replacements – and tell them to the next fool who comes along. But I have something else to do – a task put on me by a dear friend who tried to save me while she herself was dying. I'm going to look for the one who destroyed Moros, whoever it may be, if it takes the rest of my life, long or short. And I'm going to start looking on that moon of Saltrenius – with no more delay.'

He turned and moved to the door. But the alien was there before him – wings spread, sturdy fingers revealing small, sharp talons, equally sharp little teeth gleaming in the narrow mouth.

Keill halted. 'Old man, I wish no harm to you or to this creature. But I'm leaving, one way or another.'

Talis raised a hand, and some mental message must have passed between him and Glr, for the alien swirled away from the door and settled.

'I would not stop you leaving, Keill Randor,' said the old man. 'I have told you all I can tell you – I cannot force you to believe me. But certainly, the moon called Creffa is exactly where we *wish* you to go.'

Keill turned back, surprised. 'But before, on Saltrenius . . . You went to some lengths to *stop* me.'

'Of course. You were dying then – and you were going into danger unprepared. The old hand moved as before, to the side of the chair. 'Bear with me a moment longer, and observe.'

Again the surface of the nearby wall shivered. But this time it was not the silent group of hooded figures that Keill saw.

Instead the screen revealed an eerie alien landscape, stark, rock-strewn, the shadows deep black and sharply defined. In the background rose the high, curved surface of a life-support dome, sleek and shiny in the brilliant light.

In the foreground was the bulky, cylindrical shape of a spaceship – which Keill recognized at once.

The cruiser he had seen at the Saltrenius spaceport. The ship that belonged to the three men who called themselves legionaries.

'This is Creffa,' Talis said. 'I see you have recognized the ship. One of our monitoring devices recorded this scene within the last few days.'

Keill said nothing, but watched. The airlock of the ship was opening, and figures were appearing.

They were spacesuited, of course, but Keill did not need to see faces to the first man who descended to the dusty surface. A head taller than the others, enormous width of shoulder . . . The mocking giant who preferred to wear only half a legionary uniform.

Behind him from the ship, stooping under sizeable containers of what must have been supplies, came other figures. Not just the two that Keill had expected. The giant had acquired some new companions.

In all, there were nine men who left the ship and made their way, through the light gravity of Creffa, towards the dome.

'Are there more inside?' Keill asked, as the image faded from the screen.

'No,' Talis said. 'Only the nine. Six more had been recruited – from the criminal element on Saltrenius – before we took you from the planet. And hear me, Keill Randor – not one of them is a legionary.'

Keill nodded. 'As I thought. I was certain before that the first three were not.'

Surprise showed in Talis's voice. 'You knew? Yet you were going – ill as you were, and unaided – to walk into their trap?'

'A trap is no trap if it is expected,' Keill said. 'I had to go. As I still must – whether there are nine or ninety.'

'Just so,' Talis replied. 'Much could be learned, many questions answered, by patient and careful observation on Creffa.'

'Observation?' Keill echoed with a grim smile. 'Something more, Talis. It's clear that whoever destroyed Moros also sent those men to pose as legionaries, and to set up a base that would attract any survivors. I want to spring that trap before any real legionaries walk into it unknowingly.' His voice grew tense. 'Some may already have done so while I've been here.'

The cowled figure shook his head. 'None has. Our monitoring devices have kept a full-time watch. In the same way, all our devices have searched and scoured the galaxy, since the day of Moros's destruction, looking for surviving legionaries. We have found none – except yourself.'

Keill was stunned, hearing the words he had been half-dreading for so long. 'There must be some! You can't monitor the entire galaxy!'

'If there are,' Talis said softly, 'they are in hiding. They are not moving around the galaxy as you did, searching for their fellows. Had any done so, we would have located them – just as we located you.' He reached a sympathetic hand towards Keill. 'No, I greatly fear . . . that you may be the last legionary.'

Keill's face revealed little of the torment within him – only a momentary twisting of his features, a flash of anguish in his eyes. Then his control returned, and he gazed calmly at Talis.

'Even if that is true,' he said levelly, 'I am still going to this moon, to do what must be done.'

Well spoken, said the bright inner voice of Glr. *Foolish, stubborn and brave – no wonder humans are so short-lived.*

Keill ignored the interruption, for Talis had raised an admonishing hand. 'I agree, you must go. But I urge you – do not plunge into rash action. Use caution!'

Keill rose to his feet, smiling thinly. 'Talis, it is too late for caution. A time always comes when it is necessary to *act*, not merely to observe. That time has come now, for me – and for those impostors on Creffa.'

Killers' moon
chapter nine

Enveloped in the misted nothingness of Overlight, Keill Randor completed his routine check of his spaceship's systems, leaned back in the slingseat and stretched luxuriously.

He was relaxed, entirely at ease, and glad to be on the move. Inaction was nearly the worst torment of all, he thought. Especially when inaction had been forced on him, by the old man on the hidden asteroid. So much time had been lost, while he had lain unconscious, and then while he had slowly recovered, after . . . whatever had been done to him. Time that the false legionaries, in their base on the moon called Creffa, would have used to strengthen their position.

But at least they were still there, according to the Overseers' monitoring devices. And no legionaries had walked into that trap . . .

Keill pushed that thought away. He was not willing to face the possible truth of old Talis's statement that there *were* no other legionaries. He was not sure that he could ever face the possibility that he might be the last of his race – which meant living with a unique and terrible loneliness for the rest of his life.

Again he brought his thoughts under control. Loneliness of any kind was not a subject to dwell on in deep space, especially not in the emptiness of Overlight. It could do strange things to a human mind, if that mind turned to brooding and fretting. The best remedy was keeping busy.

He glanced down again at the last read-out, still showing on his computer screen from his systems check. The Overseers had certainly renewed his ship, but had sensibly left its components as they were, as Keill was used to. He knew that they could easily have built in some wonderfully advanced technology, superior to the systems in his ship – but he would have needed more time to be trained to use it. They may well have made some slight adjustments to the ship's computer guidance systems, but that did not affect Keill. The ship remained as familiar as ever, like an extension of his own body and reflexes.

He thought back to his departure from the asteroid – if it was an asteroid. As mysterious and secretive as ever, Talis had instructed Keill to keep his viewscreens blank after he entered his ship, and to keep them that way until he entered Overlight. His ship computer had been preprogrammed, Talis had said, to take the ship off the asteroid and then to enter Overlight as soon as possible.

And, Talis had added, the computer had been programmed to erase those instructions once Keill was in Overlight.

Keill had wondered about that statement. If the Overseers had intended him to go out as their emissary, as Talis had said earlier, how would he ever have contacted them, reported to them? Talis had read his puzzlement correctly, and had explained.

'If you ever have any wish to contact us,' the old man had said, 'we have provided a communications link. It will be there when you need it.'

At the time, with his doubts and disbeliefs still strong, Keill had not given much thought to the statement. He had felt that there was never likely to be a time when he would want to make any contact with the old man and his peculiar, hooded friends. But now, out in space, that vague assurance of a communications link worried him.

Communications were definitely one of the Overseers' specialities. He had been shown some of their monitoring devices, of the sort that they had scattered around the Inhabited Worlds – amazingly intricate but compact objects, some no bigger than a fist, none larger than a man's head. Operating like spy satellites, they could pick up, record and transmit most forms of broadcast media from a planet's surface, whether electronic, holo or whatever. They could also, from orbit, film and transmit visual images of a planet that were astonishingly detailed – as Keill had seen with the tape of the nine men on Creffa. And the devices were nearly undetectable by the people of any planet, because of their size and the erratic orbits that were built into them.

Also, if anyone did locate them by accident, the devices would self-destruct before they could be examined closely.

That fact especially troubled Keill.

One of the pleasures of being away from the asteroid had been the feeling of personal freedom – of not being watched. He had known, all the time he was there, that he had been under scrutiny by similar monitors. But was he still being watched? Was there a device hidden on his ship, monitoring him? Or was the communications link that Talis had mentioned merely waiting somewhere in the ship – waiting for the moment when he might need it, before somehow becoming activated?

If so, where was it? And was it, too, programmed to self-destruct if wrongly handled?

He strongly hoped that the Overseers had not planted such a device on the ship. If he came across it unknowingly, and mishandled it, he could blow himself out of the sky.

Time to make a search, he thought.

He unstrapped himself from the slingseat and stood up. The familiar drift of his body, in null-gravity, did not trouble him. The boots of his spacesuit adhered to the treated deck of the ship, keeping him from floating. He moved towards a row of compartments that extended across one side of the single inner chamber of the ship. They held all his necessities – food supplies in one, weapons in another, clothing and personal possessions in another, and so on.

One thing about a single-person fighter, he thought, there are only so many places where an object can be hidden. Besides those compartments, there were the ship's various systems – the drive, life support, ship's weapons and the rest –

behind heavy bulkheads at the nose and stern. He could go through all possible storage spaces in a few minutes. But he would be thorough, he told himself, and take his time. If the Overseers had planted a monitor, it could be extremely miniaturized. But there was time – about half an hour yet before he would come out of Overlight near the planet Saltrenius.

And then something odd happened, something totally irrational.

He began to laugh.

Not out loud, but to himself, within himself. Carefree, bubbling laughter . . .

No, he thought – and anger surged up in him, blotting out the laughter. It's not me. It's that alien – that winged, telepathic giggler of an alien.

Instantly the silent, laughing voice formed in his mind. *Now that you have discovered me, may I be released? Your weapons store does not suit my dignity.*

Keill moved swiftly to the weapons compartment and flung open its door.

The round, colourless eyes of the little alien gazed at him, unblinkingly.

Your communications link reporting for duty, sir, it said.

The alien floated out, automatically spreading its wings despite the null-gravity, and drifted over to the control panel. There it settled on the edge, gripping with the strange little feet that were like hands. And Keill followed, speechless with anger, flinging himself into the slingseat, glaring at the creature. It returned his look calmly, but the silent laughter faded.

I warned Talis you would be angry, the inner voice said. *But he felt you would not allow me to accompany you if you knew beforehand.*

'He was quite right,' said Keill coldly. 'And I don't want you to accompany me now. Give me the figures, and I'll alter course and take you back.'

I cannot, the alien said. *I do not know the coordinates.*

'You must!' Keill said. 'Surely even those senile old mad-men wouldn't send you away unless you could get back!'

I can get back, the voice replied. *But I do not know how.*

As Keill was about to explode, the alien hastily went on: *The data is in my unconscious memory. Talis can recall me by projecting a certain code to my mind. I will then automatically programme the computer for return. But I will at once forget the data, consciously – just as the computer will erase the figures from its memory once the new course is begun.*

Again Keill was speechless. More of Talis's cursed secrecy. And, like every action of the Overseers, it seemed both so plausible – and yet so wholly mad.

Then a thought struck him. 'You can reach Talis's mind from here?'

The reach of an Ehrlil mind has no limits in space. The little alien spoke matter-of-factly, without pride.

'If so,' Keill said, 'you could have remained on the asteroid, and still set up a "communications link" with me, wherever I was.'

True.

'Then why are you here?' Keill shouted.

Talis did not wish you to go into danger unaided.

'Unaided?' Keill echoed. 'I'm to face nine men who will al-most certainly try to kill me – and I must do so with you filling my mind with crazed giggling?'

I will not get in your way. The alien's silent voice seemed hurt. *But I can use a weapon, as you know. And pilot your ship.*

'You can pilot this ship?'

Human ships are child's play – even for a child like myself. The words held a trace of laughter, quickly fading. *How do you think you were taken from Saltrenius to the asteroid?*

Keill pondered. 'Perhaps then you can be of use.'

He had worried, earlier, about leaving his craft unattended after landing on Creffa. If some of his enemies located it, he would have his escape cut off. But now, with the alien . . .

79

Exactly, the inner voice said, replying to his thought. *I will guard your ship. And whatever else you wish. I am under your orders.*

'All right,' Keill said at last. 'As long as you remember that, and don't start taking orders from Talis at long range. Remember that I'm going on a task of my own choosing. I'm not the Overseers' emissary – and I want no interference, from them or from you.'

It will be as you say. The thought seemed saddened. *But you are being needlessly stubborn. All that Talis told you is the truth.*

Keill was disturbed by the words, and by the clear sincerity and earnestness behind them. Such things could not be pretended, in a telepathic voice.

'No doubt you believe it,' Keill said. 'But I'm not concerned now with tales of Warlords and the rest of it. My concern is with nine men on Creffa, and what I can get out of them about the death of my world.'

It is all the same thing, said the alien patiently. *Can you not see that the death of Moros should demand your belief in the Warlord? Such an act could only be done by someone extremely powerful, and extremely ruthless.*

Keill did not reply at once. It was a point that he himself always came back to. Who was there in the galaxy dangerous enough, insane enough, to destroy the Legions? How could an attacker get past the defences of Moros? And, most of all, *why*?

When it came down to answers, he thought ruefully, Talis's story of the Warlord was the only one he had been given, by anyone. If only it was not so unlikely . . .

Only your stubbornness makes it so, came the voice of the alien.

'That's another thing,' Keill said sharply. 'While you're here, you will keep out of my mind. My thoughts are my own.'

I told you before that I receive with difficulty from humans, the alien replied. *I could not read the deeper levels of your mind if I wished to. I can receive only those thoughts that you form clearly, on the surface of your mind, as if you were speaking them.*

'Nothing more?' Keill asked suspiciously.

*Only blurred impressions, mixtures of emotions. Indeed, that is all
I ever get from most humans. You, at least, have some clarity of mind,
if not as much as the Overseers. That is one reason why I was willing to
come with you.*

'One reason?' Keill was interested in spite of himself. 'What
are the others?'

First, because I agree with Talis that you will need me, the alien
said. *Second, because it is obvious that life in your company will never
be unexciting.*

'It might be shorter than you bargained for,' Keill said
grimly.

Possibly. But I do not fear dying – except from boredom.

Keill could not help smiling at the words, and a trace of the
alien's laughter crept into his mind in response. He leaned back
and studied the creature again. The slender, bird-like body, the
domed head, the round eyes – it was almost a clownish figure.
Yet the brightness of those eyes, and the capability of the
hands, belied the foolishness. Keill thought for a moment of
this little being, alone in its own ship, penetrating the incon-
ceivable distances from one galaxy to another, facing whatever
unknowable dangers lay on such a path . . .

He realized that beyond its appearance, beyond its zany
sense of humour, it – no, he corrected himself, *she* – deserved
respect. She was a being of high intelligence, ability and
courage.

'All right, little friend,' he said at last, still smiling. 'Glr – that
is what you are called? We'll be comrades-in-arms, for a while.
I hope neither of us will regret it.'

We will not, Keill Randor, said Glr. *For myself, I welcome your
friendship. As I will welcome even more the time when you learn that
Talis spoke the truth. I hope the knowledge is not acquired too painfully.*

A faint chill prickled Keill's spine. 'Do you read the future,
as well as minds?'

No. But I can make predictions, as you can, from the available data.

Before Keill could reply, the computer intruded with a warning tone to draw his attention, and a cluster of figures flashing on to its screen.

They were nearing the point of emerging from Overlight.

Keill turned his concentration to the controls, readying the ship for entrance into normal space, checking the course that would bypass the planet Saltrenius towards a landing on its moon, Creffa.

chapter ten

Creffa was small for a moon, but as airless, rocky, cratered and uninviting as any. Keill's course took him on one orbital sweep, far enough out so that anyone spotting him from the moon's surface would not be able to identify the ship, or imagine that he was anything other than a bypassing ship on its way to planetfall on Saltrenius.

His viewscreens, at extended magnification, showed the gleaming space-dome clearly. The bubble of sturdy metal and plastic was set on a broad, dusty plain on the moon's bright side, yet not far from the sharply defined boundary of the far side's darkness. There were no craters or rock formations within several hundred metres of the dome itself, he saw. A man on foot would have no cover approaching it.

But at least one piece of luck had come his way. The orbital sweep showed that the space cruiser which belonged to the dome's occupants was not in sight.

'Probably on Saltrenius again,' Keill decided.

Some have remained, Glr said. *I can sense human minds within the dome, though I cannot tell how many.*

'Anyway, it lowers the odds,' Keill said. 'And it gives me a chance for some exploring. Whoever's been left in the dome is likely to stay inside.'

He curved his ship to a landing – just inside the deep shadow of the moon's dark side, and over the horizon that would be visible from the dome. He knew that the landing would not be detected: its sound would not travel in the vacuum, and he had chosen a spot surrounded by upthrust clumps of rock that would swallow the vibrations.

Unstrapping himself from the slingseat, he gathered up his

helmet and went to the weapons compartment. It contained a sizeable selection of rifles and pistols, with even a few knives and other hand weapons. But Keill did not hesitate over his choice. He had no illusions about what might happen: if there was a fight, it would be no place for more civilized weapons like anaesthetic needle-guns or stun-guns. Instead he strapped on an ion-energy pistol, a beamer – a modified version of his spaceship's weapons, firing a focused beam of raw energy.

Glr watched the preparations with interest. *You are very calm, for a human,* she said.

'What did you expect?' Keill smiled. 'That my knees would tremble?'

I would have expected some worry or excitement, Glr replied. *It is the human way.*

Keill shrugged his way into his airpack. 'It isn't the Legion way. A waste of energy.'

Some day you must instruct me in the ways of the Legions, Glr said.

Keill laughed. 'Little friend, if I survive this, I'll happily put you through an entire training programme.' He fastened his helmet, swiftly ran through a final check of his equipment, then turned again to Glr, concentrating, trying to form words clearly in his mind, as if speaking them.

'*Are you receiving me?*' he asked.

Perfectly.

'*Good – then we can keep in contact. I want you to stay at the controls, but do absolutely nothing unless I tell you. Clear?*'

Perfectly.

'*And if any of the others spot the ship, and try to board it, let me know at once.*'

I hear and obey. There was a hint of laughter in the reply.

'*Keep your jokes for afterwards. And one more thing – if I don't come back . . .*'

You will be dead, Glr replied calmly, *and no longer able to give me orders. So I will use my initiative.*

Keill smiled. '*All right. Then you can go off and report to your Overseers.*'

I will, said Glr. *But first I might try out the weapons of this ship. On the dome and its occupants.*

The airlock closed silently behind him as Keill dropped to the surface of Creffa. It was a slow, dreamy drop, in the light gravity of the moon – and his progress was also like a dream, long, reaching strides that were in fact huge, slow leaps of many metres at a time. Soon he had reached the edge of the undiffused glare that was the bright side of the moon.

The plastiglass of his helmet darkened instantly, protectively, as he moved across into the light. Behind him, his ship could no longer be seen over the horizon. Ahead, somewhere beyond the jagged clusters of rocks where he stood, the dome lay.

In some ways, he thought, with the abundance of fanged rock and the absence of vegetation and water, his surroundings were like the region of the Iron Peaks on Moros, where trainee legionaries went for individual survival tests. But at least in that place there would have been the moan of a mournful wind, and the crunch and slide of your boots over the rock, to prove that you were still alive. In this dreary place, airlessness meant an inhuman silence, bleak and disturbing, so that Keill felt like a disembodied ghost.

But he shook off the oppression that gathered in his mind, and began to make his way through the rocks – slowly and stealthily, controlling his movements now so that he kept low to the ground despite the low gravity, trying to step only on rock so that no tell-tale footprints would remain in the dust behind him.

At last, edging beneath an overhang that would have collapsed long before in normal gravity, he saw the dome.

It rose from the broad expanse of dust like a blister rises from human skin, but so bright in the reflected glare that it seemed to be made of mirrors. Around it, the dust was crisscrossed with the tracks of many boots, from the comings and goings of the dome's nine occupants. But at the moment there was no one in sight, no sign of movement or activity around the dome.

He drew back behind the screening rock and began a cautious circling, wanting to examine the dome from all sides, and most especially to locate its entrance.

Keill.

Glr's voice within his mind – and a tone of some urgency in the one word.

Your ship's sensors report another ship nearby. On a course for a landing.

As before, Keill concentrated, to form the reply in his mind. 'Will it overfly your position?'

No, its course will bring it down near the dome, from the bright side. I will not be detected.

That was some luck, anyway, Keill thought to himself. But he wished that the other ship could have delayed its arrival awhile. Even so, he thought, if he could get close enough to the landing without being seen, and watch the men that disembarked, he might learn something.

He knew perfectly well, with a calm and untroubled sureness, that he would eventually have to try to enter the dome, no matter how many men were waiting inside. But he also had no intention of going in too blindly – not if he could manage a careful study of the opposition, or some of them, beforehand.

He wound his way as swiftly as he could through the rocks, still circling the dome but at no time exposing himself to it. Then he felt the ground tremble slightly beneath his feet. And at the same time Glr's voice reached into his mind again.

Sensors indicate the ship is landing. It seems to be the cruiser.

An image began to form in Keill's mind, projected by Glr – of the dome, squatting in its empty stretch of ground, and on the edge of that plain a ship coming in to land. The ship was recognizably a cruiser, but Glr's mind had added a few touches of her own – a great plume of fire from the ship's drive, and an evil face painted on to the front of the ship, all jagged teeth and cruel, slanted eyes.

'Thanks,' Keill said sardonically. '*Very artistic.*'

Better than a map, is it not? asked Glr, her laughter bubbling.

'*Much better. Be quiet now, while I go and look.*'

The heavy vibrations set up by the cruiser's landing increased steadily as he crept forward, until – crouching within the solid blackness of a tall rock's shadow – he was again at the edge of the plain.

The vibrations eased and stopped. The cruiser was down. Keill leaned forward to peer round the rock that sheltered him – and at once jerked his head back.

The cruiser had landed about three hundred metres away.

And beyond it, he had seen the entrance of the dome – its airlock open and spacesuited men emerging, moving at speed in the same long, leaping strides that Keill had used earlier.

He flattened himself against the rock. If any of those men, or the men in the ship, had glanced his way – and if his helmet had glinted even for an instant in the brilliant light . . .

It was an outside chance – but it was possible. Time to move.

But he did not retrace his steps. He drifted with slow caution from rock to rock towards where the cruiser had settled. Whatever the risk, he was not going to pass up a chance to see whatever might be seen.

Soon he had spotted another vantage point at the edge of the open area. When he reached it, he saw, he would be able to observe the ship and the dome while staying safely hidden in a bulge of deep shadow. He began to circle an outcropping, moving towards that point.

And he came face to face with two men, rounding the outcropping from the other direction.

Their faceplates, like Keill's, were darkened against the glare, revealing nothing. But one of them was wearing a spacesuit identical to Keill's – with the blue circlet of the Legions gleaming from helmet and chest.

And both men were holding weapons, ready in their hands.

Keill identified the guns at a glance, and with some distaste. Janglers, they were called – stubby pistols with ugly, flared, bell-shaped muzzles. They discharged a field that set up interference with the human nervous system – which caused, at the very least, indescribable pain. The guns were a sadist's weapon, outlawed on many worlds, and never, as Keill well knew, carried by legionaries.

He stood calmly where he was, making no motion towards his own weapon, while the other two took a tentative step towards him. The one in the Legion spacesuit lifted a gloved hand to his helmet, touching the switch that activated the man-to-man communicator.

'That you, Jiker?' The voice within Keill's helmet was metallic, distorted by the communicator.

Keill felt relieved. Of course there were two men on Creffa wearing full legionary uniform, which obviously included spacesuits. This one, seeing Keill's suit, naturally thought he was looking at his fellow impostor.

Keill flicked his own helmet switch. 'Yeah, it's me,' he said gruffly, knowing his voice would be just as distorted in the other man's ears.

But to his surprise the other raised his gun menacingly.

'The hell it is,' said the voice in Keill's helmet. '*I'm* Jiker.'

Keill's hand flashed, and his gun leaped from his belt. But the other man had only to press the firing stud on the jangler. And pure, raging agony reached out and grasped Keill's body like a monstrous fist.

Dimly he heard himself cry out, dimly he felt himself twisting, jerking, beginning to fall.

Then he heard and felt nothing at all.

chapter eleven

Keill awoke to the clamour of his own name being shouted, over and over.

No, not shouted, he realized. It was Glr's mental call, as penetrating as a cry of fear.

'*Stop it*,' he thought, raising one hand to his head, which was throbbing dully. '*I'm here.*'

Relief flooded into his mind from Glr's. *What happened? Where are you?*

Keill's probing fingers found a raised and tender bump on his head, and the slight roughness of dried blood. '*I must have bounced my head around in my helmet when I fell. As for where I am ...*'

He looked around. He was lying on a hard bunk in a small, metal-walled cubicle – which he recognized as the usual cramped sleeping quarters for men in a space-dome. The air smelled stale and musty, but was breathable – and he was his normal weight, which meant that some form of artificial gravity was operating in the dome. His spacesuit had been stripped off him and flung untidily in one corner – though his energy gun, predictably, was not with it.

'*I'm inside the dome, and I'm in one piece.*' He swung up to a sitting position, ignoring the headache. One thing about the janglers, he thought to himself – for all the pain they caused, it stopped instantly when the weapon was deactivated. Though there could sometimes be serious after-effects ...

What now? Glr asked.

'*You stay there, and stay quiet awhile. The door is probably guarded, and I'm going to ...*'

Whatever it was, he was not able to do it. The door swung

open, and two men entered. Both were carrying guns, and they separated as they entered, moving to either side of Keill and keeping their weapons trained on him, all very professionally.

One of them, holding a jangler, was thin, wiry, with a long jaw and small, glittering eyes. The other was heavy-set and swarthy, with a nose that seemed to have been broken many times. And he had Keill's own beam-gun in his hand.

Both were wearing legionary uniforms.

'Y've come round, have y'?' the thin one said. 'Thought y' might've cracked y'r skull.' He grinned, a mouthful of small, yellow teeth. 'Nice trick, that, wasn't it? Askin' y' if y' was me? Ol' Rish here, he would've answered different, wouldn't y', Rish?'

The heavy-set man grunted, never taking his eyes from Keill. So the thin one was Jiker, the one who had shot Keill. And, yes, it had been a good trick. But Keill remained silent, studying the two men, judging their abilities, doubting if he would have much of a chance to move against two guns, but poised and ready if even the edge of a chance offered itself.

'Nothin' t' say t' y'r brother legionaries?' Jiker went on. His laugh was high-pitched and ugly.

'Where did you get the uniforms?' Keill asked, his voice as expressionless as his face.

'Took 'em off a ship that just came floatin' by,' Jiker grinned. 'Boys wearin' 'em didn't have use for 'em, not any more.'

'Where was that?' Keill asked.

'Just off good ol' Moros,' Jiker said, snickering. 'You remember Moros, don't y', boy?'

'Why were you there?' Much could be learned from talkative men, Keill knew, if they could be kept talking.

Jiker seemed all too ready to chatter. 'We like it there, don't we, Rish? Quietest place y' ever saw – real peaceful now. Like the boss said, when we did the last sweep . . .'

'Jiker!'

The voice from the doorway was deep, resonant, musical,

seeming effortlessly to fill the room. Jiker's thin mouth snapped shut, and he paled slightly beneath his spacer's sunburn as he glanced towards the door.

The bare-chested man who was entering the cubicle had to stoop, and to turn his vast shoulders sideways, to pass through the doorway. Here was the leader of the original three false legionaries – the half-naked giant who had gazed at Keill, and laughed, that frustrating day on the spaceport of Saltrenius.

He was smiling now, unpleasantly. 'Jiker, one of these days I think I will send you for a walk outside without a suit, and see if you can talk in vacuum.'

The threat seemed all the more vicious for having been made in that easy, melodious voice. Then the giant turned to inspect Keill – who countered with an inspection of his own.

The enormous, smoothly muscled bulk of the man was belied by the lightness of his step, the control of his movements. Here was no lumbering man-mountain, Keill saw, but a man who was as athletic and co-ordinated as he was powerful. Which made him all the more formidable.

Probably from one of the altered worlds, Keill surmised. The hairlessness, the bronze skin were indications. But there was something else . . .

He remembered the words of the newsman back on Saltrenius, which seemed so long ago. About the strange markings round the throat and belly of the giant. The marks were plainly visible to Keill – looking very much like raised, narrow ridges of scar tissue, evenly and completely encircling the powerful neck and abdomen. Then Keill looked again, and his skin crawled.

The ridges seemed to be *moving*. Writhing, swelling slightly. As if serpentine things with lives of their own were curled round the giant's body, just beneath the skin.

The giant's malicious smile widened as he surveyed Keill.

'So we have finally caught one, have we?' His chuckle resounded in the narrow room. 'And, I believe, the very one who was hurrying to make our acquaintance on Saltrenius. What took you so long to pay us a visit, legionary?'

Keill said nothing, watching the giant impassively.

'Taking refuge in silence, I see. Very well – we shall go through the formalities. Your name and rank?'

'Keill Randor, Group Leader of the fourth Strike Group of the 41st Legion.' Keill's voice was flat and cold.

'Of the planet Moros,' said the giant. 'Is that not how the ritual went on?'

Keill let the question pass. 'Gloating is a pastime of small minds. Do you have a name, gloater?'

The giant's smile faded for an instant, then returned. 'Ah, the legendary fighting spirit of the Legions is not quelled. Yes, Keill Randor, you may know my name – for the short while that you have left to know anything. I am the Lord Thr'un of Irruq-hoa.'

Keill raised a sardonic eyebrow. He had never heard of a planet called Irruq-hoa, but then there were many planets he had never heard of. He did know that aristocratic titles were common in many human societies through the galaxy. But it was an odd distinction for the leader of a gang like this to bear.

'Why is a lord of Irruq-hoa sitting on a moon of Saltrenius pretending to be a legionary?'

The giant's laughter boomed. 'On my world, we have a species of water creature that is hardly more than a large stomach, with filters. It sits quietly across the current of the stream, and other creatures swim blindly in, to be eaten. I have been waiting here to eat you, legionary.'

'On my planet,' Keill replied coldly, 'there was a poisonous reptile that had the ability to disguise itself as other, less vicious creatures. We always killed them, whenever we discovered one.'

'I am the reptile in disguise, am I?' laughed Thr'un. 'And you would like to kill me, I am sure.' He stepped forward, looming over Keill, the eerie markings jutting and squirming beneath his skin. 'It would be interesting to let you try, Randor. I have often wondered how the famous fighting skills of the Legions would measure up to those of the . . . to mine.'

Keill had not missed the broken sentence. 'To those of the what?'

Thr'un smiled. 'So many questions. But it is I who have questions that are to be answered.' He moved back, folding his huge arms. 'First answer me this, Randor. How many other legionaries have survived?'

Keill nodded thoughtfully. 'So I am the first, as you said, to fall into your trap. I doubt if the others will be so careless.'

'What others?' the giant hissed. 'Where?'

Letting his eyes shift away from Thr'un, Keill assumed an expression of dismay, as if he had said more than he intended. 'Perhaps there are no others. I . . . I don't know.'

'You will tell me!' Thr'un bellowed.

Keill bent his head and stared steadfastly at the floor, giving a perfect portrayal of a man determined not to give away a secret.

The giant snorted, and gestured at Jiker and Rish. 'Bring him along,' he ordered. 'You may tie him down and jangle him a little until he feels more conversational.'

Thr'un turned and went abruptly out, and Keill raised his head to confront the muzzles of the guns in the other men's hands, and the unholy gleam of pleasure in their eyes.

They guided him into a corridor that ran outside the cubicle, both men staying well behind him and staying on opposite sides of the corridor, so that even Keill could not hope to turn and lunge at both together. So he went without argument, using his chance to examine what he could see of the layout of the dome.

It seemed to follow the basic, standard shape of most space-domes. It was ovoid, and on two levels. The upper one would normally be a hemisphere of metal and plastic, topped with a broad lens-like circle of plastiglass and used primarily for observation, communication and the like. So Keill knew from the flat, blank ceiling that he must be on the lower level.

Most space-domes had one wide corridor running round the circumference of the lower level, just inside the tough outer hull. That main corridor would surround all the various functioning sections of the dome – like workrooms and laboratories, sleeping quarters, communal eating and recreation areas – along with the usual life-support systems, storage rooms and so on. And these would be connected by narrower passages that would each join up at some point with the main outer corridor.

So it seemed to be, in this case. The passage they had entered from the cubicle led to a broad, curving corridor as Keill had expected. A quick glance over his shoulder and he had exactly what he needed for his bearings – because he had glimpsed, behind them, the broad and heavy hatchway of an airlock. That had to be the dome's entrance – almost certainly its only one.

They moved along the main corridor, then soon turned down another of the narrow connecting passages. There the two armed men had to walk nearly shoulder to shoulder, but even so it would have been insanely risky for Keill to turn on them. Anyway, there was too much he still wanted to find out – and, he hoped, there might be better chances for escape later.

In a moment they came to a doorway opening off the passage, and the two urged Keill through it. It might once have been a laboratory, when the dome was serving its original purpose of scientific research. Now it was disused and empty, except for a low, heavy metal platform, which had once probably held an assortment of machinery and equipment.

Now, apparently, it was to hold Keill Randor.

'Get on there,' Jiker snarled, with a gesture of the jangler. 'On y'r back.'

Keill did as he was told, calmly, though he could guess what was to come. But Rish was holding the beam-gun aimed unerringly at Keill's head, and looked only too ready to use it.

Jiker stooped and took several metal bands and clamps from beneath the platform, obviously well prepared beforehand for their purpose. He fastened the bands tightly across Keill, clamping him to the bare metal surface so that he was immobilized – held by wrists and ankles, and by bands across chest and thighs.

'Now,' Jiker said, licking thin lips, 'think about them questions the boss asked y'.'

He raised the jangler and pressed the stud.

The agony flooded in. It was as if every nerve-end was being dragged forcibly from its place, to be dipped in acid and hacked at by a saw-toothed blade. Keill's body contorted, convulsed, threshing within the confines of the bands that held him – and blood streamed from his lip where he had sunk his teeth in to keep from screaming.

Then, instantly, the pain was gone. Breathing heavily, he licked his torn lip and glared with hatred at the grinning face of Jiker.

'Nice, was it? Anythin' t' say yet?'

Wordless, Keill looked away.

'Right, take as long as y' like. Plenty more where that came from.'

Jiker raised his gun again, glee in his eyes.

And again the murderous pain.

And again . . . And again . . .

After what may have been the sixth time, or the tenth – Keill could no longer be sure – he became aware that the giant had entered the room. For a time there was a pause while Thr'un consulted with his men, and Keill could assess his damage.

His body ached with bruising where the convulsions had thrust him against the metal bands. His lip was swollen and throbbing. And his head seemed to have become a size larger, so ferocious was the ache that filled it. But, tentatively moving his neck and as much of the rest of himself as he could, he knew that he still had command of his body, that he was not seriously injured.

Then the giant loomed over him.

'You seem determined to suffer,' said the melodious bass voice. 'As I would have expected. Are you any closer to telling me what I wish to know?'

Keill neither spoke nor looked at him.

'Also as I would have expected,' Thr'un said with an exaggerated sigh. 'The Legions made their men little more than robots, blindly following the demands of their masters.'

An odd emphasis in the words gave Keill the glimmer of an idea. Finding what was left of his voice, he croaked, 'Do you not follow *your* masters?'

Thr'un took the bait. 'My Master,' he began, 'does not require me . . .'

He stopped abruptly, glowering down at Keill. 'Very crafty, legionary.' The voice rumbled deep and deadly. 'You have been trying hard, have you not, to learn what you can. But you have learned nothing. And even if I were able to reveal to you the name and whereabouts of the Master, you would not live long enough to make use of that knowledge.'

Keill ignored the death threat, his mind grasping and examining the rest of the speech. A 'Master'? Who set up this trap on Creffa, and also sent the men on sweeps near Moros, as Jiker had said? Who seemed to give his minions something of a free hand? And whose name and whereabouts Thr'un was not 'able' to reveal?

It was all beginning to sound like something he had heard before.

He tried to focus his mind, to contact Glr and pass on what he had learned. Perhaps the little alien could make more sense out of these vague hints. Or perhaps the Overseers . . .

But then the giant was speaking again, distracting him. 'You may now decide, Randor. Tell me of these other survivors, and you have a chance to keep your useless life. Stay silent, and you will die, now, in a most unpleasant manner.'

Keill smiled coldly. 'As far as I know, there are no others. I have met none, I have heard of none.'

'Lies!' boomed the giant, and gestured to Jiker. The thin man hurried forward, grinning.

While Rish kept his beam-gun steadily on Keill, Jiker removed two of the bonds – those across his body – leaving him clamped only by his wrists and ankles.

'As you know,' Thr'un said malevolently, 'janglers do not themselves kill. But you will also know that the convulsions they cause can be very severe. A man who might happen to be held by hands and feet might suffer a great deal of damage. He is likely to bend himself almost in two – and his neck or his spine will snap as if they were glass.'

Keill said nothing, still striving to gather his concentration, to reach Glr.

'Have you an answer now to my question?' Thr'un bellowed.

But Keill ignored him, for the voice of Glr had slid into his mind.

Keill, if you are projecting, I cannot fix on it. It is too muzzy. Try harder – because there is trouble. I sense two humans moving nearby, probably searching for the ship.

As expected, Keill thought, the giant had sent men out to look for their captive's ship. With a supreme effort, he gathered his thought. *'Glr, take off at once, and stay in space on the dark side. If you hear nothing more from me, tell the Overseers that I . . .'*

But he was unable to continue the message, for Thr'un was bellowing again, drawing his attention.

'As you wish, legionary! If there are others, some will no doubt visit me soon. They may prove more co-operative. I have no more use for you!' He turned to Jiker. 'Go ahead.'

Jiker began his high-pitched titter as he took aim. Then the jangler flared.

As before, Keill's body twisted, writhed, flexed – and now

97

arched high off the metal surface. Arched in an impossible curve, jerking and threshing, only his arms and his feet held still.

Then there was a sickening, grinding crack.

Jiker released the firing stud, and Keill's body slumped down, limp and motionless.

chapter twelve

The intense, crushing pain that continued within his body proved, to Keill's half-conscious surprise, that he was still alive. It also told him that he would probably not live for much longer.

The pain clawed at every segment of his body. Each muscle and joint was in torment, but most of all his neck and lower back. He had clearly broken his spine, as Thr'un had indicated. Perhaps his spinal cord still held, temporarily, but he would not have long before it too gave way. He would probably be dead even before Thr'un or his men got round to finishing him off.

He felt no fear, no self-pity – just an edge of regret that he had achieved so little against Thr'un and his false legionaries. But at least he had gathered a few hints, which he still had to pass on to Glr. He fought with the haze in his mind, fought to focus his thoughts, to make contact again with the alien. But the pain, and voices dimly heard, intruded. One of the voices was Thr'un's, from some distance away – as if the giant had turned to leave, after Keill's collapse, and was issuing orders from the doorway.

'. . . won't have survived that,' the deep bass voice was saying. 'Strip off the uniform for one of the other men to use.'

'Whatd' we do with th' body?' Jiker's thin voice.

'Put it in the airlock, and some of the others can take it to the ship. We'll throw it out when we next visit the planet, and let it burn in atmosphere.'

Jiker began to say something else, but Keill didn't hear – for Glr was in his mind, fear and worry plain in the inner voice.

Keill clutched at his concentration, and in pain-filled bursts of thought, told Glr what had happened.

In the midst of the anxiety pouring from Glr's mind, he heard – astonishingly – the rise of the alien's silent laughter.

Keill, you are a hardhead! Glr cried. *Clinging to your doubts still – even to convince yourself that you're dying!*

Clearly, Keill thought, he had not managed to project properly, and Glr had misunderstood. He began to try again, but the alien interrupted.

No, I received you properly. Don't you see? Talis told you the simple truth. Nothing those men could do could break so much as your little finger!

The hope that ballooned up within Keill was instantly crushed by disbelief. The agony in his back was very real . . .

Of course it is! Glr replied. *The weapon put every muscle and tendon under terrible stress – that is what hurts! But nothing is broken! Nothing can be!*

Hope seeped back, determined. The pain from aching ligaments? The terrible cracking sound merely from joints shifting under the strain, as a man can crack his knuckles without damage?

He tried tentatively to move his body, half-expecting that he might be paralysed. But it moved – torso shifting, knees rising. As he moved, the pain flared, then eased, slightly. And hope burst forth undiminished.

It seemed to be true! He was probably suffering only from a ferocious stretching and twisting. And a lifetime of gruelling Legion exercises, which were focused on stretching and twisting, had made his body supple beyond most people's imaginings. He had very likely pulled a muscle or two, strained ligaments – but he was intact, he was functional. It might hurt, but his body would do his bidding.

By then it was time for it to do so. The whole exchange with Glr, at the incalculable speed of thought, had taken place while Jiker and Rish were turning back towards him from the door. The giant Thr'un had presumably left the room. And his two men, only glancing at Keill who was again lying as limp as he could, began at once to release the clamps that held him to the metal platform.

Then Jiker's sharp eyes registered the faint movement of Keill's chest, with his breathing.

'Sunfires,' Jiker gasped, 'he's still alive!'

Keill remained motionless, and made his breath rasp in his throat.

'Not f'r long, I reckon,' Rish grunted. 'Give him another burst.'

Keill sent out a sharp mental call. '*Glr, come in now, quickly, and overfly the dome, as low as you can.*'

I hear and obey, came the laughing reply.

Jiker was taking a tentative step forward. 'Can't be faking – not after what we gave him. Must be a lot stronger 'n he looks.'

Keill made his chest heave, gave a choking rattle in his throat, then sagged, not breathing.

Jiker took another stride forward, and bent over him, listening.

And with the howling, throbbing roar of a thousand devils, Keill's spaceship thundered past overhead, no more than a man's height from the upper surface of the dome.

Both men jerked their heads up, gaping fearfully.

And Keill reached, grasped Jiker's tunic, shifted his hips for leverage, and flung the skinny man into Rish's face.

Every muscle of his back shrieked its displeasure, but it was an entirely bearable pain. He swung round and came to his feet, just as Rish, face contorted with anger, also scrambled upright. Both men had dropped their guns as they sprawled, but Rish was too enraged to think about weapons. He lowered his head like a bull, and charged.

Keill swayed aside, grasped and jerked at a meaty shoulder so that the charge became a headlong plunge.

The impact of Rish's forehead on the corner of the metal platform echoed dully in the room. The heavy man sagged to the floor, his face a mask of blood, an indentation showing where a segment of his skull had been crushed back into his brain.

Keill did not glance at the corpse, for Jiker was scrabbling across the floor towards one of the guns. Keill sprang to intercept him – grasping him by the belt and hurling him across the room, where he bounced from the wall and lay huddled. Then Keill scooped up both the jangler and his own energy-gun.

'Now it's your turn to do a little dance,' he growled.

Jiker was jibbering with fear. 'How . . . how c'n you be alive?'

'Worry about your own life,' Keill said. 'The other men – where will they be?'

'Dunno,' Jiker gabbled. 'Canteen, maybe – no!' His voice rose thinly as Keill aimed the jangler at him. 'They'll be suitin' up – to go out an' see what that was just went by!'

Keill flung out a mental message. '*Glr, circle back and disable their ship. Then bring the ship down and fire a blast or two just in front of the dome's entrance.*'

To keep them penned up inside? Glr said, doubtfully.

'*Yes.*' There was a cold deadliness in the mental tone. '*I want them all in here, with me.*'

As you wish, said Glr.

Keill had not taken his eyes from Jiker. 'Where will the men be, suiting up?'

'Equipment room, down th' other end by th' entrance.'

'And Thr'un?'

'Maybe with 'em . . . Maybe up in th' dome, where he stays most 'f th' time . . .' An evil glint lit up Jiker's eyes. 'Y' won't get past him, y'know! He'll take y' apart! He ain't human!'

Keill was about to demand more detail on that interesting point when the door to the chamber was flung open.

One of the other men burst in, obviously sent to collect Jiker and Rish. The pass Glr had made in the ship had produced action. Thr'un would be organizing his men to face a possible attack.

But Keill spun and fired – with the beam-gun – before the

newcomer could open his mouth. The man screamed and toppled, a small flame licking for an instant at the edge of the hole burned by the energy gun in the centre of his chest. And in that instant Jiker scrambled to his feet and lunged desperately at Keill.

Effortlessly Keill stepped within the reach of the frantically clawing fingers and drove a short, jabbing punch at the side of the long jaw. Anger and left-over pain put extra venom behind his fist – and the angle of Jiker's head, as his body sprawled, showed that it was not only janglers that broke necks.

Beneath his feet the floor quivered, heavy vibrations shaking the rock foundation of the dome. That would be Glr, making short work of the cruiser.

Keill moved quickly towards the door, bending over the man he had shot, freeing his gun. A needler, just for variety. But not much more useful to Keill than the jangler. He dropped both weapons on the floor, and smashed them with two driving blows of his heel. His own beam-gun would be all the weapon he would need.

There had been eight men, and Thr'un had made nine. Now there were five, besides the giant.

More vibrations underfoot – and then the voice of Glr in Keill's mind.

At the entrance, as requested. Two men in spacesuits had started to come out. They have gone back in at some speed.

'Good,' Keill replied. '*Stay there and keep watch. And don't speak for a while – I'm going to be busy.*'

Gun in hand, he sprang through the door and moved away along the narrow passage.

There had been no one in the passage – and as Keill came to its junction with the wide outer corridor, and peered carefully round the corner, there was still no one in sight. No doubt most of the remaining men were collected at the other end of the dome, near the airlocks, as Jiker had said. All their attention would be on the spaceship – with its Legion markings –

guarding the dome's entrance. The last thing they would expect would be one man attacking them from within.

And, because that one man was an armed legionary of Moros, in full fighting readiness and with a good many scores to settle, it was all too likely that it would be the *last* thing they would expect.

Keill turned into the corridor and moved swiftly and silently along it, hugging the inner wall. His movements seemed to have eased the pain from his strained and tortured muscles, and he moved as lightly and fluidly as he ever did. He slowed his pace as he neared the opening of another connecting passage. A careful glance round – and again no one. But soon, he was certain, the curving main corridor would reveal the opening of the airlock at the dome's entrance . . .

And there it was; and two men in space suits, with guns in their hands – energy guns. They hesitated only for a second, astonished at the sight of him, then jerked up their guns and fired.

Keill dived full length straight ahead. His left hand slapped on the smooth metal floor to break his fall, as the beams from the others' guns sizzled above his head. Then he was sliding a few paces, full length on the floor, but his own gun was rock-steady in his right hand, blazing out its deadliness.

The two men dropped with a clatter, and Keill was up again. To the left of the spacesuited bodies, a doorway that had to be the end chamber where the others were gathered. Three left now, besides the giant.

He flattened against the wall, swiftly glanced round the edge of the door and drew back. Energy beams hissed past, biting into the doorframe, the metal sliding and dripping as it melted. Two of them, waiting, hidden behind metal cases in what must be the equipment room. He could hear their voices, high-pitched and nervous in the face of this unexpected attack.

Beyond them, he had seen in that lightning glance, had been another doorway. And somewhere there was a third man . . .

He moved quietly away from the door. The two inside the

equipment room would keep for a moment – they were not likely to move. But the third man was probably trying to circle, to get behind Keill. Would he use the nearest connecting passage, the one Keill had just come past?

Apparently he would. Keill waited at the corner of the passage, ears straining, and caught the muffled slide of boots on metal as the man crept forward. Listening carefully, Keill waited – not a muscle moving, hardly breathing, as if he were carved in stone.

Another soft shuffle of a foot – nearer now. Carefully Keill weighed the distance and the timing, poising himself, silently shifting his gun to his left hand . . .

Then the other man put his head round the corner, and met the axe-edge of Keill's hand across his throat.

Keill caught the body as it collapsed, easing it soundlessly to the floor, ignoring the purple-black of the face as the man died swiftly from a crushed larynx. Silent as before, he drifted along the narrow connecting passage, rounded the corner, then let his boots ring solidly on the metal as he stepped through the doorway into the chamber behind the last two men who waited, watching nervously in the wrong direction.

They swung round in panic, wildly trying to bring their guns to bear, and Keill dropped them with one shot apiece.

And now there was only Thr'un.

A quick but careful survey of the remainder of the dome's lower level confirmed what Jiker had said. The giant was certainly on the upper level – where he had no doubt gone to look out at the Legion ship that lay in wait at the dome's entrance.

Keill paused at the bottom of the stairs that led to the upper level, staring up at the curving wall, with a patch of stars glinting through the plastiglass at the crest of the dome. One set of stairs, which emerged through the floor of the top level, so that at the top Keill would be in full view of the waiting Thr'un.

He ghosted up a few steps in total silence, then halted,

crouching, and projected a call. '*Glr – another diversion. Fire a blast over the dome, as close as you can.*'

At your service, came the cheerful reply.

The plastiglass flared with eerie light as the narrow beam of energy blazed past overhead. In the same instant Keill sprang up the remaining stairs, dived and rolled.

Another, narrower beam flashed centimetres away from where he had been, burning deep into the floor. But Keill had found refuge behind a heap of discarded cases, and lay there, listening carefully, looking over his surroundings.

Clearly Thr'un's men had seen no need to be tidy-minded in their occupancy of the dome. Nor had the scientific group who had first used the structure been any more inclined to neatness when they left. The upper level, which was one large chamber with the dome itself as ceiling, was filled with clutter and rubble.

There were discarded cases and containers of every size and shape, scattered and heaped at random. There were what seemed to be stacks of spare parts for machinery, and segments of scientific equipment, probably damaged and thrown aside as irreparable. There were even a few mounds of rock – no doubt samples from the surface of the moon, left behind after examination.

It all meant useful cover, for anyone wishing to keep hidden in the wide chamber. But it was cover for Thr'un as much as Keill.

Then Keill saw that there was a considerable cleared space along one side of the chamber – a space that was dominated by a tall bank of equipment, apparently in working order.

Communications equipment, without doubt. Perhaps for Thr'un to maintain contact with his 'Master'?

A faint rustle to Keill's left. The giant was circling, stalking, seeking a chance for another shot with his beam-gun.

Keep moving, Keill told himself, edging soundlessly away to his right. It was his only direction – yet he regretted it, for he was being driven away from the stairs, being cut off from the only way out. No matter, he thought. If he'd been sensible, he would never have climbed the stairs – but merely have gone out to his ship and blasted the dome to cinders. But somehow he had wanted to face the giant this way. And there was always the chance that more useful information might be forthcoming.

The energy beam hissed past him, and a metal canister on a heap of rubbish fell away, a gaping hole melted into its surface. Keill ducked, moving swiftly – and as he did so, the rich bass voice of Thr'un echoed musically through the chamber.

'Welcome, legionary. You seem amazingly difficult to kill – but I promise you, you will not leave here alive.'

chapter thirteen

Keill did not reply, but took advantage of the sound of the resonant voice to move more swiftly. Only a few strides now, and he would be behind the heavy bank of equipment that was some complex form of communicator. There was a chance that Thr'un would not wish to burn through that, to reach him.

'As close-mouthed as ever, Randor?' called the giant. He, too, had moved, as the direction of his voice showed. 'I would have thought you would have a few last words.'

Again, covered by the rolling echoes of Thr'un's voice, Keill moved. For an instant he was fully exposed in the cleared area, but his speed saved him. He felt the blistering heat of the energy beam just above his head as he dived and rolled, coming to rest behind the communicator cabinet. Its metal bulk rose comfortingly above him, nearly his own height.

'You are mistaken,' Thr'un said, 'if you think that will protect you.' To underline the words, the energy beam bit at the corner of the communicator. Molten metal hissed and dripped.

'And you are mistaken,' Keill shouted, 'if you think killing me will save you. My . . . companion in the ship still has you trapped.'

'Yes, that was clever of you,' Thr'un mocked. His voice indicated that he was moving slowly closer. 'I had not imagined that there was someone in your ship – you were alone, were you not, on Saltrenius? Who is it out there, another legionary?'

'As full of questions as ever, Thr'un?' Keill said, mimicking the giant's earlier words. 'Still intending to report dutifully to your Master?'

Keill was aware that the giant wanted to keep him talking, to put him off-guard when the final attack came. But the trick might work in reverse. Certainly Thr'un seemed to enjoy the sound of his own voice . . .

'I do not report to the Master,' Thr'un sneered. 'Only the One reports.'

Keill sat up at that. More intriguing hints and mysteries. Could he jolt more information out of the giant – providing he had time to do so?

'And the "One" would be the head of your group that you nearly told me about?'

'Clever again,' Thr'un growled. He was even closer now. His energy gun crackled again, and a corner of the communicator sagged, something within it bursting briefly into flame. Keill paid scant attention.

'Is he as insane as you, or your cowardly Master?' he called.

'You prattle of things beyond your knowledge!' Th'run replied, voice rumbling deep with anger.

'Knowledge?' Keill said. He sensed that the moment of attack was near, and spoke quickly, hardly thinking about what he was saying. 'I know what you are, and who you serve. I know your Master is the destroyer of my world and my people. And I know that he has a madman's dream of wrecking the galaxy with warfare, and ruling over its ruins!'

Surprise joined the anger in Thr'un's voice. 'You know more than you should, legionary. More than I imagined. The Master will be interested.'

Again his beam-gun blazed, and there was a flash and a muffled explosion deep in the bowels of the bank of equipment. Keill drew back slightly as the metal that sheltered him grew hot to the touch. But he moved by reflex, hardly aware – for his mind was dazedly trying to assimilate what had just been said.

He had hurled his wild accusations, based on the story old Talis had told, in order to provoke Thr'un into revealing the true nature of the 'Master' who directed him. He had not imagined for a moment . . .

But it had happened. Thr'un had *confirmed* the fantastic things Keill had said.

Which meant that the Overseers' story about the Warlord . . . was true.

As true as Talis's statement about the bones of Keill's body.

He shook his head, trying to clear it, to re-orient himself. Think about it later, he told himself savagely, or you won't live to think at all.

Thr'un's voice had last come from a point that must be on, or near, the edge of the cleared area. Silently Keill eased his way to the right, crouching at the corner of the communicator, concentrating, focusing energy and power into his legs. Make him speak again, he thought. Pinpoint his position.

'Your Master won't be pleased at what has happened here, Thr'un,' he called. 'A failure is executed – isn't that the way of the Warlord?'

'Warlord, you call him?' Thr'un rumbled. 'An apt name. Yes, he has his way with failure. But I have not failed, legionary. I was sent here to complete the task I began – to clear the galaxy of your Legions. And I will complete it!'

The implication of the words struck Keill at once, and the hatred and rage that rose in him seemed to fill his veins with fire. '*You*? You are the destroyer?'

'It was I,' the giant gloated, 'who sent the radiation capsules into the atmosphere of Moros. A laughably simple task. Miniature capsules, made by the genius of the Master, hidden in an innocent shipment of grain. Your Legions suspected nothing. And then, on the signal, the chain reaction . . .'

But Keill did not let him finish. Fury reinforced his strength as he exploded into a surging leap – not sideways round the corner of the communicator, but straight up, in a mighty standing jump.

He was firing as he leaped, firing as his feet struck the top of the melting, blackened machine, firing still as he sprang without pause out across the cleared area, at the throat of his enemy.

The giant had flung himself to one side to dodge the deluge of energy blasts, and that movement and Keill's speed threw his own aim off. Energy beams sizzled past Keill as he charged – and then scalding pain bit deep into his right shoulder as one of the erratic beams found him, spinning him off-balance, hurling him to the floor.

His gun fell and slid out of reach – and then the giant, moving with his own astonishing speed, was towering over him, gun levelled at Keill's face.

Keill waited for the death shot, but Thr'un did nothing, except let a cruel smile of satisfaction grow across his face.

'You see?' he said. 'I have not failed, after all.'

Keill looked at him with contempt. 'You won't have long to gloat. My companion will know the moment I am dead – and will destroy the dome with you in it.'

'Indeed? I doubt if he will know so quickly. No, I will have no trouble in burning my way out of the rear of the dome and dealing with your companion – after I have dealt with you.'

He widened his mocking smile, then glanced down at Keill's shoulder, where blood seeped steadily through the seared flesh.

'You are injured, which is a shame,' Thr'un said. 'Yet you have proved a dangerous and resourceful opponent, and so you can still be deemed worthy.'

To Keill's astonishment, Thr'un stepped back, and tossed his beam-gun aside. 'Come, Randor, let me show you what I know to be true – that the much-admired skill of the Legions is nothing to the power of the Deathwing!'

Keill rose slowly to his feet, hardly able to believe what was happening. 'Deathwing?'

Thr'un laughed expansively. 'You have not heard the name? It is the Master's select force – his chosen lieutenants, who serve his will throughout the galaxy. Men like myself, Randor, from the altered worlds. Men to whom the Master has given skills, and strengths, and power, beyond anything dreamed of by a puny legionary!' He raised his arms at his sides, muscles rolling under the naked bronze skin. 'See, Randor! See how your death will come!'

Keill's eyes widened with amazement and horror. The weird, ridged markings on the giant's body were moving again. Writhing, swelling – *opening* . . .

From beneath the skin, where the ridges encircled Thr'un's body, erupted *growths*. Swiftly they extended, upwards and downwards, flaring, fanning out. They were like slabs of thick and heavy leather, solid linked plates of a dark, unpleasantly muddy colour. And they protected the giant like armour.

From the band around the neck they spread out to cover the throat and the base of the skull, reaching down over the upper chest and back. Below, the abdominal armour extended to cover the loins, the belly and the kidneys, stretching up over the solar plexus and the lower ribs.

All the weaker points on the human body – from neck to thigh – were, on Thr'un, protected from harm.

Keill had backed away a step, involuntarily. But he saw the sadistic light in the giant's eyes, and fought to bring his shock and revulsion under control – willing his aching, wounded body into the poised relaxation of combat readiness. His right shoulder felt as if naked flame was still eating at his flesh. But it was not a crippling wound, he knew. Beyond the pain, he still had the use of the arm.

Yet he let it dangle limply, as if the shoulder was shattered. Over-confidence might be the only weakness that Thr'un would show.

Then the giant attacked, without warning.

Keill was nearly trapped by the speed and power of the rush. But he managed to dodge one blow, block another, and spin away out of reach. Instantly Thr'un was upon him again – and again Keill evaded the attack, twisting away.

It became the pattern of the fight. Keill remained on the defensive – dodging, blocking, circling, relying on his balance and speed of reflexes to preserve him. But it was a dangerous game. With his injury and loss of blood, and the after-effects of the jangler, he was likely to tire and weaken before Thr'un did. And he was still persisting in using only his left arm to defend himself.

Also, Thr'un was swift, immensely strong, and considerably skilled. Not, for all his boasting, up to Legion standards, Keill had soon realized. Thr'un's combat skills were a little too orthodox, a little too predictable and unimaginative.

But that offered small advantage – when the uncanny body armour protected him so well.

And Keill soon found out how well. Knowing that he could not last in a prolonged battle, he took the fight to Thr'un more and more, counter-attacking out of defence. But he found that striking the armour was like hitting a padded wall. The thick, leathery substance seemed to give slightly under any blow, absorbing its power, so that Thr'un was hardly troubled. Keill had to look for targets on the head or legs – and the giant, knowing he could leave his torso virtually undefended, could more easily block or evade, preventing Keill from landing an effective blow.

So they fought on, Keill still circling, defending, probing for an opening that seemed never to come – the giant still aggressive, confident. Each attack was a flurry of blows and counters, a blur of weaving, swaying bodies. The giant feinting with a straight right-hand slash at the belly, the left hand whipping across to chop at the neck – Keill sliding inside the blow, heel of the left hand driving up – Thr'un blocking and striking for the face in the same fluid motion – Keill dropping almost to one knee, a foot lashing out at a kneecap – Thr'un swivelling away from the kick, his own foot countering to smash at Keill's jaw – Keill rolling away, coming to his feet, fingers flickering out in a stab at the eyes as the giant leaped again, huge hands clutching . . .

Weariness began to seep into Keill's limbs, and his breathing grew heavier. His time was running out. Now the giant was reaching him more often, as Keill's energy flagged. Time and again only desperate reflex turned a crushing elbow-smash from Thr'un into a glancing graze, only reflex dragged his thigh around to deflect a hurtling kick to the groin. And each of these times Keill staggered, and a little more strength drained from his weary, damaged body.

But his mind was still a legionary's mind – controlled, disciplined, aware. He did not miss the glitter of anticipation and triumph in Thr'un's eyes whenever Keill staggered, or when one of Keill's attacks failed. And Keill did not hesitate when his mind weighed up the danger, and produced what could be his only, desperately risky chance to survive.

The giant was given to gloating, to over-confidence. He had already been led to believe that Keill had only one usable arm. Lead him on a little further . . .

Now as he circled and countered, Keill let his body sag even more, let himself stumble and catch himself more often, let his breathing become ragged panting.

The gleam grew in Thr'un's eyes, his teeth flashed in a victory smile, as he plunged in pursuit of his apparently collapsing opponent.

Any moment now, Keill told himself as he weakly swayed aside from a flailing boot, pretending to half-stagger before recovering. He circled again, moving carefully. The timing had to be perfect, Thr'un had to approach at exactly the right angle, and had to respond in exactly the right, orthodox, predictable way . . .

The giant hurtled forward, just as Keill wanted him to. And Keill swung his left fist, slowing the punch slightly, invitingly.

Thr'un took the invitation. One hand flashed up and grasped Keill's wrist, the other huge arm clamped his elbow. Then the giant pivoted, twisted, and threw.

In the microsecond before his feet left the floor, a flurry of images passed through Keill's mind. The unbelievable words of Talis, on the Overseers' asteroid – the aftermath of the torture session at the hands of Jiker and Rish – the reassuring words of Glr . . .

He had manoeuvred Thr'un into using a standard hold-and-throw, so basic in unarmed combat as to be almost instinctive. If performed properly, as Keill's body was swung up and across his arm should break neatly in about three places.

He had been sure that Thr'un, with the orthodoxy of his technique, would use the hold. And he had been sure that the giant would not miss a chance to cripple his opponent's other arm, after which he would no doubt take his time at kicking Keill to death.

But the arm . . . did not break.

Keill flexed his body as he arched through the air, and his feet thudded firmly on to the floor, instantly finding balance and leverage. The tendons in his left elbow shrieked with the wrenching pain, but held.

Thr'un, expecting a shattered arm within his grasp, but finding instead that he was holding an arm like a steel bar, was dragged forward for a fleeting instant, off-balance, exposed.

And Keill, oblivious to the blaze of agony in his injured shoulder, swung his right fist across in a short arc with precise timing, swivelling his perfectly poised body as he struck, so that all his weight, all his fury, all his vengeful hatred followed into and through the blow.

In the Martial Games of Moros, such a blow from the fist of Keill Randor had smashed through slabs of plasticrete piled nearly a metre high – had splintered a wooden post as thick as Keill's own waist – had once even crumpled and cracked a plate of niconium steel.

Now that fist struck lethally at Thr'un's temple, just above the ear where the skull is thinnest, and crushed it like paper.

The huge armoured body was flung away like a dry leaf in a storm, crashing to the floor with a heavy, echoing finality.

Aftermath and beginning

chapter fourteen

The viewscreens showed the peaceful, star-glittering vastness of deep space. Far behind, on a tiny moon called Creffa, lay the molten, crumbled ruins of what had once been a gleaming space-dome, flattened by the guns of Keill's spaceship – the last thing Keill had done before his battle fury was spent, before he had sagged back to let Glr take the controls.

The little alien had taken the ship leaping out beyond the planetary system of Saltrenius, far into the welcoming reaches of space. There her strange, small hands had dressed Keill's shoulder, rubbed medication on his aching, tormented muscles and generally attended to all his hurts. Now Keill lay back, luxuriating in the restful clasp of the slingseat, and – with the ship under computer guidance – waited while Glr finished her long-range telepathic report to the Overseers.

At last the round eyes opened. *Talis regrets that the communicator on the dome had to be destroyed. It might have provided some directional fix.*

Keill shook his head. 'There wasn't much left of it before I destroyed the dome,' he said aloud.

Certainly the Overseers approve the dome's destruction, Glr said. *They wished no hints of what happened there left to be found by searchers from the Warlord.*

'Secrecy at all costs,' Keill intoned, hearing Glr's soft laughter in his mind.

Talis is very interested in your mention of the group called the Deathwing. He regrets you were not able to learn more about it.

'I beg his pardon,' Keill said sourly. 'That conversation ended a little abruptly.'

The mental laughter rose. *He understands that the Deathwing is a special force from which the Warlord selects his emissaries. But he wonders if you have any theories about the others in the group – especially the person whom Thr'un called 'the One'.*

'Not really. Except that if he's the leader of that group, and someone like Thr'un only a follower, he must be fairly impressive.'

Just so. Glr's imitation of Talis's favourite phrase made Keill grin. *The Overseers also ask if you have any doubts remaining, about what Talis told you during your stay with them.*

Doubts? Keill felt again the chill that had swept over him in that desperate moment of realization when, facing Thr'un, he had learned that the whole fearful story of the Warlord was true beyond all doubt.

'Only one,' he said grimly. 'That if I meet any more members of this Deathwing, I doubt if I'll survive the encounter.'

Glr's bright eyes shone with amusement as she relayed the message. *Talis is sure you will, now that you know more about what to expect. He is very pleased at being right about his assessment of your survival potential.*

'Fine,' Keill muttered. 'Tell him we're all very pleased here, too.'

He also hopes you will now confirm, Glr went on, *that you will act as the Overseers' emissary. To go on their behalf to worlds that are threatened by the Warlord – and to do what you can to oppose the threat.*

Keill knew what his answer was, yet he hesitated. On *their* behalf? But he was still a legionary, if alone – and he had a job to do, an unspoken promise to keep, to the dead of Moros. He did not delude himself that the defeat of Thr'un was anything but a first, small step in keeping that promise. Somewhere the real enemy, the real destroyer, still lived, still strove to spread his deadly infection of violence and murder.

'Tell Talis,' he said slowly, 'that it is as much my fight as his – or more. Tell him that I will work with the Overseers, but not *for* them. I will accept advice and assistance, but not orders.

Tell him that wherever I go, I will do what I can and what I must – but *my* way, without interference.'

Talis understands the conditions, and agrees.

'And do you come along as well?'

Of course, Glr laughed. *You would certainly never survive without me.*

Keill lay back in the slingseat. In his mind's eye an image formed – an image that always lurked on the edge of his imagination, that would probably always continue to lurk there. The image of the planet Moros as he last saw it – bathed in a glowing haze of lethal radiation, in which everything and everyone that Keill had loved had met their deaths.

And beyond that image, another, newer one. Like a black shadow across his inner vision. The dark mystery of the Warlord – and the shadow of the Deathwing.

The Overseers are waiting for your confirmation, Glr broke in.

'Tell the Overseers,' Keill said, 'confirmed. Absolutely confirmed.'

book two

Deathwing over Veynaa

Rebels of the Cluster
chapter one

The watcher among the rocks had not noticed the point of
light when it had first appeared, high in the pale yellow sky.
Only when it had fallen further, enlarging, brightening, did
the watcher's one huge eye glimpse it.

The watcher's six arms halted their activity. Within its
cold brain messages were relayed and received. Silently it
moved backwards, into a shadowed cleft among the rocks, its
eye fixed unblinkingly on the hurtling object in the sky.

In seconds the object revealed itself as a metal capsule, man-
sized and coffin-shaped. It fell bathed in fire as the atmosphere
flared along its metal skin. And it fell with a high-pitched
howl as its small retro rockets cut in, slowing its plunge – and
at last depositing it with a bump and a slide among the rocks.

It was a standard escape capsule, in use on many of the
spacecraft in the Inhabited Worlds. It had a tiny power supply,
enough for some guidance control, for its retros and for a
continuous 'Mayday' broadcast while in flight. It was a spaceman's last resort when his ship was dangerously malfunction-
ing, beyond repair.

The capsule came to rest less than a hundred metres from
the watcher. The great eye observed steadily as a seam opened
in the capsule's hull, parting it into two halves. From within
it, as if hatching from an egg, a spacesuited man emerged.

The man unfastened his helmet and took a deep, grateful
breath of the cold air, then began to peel off the spacesuit,
indifferent to the biting wind that swirled and moaned
around him. He was a tall, lean young man with a strong-
boned face, wearing what seemed to be a uniform – dark-

grey tunic and close-fitting trousers tucked into boots. On the cuffs of the tunic were flashes and stripes of colour, and a sky-blue circlet decorated the upper chest. The same circlet appeared on the spacesuit helmet, and on the open and now useless capsule.

The man folded the spacesuit into a manageable bundle with the helmet and breathing pack, then straightened, studying his surroundings. It was an uninviting landscape of dark, bare rock, so ridged and creased and corrugated that, from above, it would look like badly crumpled cloth. Much of the rock was discoloured with broad smears of a substance that gleamed a sickly blue under the pale sun.

Yet, for all its dismal appearance, it was a place with an oxygen atmosphere, able to support human life – even if not comfortably. If the man from the capsule had been an ordinary spaceman, who had ejected from a crippled ship, he could have counted himself lucky.

But luck had nothing to do with it. His ship was intact – orbiting in deep space, under the guidance of the most unusual pilot in the Inhabited Worlds.

And the man from the capsule was no ordinary spaceman.

He was Keill Randor, the sole survivor of a race of people who had once been the galaxy's most renowned and most supremely skilled fighting force – the Legions of the planet Moros.

And he had chosen to land as he had done for a purpose – as part of a task he had to accomplish in this bleak place.

As his gaze swept across his surroundings, he caught a glint of metal deep in a shadowed cleft. He moved closer, warily – and saw the watcher.

And he knew that his task had begun.

The watcher was a robot – a work-robot, he recognized, probably with a limited programme and no decision faculties. Its body was wide and pyramid-shaped, with a low centre of gravity to keep it upright on rough terrain. It had six arms –

flexible, whippy tentacles of metal – with tools on their extremities, mining tools like drills, scoops, pincer-like grabs. Surmounting the body, some two metres from the ground, was a scanner 'eye' – which relayed pictures to screens that humans would monitor.

The robot moved slowly out from the shadow, rolling on heavy, rubbery treads that made its advance eerily silent.

Keill Randor stood still, watchful but relaxed, fairly sure that the heavy robot was no danger to him.

But he was less sure of his safety when, looking up, he saw two human figures who had appeared on a nearby rise, with old-fashioned laserifles held ready in their hands.

The smaller of the two figures waved an arm in a beckoning gesture. Keill gathered up his spacesuit and obeyed, moving with sure-footed, athletic speed up the uneven slope.

Both of the others wore hooded, one-piece coveralls, shiny and metallic, and probably thermally controlled. Garments like them were commonplace on many planets in the Inhabited Worlds. And the smaller of the two was a woman, for the coverall did nothing to hide the shapeliness of her figure – no more than it hid the bulk and muscle of her taller companion.

As Keill drew near, he saw an open, balloon-wheeled ground-car – of a make almost as out-of-date as the laserifles – standing a short distance beyond the two figures. He also saw the bulky man swing the rifle to fix its ugly muzzle on his chest.

But the woman merely looked him up and down, then nodded. She had large, dark eyes in a delicately oval face, but they held an expression of cool and competent authority.

'We picked up your mayday,' she said. 'My name's Joss – this is Groll.'

'Keill Randor. Thanks for coming out.' He glanced briefly at the rifle held by the bigger man. 'No need for that – I'm not armed.'

'Precautions,' the woman said. 'You've dropped into the middle of a war.'

'I know,' Keill said. 'That's why I'm here.' As the woman raised her eyebrows, he added, 'I heard some news about trouble here on the Cluster, and thought I could find work. But my ship's drive overloaded and I had to come the rest of the way in the capsule.'

The woman called Joss studied him curiously. 'Work? Are you some sort of soldier?'

'Some sort.'

'Mercenary!' spat the big man named Groll, a sneer on his coarse-featured face.

Keill looked at him coldly. 'Nothing wrong with being a mercenary – depending on who you fight for, and why.'

Groll was about to reply when the woman silenced him with a gesture. 'You'd better come and talk to the Council,' she said thoughtfully, motioning to the ground-car.

The vehicle was not only old-fashioned but old. Its drive stuttered and bellowed, its body rattled with every bump, and there was a bump every few centimetres. Conversation would have been impossible even if the biting wind had not snatched words away from mouths. So Keill sat back, staring out at the dismal vista of blue-smeared rock, wrapping himself in his thoughts.

He knew a good deal about this place where he had landed – more than he would admit to its people. He had come as prepared as possible, yet ahead of him remained a huge range of unknowns, of questions and mysteries. He would have to deal with them as they came up, while posing as a wrecked spaceman, a drifter, a soldier of fortune.

If they accepted him, his task would be that much easier. If not ... then his ship and its strange pilot were near enough to scoop him up if he ran into dangers that even he could not overcome. So he was not alone.

Certainly not as alone as he once had been, totally, overwhelmingly, when he had learned that he was the only living remnant of an entire race of people. A race that had been deliberately, inhumanly, murdered.

At the time, he had not expected to feel that mind-numbing loneliness for long. The deadly radiation that had enveloped his world, the planet Moros, had brushed lightly against him, enough to plant a slow death within him. He had set out then, alone, with a steely determination, to use what time he had left to find out who had destroyed his world, and why.

But he had been diverted. And his life had been altered in ways that he would once have thought beyond belief.

He had been gathered up by a group of strange, elderly scientists, brilliant beyond the level of genius, whom he had come to know as the 'Overseers'. In their secret base, hidden within a small, uncharted asteroid, he had been cured of the radiation's lethal effects – and had learned the truth behind the murder of Moros.

The Overseers, tirelessly keeping watch over the Inhabited Worlds with uncanny monitoring devices, had discovered the existence of a mysterious being who was the single most malignant danger to the well-being of the unsuspecting galaxy. Knowing little else about this being – neither where, nor what, nor who he was – they had given him a name of their own: the Warlord.

But the Overseers at least knew the intentions of the Warlord. He was sending out emissaries and agents to spread the infection of war throughout the galaxy – to set nation against nation, race against race, planet against planet. Until, if he had his way, all the Inhabited Worlds would be ablaze with an ultimate war – and the Warlord would be waiting to emerge and rule whatever was left after that final catastrophe.

It was the Warlord, the Overseers were sure, who had destroyed Moros – before the Legions too could learn of his existence, and turn their might against him.

So the Overseers had sought and found Keill Randor, the

last legionary – and probably the most skilled fighting man in the galaxy, whether piloting his one-person space fighter or in individual, hand-to-hand combat. They wanted Keill to be *their* emissary – to go to worlds where they suspected the Warlord's influence was at work, and there to learn more about him and wherever possible to thwart his plans.

Keill had agreed – for the fight against the Warlord was *his* fight, too, against the murderer of Moros. But when he had left the secret asteroid to begin that fight, he had left considerably changed.

For one thing, the Overseers' scientific genius had not merely healed him of the radiation's effects. That deadliness had settled in Keill's bones – so the Overseers had *replaced* his entire skeletal structure, with a unique organic alloy. It was stronger and more resilient than even the toughest metal. As far as the most demanding tests showed, it was unbreakable.

And for another thing, his loneliness had ended. On the asteroid he had met an alien visitor – an intelligent being from another galaxy, for there were no intelligent life-forms other than man within the Inhabited Worlds.

Glr was the name of the alien, a female of a race called the Ehrlil – a race of long-lived explorers of the unfathomable intergalactic spaces, a race of small, winged beings who communicated telepathically. Glr herself, Keill soon found, had special qualities of her own – among them a boundless curiosity and an unquenchable sense of humour.

Glr became Keill's friend and companion when he left the Overseers' asteroid. Now she was at the controls of his ship, immensely distant, yet in contact with his mind through her telepathic power, which had no limits in space. She was also his only link with the Overseers – for they had kept the position of the asteroid a secret even from Keill, for fear that he might fall into the hands of their enemy, the Warlord, and be forced to betray them.

Keill and Glr had already had one encounter with forces of

the Warlord, and had defeated them. And in doing so Keill had learned a valuable fact. The Warlord's most important agents were organized into a special élite force, whose leader was known only as 'The One'. Many of its members came from the Altered Worlds, planets where mutations had taken place among the human inhabitants. But all of the members of that force, mutants or not, were skilled and powerful, and as malignantly evil as their Master. The nature of that force was revealed by its name – the Deathwing.

Beneath him, the ground-car's rumble altered, jolting Keill out of his memories. The big man called Groll, at the controls, had been guiding it through a winding series of gullies and low ravines. Now he had aimed it towards a low, flat slope, increasing its power. The wheels skidded slightly on the smeared blue substance, and Keill glanced down at it.

It was, he knew, a simple lichenous form of vegetation. It was also why he was there.

Because of that harmless lichen, war was brewing in this cold, rocky place. A war that showed all the signs of the insidious, poisonous influence of the Warlord.

Which meant that somewhere, sometime – perhaps very soon – Keill Randor would once again come face to face with the Deathwing.

The ground-car roared up to the top of the low ridge, and had begun its plunge down the far slope when Groll urgently brought it to a jerking, sliding halt.

Beyond the foot of the slope, from a broad, low area like a vast shallow basin within the rocks, rose a massive structure. It was cylindrical and flat-topped, resembling an enormous drum – some eight storeys high, with a frontage at least three hundred metres wide. Windows gleamed at regular intervals in its sturdy plasticrete walls, and at its base, between huge supporting buttresses, were wide openings that were more like loading bays than doorways.

On top of the building was a landing pad for spacecraft, on which was resting the bulbous oval shape of a cargo shuttle ship. Around the edge of the roof was a series of unsightly humps that Keill recognized as reinforced gun emplacements.

The weapons within them were heavy-duty laser cannon. And they were firing.

The building was under attack.

High in the yellow sky a silvery dart-shape veered and plunged. A one- or two-person fighter, Keill saw, with what seemed to be a skilled hand at the controls – and with more advanced weaponry than the out-dated lasers of the defenders. It was the crackling blast of an ion-energy gun that spat from the slender ship's nose as it dived towards the huge building.

Gobs of molten plasticrete exploded from the flat roof, within dangerous metres of the exposed shuttle ship. The silvery shape flashed over, curving and zig-zagging, while the laser cannon hissed and flared, the bright beams slashing in vain through the sky around the attacker.

Then the pilot of the gleaming ship pulled it around in a tight loop, on to a different course. Something had attracted his eye. Something like ... a ground-car in full view on a nearby rocky slope.

'Get out of here!' Keill shouted, as the slim, menacing shape arrowed towards them.

Groll dragged brutally at the car's controls, to force it back over the protecting lip of the ridge. But the elderly drive sputtered and hiccoughed, and the wheels slid beneath it.

Above them, the attacking ship swooped for the kill.

Groll yelled with fear, trying to scramble free of the car, ignoring Joss, who seemed frozen, unable to move.

But Keill Randor was a legionary of Moros – his reflexes, his muscles, his entire physique honed by a lifetime's training to a degree beyond most men's imagining.

In the fractional instant before flame blossomed from the ship's forward gun, he had grasped the back of Joss's coverall, braced himself, and flung her one-handed out of the open car, sprawling and tumbling down the slope, And in a follow-through to the same motion, he dived headlong after her.

Behind them, the entire slope seemed to erupt in a volcanic explosion of fire and shattered rock.

chapter two

The tumbling slide of Joss and Keill, over the greasy blue lichen, had ended in a shallow cleft in the rock – where they crouched while rock fragments, molten or splintered, hurtled around them. So they arose unharmed when the attacking ship had swept upwards after its pass at them and vanished.

Above them, the ground-car lay tilted crazily, the front end rearing up, crushed and smoking. The energy blast had struck just in front of it, but close enough to wreck it beyond repair – and to have killed any occupants.

Joss rubbed a grazed elbow, showing through a rent in her coverall's sleeve, and looked at Keill with new interest. 'Thanks for that. You're stronger than you look.'

Keill shrugged. 'It's more balance and leverage.'

'Perhaps. But I don't know many who could have done that.' She pointed up the slope. 'Not even him.'

Beyond the shattered car, the huge figure of Gröll lay, stirring slightly. The force of the blast had flung him up the slope – but he had been far enough to one side to escape the full impact. As they watched, he struggled slowly to hands and knees, shaking his head dazedly.

Motioning to Keill, Joss started up the slope towards Gröll – while in the distance, from the openings at the base of the mighty building, a crowd of people were surging out on to the rock.

In no time another ground-car had thundered up on to the slope and gathered them up. As they roared back down, Keill glanced over at Joss, seated beside him. Her hood had been pushed back, and her thick dark hair flowed free in the wind.

She seemed more excited than distressed by the narrow escape from danger – her eyes were sparkling, her fine-featured face glowing, and her smile as she turned towards Keill was radiant.

She leaned forward and put her lips to his ear. 'That's Home,' she shouted above the car's roar, pointing to the building that was looming ever closer. 'Where the Clusterfolk live.'

Keill blinked. 'All of them?'

'All.' She nodded, her smile widening. Keill grinned back in return – but the grin faded slightly when he caught the edge of a look from Groll, in the front seat. It was a look filled with a sullen, brooding dislike.

The big man had suffered no serious harm – but now he was clearly feeling that he had been shown up somehow, out on the slope. Keill sighed inwardly. Not an ideal start. Out of two people, he had made one friend, one enemy.

But, glancing at the lovely woman beside him, he was just as glad it hadn't worked out the other way round.

He settled back for the rest of the ride. As he did so, another thought formed within him. But it was not one of his own. It was the silent, inner voice of Glr, reaching into his mind.

I take it you are still alive, said the alien voice with an edge of sarcasm, *despite all the alarms I sensed in your mind just now.*

Keill began forming a silent reply, sorting through the events since his landing. He had no telepathic ability, but Glr could reach into his mind and pick up some of his thoughts.

More clarity, mudhead! scolded the inner voice.

Keill's mouth quirked in a private smile. For Glr, most human minds were too alien to read, too much a clutter of swirling, overlapping, jumbled thoughts and images – thick mud, Glr called it. She could read only surface thoughts and in only a few minds – those that could form their thoughts clearly and precisely, like unspoken words.

So Keill gathered his concentration, and related to Glr what had happened since his landing.

Then the war down there seems well under way, Glr commented when he was done.

'*So it seems,*' Keill agreed.

And you are still going to reveal yourself as a legionary?

'*It's the best way, as I said before,*' Keill replied. '*It should help to ease some suspicion.*'

But if there is a Deathwing agent there, Glr said worriedly, *you will be in grave danger from the outset.*

'*I've already been in danger,*' Keill said. '*I didn't come here to avoid danger.*'

He felt the ground-car slowing, and looked up to see that they were approaching one of the doorways at the base of the huge building. '*Enough for now – we've arrived.*'

Be wary, said Glr. Then her voice withdrew, as the car stopped.

The crowd surged forward round the vehicle, in a clamour of shouted concern and questions. As they climbed out of the car, Joss held up a hand, and the babble quietened.

'You'll hear all about it later,' she called. 'Right now the Council has to meet.'

'They're already gathered, Joss,' shouted a voice from among the throng. 'In the meetin' room.'

She waved her thanks with a smile, and Keill noted again the calm air of authority that she wore, and the admiring deference in the faces of the crowd around her – as obvious as the open curiosity with which they stared at him.

Then she was taking his arm and leading him through the crowd into the building, with Groll lumbering stolidly in their wake.

They entered a broad, low-ceilinged area where a number of other ground-cars were parked, with a few people and some of the six-armed work-robots moving among them. Beyond this area they passed through a doorway into a long, low brightly lit corridor, with more doorways and intersecting passages along its length.

The interior of the Home seemed cheerful but almost entirely functional, the bright plastic of its walls only rarely interrupted by metal or ceramic designs. And the people that Keill glimpsed through the doorways, or passed in the corridor, seemed equally functional in their shiny coveralls – though all had time to call a friendly greeting to Joss, and to peer curiously at Keill.

'How many are there?' Keill asked.

'The Clusterfolk? Six hundred and forty-one.'

'Make it forty-two,' Keill said, and was pleased when her smile glinted.

But it seemed a laughably small number of people, he thought, to go to war against a world.

At the corridor's end they stepped on to a moving walkway, rising upwards, twining round a descending walkway to make a double spiral. It took them rapidly up to the topmost level, where they followed another broad corridor to its end. Gleaming metal double doors stood closed before them.

Joss let her hand rest lightly on Keill's arm. 'Will you wait here while I speak with the Council? Just a few moments. And Groll—' she glanced at the big man '—you too.'

'Are you a Councillor?' Keill asked her.

'One of several. You'll meet them.' Her smile flashed, and she turned away.

When the double doors had closed behind her Keill leaned back against the wall of the corridor, patient, relaxed. He knew that Groll was glowering in his direction, and had no doubt that the big man had something to say. He did not have to wait long.

'Reckon you're a spy, that's what,' Groll rumbled aggressively. 'Dirty Veynaan spy.'

Keill said nothing. Veynaa, he knew, was the large neighbouring planet on which the Cluster's six hundred folk had declared war. It was not surprising that a Clusterman might be wary of spies. Or perhaps Groll merely had an ignorant man's aversion to strangers.

Then again, there might be something more to the big man's hostility. Something deeper and more deadly. It might be worthwhile, Keill thought, to stir him up a little and see what emerged.

'Got nothin' to say?' Groll sneered, stepping closer.

Keill looked at him without expression. 'I'll say this,' he replied flatly. 'You've managed something I didn't think possible.'

A puzzled frown wrinkled Groll's brow. 'Whassat?' he demanded suspiciously.

'To be even stupider than you look.'

Groll was fairly fast for a man of his bulk. His knotted fist swung without warning in a savage, clubbing punch.

It was a grave mistake – but Groll did not have time to realize it. He did not even have time to register that the punch had missed, that Keill had swayed aside just far enough.

Then Keill struck him, twice, his hands blurring past any eye's ability to follow their speed. He struck with fingertips only, not wishing to kill, the fingers of one hand jabbing deep into Groll's bulging belly, those of the other hand driving into the small of Groll's back as the first blow doubled him over. The second impact and Groll's own impetus sent the big man lurching forward, his head meeting the hard plastic wall with a meaty thud.

As the unconscious bulk of Groll slid to the floor, a sound behind Keill brought his head round. Joss was standing framed in the open double doors, staring wide-eyed.

'Sorry,' Keill said. 'He got a little . . . aggressive.'

'He usually does.' For all her surprise, she did not seem perturbed, Keill saw, and she hardly spared a glance for the fallen Groll. 'You're a very unusual man. I could barely see you move.'

Keill waited, saying nothing.

She smiled quickly, stepping aside. 'You'd better come and meet the others.'

The room beyond the doors was sizeable, but no less functional than the other parts of the building Keill had seen. It was dominated by a long, low table, behind which stood a few metal cabinets and some standard equipment including a computer outlet and a holo-tape viewer. But Keill's attention was on the four people at the table.

Two were older men, grey-haired and stringy. A third was an equally grey-haired woman, but heavy-bodied, with a cheerful ruddy face and bright eyes. The fourth was a younger man, tall, dark-haired, with a narrow intense face. They all wore variants of the shiny coverall favoured by the Cluster-folk; there were no signs of rank or authority.

'The Council of the Cluster,' Joss said formally as they approached the table. 'This is Shalet, Council leader,' she went on, indicating the big grey-haired woman. 'This is Fillon.' The young, thin-faced man. 'And this is Bennen, and Rint.' The two older men.

Keill nodded to them all agreeably, but had not missed the subtle ordering of the introductions. It was the leader, Shalet, and Fillon who – besides Joss herself – were the important members of this Council.

There was a brief silence while the five inspected Keill and he studied them. Keill broke it first. 'I'm Keill Randor. Joss will have told you how I came here, and why I was coming in the first place.'

'She did,' Shalet replied in a resonant baritone. 'Says you're a professional soldier.'

Keill smiled wryly. 'Mercenary was Groll's word.'

Shalet shrugged beefy shoulders. 'Don't matter. Joss says you're pretty good. Saved her life – we got to thank you for that.'

'And Groll just found out,' Joss put in, 'how good he is.'

One of the old men leaned forward. 'Y' mean big Groll got nasty, and you're still standin'?' He shook his head wonderingly. 'You're more'n pretty good, boy.'

'Where'd you learn soldierin'?' Shalet asked.

Keill had been expecting the question. 'On the planet Moros,' he said levelly.

Above the mutters of surprise, Fillon's snort of derision rang out. 'The Legions?' There was an edge of a sneer on the narrow face. 'They died out, not so long ago. Everybody knows that.'

'Perhaps some survived,' Joss said softly.

'One did, anyway,' Keill said. He slipped a hand into his tunic, and took out a disc fastened to a thin chain. Around the edge of the disc was the same blue circlet as on his uniform, and within the ring of blue was a tiny, colour holo-pic of Keill's face, with details of his name and rank, embedded deep in the plastic. 'This is a Legion ID, if it means anything to you.'

'Does to me, boy,' said the older man named Rint. 'Seen 'em before, on the vid. Uniform too, now I recollect.'

Fillon snorted again. 'So you're a legionary turned mercenary?'

'My people are dead, and I have to earn my keep,' Keill said quietly. 'It's the only work I know.'

'And how do we know,' Fillon snapped, 'that you didn't hire out to Veynaa, first?'

Keill allowed a puzzled expression to form on his face, and Shalet saw it. 'Veynaa's the planet we're at war with,' she explained. Then she turned impatiently to Fillon. 'And you know better'n that about the Legions. Never fought in an unjust war. If they was around, they'd likely fight for *us*, if we could afford 'em. Spyin' wasn't their trade, neither.'

'It still isn't,' Keill said firmly.

'I'll need more than words,' Fillon sneered, 'to convince me.'

Shalet slapped a broad hand on the table. 'Not me! I get a good feeling from you, Randor. Reckon the Cluster could do with a fightin' man like you.'

'Don't be naive,' Fillon objected. 'He could be dangerous!'

''Course he could!' Shalet boomed. 'If he's the only legionary left, maybe he's the most dangerous man around! So let him join us, an' be dangerous to Veynaa! We can tell 'em we got *two* weapons . . .'

'Shalet!' Joss broke in sharply.

'Oh, right – sorry.' Shalet subsided. 'Anyway, what's the decision?'

Fillon stood up abruptly, eyes burning. 'I tell you this man should be kept under guard, till we're sure of him!'

'An' how're we gonna be sure?' Shalet asked.

'Wait till Quern gets back!' Fillon snapped. 'Quern will know.'

The others all began talking at once, but Joss's clear voice sliced through the hubbub. 'If Keill Randor had been locked up earlier today,' she said, 'I would be dead.'

'True enough,' Shalet agreed. 'But maybe Fillon's got a point. Wouldn't hurt to wait till Quern can have a talk with him.' She glanced around, the two old men nodding in agreement. 'Right – let's be fair. Randor, I don't think myself you got anythin' t' do with Veynaa, but we can't take chances. You can be free to come and go as you like around the Home, but there's gotta be someone with you all the time. An' we'll talk about it again when Quern's back. All right?'

Keill glanced at Joss, who looked sympathetic, then at Fillon, who looked annoyed. 'If that's what you want,' he said calmly.

'Reckon it won't be so bad,' Shalet added with a broad grin, 'if Joss volunteers to keep an eye on y'.'

'I will,' Joss said readily. Then she grimaced down at her torn coverall. 'But first I need to change.'

'Then while Joss is prettyin' herself,' Shalet chortled, 'you come on with me, Randor. I'll give you a personal guided tour of the Home.'

She clapped a powerful hand on Keill's shoulder and propelled him towards the door, talking boisterously. But Keill's mind was still fixed on the words that the big woman had spoken earlier – words charged with menace.

Two weapons . . .

chapter three

On their way through the doors, Keill saw that the corridor was empty, which meant either that Groll had recovered or that he had been carried elsewhere. In either case, Keill knew, he had stored up trouble for himself from that source. Not that one more bit of trouble, he thought, would make much difference.

Preoccupied with such thoughts he walked with Shalet back towards the moving walkway and down to the lower levels. So he was only half-hearing her voluble stream of information – much of which he had learned earlier from the Overseers, while preparing for his mission.

Shalet had begun with the basic fact that the small planet on which they stood was the largest body of a collection of planetoids, asteroids and bits of space rubble which had been drawn by various cosmic forces to cling together, so that the whole came to be called the Cluster.

It moved through space as a single object, rotating round a common axis. And the larger bodies had, over the millennia, developed simple forms of life, mostly various lichenous growths including the blue substance Keill had seen, and a thin but breathable atmosphere.

The Cluster orbited its sun quite near, in astronomical terms, to a larger planet. When mankind's early starships had brought colonists to this system – during the ancient Millennium of the Scattering which had spread man through the galaxy – they had found the large planet, which they named Veynaa, suitable in every way to support human life.

They also explored the Cluster thoroughly – with one priceless result. A scientist, named Ossid, studying the blue lichen, found it to be a rich source of an amazingly broad-spectrum antibiotic – which the Veynaan colonists named *ossidin* after its discoverer.

So the colony's fortune was made. In the centuries after the Scattering, when the colonized planets were forming contacts, trading links and so on, ossidin proved a valuable resource. The Veynaans planted a small sub-colony of workers on the Cluster to gather the lichen and ship it back to Veynaa for processing. And Veynaa prospered hugely on the ossidin trade.

Eventually, though, the people of the Cluster – never more than a few hundred – stopped thinking of themselves as Veynaans. They enlarged their central base into the present massive structure, named it Home, and called themselves Clusterfolk. And a time came when those tough and in-dependent-minded men and women wanted to break free of Veynaan control. They wanted to govern themselves, and to take a fairer share of the rich profits from the ossidin trade.

When the Veynaans refused, anger and unrest swept the Cluster. Relations grew more bitter when the Clusterfolk went on strike, refusing to ship ossidin. A few violent attacks on visiting Veynaan officials were followed by retaliatory raids. Unrest became rebellion.

Then recently, without warning, the Clusterfolk had issued a threat. If their independence was not granted, they said, they would declare war on Veynaa.

At this point Keill restored his full attention to Shalet, since the war was why he was there. Shalet went on to say that, for a while, Veynaa had been leaving the Cluster mostly alone – except for occasional overflights and minor harassments by Veynaan ships, like the one Keill had run into that day.

'They think it's comical,' the big woman grumbled, 'us folk declarin' war on them. They figure it's just a lotta noise, an' we'll come to our senses soon.'

'Still,' Keill said carefully, 'it does seem a fairly unequal fight.'

'Sure it does.' Shalet set her jaw. 'But not if we've got ourselves an equalizer.'

'Is that what you hinted at before?' Keill asked, trying to sound casual. 'Some weapon?'

'Somethin' like that. But I shouldn't be talkin' about it. I'll leave it to Quern to tell y' about it, when he figures it's all right.'

Keill paused for a moment, so as not to seem too eagerly curious. 'This Quern sounds important.'

'He is,' Shalet assured him. 'Been a big help to us ever since he came. Gonna win this war for us, Quern is.'

A premonition stirred behind Keill's calm control. 'Since he came? He's not from the Cluster?'

'Nope – offworlder, like you,' Shalet grinned.

'I got the impression,' Keill said lightly, 'that some Clusterfolk don't like offworlders too well.'

Shalet snorted. 'Don't judge the Cluster from the likes of Groll, or Fillon. Lots of folk here are from offworld, come to get work before the trouble started. Must be a hundred or so.' Her laugh boomed. 'Fillon himself, he's one of 'em, an' Joss too. All good Clusterfolk, now – even if Fillon gets a bit prickly sometimes.'

Keill nodded, storing the information away. It was an interesting fact about Fillon, though not fully explaining the young man's hostility to Keill. And the mystery man Quern was even more interesting . . .

But he knew better than to arouse suspicion by pressing Shalet with even more questions. He regained his expression of polite interest as the guided tour continued.

They descended at first to the lowest levels of the great structure, where Shalet led him through the sizeable areas where much of the work of the Home went on. Keill watched the work-robots disgorge their heaps of fragmented, lichen-covered rock, which were gathered up to be powdered in mighty machines and packed into storage containers.

Shalet explained that the Cluster was stockpiling the raw ossidin, while the rebellion continued. 'When we're free,' she said, 'we'll get the stuff processed offplanet, and market it ourselves. An' we'll get some new equipment – not all this out-of-date stuff the Veynaans put on us. Quern's makin' all the arrangements.'

'He seems to know his way around,' Keill commented.

'Quern's been a trader all over the galaxy,' Shalet said proudly. 'Knows more about trade than any of us.'

Keill nodded, making no further comment, but adding another fragment to the mystery of Quern.

Shalet went on to describe the shipping process. An elevator, rising in a huge vertical shaft up through the Home, lifted the containers of raw ossidin to the roof, to be loaded on to the shuttles.

'You said shuttles,' Keill put in. 'I saw only one.'

'There're two – but Quern's got the other one. Makin' a trip,' Shalet said vaguely.

The shuttles, she continued, carried the containers up to a giant ultrafreighter, in a parking orbit round the Cluster. And when it was fully loaded, it transported the raw ossidin to be processed – to Veynaa, before the rebellion.

More information for Keill to tuck away. He knew something of the enormous interplanetary ultrafreighters – ten times as long as his own spaceship, and proportionately as wide. It seemed that the Cluster had everything they needed for running the ossidin trade – once they had gained their independence.

Farther on among the lower levels, Shalet took him through maintenance areas, workshops, laboratories, clerical rooms and more. All of these areas were swarming with busy Clusterfolk and their robots. And everyone had a cheery greeting for Shalet, and took time also for a careful look at

Keill, accompanied often enough by a friendly nod. Keill smiled to himself at the buzz of talk that arose in their wake as they continued – talk in which he could hear the word 'legionary'. News never travels faster, he thought, than in a closed community.

On another level they glanced into a chamber full of huge tanks that produced the basics of the Home's food.

'Food's mostly recycled and synthetic,' Shalet remarked, 'but it keeps the belly full – and keeps us goin' since Veynaa cut off supplies. There's water under the rock outside so we could last a couple more years, if we needed, on our own.'

'But you won't need to?' Keill asked.

'Uh-uh. We're gonna finish off the Veynaans quick.'

The words seemed all the more chilling for being spoken so casually. Of course it might just have been a figure of speech, Keill knew. But he wondered . . .

The upper levels of the enormous honeycombed building held a variety of communal rooms – recreation rooms, eating areas and sleeping quarters; the last ranging from sizeable apartments for families to tiny one-person cubicles. The tour ended in front of the narrow door to one of these cubicles. It offered little more than a narrow bunk and storage niches, with a slit of window in one wall.

'This can be yours,' Shalet said. 'Ain't much, maybe, but at least the singles get a place of their own. Privacy's a luxury in a place like this.'

Keill agreed, gratefully, knowing how he would have been limited if he had had to share accommodation with several curious Clusterfolk.

'Showers an' so on are along there,' Shalet added, pointing. 'An' we eat pretty soon. Someone'll come an' show you, but I reckon you're all right on your own till then. Stay put, though, don't want to upset Fillon by wanderin' round alone, do y'?'

She grinned, and turned away.

Keill sank thankfully on to the hard bunk, glad for the chance to digest all that he had learned that day, to examine it for facts that related to his purpose on the Cluster. The window-slit showed that, outside, night had fallen – so it had been a long day, as well as an active one.

And it had been mostly enjoyable. The Clusterfolk were likeable, good people – Keill had considerable respect for their sturdy, hard-working, determined approach to life. But with the respect came sadness. Normally, they would have little chance of carrying through their impossible dream of independence. They were too few and Veynaa was too strong.

How could six hundred people with laserifles and two cargo shuttles fight a whole world? When Veynaa finally decided to squash their rebellion, the end of the Cluster's dream would be tragic – and calamitous.

Yet Shalet had let those hints slip – of a weapon, an 'equalizer', and finishing the Veynaans off.

In the midst of those disturbing thoughts, Glr slipped into Keill's mind. And she seemed no less disturbed, when Keill told her what Shalet had been saying.

It all forms a most unpleasant equation, she said. *With a weapon, and a human called Quern, as the unknown factors.*

'I'll find out more,' Keill assured her. 'But I need to be careful about asking questions.'

True. But time is short.

'This Quern will return to the Cluster sometime,' Keill replied. 'I'll surely learn more then.'

It will be an interesting meeting, Glr commented.

Keill caught the hint of anxiety in the alien's inner voice. '*About Quern – are you thinking what I'm thinking?*'

Indeed – literally so, at this moment. There was a trace of Glr's laughter, quickly fading. *Certainly he follows the pattern. An outsider, gaining a position of influence and power, guiding the people around him to accelerate the progress towards war. There can be little doubt.*

'*Deathwing.*' The word resounded hollowly within Keill's mind.

It is the way that the Warlord works, Glr agreed. *And it seems we have come none too soon.*

Keill was silent for a moment, weighing the grim conclusion. Before he could reply, there was a subdued tap at the door of his cubicle. He felt Glr slip out of his mind as he moved to the door.

Joss was standing there, looking restored and lovely, her smile warm.

'Hungry?' she said. 'The food hall is serving in a few minutes.'

'Starving,' Keill said truthfully, returning her smile.

The food hall's plain, functional plastic tables and stools were crowded when they reached it. Keill followed Joss's slender form through the throng, to the central automated counter where they collected their meals in closed containers. As they found a table, Keill saw Shalet across the room, who gave him a wave and a broad wink.

Joss laughed. 'I hope Shalet's tour didn't weary you.'

'Not for a minute,' Keill said. 'Very informative.' Catching Joss's quick glance, he smiled and added, 'Don't worry, she didn't spill any secrets.'

'There's a saying in the Home,' Joss said wryly. 'A secret can be kept for five minutes – an important secret for half as long.'

Keill chuckled. 'And will a time come,' he asked lightly, 'when I can be trusted with Cluster secrets?'

'Oh yes, soon,' Joss said. 'The folk have accepted you already. They're delighted to have a legionary on their side.'

'Not all of them,' Keill said. He had caught sight of the bulky form of Groll, in a far corner, glowering darkly under a livid bruise on his forehead.

Joss followed his gaze. 'Groll won't forget what you did to him,' she warned.

Keill shrugged. 'Tell him to keep his fighting for the Veynaans.'

The conversation declined a little as they turned to their meal. Shalet had been right, Keill found, eating in the Home was more like refuelling than enjoyment. But fuel was necessary, and he dutifully worked his way through what was before him.

When they had done, Joss looked up, hesitating a moment. 'Would you like to walk awhile,' she said tentatively, 'if you're not tired?'

'I'd like to,' Keill said quickly. 'But won't you get bored with keeping watch on me?'

Joss laughed softly. 'I'm not. Whatever Fillon says, I don't think you need to be watched.'

Keill felt pleased at the implication that she was there for his company, not for security reasons, and even more pleased when she calmly and naturally slipped her arm into his.

They strolled the corridors awhile, talking – or at least Keill was talking, for Joss was a superb listener, attentive and responsive. She seemed especially fascinated by Keill's life as a legionary, and it was a subject he was happy to talk about – up to a point. While tales of past adventures with the Legions were one thing, he had to be vague and evasive when Joss sought to know more about what he had been doing since the destruction of Moros. Secrets, he thought darkly, on both sides. But he knew it could not be otherwise.

Eventually they made their way to one of the small recreation rooms. A broad window occupied much of one wall, and Joss led him to it, to gaze out in silence at the starbrilliant night. It was an impressive view, Keill admitted. The starlight glinting on the stark and rugged rock slopes around the Home gave them a delicate, eerie beauty.

Joss lifted a slim finger to point at the sky, where one fat golden spot of light stood out, smaller than a moon but larger than any of the stars.

'Veynaa,' she said quietly.

As Keill obediently looked a voice from the doorway broke in. 'Joss?'

Keill turned to see an anxious-looking Clusterman hurrying towards them, bending to mutter something in Joss's ear.

She looked at Keill regretfully. 'I'm sorry. I must go.'

'Trouble?' he asked.

'No – just the opposite. I'll tell you tomorrow, if I can.'

'Are you going to let me find my way back, unguarded?' Keill grinned.

She laughed. 'As long as you don't get lost.'

Keill returned to his cubicle directly. Wandering around alone would be pointless, he decided – it might reawaken suspicion, and he did not yet know where to begin searching for answers to his questions. In any case, he realized, it had been quite a day, and the thought even of the hard bunk in his cubicle was appealing.

But as he reached it, Glr's inner voice spoke to him, laughter bubbling behind the silent words.

I have always wondered about human courting rituals, she teased. *They seem more dull than those of my race.*

'If I ever do any courting, as you call it,' Keill replied, 'you can stay out of my head.'

Willingly, Glr laughed. *But one day I must tell you about the mating flights of the Ehrlil.*

'Can we change the subject?' Keill said sourly. 'I'm sleepy.'

Before you sleep, Glr said more soberly, *you might want to know that your ship's sensors have detected a spacecraft nearby, on a course for the Cluster.*

Keill sat up quickly. '*Any identification?*'

Not yet. But it will soon be near enough for more accurate scanning.

'It might be another Veynaan raider,' Keill said. 'But it could also be . . .'

The mysterious Quern, Glr put in. *Wait, now – the ship is closer. It has . . .* She seemed to hesitate.

149

'*It has what?*' Keill asked.

Glr did not reply.

'*What is it?*' Keill asked, puzzled.

Silence.

'*Glr?*' Unease trailed a cold finger down Keill's spine. Gathering his concentration, he formed the mental words with the utmost care. '*Glr – are you reading me?*'

Silence still – as empty and total as the silence of infinite space.

Communication had been cut off. And, since Glr was the communicator, that meant only one thing.

Something – far out in the depths of space, unknowable to Keill, beyond any guessing – had happened to Glr.

chapter four

Keill did not sleep that night. He spent much of it staring out of the window-slit, at the star-stippled depths that concealed his ship, far beyond the range of human vision. Tension and anxiety seethed behind his iron control, and his imagination went into over-drive.

Perhaps a real malfunction had developed in his ship, he thought. Or perhaps Glr's telepathic power – still mostly a mystery to Keill – had failed her. Or, again, perhaps that in-coming spacecraft had been a Veynaan raider after all, who had spotted Glr and attacked.

Keill did not even let himself think about the chance that the strange ship might well have been carrying the man called Quern and that *he*, for some unknown reason, might have attacked Glr.

Throughout the long night, he regularly formed the inner mental call to Glr. As regularly, no response came to break the silence. For a wild moment he thought of stealing the remaining shuttle from the roof of the Home and hurtling out to where Glr had been orbiting. But that would finish his mission on the Cluster before it had started. And Glr would not want that, even if she was . . .

He could not bring himself to confront the word. Instead, he clung to the possibility that there was some simple ex-planation for Glr's silence. And, since there was nothing else to do, he waited.

It was a basic element in every legionary's training. When waiting was necessary, you waited – calmly, patiently, un-complainingly.

And you remained alert, ready at all times for the moment that put an end to waiting.

When Joss appeared at Keill's door in the morning, he greeted her with relaxed calm, showing no signs of his night-long turmoil. Nor did he fail to notice a difference in her – a suppressed excitement, shining in the depths of her large eyes. Somehow, on this morning, Keill doubted whether it had anything to do with him.

'Come and eat with me,' Joss said brightly. 'The Council's meeting early today, and they want you there.'

Keill raised his eyebrows. 'Again? Why?'

Her excitement threatened to burst its restraints. 'Quern's back.'

'Is he?' More anxiety clamoured behind the barrier of Keill's control. So the strange ship last night had been Quern's. Then Glr could be . . .

But again he pushed that thought away. If Quern was what Keill thought he was, every fragment of his alertness and wariness would be needed in that confrontation. 'Let's not keep him waiting, then,' he said, with a convincingly light-hearted smile.

They made short work of breakfast, no more tasty than the previous evening's meal, and were soon entering the heavy double doors of the meeting room. The Council was seated as before, at the long table, and Keill again stood facing them as Joss slipped into her place. He nodded his greetings to Shalet and the two old men, let his glance slide easily across Fillon's chill scowl, then focused his attention on the stranger seated in their midst.

The man was tall, taller even than Keill, but unnaturally, skeletally thin, fleshless skin drawn tightly over the jutting bones of his face. He wore a high-collared, loose tunic with flowing sleeves, almost a short robe, loose-fitting trousers and light shoes like slippers on his long feet. The clothing was bright and colourful – incongruously so, for the man was an albino. His skin was an unrelieved, corpse-like white – and white, too, was the thinning hair that straggled nearly to shoulder-length. Yet Keill guessed that the man was only in early middle age – his movements were brisk, his back martially straight.

The albino examined Keill silently for a moment. And Keill noted a flicker of something like puzzlement, even unease, within the unpleasantly red-rimmed eyes in their deep, bony sockets.

'A legionary, I am told?' the man said at last, his voice as colourless as his skin.

'Keill Randor.' Keill kept his own voice and face expressionless, standing relaxed and still, though the adrenalin was surging in his veins.

'You are fortunate to have survived the end of your world,' the cold voice said. Another flicker showed in the red eyes. 'Were there other survivors?'

'There may have been.'

'Ah. Presumably then you have not encountered any. How tragic.' The words were spoken with a total absence of feeling. 'I am Quern, as you will know.' The albino paused, but Keill said nothing. 'I have been told of the … interesting way you came among us. And of how … keen you are to join the Cluster's fight against oppression.'

Again the words sounded false, unnatural, in that dead voice. Again Keill made no reply, but his eyes locked with the red-gleaming eyes of Quern.

And he knew – instinctively, but beyond any doubt – that he was looking into the eyes of the Deathwing.

'Are you not going to answer?' Quern asked.

'I wasn't aware you had asked a question,' Keill said calmly.

He saw that the others were looking at one another, worried by the hostility that had appeared between the two men. Joss especially looked upset – but then relieved when Quern uttered a short, barking laugh.

'Good. At least you are not pouring out assurances of how devoted you are to our cause.'

Keill's expression did not change. 'I came to offer my services as a soldier. I'm still finding out about your cause.'

'Indeed. And your services will be welcome.' The albino's thin lips twisted in a half-smile. 'We would not be so unwise as to reject a legionary. Even though some of us—' he waved a bony hand towards the still scowling Fillon '—are still a trifle unsure of your . . . trustworthiness.'

'I'd be glad,' Keill said dryly, 'if you could suggest how I might prove myself trustworthy.'

'So speaks a man of action.' Quern's sardonic smile broadened. 'And I shall do just that. There is a task which you can perform for us – after which, if it is completed properly, we will be satisfied.'

'Name it,' Keill said curtly.

'At the suitable time,' Quern replied. 'There are preparations to be made and I must soon leave the Cluster again, briefly. When I return, all will be made clear. Until then—' he raised a long white finger, for emphasis '—I must ask you to continue to restrict your movements, and remain within the Home. The outside areas, including the roof, must be off limits.'

Keill shrugged. 'As you wish.'

'Excellent.' The red eyes flicked towards Joss, a gleam of malicious laughter within them. 'I'm sure that restriction will not prevent you from . . . occupying yourself pleasurably.'

As he spoke he rose to his feet, making clear that the meeting had ended. Keill turned to the door with the others, and Joss moved to join him. They walked together wordlessly for a while, Keill wrapped in thought, Joss glancing at him concernedly now and then.

Finally she broke the silence. 'Quern's an unusual person,' she said, almost defensively.

'He is,' Keill agreed wryly. 'Unusual.'

'He upsets people sometimes,' Joss went on quickly. 'He can seem strange, unpleasant. But he's completely dedicated to the Cluster. And he says there's no room in a war like ours for . . . finer feelings. We need to be hard, ruthless, single-minded – ready to make any sacrifice.'

Keill shook his head wearily. 'I've heard many military leaders say the same thing. That only victory is important, no matter how it's achieved.'

'You sound disapproving,' Joss replied. 'But we have no choice. Against an enemy as powerful as Veynaa, we must fight any way we can.'

'My people believed,' Keill said, 'that if you sacrifice every-thing to win – all principles, all sense of right – you end up with a pretty hollow victory. There's a line in a Legion song – better to lose like men than win like beasts.'

'But the Legions never lost,' Joss murmured.

'They lost, and they died, in a war they didn't know they were fighting,' Keill said harshly. 'Against an enemy who knew all about single-minded ruthlessness – and worse.'

Joss looked up at him, her eyes dark and clouded. 'I'm sorry.'

'Don't be.' Keill gathered his control, forced a half-smile. 'I'm a little edgy, that's all. It's being kept in the dark about everything – including now this task Quern has in mind for me.'

'Don't worry,' Joss assured him. 'You'll know what's happening soon. Just wait a while.'

'Of course,' Keill replied flatly. 'I'll wait.'

Two days of waiting later, even Keill's patience was wearing thin, his trained control fraying at the edges.

Nothing had happened in that time that furthered his mission, or that answered any of his questions.

He had not seen Quern again, nor heard anything more from him.

And, worse, a deathly silence had remained the only response to all of his mental calls to Glr.

Of course his days had not been entirely empty. He had continued to see much of Joss, when she was not occupied with Quern and the Council. They ate together, strolled the corridors, chatted to other Clusterfolk, watched occasional old holo-tapes. Once they had visited the gymnasium to play an intricate variation of hand-ball that was popular in the Home. Keill, with his legionary's reflexes, had eventually won – but Joss had proved lithe, athletic and astonishingly quick.

To an outsider, then, they would have seemed like any young man and woman who enjoyed being together. And Keill might have been happy during those days – had he not carried within him a storm of frustration and anxiety.

It was even worse during those hours when Joss left him to his own devices, and when everyone in the Home seemed to have something to do except him. Then he would wander the corridors and walkways, or more often sit at a window – in his cubicle or in a recreation room – brooding over the bleak landscape of the Cluster, or at night staring ever more despairingly at the starry expanses of sky.

Late in the afternoon of the third day, he was in his cubicle when the walls trembled minutely with a distant, rumbling vibration. For an instant he wondered if another Veynaan raider had swooped down on the Home. But when the sound was not repeated, he guessed its real cause.

One of the shuttles had lifted off from the pad on the building's roof.

And Quern had said he was leaving again, briefly.

A thought that had been germinating in the back of his mind flowered suddenly. He remembered Quern's words, when the albino had confirmed the restrictions on Keill's movements. The outside of the Home was off limits – especially the *roof*.

So possibly something was up there that Keill was particularly not allowed to see. And possibly it was still there, though Quern was absent.

If he could get on to the roof unseen – at night . . . At least, he thought sourly, it would be something to do. Aside from going insane with waiting.

On the very heels of that thought came another.

But this time – not his own.

Keill. I am here.

He sprang up with a shout, relief and gratitude flooding through him like a tide.

'Glr! What happened? Where have you been?'

I have had to be silent, Glr replied, *and later I will have to be silent again. The human called Quern is an extremely powerful short-range telepath.*

Keill sat down again slowly, unnerved by the grave tone of Glr's mental voice. 'I don't understand.'

I became aware of his power only when his ship entered the Cluster's atmosphere, Glr replied, *because his mental reach is limited. But then I had to shield my mind at once – and yours as well. And communication is impossible through a shield.*

Chill realization struck Keill of what it would have meant – to the Overseers' secrecy, to his own chances – if Quern had freely been able to read his mind. 'So he *must* be from the Deathwing. And from one of the Altered Worlds – a mutant.'

Without doubt.

'But aren't you in danger?' Keill asked.

I do not think he is aware of me. I touched his mind only for an instant – and my mind may be too alien for him to have recognized the touch, or my shield. But he is aware of your shielding, and is puzzled by it. He probably believes it is a natural barrier. And he has probed and struck at it many times.

'Struck? I felt nothing.'

You are not a telepath, Glr said. *But to another telepath, a mind-blow can be as violent and painful as a physical blow. And within his limits, Quern's power is enormous. I feel – battered.*

Only then, guiltily, did Keill become aware of the intense weariness that lay behind Glr's words.

'I'm sorry. How can I help?'

You cannot. I will rest soon – and hope that his next visit is as brief as this one. But the Overseers are worried – for Quern will certainly have informed the Deathwing of his encounter with a legionary.

Keill nodded. The only other member of the Deathwing he had met had had no chance to communicate with his leader – the nameless 'One' – before he met his death at Keill's hands. But now. . .

'*Does it matter? Quern has no reason to think I'm anything other than I seem to be – a surviving legionary turned drifter.*'

Perhaps. But the Deathwing, as you know, does not always act reasonably. And I believe that Quern is particularly unbalanced – his mind is repulsive. Glr's voice was sharp with distaste. *It may be a cause of his heightened power. You must take extreme care, Keill. And we will not be able to speak when Quern is on the Cluster.*

'I understand,' Keill said grimly. 'Let me tell you now what's been happening. And one other thing – while Quern's away, I'm going to have a look up on that roof. Tonight.'

Betrayal in space
chapter five

Keill stepped out of his cubicle into the deserted corridor. The night was well advanced and the hard-working Cluster-folk believed in going to bed early. Keill knew that there was no security force, as such, within the Home – the main danger to security was Veynaan attack from the air – and the few folk who worked night shifts, tending the food tanks and other parts of the life support system, would be on the lower levels. And Keill was going upwards.

He walked quickly but boldly to the ascending walkway, and sped up the moving spiral. It ended, of course, at the main corridor that led to the meeting room, on the top level. But a quick search of intersecting passages located a ramp leading upwards, and a heavy door.

He eased the door open with infinite care, an eye pressed to the opening. Beyond, on the roof, he saw only blackness and a sky full of stars, heard only the moan of the bitter night wind.

Slipping out on to the roof, he paused in deep shadow, letting his eyes adjust. Soon the starlight showed him the bulky outlines of the laser cannon emplacements on the roof's edge, and the upthrust of the landing pad where one of the shuttle ships rested. He moved forward soundlessly. The pad was raised from the roof – at about his shoulder height. Ignoring the broad ramp that led up to the shuttle, he circled the pad, watching and listening. Only when he was satisfied that the shuttle was deserted did he slide up over the edge of the pad and move, a shadow among shadows, to the shuttle.

The loading bay was firmly closed, but the personnel airlock gave him no trouble. Inside the ship, the blackness balked even his night vision, but he moved by touch from the control room through the hatch leading to the broad area of the cargo hold. And there his exploring hand found switches that turned on dim illumination.

The hold was nearly empty, save for a metal container, like a solid block no larger than a cubic metre. Keill inspected it closely. There seemed to be no seams which indicated an opening, but there were two slight depressions on either side. When he touched these, the top of the container slid aside.

Within, carefully gripped by contoured ceramic, lay a shiny metal ovoid. It was no more than half a metre long, and had fine filaments of circuitry and electronic hook-ups trailing from one end like the roots of a plant.

It looked like an innocent, commonplace piece of technology. But an instinctive certainty turned Keill colder than the bitter wind outside could ever do.

Shalet had hinted at some fearsome weapon. And Keill knew beyond doubt that he was looking at it.

But what was it? A bomb of some sort? Could an explosive device of that size be likely to 'finish off' the Veynaans, as Shalet had put it?

He reached a hand down gingerly, intending to turn the ovoid round and examine it more closely. But he did not complete the movement.

From outside, a sound had penetrated to his keen hearing. A muffled, metallic scrape.

Instantly Keill sent the container's heavy lid sliding back into place, switched off the illumination and moved without a sound into the control room, to crouch by the personnel airlock.

Footsteps sounded on the surface of the landing pad outside the ship.

Keill moved back into shadow. There was a chance that, if the unknown person entered, he might turn into the cargo hold and allow Keill to slide out, unseen, through the airlock.

But in the event his luck extended even further. It was the shuttle's cargo bay that swung open, in the hold – and while it moved Keill took advantage of its sound to open the airlock, and slipped out of the ship just as the boots of the unknown visitor sounded within the hold.

Stealthily he crossed the hard, roughened surface of the landing pad and lowered himself over its edge into the deeper blackness of the roof beneath it.

And then his luck ran out.

With a faint humming the surface of the roof seemed to fall slowly away beneath his feet.

His reflexes urged him to leap upwards and away like a startled wild creature. But realization held him back.

The elevator.

He thought back to Shalet's guided tour. The elevator moved along a sizeable cylindrical vertical shaft, which would make the elevator a plain circular disc, auto-magnetically supported, and flush with the roof's surface when at the top of the shaft. So he had not noticed it in the darkness until he had stepped on to it and his weight had somehow triggered it.

The elevator slid smoothly downwards. But above, Keill heard the thud of hurrying boots. The mysterious visitor to the shuttle had not missed the hum of the mechanism.

A hand-torch flashed above, the light spilling down the smooth metal sides of the elevator shaft. Keill crouched, hugging the opposite side, while the light probed down. But the elevator had dropped farther, and the torch-beam seemed never quite to overtake it enough to pick out Keill's crouching form. He felt sure he had not been seen.

But there were no other openings into the elevator shaft. Keill rode it to the bottom, knowing that he was still in danger, if some night worker was waiting on the lowest level to see why the elevator was working.

When it came to rest at last, part of the cylinder wall – a

hatchway through which the elevator could be loaded – clicked open automatically. Dim light filtered through the opening, but nothing else. No sound, no shout of alarm.

He moved silently out of the shaft. The broad expanse of the loading area was cluttered with piled containers of ossidin. Here and there work-robots stood, inactive for the night, and banks of machinery and equipment rested equally silent in their pools of shadow.

There were no Clusterfolk visible, yet Keill took no chances, making full use of cover as he ghosted across the area. The corridor beyond was also empty as he sped to the walkway. But once on its upward spiral, he halted, hardly breathing. A sound from above – on the descending walkway, that twisted around the one he was on – so that he would be fully exposed to anyone coming down.

He sprang off the walkway on the next level, moving swiftly into the empty corridor. Pushing against the nearest doorway, he found it open, and peered through. Two rows of high, bulky tanks confronted him – the containers in which the basic nutrients that made up the Home's synthesized food were cultured.

Each tank's lip was higher than Keill's head, and they were packed close together, except for a wide passage down the centre of the chamber. Overhead, a system of narrow metal catwalks allowed supervisors to keep watch on the contents of the tanks.

Keill saw no one, though the chamber was well-lit. He heard nothing except the low gurglings and bubblings from the great tanks, and a background hum from the machinery that maintained conditions within each tank.

Silently he drifted forward along the central passage between the two rows of tanks, then halted. Faintly, from the far end of the chamber, he heard voices.

He moved further forward, crouching, listening. Two of the night supervisors, he judged, idly chatting at the end of one row of tanks. At any minute they might move towards him – along the passage, or along one of the overhead catwalks.

He retraced his steps to the door where he had entered, and tugged at it gently. It did not move. He pulled more firmly. It remained solidly closed.

Somehow, while he had been in the chamber, it had been locked.

There would surely be another door out of the chamber. But that would mean going past the workmen at the far end. Perhaps, he thought, he could bluff his way past them, tell them he had lost his way.

He turned back towards the passage – and froze.

A work-robot was rolling in ominous near-silence along the passage, its scanner eye fixed on him, its six long metal arms stretching out threateningly towards him.

Keill stood still, studying the robot. It was a different design from the others he had seen. Its body was narrower and far taller, nearly three metres. And on the ends of the six tentacle arms were some different attachments, for use with the tanks – ladle-like scoops, flat paddle-like devices, but also two of the pincer-like grabs, resembling the claws of some weird crustacean.

It was almost upon him. And he knew there was no chance that it might just be going on its way harmlessly past him, in the course of its work. The eye was too firmly fixed on him. The arms were extending too obviously in his direction.

It was certainly being controlled. Which meant that someone, on a nearby monitor screen, was watching him through the scanner. And guiding those arms.

Abruptly he took a step towards the robot and leaped – straight upwards. Catching the lip of the nearest tank, he swung lithely up on to its edge, and rose to his feet, gauging his next leap to the edge of the catwalk above.

He had moved with all his uncanny speed. But the lip of the tank was narrow, sloping and slippery – and whoever was controlling the robot was also dangerously quick.

In the fractional instant while he found his footing for the next leap, one of the tentacle arms – bearing a pincer grab – swept up at him. It moved like some metallic serpent, with gaping jaws, and the jaws struck at Keill's throat.

He swayed aside, evading the grab. As he did so, the other pincer-bearing tentacle struck. He parried that lunge with a forearm block.

But the metal arm twisted back on itself, and the powerful pincers clamped on to his wrist.

Effortlessly it jerked him up, off the tank's lip, dangling him by his wrist, helplessly, over the edge of the tank.

Below him the pungent, viscous fluid bubbled and heaved. For a moment he thought he was to be dropped into the thick sludge, which would be unpleasant but hardly fatal.

Then the robot's other arms were slashing and striking at him, the second grab again seeking his throat. As he dangled painfully from one wrist, he fought – swinging and spinning aside from the attacks, blocking or chopping at the twisting, serpentine arms.

Until, without warning, the arm that gripped his wrist swung him viciously downwards – intending to smash his body against the edge of the tank, as if he were a flapping fish on a line, to break his back with the impact.

He arched the muscles of his back just in time. Not his body but the soles of his boots took the force of the slamming impact against the tank. Every cell in his body seemed to be jarred out of place, but he had suffered no harm – save for the grinding pain from the relentless grip on his arm.

Again the robot lifted him and swung him violently down. Again Keill tried to blunt the impact with his feet. But the robot had slightly shifted its position. Keill's feet only plunged knee-deep into the thick, sticky nutrient. And, savagely, the robot's pincer smashed his right forearm against the lip of the tank.

The blow was intended to shatter the arm, so that Keill could no longer use its support to save himself from being beaten murderously against the tank.

But the arm did not break.

For a frozen moment the robot was motionless – as if its controller could not grasp what had happened, or what had not.

And Keill – despite the blazing, screaming pain from his bruised and torn right arm – did not miss his chance.

In that frozen instant, using his agonized wrist as a pivot, he flung his body backwards like a gymnast in a back roll over a horizontal bar. At the top of the backward curve, he straightened his legs, his body arrowing horizontally through the air.

Before the robot's controller could react, both boots smashed into the robot's scanner eye.

Shattered circuits spat sparks and smoke through the gaping hole in the plastiglass. The robot's controller, blinded now, threshed its arms wildly, furiously. But Keill had followed through the destruction of the eye by clamping his free hand on to the tentacle that gripped him. While it lashed and flailed, he rode it tenaciously – waiting his next chance.

It came soon. Each of the robot's arms sprouted out of a socket on the tall body that was guarded with a housing of plastic. Keill's eyes were fixed on that.

And when for a fractional second the arm he rode twisted and bent near to the body, he struck.

His boot flashed down with terrifying power, and a perfect aim. The heel drove irresistibly against the joint of arm and body.

And the metal arm sheared cleanly off.

Keill dropped to the floor, rolling swiftly away, still clutching what was now a limp length of flexible metal. The pincer-grip on his tormented wrist had opened, freeing him.

For a moment the blind robot still frantically struck and threshed around itself, twisting on its treads. But, when Keill easily evaded it, its arms dropped, its treads halted, and it was still.

Clearly its controller, lacking vision, had given up the attempt at murder.

Only then – crouched and wary, half-dazed with the pain in his right arm – did Keill hear the pounding feet in the passageway, the shouts of hurrying people.

Half the Clusterfolk seemed to have been aroused by the clamour, and to be crowding the corridors as the two pale and frightened workers took Keill to the Home's infirmary. He had rejected the idea of a stretcher and walked calmly through the throngs, paying them little attention, showing no exterior sign of the agony from his swollen, bleeding right arm.

The two workers, hurrying beside him, alternated between alarmed and puzzled apologies to Keill and explanations to the crowd. 'Can't understand it,' they were babbling. 'Don't have many robots go rogue. An' what you did – never saw the like. With a busted arm an' all.' And to the crowd, 'Robot went crazy. Nearly killed him. Sure, saw it all. Happened so quick – smashed it, he did. Bare-handed!'

And the crowd was still oohing and marvelling and staring avidly as Keill closed the infirmary door behind him.

He sat quiet and unmoving, while a sleepy medic fussed over his arm. Finally the medic stood back, shaking his head wonderingly.

'That's near miraculous,' he said. 'With these contusions and lacerations, and with what those supervisors are saying happened, you should have a severe compound fracture. You're very lucky.'

'As you say,' Keill nodded wearily. 'Lucky.'

'I've given you an injection,' the medic went on, 'that will reduce the pain and swelling, and I've put on a light syntha-skin bandage. You should have full use of the arm in a day or two.'

As the medic turned away, Keill flexed the fingers of his right hand. The pain was distant, smothered, and already the forearm had returned to normal size thanks to the injection. No, he thought fiercely, I have full use of the arm *now*. And he made a mental note to send his thanks once again to the Overseers, for the unbreakable alloy that he bore within his body.

He turned as the door of the infirmary slammed open. Joss, her lovely face pale with concern, burst in with Shalet striding close behind her. As Keill stood up, Joss moved close to him, her eyes anxious as they moved from his face to his bandaged arm.

'You might have been killed!' she said.

Keill smiled, lifting his bandaged arm. 'I wasn't. Not even badly hurt.'

Joss looked startled. 'But everyone's saying that your arm was crushed!'

'Just cuts and bruises.' He waggled his fingers. 'The medic says it'll be fine in a day or two.'

'Takes more'n a rogue robot to beat a legionary, eh?' Shalet chortled.

Joss was frowning slightly. 'But what were you doing down there, anyway?'

That was the question Keill had been dreading. But there was no sign of strain in his voice or face as he replied. 'Couldn't sleep, so I was wandering,' he said easily. 'Anything to get out of that cubicle – it's worse than the escape capsule.'

Shalet's laughter boomed. 'Often feel that way m'self! What'd you do – forget which level y'were on?'

Keill nodded, putting on an embarrassed look. 'I must have miscounted, or got confused somehow.'

'Happens to strangers every time!' Shalet laughed. 'Joss, you better take him back to his cubicle, so he don't get lost again!'

Joss smiled. 'He won't. I'll see to that.'

Later, as sunrise was pushing wan grey light through the window-slit, Keill lay on his narrow bunk being scolded by a worried Glr.

I fail to see the value of being nearly caught, and nearly killed, just for a glimpse of a mysterious metal container, she was saying.

'No value at all,' Keill replied agreeably.

There was a pause. *I am glad you are unharmed,* Glr added, in a gentler tone.

Keill grinned. *'I am too.'*

And the arm will not affect you, regarding the 'task' that Quern mentioned?

'No. It's not badly hurt – and I heal quickly.'

Good, Glr said. *The Overseers are extremely anxious to learn the nature of the weapon. Your 'task' may expose some of Quern's secrets.*

'I've already learned one thing,' Keill said darkly. 'Someone on the Cluster doesn't want me alive. That robot was controlled, no question of it. My guess would be by Fillon – or Groll, if he can handle robots.'

Whoever it was, Glr replied, *he was no doubt acting on Quern's orders. So we cannot discount a sinister possibility.* She paused for a moment, then went on sombrely: *There may well be a second Deathwing agent on the Cluster.*

chapter six

Keill spent most of the next day resting in his cubicle, to speed the healing of his injury, and also to avoid more awed curiosity from the Clusterfolk, who would all have heard of the robot's attack. Joss visited him briefly at midday, bringing a meal that they shared – but she seemed slightly nervous, preoccupied with her own thoughts, and Keill commented on it.

She smiled wanly. 'Sorry. There's a great deal to do. Everything seems to be coming to a head so quickly.'

Interest sparked in Keill, but he kept his voice light. 'You seem to have a lot of responsibility.'

She nodded. 'Quern relies on me to coordinate everything when he's not here. I seem to spend all my time at it.'

'Don't the other Councillors help?'

'When they can. But all of them have their Cluster jobs as well.'

'And you don't?'

'Not really. I've had a lot of jobs on the Cluster, but just before we broke with Veynaa I was mostly piloting the ultra-freighter. And of course it's not in use now.'

'Nice job,' Keill said, trying to sound casual. 'What do the other Councillors do?'

'They're all fairly specialized. Shalet supervises a clerical section, Bennen and Rint are technicians in the ventilation and cleaning works. Fillon's more special – he's probably the best computer person in the Home.'

Keill's face was blank, but within he was grimly exultant. Every aspect of the Home's technology involved computers – including the robots.

'Maybe he ought to have a look at that robot,' Keill said calmly. 'To see what went wrong.'

'That's been done,' she said. 'Maintenance took it apart this morning. But the damage you caused made it hard for them to spot any earlier malfunction.'

He nodded, pretending indifference. 'On the subject of jobs, what does my friend Groll do? Just hit people?'

'No,' she smiled, 'he's a manual worker in the loading bay. Why?'

'No reason.' Not Groll, then, he thought – but very possibly Fillon. 'Just so I know where to avoid. I don't think he likes my company.'

Joss shook her head, laughing. 'Not even Groll would look for trouble with a man who can wreck a robot bare-handed.' She glanced down at his arm. 'How are the after-effects?'

'It aches a little,' Keill said, flexing his fingers, 'but it does what I tell it to.'

'Good. Because Quern's due back this evening – and I think he'll want to get things started right away.'

Those words, after she left, began an anticipation within Keill that grew throughout the afternoon – and rose even higher when, near sunset, he received no response to an attempt to reach Glr.

So Quern was on his way, within his own mental range of the Cluster, and Glr had set up the shielding again in her own and Keill's minds.

His anticipation reached a new peak soon afterwards when Joss returned to Keill's cubicle. No longer preoccupied, she showed the same barely contained excitement Keill had seen before. She glowed and sparkled, and Keill could hardly take his eyes off her as they went towards the meeting room, where, she said, Quern was waiting.

The albino sat as before at the long table, with the full Council in attendance. To Keill's surprise, Groll was there as well, lounging sullenly against the far wall.

'I'm told we nearly lost you,' Quern said, without a trace of concern in his cold voice.

'Nearly,' Keill said. Then, on impulse, he added: 'For a moment I felt the wing of death upon me.'

He had no doubt that a flicker of response showed in the red-rimmed, deep-set eyes. Surprise, perhaps, or wariness – but also, oddly, a trace of sardonic amusement.

'Most poetic,' Quern murmured. 'And is it true that you have not been . . . put out of action?'

Keill lifted his lightly bandaged arm. 'It's healing.'

'How fortunate. And, from what I hear of the occurrence, how extremely . . . astonishing, that your injury should be so minor.' He studied Keill coldly for a moment. 'You are a very unusual man, in many ways.'

Keill felt certain that Quern was alluding partly to the mind-shield, which would be a mystery still to the albino. And he was also certain, though he felt nothing, that at that moment Glr would be resisting another of Quern's battering probes at Keill's mind.

To distract him, Keill said curtly, 'I doubt if you brought me here to inquire after my health.'

'No, indeed.' Quern leaned back, folding his bony hands. 'Our preparations are now complete and before another day has passed we will have brought the planet Veynaa to its knees. Only the final steps in my . . . in *our* plan remain to be taken.'

Keill waited, saying nothing.

'Tonight,' the chill voice went on, 'a raiding party from the Cluster will visit one of the communication satellites above Veynaa. The party will intrude a tape into the planetary vid system, which will issue our ultimatum to the Veynaan authorities.'

Keill raised an eyebrow. 'And the whole planet will simply lie down and surrender?'

'Precisely.' Quern's smile was icy. 'Because the vid tape will also inform the Veynaans what will happen if they do not.'

'Are you going to let me in on the secret?' Keill asked.

'I think you have an inkling of it already,' Quern said, glancing coldly at Shalet. 'Hints have been dropped that you will not have missed – about the weapon that I have provided for the Cluster.'

Keill waited, his face a mask.

'The weapon is extremely powerful, and quite irresistible,' Quern continued. 'Were it used, it could . . . damage much of the planet.'

Keill stared coldly round the table at the Councillors. 'You would consider using such a thing? Shalet? Joss?'

Neither replied. Shalet gnawed her lower lip unhappily, looking down at the table, but Joss met his gaze firmly, her face pale and determined. Quern raised a long hand.

'It will not need to be used. I have arranged a . . . demonstration of the weapon's effect, on one of the dead outer planets of this system. That will be enough to convince the Veynaans.'

'What if it isn't?' Keill asked angrily, aware of a subtly false tone in Quern's voice. 'What if the Veynaans refuse to give way? Will you use the weapon then?'

'They will *not* refuse,' Quern snapped. 'Veynaans are realists, not romantic fools. They will see that they have no choice.'

Again Keill's gaze swept the table, but there was to be no help there. Joss's eyes were hard and bright with the zeal of a revolutionary; Fillon was smiling with smug delight. Shalet and the two old men looked nervous, but Quern's influence seemed to have overwhelmed them.

Keill controlled his anger. Quern and his deadly plan would have to be stopped – but not here, he knew. And not with words. 'And what's my role in all this?' he asked curtly. 'This task you mentioned?'

'Your task is the one most suitable for a legionary,' Quern said, the icy smile returning. 'You are to lead the raid on the Veynaan satellite.'

The plan, as Quern unfolded it, was devastatingly simple. A group of five would take a shuttle up to the ultrafreighter. They would then transfer the mysterious weapon to the freighter and would pilot it away from the Cluster and into a parking orbit around Veynaa.

Three of them would then take the shuttle for the raid on the communications satellite, while the remaining two completed adjustments to the weapon.

The three raiders would then pick up the other two from the freighter and return to the Cluster. And the freighter would remain, orbiting Veynaa with its cargo of death.

Keill could see problems and flaws, but he left them unspoken. 'Who else is coming?' he asked, when the albino had finished.

'Myself, of course,' Quern smiled, 'in charge of the weapon. Our lovely Joss will pilot the freighter, and will stay on it to lend me her ... delicate skills. Fillon will go with you, and will insert the tape into the vid system. And Groll, here, will accompany you as well – to ensure that you do not forget where your ... loyalties lie.'

'If you still distrust me, Quern,' Keill said flatly, 'why tell me all this? Why include me at all?'

Quern leaned forward, all humour banished from the death-white face. 'Because your skills will be useful, and because it is the best way to keep an eye on you, Randor. Nor is there any harm in telling you the plan – because it will go forward this very night, and the five of us will remain together every second from now till we enter the shuttle.'

The red-rimmed eyes glittered. 'One more thing, Randor,' Quern went on. 'You will not be armed during the raid, but Groll will be. Should you show the slightest sign of interfering with the plan, Groll has been instructed to kill you without hesitation.'

*

Keill leaned forward from the narrow acceleration seat to peer past Quern through the shuttle's viewpoint. Ahead, the ultrafreighter loomed, a vast silhouette against the stars, dwarfing the shuttle.

Quern, at the shuttle's controls, glanced back. 'Growing impatient, Randor?' he sneered.

Keill ignored the question. 'You realize that the moment Fillon puts that tape into the vid system, the Veynaans will throw ships up at the satellite.'

'No doubt. But they will not at first know *which* of their satellites has been attacked. By the time they do, you will have made your escape and be out of range.'

'Even so, they'll look for us,' Keill persisted. 'And they're likely to spot the freighter. What's to stop them blasting it to atoms?'

'Two things,' Quern replied with a frozen smile. 'The tape will have told them that the weapon will activate if tampered with. And to be doubly sure, I will have specially programmed the freighter. It will move in and out of Overlight at random points on its orbit – so the Veynaans will never pinpoint where it is, or where it will be.'

Keill sat back, considering. The freighter was not equipped with the standard ion-energy drive for short-run planetary travel – it had only minimal boosters, to keep its orbit constant around a planet when it was stationary. But it was equipped with the Overlight drive, for interstellar flight. So it could move cargo across the galaxy as quickly as a ship with planetary drive could cross a solar system.

Keill grudgingly realized that Quern had covered most possibilities, that the plan had every chance of succeeding. But if the Veynaans bowed to the threat, and gave way to the Cluster's demands, Keill also knew that the Cluster would merely find itself in the grip of new, far more deadly rulers. And the Warlord would have control of the priceless supply of ossidin.

No, he told himself fiercely, there will be a time – somewhere along the stages of the plan – when Quern can be stopped. And will be.

The shuttle was nosing up now to the huge sweep of the freighter's hull. A docking bay opened automatically, like a vast maw, at the stern of the giant ship, and the shuttle drifted in, retros throbbing, to settle on a landing pad. The bay closed, sealing itself against the vacuum of space, and the shuttle's drive faded into silence.

They waited in that silence for several moments. Again Keill peered out, studying the shadowy interior of the freighter. It was little more than an enormous shell, he knew, with solid bulkheads extending its full height and breadth to divide it into several separate compartments.

He also knew that such freighters had basic life-support systems and minimal gravity, not only in their control rooms but throughout the whole of the great shell, to maintain the condition of cargo. They were waiting now for atmosphere and pressure to be restored after the docking bay had closed.

Shortly Quern and Joss rose and moved towards the airlock of the shuttle. Quern looked down at Keill. 'You three will remain here – and try not to let your curiosity get the better of you, Randor. When I signal, your work begins.'

Keill did not reply, but merely slid forward into the pilot's seat. Behind him Groll stirred, and Keill glanced briefly back. The big man sat glowering, once again cradling a laserifle, while next to him Fillon stared worriedly after Quern.

All three were spacesuited, in readiness for their attack on the satellite. And Keill was glad that he had been able to collect his own spacesuit before leaving the Cluster. Legion spacesuits were specially made, unusually light and flexible so they would not hamper a legionary's movements. Keill had no doubt that, unarmed in Groll's company, there might come a time when he would need to move with all his speed.

He turned back and looked again through the viewport.

The great shell of the freighter was deserted – though in the gloomy depths next to the wall of the nearest bulkhead he could see the forms of some work-robots, motionless, inactive.

He could also see, stretching out from the landing pad, the metallic shine of two parallel auto-magnetic strips, on a trackway that presumably ran all the way to the control room in the freighter's distant nose. The trackway was fixed high along the side of the freighter, many metres above the deck of the hold where the robots stood. Along the strips ran low, wheel-less, two-seater vehicles that carried personnel back and forth within the freighter.

And as Keill watched, Quern and Joss came into view, riding one of the personnel carriers as they moved away from the shuttle.

Keill's eyes shifted downwards, to a work-robot, rolling along in the gloom of the deck below, bearing the metal container he had seen before on the shuttle.

Both carrier and robot vanished through openings in the great bulkhead. Several silent minutes later, Keill felt an eerie sensation deep within his body, as if at the nucleus of each cell. But he hardly noticed it, for it was long familiar to him. It meant that the freighter had entered Overlight.

There was no sense of movement within Overlight. It was not so much travel as transference. When that unique field came into being round a ship, the ship no longer existed in any real sense. It had left the known universe, where the laws of nature held true, and had begun something like a shortcut through a realm where no one knew for certain what sort of laws operated, if any. In Overlight a ship was in nothingness, in a non-place, beyond human imagining.

Keill knew that, had they been able to see outside the freighter just then, the viewscreens would have revealed only a void, a total, empty formlessness without colour, texture or depth. By comparison, even the blank vacuum of deep space at the rim of the galaxy seemed lively and welcoming.

Because the freighter was moving only from one planet to another within the same system, the almost unfelt physical sensation occurred again within only a few seconds. So the freighter had arrived in an orbit around Veynaa, and had returned to normal space. It would have to be well beyond the planet, Keill knew. Ships did not risk entering or leaving Overlight when they were within a planet's gravitational pull. It did strange things to the Overlight field, and no one took risks with Overlight.

Quern's cold voice sounded from the communicator.

'You will lift off now.' The voice grew even colder. 'And remember, Randor – no mistakes, or you die.'

chapter seven

Keill swept the shuttle along the course that its computer, pre-set by Quern, had worked out, towards the Veynaan communication satellite. Within a few minutes the freighter's bulk had vanished into the glimmering black depths behind them. Many long minutes later, the pinpoint of light that was the satellite winked into view ahead.

The retros boomed into action, and Keill delicately jockeyed the shuttle, swinging it close to the satellite, reducing speed, until at last it came to what seemed like rest in a perfect parking orbit less than thirty metres from their goal.

All three wordlessly checked their suits and fastened their helmets. Keill noticed beads of sweat on Fillon's forehead and recognized the groundsman's terror of leaving a ship in vacuum. But there was no risk. They would move across the intervening space with flitters – small, hand-held cylinders that released bursts of compressed gas, enough to propel them ahead and to control their free-fall movements.

Only when they reached the satellite would an element of risk occur. But Quern had assured them that such satellites contained at most a maintenance and control staff of two men, only one of whom was on duty at a time. And the shuttle's arrival would not have alerted them: Keill had brought it in from the rear, out of sight from the satellite's viewports, while the noise of their arrival could not, of course, travel in vacuum.

He reached to the sleeve pocket of his suit and took out the flitter cylinder. Opening the airlock, he jerked his head at the other two, and stepped out into space. He sailed ahead slowly, staring at the immense wheeling curve of the planet Veynaa, dominating his range of vision, the thin cloud cover in its atmosphere drawn like veils across clearly visible land masses.

Then he let his body curve slightly to glance back. Fillon had clearly been reluctant, for Groll had a tight grip on one of his arms as if he had had to drag the other man out. They, too, curved in free-fall, the laserifle swinging slowly where it was slung across Groll's shoulders, until a burst of ice crystals showed that Groll had fired his flitter, to bring their glide on target.

Keill fired his own flitter, and the three figures surged silently towards the satellite.

It was more precisely a space station, resembling two slightly flattened eggs joined at their sides and bristling with aerials, solar panels and a complicated tangle of other equipment. Keill had no difficulty in opening the outer door of its airlock, and then they were standing in the chamber of the lock, already feeling the artificial gravity grip them, waiting for the inner door to open.

If something had gone wrong, Keill knew, they might well find themselves staring at the muzzle of a gun. He gathered himself on a fine edge of readiness.

But it seemed that the Veynaan who was on duty had been dulled by tedium and sleepiness. The inner door was halfway open before his frozen, horrified stare at the men in the airlock changed into a scrambling lunge for a hand-gun, resting on a nearby panel.

By then Keill had almost reached him. But in the last second, Groll's laserbeam scorched past Keill's shoulder and drilled a small, neat hole in the Veynaan's head. The man collapsed face forward on to the panel, a thread of smoke rising from the singed hair.

Keill whirled in fury. 'You didn't need to kill him!' he shouted into his helmet communicator.

'Ain't takin' chances,' Groll snarled, his finger still curled over the firing stud.

'Try to fire that thing again,' Keill told him coldly, 'and I'll take it away from you and stuff it down your throat.'

His eyes locked with Groll's, and for a moment the big man seemed about to take the challenge. But then Groll's eyes shifted, and his finger slid away from the stud.

Keill turned away, in time to see the hatchway connecting the two segments of the satellite swing open. Through it stumbled the second Veynaan, half-asleep, yawning and rubbing his eyes.

He had no time even to open those eyes before Keill sprang. Nor did Groll have time to swing his rifle round. The knuckle of Keill's middle finger struck a perfectly weighted blow just behind the Veynaan's ear. He sighed and crumpled, and Keill eased him to the floor.

'You sure keen on keepin' Veynaans alive,' Groll rumbled.

Keill ignored him. 'Fillon – get moving!' he barked.

Fillon, who had been watching tremulously, jumped and scuttled quickly over to the panel where the dead Veynaan had been sitting. For Keill, even with his fair grounding in computer and communication systems, the tangle of equipment was a maze that would have taken weeks to sort through. But Fillon's hands moved unerringly among the circuits, making the cross-connections that would allow the inserted tape to override the system.

As he watched, Keill toyed with the idea of disarming Groll and preventing the tape from being broadcast. But in the end he rejected it. Quern would certainly be alerted by such an action – and stopping the Cluster's taped ultimatum was far less important than stopping Quern.

He stepped towards the hatch into the other section. Quern had said there were only two men on the satellite, but no professional fighting man would take another's word on such a matter – even less Quern's. Silently he entered the compartment, his eyes sweeping over the unmade bunks, the discarded clothing, the clutter and mess created by two bored men living together in a tiny capsule in space. But only two.

Satisfied, Keill turned back towards the hatch. It had swung shut behind him. But when he grasped the handle and twisted it, the hatch did not budge.

It was locked, or jammed. And Keill knew beyond doubt that it was no accident.

'Groll!' he shouted.

No reply. His helmet communicator remained silent.

'Don't be stupid, Groll! Open it!'

Silence.

Keill took a step backwards, and another. He neither knew nor cared, just then, what Groll was trying to do, whether he was carrying out Quern's orders or acting on his own. Within Keill at that moment there was no room for analytic thought. There was merely a controlled but towering anger.

He breathed deeply, gathering that anger, channelling it, letting it flow and mix with the adrenalin that was pouring power through his body. Then he exploded into movement, leaping at the hatch.

At the instant that a sharp yell burst from his lips, focusing the release of power, his booted foot smashed with terrifying force just above the hatchway's handle.

The hatch was made of the same metal as the satellite's hull, as the hull of most spacecraft. True, the hatch contained only one layer – but it was the strongest, most resistant metal that technological man had yet devised.

But the metal bulged like a blister beneath the impact of Keill's boot. And the hatch flew open as if on springs, slamming back resoundingly against the wall on the far side.

Keill leaped through the opening. The dead Veynaan had slid to the floor, the unconscious one lay where Keill had left him. Otherwise the compartment was empty.

He hurtled to the airlock, willing it to more speed as the inner door opened, closed, and the outer door slid aside.

Snatching the flitter from his sleeve pocket, Keill stepped

out into space – in time to see the shuttle just beginning to edge away from its parking orbit. Helpless, he ground his teeth in rage as he watched the bulbous ship curve away, accelerating, the flame of its drive dwindling into a light-speck as it sped away into the distance.

Then from another part of the limitlessness around him, Keill's eye caught sight of other points of light.

Spacecraft – five at least – hurtling up from the surface of the planet, clearly on a course that would bring them to the satellite.

Keill drifted for a moment, just beyond the airlock, knowing that the Veynaans were still too far away to see him, a comparatively minute speck in the vastness. As he watched, the five ships changed course. Their detectors had clearly picked up the fleeing shuttle, and they swept away in pursuit.

They would be very unlikely to catch it, he thought, before it could reach the freighter. And the freighter would simply go into Overlight, to reappear on the other side of the planet, beyond the reach of the pursuers.

Then, of course, the Veynaans would turn back to the satellite.

More calmly, he weighed his chances.

He could use the flitter to get out into space, far enough away to be undetectable by the ships when they returned. But that would exhaust the flitter and he would be stranded – and a call to Glr would be his only hope.

But he could not reach Glr until Quern returned to the Cluster. Only then would she know that Keill, whose mind she would still be shielding, had been left behind in space.

Then, of course, she would come at once, being able to drop the shields when she and Keill were both out of Quern's telepathic range. But it would all depend on Quern moving back to the Cluster quickly – before the airpack on Keill's spacesuit became exhausted.

Otherwise . . .

He grimaced, disliking the idea of floating helplessly in space and merely hoping that Quern would move in time. No, far better to stay on the satellite, Veynaans or not.

After all, they would not expect to find anyone there but their own men. He would have the element of surprise, at first, and he would have the gun of the dead Veynaan inside if he needed it. The ships would not blast the satellite itself, not with a Veynaan alive inside as a hostage. At least, he hoped they wouldn't.

In any case, he thought fiercely, I'd rather make a fight of it here, whatever happens, than drift around out there and suffocate.

The flitter fired, and he dived back into the satellite's airlock.

Back inside, he unfastened his helmet and placed it within reach, then picked up the dead Veynaan's gun – an energy gun, he saw gratefully – and tucked it into a leg pocket on his suit.

The other Veynaan was beginning to stir and moan. Keill bent and lifted him effortlessly, carrying him into the other compartment and dumping him on a bunk, then tying his hands with the sleeves of a dirty shirt plucked from the floor.

Returning to the main compartment, he glanced round, establishing the layout in his mind. The communication equipment almost encircled him, in banks and cabinets against the hull of the satellite, leaving a sizeable clear area directly in front of the airlock. He would be better off in the other compartment, he thought, when the Veynaans arrived.

But before he could move, his attention was caught by the picture on the broad display of monitor screens, above the place where the dead Veynaan had sat. A large, florid man was pictured on all the screens – a man wearing a lavishly decorated uniform of some sort, and a ferociously angry expression.

Curious, Keill moved closer to watch and listen.

'. . . have heard the demands and threats of the Cluster rebels,' the uniformed Veynaan was saying. 'The people of Veynaa will not need me to tell them that these demands are outrageous. In fact, they are insane.' His voice grated. 'That is what has overtaken the leaders of the rebellion – insanity, and evil.'

If you knew how right you were, Keill thought, watching.

'You will also have heard the ultimatum from the rebels,' the man on the screen went on, 'which gives us twenty-four hours to submit to their terms. Submit!' The man spat the word as if it were poison. 'But the government and military authorities have authorized me to tell you this: we will not submit. Veynaa will not give away its most priceless asset – it will not bow down to madmen and murderers.'

Quern had said the Veynaans were hard-headed realists, Keill remembered. Hard-headed they certainly seemed to be.

The man on the screen was growing more furious with every word. 'All Veynaans will also have heard the rebels' threat – to attack our world if we do not accept their terms. Most of you will have felt that threat to be absurd, impossible. But I must tell you that it is a serious threat – and the authorities are taking it seriously.' His voice darkened. 'The rebels have acquired some sort of destructive device – and they demonstrated its power, for us, on the dead outer planet of this system, Xentain. But they did not know – or did not care, if they knew – that our exploratory team had landed on Xentain some weeks ago. That there were two hundred and thirty Veynaans on Xentain when the rebels launched their . . . demonstration. Today the planet is as dead as it ever was, and all of them with it.'

The man's voice was ragged with pain as well as rage. And Keill too felt chilled by the revelation, by the pointless, unnecessary killing. He knew that the speaker was right – that Quern would not have cared, if he had known, about the exploratory team.

184

'We sent a robot ship to relay back pictures of Xentain as it now is,' the man went on. His image began to fade, and another image to replace it.

And though the Veynaan's voice went on speaking, Keill heard no more words. He was staring rigidly at the screen, pale with shock, clenched fists white-knuckled, his mind a swirling tumult of horror.

It was a sight he had seen once before in reality, and a thousand times since in nightmare.

A planet surrounded by a glowing, pulsating, golden nimbus of lethal radiation.

Just as his world, Moros, had been, on that terrible day when the Legions had died.

Through the waves of horror and shock, Keill fought for control, and found it, as, deeper within him, a steel-cold, hate-filled, relentless rage began to form and build. Final proof was there on the screen, if it had been needed, that Quern was of the Deathwing, an agent of the Warlord, and that he was threatening to do to Veynaa what had been done to Moros.

The ghastly image of glowing death vanished from the screen, and the uniformed Veynaan returned. 'Our scientists say that this is a totally new form of radiation. They cannot say what it is, or how it is formed – only that it is lethal, and long-lasting.' His fist slammed fiercely on to the table before him. 'But we will not panic – and we will not *submit*! We will meet this monstrosity with our anger – our courage – our strength!'

The speaker also now struggled for control, rubbing a hand across his face. 'Your local governors have begun preparations. Protective clothing will be issued, shelters will be prepared, as far as possible in the time we have. Key personnel from each district will be evacuated offplanet, as many as the available spacecraft can take. But these, people of Veynaa, are merely precautions. Your government is convinced, without any doubt, that the rebels' threat is a *bluff* – that not even they would dare to use such a weapon against a planet of six million people!'

Fool, thought Keill coldly. You don't know who you're fighting – or what.

'In any case,' the Veynaan went on grimly, 'they will not get a chance to do so. They will be stopped – and our dead, on Xentain, will be avenged. Plans are now well advanced for a *full military strike* against the Cluster. We will wipe those vermin off the face of their planet, and reduce their nest to rubble!'

'You can't!' Keill heard himself shout. Fools twice over, he thought – for the moment that attack is launched, Quern will activate the weapon, and every living thing on Veynaa will die!

His mind raced. He could hardly set out to stop the Veynaans and their blindly vengeful plans. Which meant that he would have to stop Quern – and somehow also warn the Cluster.

And that meant returning to the Cluster – back into Quern's grip.

As his mind feverishly began to make plans, the inner door of the airlock hissed open behind him.

chapter eight

Keill spun, reaching for the gun in his pocket, but as instantly letting his hand drop. The two spacesuited men in the airlock were both armed – and their surprise at seeing him had not prevented them from levelling their energy guns at him.

They stepped in warily, glancing round, their guns unwavering as they unfastened the visors of their space helmets and raised them. Their faces were brown, leathery, seamed – the faces of experienced spacemen, veteran regulars in the Veynaan armed forces.

'Lookit this,' the taller of the two said. 'They left one behind.'

Keill neither moved nor spoke.

'I'll take a look around,' the shorter one said. 'Watch him.'

The short man moved to one side, professionally cautious, staying well out of Keill's reach. 'Should be two technicians,' he growled. 'What've you . . .'

He stopped, catching sight of the body of the dead Veynaan. His eyes narrowed and his brown face flushed with rage as he saw the entry wound, the darkened stream of blood on the dead man's hair. 'They killed one!'

The taller Veynaan, glaring, raised his gun to sight carefully at Keill's face. 'Make it one for one.'

'Wait,' said the short man – a fractional instant before Keill moved.

The gun was lowered, and Keill held back, still standing relaxed and silent.

'Somebody's gonna want to talk to this one,' the short one explained.

'Yeh.' The tall one looked disappointed. 'Have a look in the other part. And call the other ships, tell 'em what we found.'

As the shorter one moved to the hatch of the other compartment, Keill was savouring the meaning of his words. The other ships of the squad he had seen were elsewhere – probably still seeking the shuttle. These two Veynaans had come alone to the satellite.

'Hey!' The shorter one was staring at the bulging dent in the hatch, the shattered lock. 'What could've done this?'

The surprise in his voice made the taller man involuntarily begin to turn his head. Before he realized his mistake, Keill had dived.

It was a headlong, flat, low tackle that swept the Veynaan's legs from under him while his gun flared harmlessly above Keill's head. The tall man sprawled on top of Keill in a tangle of threshing arms and legs, until Keill slammed an elbow into his belly and drove all breath and fight out of him.

The shorter man was cursing and bobbing back and forth, trying to get a clear shot that would not endanger his friend. But Keill's own gun seemed to leap into his hand, and its energy beam bit into the Veynaan's upper arm.

He shrieked and dropped his gun, staggering backwards, clutching his seared arm, and overbalanced as he stumbled through the hatchway. Then Keill was on his feet, snatching up his helmet and leaping for the airlock.

By the time the outer door had opened his helmet was fastened and the flitter was in his hand. Beyond, a slender, needle-nosed Veynaan fighter floated silently, keeping pace with the satellite. Keill hurled himself into space towards it.

As he did so, the inner voice of Glr clamoured into his mind.

Keill! What in the cosmos are you doing out there?

'*At the moment,*' Keill said laconically, '*stealing a Veynaan fighter. What are you doing?*'

Coming to find you, Glr replied. *The sensors told me that Quern and the shuttle have returned to the Cluster. Yet I knew that your mind – which I was still shielding – was in space near Veynaa. What happened?*

'Tell you later,' Keill said quickly. In the distance he had caught sight of five tell-tale points of light, moving in his direction. *'In a minute I'll have five other fighters on my tail. Keep coming.'*

I am ready to enter Overlight now, Glr said.

'Will you be able to locate me?'

Keill, I could pinpoint your mind from across the galaxy, Glr said calmly.

Her mind withdrew as Keill plunged through the airlock of the Veynaan ship and into its narrow, tunnel-like interior, flinging himself into one of the two contoured seats at the control panel. It was a compact, up-to-date ship, much like fighters that Keill had often flown with the Legions. Rather have my own, he thought, but it'll do.

As he fed power to the drive, veering the ship away from the satellite, the viewscreens showed a spacesuited figure framed in the satellite's airlock. A gun in the figure's hand spat an energy beam, but it crackled harmlessly past as Keill swung the ship up and out of range.

But the other five Veynaan ships had sighted him, no doubt being told by the men in the satellite what had happened to their ship. They were closing fast, in battle formation.

Without hesitation, Keill sent his ship leaping ahead, its drive bellowing like a challenge – straight at the centre of the formation.

The manoeuvre clearly took the others by surprise. The formation wobbled a bit, then tightened as Keill flashed towards them.

They've recovered well, Keill thought to himself. They'll be ready to fire just about . . .

Now.

Hands flashing over the controls, Keill cut power and brutally forced the nose of the ship down. It fell away, twisting and fishtailing – as five energy beams blazed through the space it had vacated.

At once Keill slammed on full power and jerked the ship up again, its drive howling, its own beam raking upwards.

Bright flame exploded from the sterns of the two ships in the middle of the attacking group. As they faltered, Keill flashed between them, neatly intersecting the path of the attackers.

The two damaged ships spiralled away. Keill ignored them, knowing that they were only disabled, and should reach the planet safely if the pilots were good enough. He dragged the ship over in a tight loop, his eyes blurring darkly for a moment as the gravs clutched him, the ship shuddering and vibrating in protest. The three remaining Veynaans had also begun to wheel, in a gentler curve, but then frantically tried to twist round to bring their guns to bear as they found Keill sweeping down on top of them.

Before they could find their aim, Keill's gun fired again, slashing into the body of one of the ships – which whirled crazily away, out of control.

In the same moment, thundering out of the emptiness, Glr was there, the forward guns of Keill's fighter ablaze.

One of the two remaining Veynaan ships jerked upwards as if it had run into an invisible wall. Keill felt rather than heard the explosion as flame gushed from a gaping rent in its hull.

And the fifth and last ship lost no time in changing course, fleeing at top speed into the distance.

We missed one, Glr's voice said.

'*We must be out of practice*,' Keill replied with a grin.

Glr's laughter bubbled as she swung Keill's ship near. Keill thought he had never seen anything so welcome as that sleek, blunt-nosed, wedge shape, its blue Legion circlet gleaming.

He set the Veynaan ship's computer, to leave it drifting, and once again leaped out into space, to float across into the opening airlock of his own ship.

*

As he stepped into his ship's interior, Glr rose to greet him – whirling around the cramped space in one wild, delighted circuit, the tips of her wide, diaphanous wings clattering against the bulkheads. Then she settled abruptly on to his shoulder, her little hands gripping him with painful strength, making Keill glad that she had remembered to keep her talons retracted.

He craned round to look at her, grinning, and her round eyes glowed at him like small moons. He reached up to run an affectionate hand over the overlapping plates of skin like soft leather that covered her domed head and small, compact body – then snatched his hand away as she playfully snapped at him, a glint of sharp little fangs within her short muzzle.

I suppose I should be glad to see you, her mental voice said, striving for a grumbling tone. *But I am not happy at being caged in this ship for so long. I have nearly forgotten what it is like to spread my wings fully.*

Keill moved towards the controls. 'When this is over,' he promised, '*I'll take you somewhere that is the most perfect place for flying in the galaxy.*'

How would you know, ground-crawler? she replied, her laughter rising.

As Keill slid into the familiar supporting grip of his sling-seat, Glr hopped from his shoulder to her own place, which Keill had rigged for her, above the control panel. It supported her small body, and also had attachments to which she could fasten the finger-hooks on the upper joints of her membranous wings, leaving her hands – which were also her feet – free to handle the controls. Not so much a sling-seat, Keill had said when he had finished it, as a sling-perch.

Settled, she turned her bright round eyes to Keill again, her silent merriment fading to seriousness. *Now,* she said, *tell me.*

Quickly Keill related everything that had happened from the moment that he had left the Cluster on the shuttle with

Quern and the others, up to the nature of the monstrous weapon now orbiting Veynaa, and also what he had learned from the satellite's monitor screens.

Glr was gravely silent for a moment. *Do you think*, she asked at last, *the Veynaan humans will be foolish enough to risk attacking the Cluster?*

'Not much doubt of it,' Keill said. 'They're angry, and they're looking for revenge. People do foolish things when they feel like that.'

Humans do foolish things much of the time, Glr replied primly. *For example, you are doubtless now going to return to the Cluster, although Quern will surely have you killed on sight.*

'He can try,' Keill said. 'But he has to be stopped – and I can't do that sitting out here.'

Very well. There was a troubled note in Glr's silent voice. *Will you land your ship openly?*

'I'll have to. But I'll put it down somewhere safely out of sight of the Home, and those cannon.'

Then he realized what was troubling Glr. 'I'm sorry,' he added gently. 'I don't like taking you back into Quern's range.'

No matter, Glr sighed. *He was probing your shield constantly, when you were near him – it is a relief to be away from that power. But the shields will withstand him, for as long as is necessary. And it will be useful if I am near to hand with the ship, in case you need help.*

Keill nodded, reaching for the controls. But Glr stopped him.

Before you enter Overlight, give me time to report to the Overseers. They will be growing anxious.

'Fine. I'll get myself some food while you do so – I don't expect much hospitality on the Cluster.'

The Overseers will want to know what you intend to do, Glr added.

'Tell them I'm going to get into the Home, one way or another, and warn the Clusterfolk – against Quern as much as against the Veynaans.'

And if the Clusterfolk will not listen?

'Then – whoever tries to stop me – I'll have to kill Quern.'

To save a world
chapter nine

Emerging from Overlight, Keill sent his ship arrowing down towards the misshapen collection of planetoids and asteroids that was the Cluster. Glr stirred, her inner voice sounding strained.

Keill, the Overseers are deeply concerned. They think that the aggressive reaction of Veynaa was foreseen by the Warlord, and was a part of his plan all along. One way or another, Quern will seek to destroy the planet, to give the Warlord total control over the Cluster. And the Overseers fear that the memory of Moros, and its similar destruction, will make you reckless.

Keill grinned tightly. 'Let Quern worry about that.'

But Glr did not reply, for then they were nearing atmosphere, at the threshold of Quern's telepathic reach.

On the control panel the communicator crackled into life.

'This is Clusterhome. Identify yourself.'

'Keill Randor,' he snapped. 'I'm coming in.'

A gasp of surprise from the voice at the other end. 'Randor! They said you were dead!'

'They were wrong. Let me speak to Joss, or Shalet.'

'They're all in the meetin' room, next level,' said the Clusterman. 'I'll get 'em.'

A pause, while the image of the Cluster on the viewscreens seemed to be rushing towards the ship, ever larger.

Then Joss's voice, breathless with astonishment. 'Keill! Groll said you'd been killed!'

'Groll's wishful thinking,' Keill said. 'Is Quern with you?'

'The Council is in the meeting room,' she replied. 'Quern too – finalizing plans for when the Veynaans reply to the ultimatum.'

'They'll reply all right.' Quickly he outlined what he had heard on the satellite. 'Joss, the Home will have to be evacuated – and Quern must be prevented from using that weapon!'

'No, Keill.' Joss's voice was low but determined. 'The Veynaans may talk bravely of attacking, but Quern is certain that they will not dare. And no matter what happens – the Cluster will not back down!'

'Joss, you're wrong. Quern's wrong – if he really believes what he says. Just tell the Council that I'm coming in, with a message that their lives will depend on.'

'I'll tell them,' Joss said doubtfully. Then she added, 'Keill, how did you get here? What ship is that?'

He had been prepared for the question. 'Some kind of Veynaan ship. After Groll left me behind, I took it away from the men who came up to the satellite. Tell you about it later.'

He broke the connection, and turned his attention to landing as his ship hurtled down through the Cluster's yellow sky.

Skimming the upthrust crags of the rocks near the Home, he quickly found what he sought – the flat slope on the other side of the ridge where the Veynaan ship had attacked the ground-car, just after his arrival. Retros booming, landing jets screaming, in a cloud of billowing dust and flame he swept to a landing on the slope, hidden by the ridge from the Clusterhome beyond.

As he rose, Glr looked at him, a wistful, worried expression in the round eyes. He stroked her head reassuringly, wishing he could speak to her. Then he took an energy gun from his weapons compartment, clipped it to his belt and left the ship. Behind him, the airlock slid shut with a sound like finality.

At the Home, a crowd had gathered in the lower area. Nervousness as well as excitement sounded in the buzzing murmur that swept through them as Keill entered. No one spoke to him directly, but they fell back, making a passage for him as he strode quickly through, staring worriedly after him as he moved out of their sight up the spiral walkway.

In the corridor leading to the meeting room, Joss was waiting – pale and lovely, her dark eyes clouded with doubt and concern. She moved swiftly to him, her hands a feather-touch on his shoulders.

'Keill, I'm glad you're safe. But I'm not sure it was wise for you to come.'

'Maybe not,' he said. 'But I have to find a way to stop the insanity that you people have got yourselves into. Will the Council listen?'

'They'll listen – but I don't think you'll convince them.' She stepped away, and held out a hand. 'And, Keill – Quern has insisted that you shouldn't enter the meeting room armed. I have to ask you to give me your gun.'

Keill hesitated for only a moment. Speaking to the Council was the important thing. If the worst came to the worst, he knew he could deal with Quern as easily with his bare hands. He freed the gun from its belt-grip and handed it to Joss, then walked wordlessly into the meeting room.

As before, the Council sat at the long table, as if they had not moved since he was last there. The two old men seemed distinctly nervous, Fillon smouldered with ill-concealed anger, and even Shalet would not meet Keill's eyes. He was briefly grateful that, this time, Joss did not take her seat, but remained beside him, as if to lend her support to his words.

And, in the central seat, Quern was smiling.

'So glad to see you safe, Randor. Groll has felt the edge of my anger for his . . . hasty action.'

Keill looked at him silently, his eyes moving to the compact case of dark metal that the albino held, attached to a strap slung across his bony shoulders. No doubt it was the remote activator for the controls of the orbiting ultrafreighter, and its terrible cargo.

He swung his eyes to take in the rest of the Council. 'Joss

will have told you what I want to say. The Veynaans are going to attack the Cluster, before the time limit on your ultimatum runs out. Maybe any moment. And it won't be just a hit-and-run raid. They're coming in force to level the Home, to wipe you out.'

Fillon leaned back, sneering. 'Are you carrying messages from the Veynaans now?'

'My message is *about* the Veynaans, not from them,' Keill snapped. 'Listen to me! I'm trying to save your lives, and the lives of all the Clusterfolk!'

'Sounds more like you're trying to save the Veynaans!' Fillon spat.

'I'm trying to prevent more slaughter,' Keill replied. 'Slaughter that would horrify you – some of you – if you stopped to think about it.'

Beside him Joss stirred. 'You said *more* slaughter.'

'There were two hundred and thirty Veynaans on that planet Quern used to demonstrate your weapon on. An exploratory team. And I don't doubt Quern knew it.'

The others turned to the albino, shock registering on the faces of Shalet and the two old men.

Quern shrugged coldly. 'There are casualties in every war.'

'Casualties?' Keill said bitterly. 'You're sitting there with the power to murder *millions* of people – and you're planning to use it!'

Shalet interrupted, her broad face frightened. 'But Keill – Quern has said all along that the Veynaans'll give way, that the weapon won't ever be used.'

'And I say it again,' Quern put in. 'The Veynaans may make warlike noises among themselves, but they will not move against us.'

'Even if they do,' Fillon added darkly, 'we can't just run and hide and give them the victory. Not if we and our children are going to have the kind of future that we have been fighting for!'

Keill clenched his fists angrily. 'There will be no future, for any of you, if you give Quern his way. You must all see that. You must realize that Quern *wants* to use that weapon – just as he has been using your revolution. For his own insane, evil purposes!'

There was a blank, stunned silence. Then Fillon's lip curled again. 'That's an absurd statement. What are these purposes Quern is supposed to have?'

In that moment, Keill knew that he had lost them. He could not introduce into this gathering the truth about the Death-wing and its evil Master. He had no way of proving such statements – and even in making them he would be revealing more about himself, and why he was there, than he dared.

And Quern laughed. 'See, he has no answer.' He rose to his full height, the icy smile fading. 'We have listened to this foolishness long enough. To my mind, it is deeply suspicious. Here is Randor, returning in a ship that he admits is Veynaan, filled with wild tales about a Veynaan attack, seeking to undermine our courage, our will to win!' One skeletal white hand slapped down on the table. 'That, to me, is no less than treachery!'

A further silence fell. Keill glared round the table, but saw that even Shalet seemed confused and worried by Quern's words, while the faces of the others had hardened, as if convinced that the albino was right.

Quern cocked a white eyebrow, his mouth twisting in an acid, triumphant grin. And once again within Keill an incandescent fury began to build, channelled and controlled to feed the power that was on the verge of exploding. He poised himself to do what he had to do – the only alternative left to him.

'I haven't come to betray you,' he said, eyes blazing. 'I've come to save you from betrayal – and worse. And I will.'

His muscles tensed for the final leap at Quern's skinny throat. But in that instant he sensed movement behind and beside him. And he held back, trying to turn, to redirect his forward lunge.

He did not see the blow. But he felt it, like a sunburst in his head. Then he felt nothing more.

chapter ten

He awoke with what seemed to be laughter all around him, dying away as his consciousness returned. Deathwing laughter, cruel and gloating. Or perhaps, out of some nightmare, the laughter of death itself, drawing near – his own death, that of many Clusterfolk, the megadeaths of Veynaans.

He sat up carefully, letting dizziness and the pounding of his head subside. He was lying on a bunk in a cubicle – perhaps the same one that he had used before. The door was no doubt locked, and probably guarded, though no sound penetrated from the corridor outside. And he was manacled.

His hands and feet were embedded in two blocks of clear plastic, a familiar enough form of restraint on the Inhabited Worlds. The plastic would have been liquefied until his hands and feet had been placed within it – then a molecular hardener would have been added, to transform it into solid, unbreakable blocks. Somewhere there would be a key, a sonic device that would alter the stresses within the plastic and crumble it into dust. But he had no doubt that Quern would be in charge of the key.

His Legion training rallied, bringing a clear-minded calm to rinse away the frustration and fury that threatened to build within him. Coolly, he assessed his position.

He had failed, of course, completely. The Home would not have been evacuated, even though the Veynaan attack might come at any second. Quern was still fully in charge. And even Joss had turned against him, at the last – probably swayed by Quern's accusation of treachery, or driven by her own fierce dedication to the Cluster's aims.

Worst of all, he thought sourly, she had even hit him with his own gun. He might have done well to remember, sooner, how quickly she could move.

Look for positive factors, he told himself. But he knew they were few, and thin. At least Quern had allowed him to remain alive, for unknown reasons – though the plastic manacles reduced the value of that fact. And, more positively, Glr was nearby – though, again, she would not know what had happened and so would not know what action to take, until, perhaps, it was too late.

In a way, Keill thought, it's too bad I wasn't killed. Glr would have sensed that, and then she would have moved against Quern. Probably more effectively than I have.

He surveyed his surroundings – but could see nothing of use in the nearly empty cubicle. Pointlessly he strained every gram of his strength against the confining plastic. He rolled off the bunk and struck the cube that gripped his arms, in front of his body, fiercely against the floor, then against the metal base of the bunk. The hard plastic was not even scratched.

He lay still, his mind searching for even a hint of a possibility.

And the cubicle door opened.

Shalet came in. Gone was all the bluff cheeriness that was normal to the big woman. She seemed hunched, older. Worry had etched deeper lines in her broad face, and her clenched hands were trembling slightly.

Keill hoisted himself to a sitting position on the floor. 'How did you get in? Isn't there a guard?'

She nodded. 'Friend of mine. Told him official business.' Her mouth twisted. 'Maybe it is, too. Keill, I got to talk to you!'

'All right,' Keill said wryly. 'I'm not going anywhere.'

Shalet wrung her hands. 'I'm scared, that's what! Quern's been sayin' some funny things, actin' odd, ever since he got back last time. He acts – I dunno – he acts *hungry*, sort of, an' *eager*, like as if everythin' that's happenin' makes him real happy and excited. An' he's got that Groll doin' whatever he says, and Fillon – and Joss, too. You know she hit you?'

Keill nodded, grimacing.

'Whole Council's under his thumb now. 'Cept me, I guess. But I got to noticin', whenever Quern talked about what'd happen in the Cluster once we'd won, he started sayin' "I", not "we". As if he'll be runnin' things, alone. An' then when you came back, an' said what you did. . .' Her heavy jaw set solidly. 'I always had a good feelin' about you, Keill, an' I don't think you're a traitor!'

'Thanks for that,' Keill said quietly.

'An' I tell you what I do think – I think Quern's sick, that's what! I think he's out for power, like you said – an' doesn't care who he hurts, or how many he kills!'

'You don't know how right you are, Shalet,' Keill said. 'Do any other Clusterfolk feel like that?'

She shrugged. 'Dunno. Everybody knows what you said about the Veynaans comin' – you know how news gets round the Home. Lots of people have left – scattered out in the rocks somewhere, just in case. I'm thinkin' of goin', too. But I didn't want to leave you here. Quern said somethin' about havin' a lot of questions to ask you – an' he didn't look like he was goin' to ask them nice.'

'I can imagine.' Keill held up his plastic-encased hands. 'But how can you get me out?'

Shalet glanced over her shoulder at the door, then tugged something out of a pocket. Not a weapon, but a short, thin tube with an oddly shaped bulge at one end.

The sonic key.

Keill stared at it, amazed, then grinned at the grey-haired woman. 'Shalet, I could kiss you. How did you get it?'

She beamed. 'Groll had it – he was the one who put you in them things after Joss whacked you. I just told him I'd look after it, and he handed it over. After all, I'm still head of the Council – an' Groll's as stupid as he is big.'

'You're a genius.' Keill held out the manacles on his hands, Shalet raised the sonic key – then they both halted, listening.

The sky outside the Home seemed at once to be filled with a throbbing, rumbling roar – as if the grandfather of all thunderstorms was unleashing its wrath.

The massive building vibrated. It shook again, and again, as if pounded by some gigantic fist. The corridor beyond the cubicle filled with the sounds of plastiglass smashing, people screaming, the clatter of running feet.

'Keill!' Shalet yelled. 'The Veynaans!'

Beneath them the floor rippled and heaved. Shalet, ashen-faced, lost her balance, stumbled to her knees moaning in fright.

'Quick!' Keill's voice slashed across her hysteria like a whip, as he held up his trapped hands. Fumbling, weeping, Shalet brought the key into position. It made no sound above the violent tumult beyond the cubicle, but the plastic fell away, crumbling to powder.

He snatched the key, freed his legs, then sprang up, grasping Shalet's arm, dragging her roughly to her feet.

Then he flung open the cubicle door. The guard was standing in panic-stricken indecision, watching the terrified Clusterfolk pouring past him in a huddled, screaming mass. He began to turn as the cubicle door opened, but Keill effortlessly plucked the laserifle from his hands.

'Get out while you can, friend,' Keill said gently.

The guard looked around wildly, then turned and fled into the throng. Keill pulled Shalet out of the cubicle, thrusting the laserifle at her.

'Shalet, if these people panic completely, most of them will die inside the Home! They need direction now – they need you!'

The big woman steadied herself, eyes clearing, jaw setting firm. 'Right – I'm all right now.'

Keill gripped her shoulder in reassurance, then turned and plunged into the crowd. Behind him he heard Shalet's powerful voice booming, rising even above the thunderous, crashing explosions that spelled the end of the Home.

He moved through the packed, stampeding people with desperate speed, pushing, shouldering, dodging. At last he was on the walkway, springing up the deserted ascending spiral, ignoring the frenzied stream of people pouring down the descender.

He was remembering what Joss had said about the Council waiting in the meeting room for the Veynaan reply to the ultimatum. They might still be there, now that the Veynaans had replied with violence and death. He might still have a chance to stop Quern, and to save Joss and the others.

The upper levels of the Home were nearly empty when he reached them, and the wreckage more complete. Cracked and shattered walls, lumps of plasticrete flung from the Home's exterior, littered the corridor. But he did not slacken speed, sidestepping or hurdling the obstacles. Beneath him the floor leaped and bucked, like a living thing, as a heavy explosion nearby ripped at the building. But he kept his balance, hurtling through the meeting room's doors that hung twisted and askew.

Within was chaos and destruction. One wall of the room no longer existed, and smoking, half-molten rubble lay heaped on the floor where the table had stood. Keill feverishly kicked through the wreckage, but found only broken shards of the table. No bodies.

So all the Council had got out.

They might have tried to make it to the shuttles, he thought. Or they might have been on the descending walkway, among the crowds, even as he had rushed up the ascender.

But one way or another he knew that, as he stood there,

Quern might be pressing the switches that would murder a world.

He sprinted back to the walkway, ignoring the continuing blasts that tore at the fabric of the upper levels all around him. The descending walkway was nearly empty now, save for a few stragglers. And the lower levels were emptying fast, as the Clusterfolk streamed out of the many exits, away from their dying Home.

Outside, it was a scene from an inferno. Flame and smoke darkened the sky, the screams of terrified and injured people cut shrilly through the manic bellow of attacking spacecraft. Above the Home, the dart-shapes of a dozen Veynaan fighters wheeled and dived, energy beams slashing and pounding at the building. On the roof of the Home, a few remaining laser cannon bravely spat defiance – but even as Keill looked up, the whole of the two upper levels collapsed in a deafening eruption of smoke and dust.

And in the distance, Veynaan warships were settling on to the rocks, armed men in full battledress pouring from their airlocks as they touched down.

The Veynaans were landing on the far side of the basin where the Home stood, away from the ridge that sheltered his ship. If any Veynaan fighters had spotted his ship, it would have been a sitting target. But more likely the Veynaans were concentrating on levelling the Home. And Keill knew that Glr would wait for him until the very last minute – and, if necessary, longer.

He rounded a spur of rock, seeing that the Veynaan foot soldiers had rapidly moved closer, spreading their formation into a wide, sweeping, relentless curve. But some of the Clusterfolk were rallying, forming small pockets of resistance – tucking themselves into the shelter of the rocks, laserifles blazing at the attackers.

A group of such rifles was firing from an outcrop to Keill's right. Crouching, he moved towards them – and heard with pleased surprise the resonant voice of Shalet, directing the fire.

There were five in the group, including Shalet – their smoke-blackened faces set like stone with fierce determination. Shalet greeted Keill with a whoop of joy, and almost in the same instant dropped a Veynaan with a lancing beam from her rifle.

'Shalet, do you know what happened to Quern, or the others?'

She shook her head. 'Haven't seen 'em. I heard old Bennen was killed, in the Home – and Rint's out here somewhere, with a rifle. Don't know about Quern.' She fired again, missed, cursed richly. 'But somebody said one of the shuttles lifted off just before the Veynaans got here.'

The galling taste of failure rose in Keill again. He guessed that Quern had paid more heed to Keill's warning than the albino had been willing to admit, and had made his getaway – most likely taking Joss along.

It was past time, Keill thought dismally, to make his own getaway.

He glanced round the bulwark of the outcrop. The Veynaans were almost on them – and carrying hand beamers and energy guns, far more powerful than the out-dated lasers.

'You'll have to move, Shalet!' he shouted urgently. 'You'll be cut off in a couple of minutes!'

The big woman nodded and bellowed at her group. They slid down into a gully that ran beneath the outcrop, then hesitated.

'This way,' Keill barked. 'There's a good ridge not so far from here, and my ship is just beyond it. Let's move!'

Instinctively his voice had taken on the commanding tone of a Legion officer. As instinctively, the five formed up behind him, trotting obediently along as Keill moved ahead along the gully.

The wrinkled, creased slopes of the basin that contained

the Home produced plenty of gullies, furrows and shallow ravines, interspersed between its ridges and crests. These low areas offered shelter and a tangled network of paths that might take them near Keill's ship with a minimum of exposure.

And one quick glance around from the height of the outcrop had given Keill a picture of the terrain, now printed like a three-dimensional map on his mind's eye. He could see the twisting, mazy route that he must take as if it were a bright red meandering line on that map.

Urging Shalet and the others to greater speed, he raced ahead of them along that route, more and more desperate to get out of the basin, up on to the ridge where Glr was waiting.

But around a craggy shoulder of rock, where one gully intersected another, the way was blocked.

Two Veynaan soldiers, on the level floor of the gully, spun towards him, guns sweeping round.

Keill was still unarmed. But the Veynaan beams blasted nothing but rock behind him as he flung himself into a flat dive to one side, against the rough, sloping rock at the side of the gully.

His hands struck for an instant, and then he rebounded as if his arms were springs. The battering-ram impact of his boots flung the first Veynaan off his feet – and Keill followed through into a twisting roll, reaching for the first soldier's dropped gun as that of the second man spurted flame.

The beam blistered rock only centimetres away from Keill's rolling form, but the Veynaan had no second chance. Behind Keill, Shalet's laser fizzed, and the Veynaan dropped.

Keill sprang up, holding the first soldier's gun, grinning tautly at Shalet. 'I've got a lot to thank you for.'

Her echoing smile flashed. 'I reckon we're about even.' Then the smile faded to seriousness. 'Keill – that ship of yours. I reckon we ain't comin'.'

Keill looked surprised. Beyond the gully, the thunderous

fire of the Veynaan fighters had become only sporadic now. But the air was torn with the blazing crackle of energy guns, the shrieks of fleeing and dying people and scattered bursts of answering laser fire, as the Veynaan forces advanced upon the overwhelmingly outnumbered Clusterfolk.

Shalet shrugged. 'We ain't gonna win this fight, but we ain't gonna run from it either.' Her eyes misted slightly. 'I wish we'd listened to you. I wish we'd stopped Quern.'

'So do I.' He took her hand, groping for the right words to say. But the words never came.

Instead, a heart-stopping sound froze him in his tracks.

A scream. His own name, in a scream of pure agony and terror, drawn-out, weakening, trailing away.

And a scream that was silent. That was heard only in his mind.

Glr.

chapter eleven

Keill raced over the rocks like a blind, unstoppable projectile, arrowing in a perfectly straight line towards the steep ridge that hid his ship.

He had hardly been aware of Shalet's grunt of surprise as he had suddenly flung himself away, up the slope of the gully at top speed. He hardly looked at the crumbling, cracked, treacherous surface of the rocks beneath him, letting instinct and reflexes maintain his sure-footed balance. He was unaware of the occasional random energy beam that sizzled past him or splintered rock at his feet, as he sprinted across the furrowed terrain. He did not even think of the Veynaan gun that he had acquired, and that he had thrust into his belt at his back, to keep it out of the way during his half-crouched, headlong dash.

But for all his blazing speed, for all the unthinking cold fear and fury that gripped him, he was still a legionary. Though he leaped without slowing up the near slope of the ridge that he sought, he slid at once to a halt before reaching the top, and raised his head with slow caution to peer over the crest towards his ship.

It rested as he had left it. No Veynaan energy beam seemed to have been flung at it; no sound or sign of movement came from it.

But the ship had been landed so that the airlock was on the far side, not visible from where Keill crouched. He ghosted over the lip of the ridge, down the far slope, circling the ship.

The airlock was open, the landing ramp extended. And at the foot of the ramp stood a menacing, hulking figure.

Groll – with a laserifle levelled at Keill's chest, and a brutal smile twisting his thick lips.

'Master Quern said you'd be along.' The smile broadened. 'Always right, him.'

Groll could not have seen the Veynaan gun, in Keill's belt at the back. But Keill did not reach for it – did not respond directly in any way. Instead, the strength seemed to drain out of him. His head dropped, his shoulders slumped, his hands dangled limply at his sides. He stumbled slightly as he moved towards the ship.

Groll grinned cruelly at the visible signs of defeat. 'Took on more'n y' c'd handle, didn't y', legionary?' He motioned abruptly with the rifle towards the ramp. 'In y' go.'

Keill moved forward like a sleepwalker. Groll stepped aside, the rifle unwavering, as Keill reached the foot of the ramp. He took a plodding step up, then another. One more would bring him level with the watchful Groll, and the gun at Keill's back would be visible.

He began the next step, then seemed to stumble again, sagging forward.

Groll, chuckling coarsely, swung the rifle around, the heavy butt lashing out brutally to drive Keill forward.

But it missed its target.

In that fragment of time Keill's right hand blurred – reaching back, plucking the Veynaan gun from his belt, firing unerringly across his back.

And Groll's heavy body crashed backwards to the ground, his chest a smoking ruin.

Keill turned towards the airlock. But before he could take the four paces into his ship, a voice floated out to him from within.

A voice cold as death itself, tinged with laughter that bore an infinity of malice.

The voice of Quern.

'If that was your gun, Randor – and I'm sure it was –

throw it into the ship. And then follow it in *very* carefully. Or I shall turn this creature of yours into ashes.'

Keill scarcely hesitated. The gun went clattering in through the airlock, and he walked in after it, keeping his hands visible.

But as he stepped through the inner door, he stopped as if he had been struck. The blood congealed in his veins, his mind reeled.

Glr lay in a crumpled heap on top of the control panel.

She lay on her side, motionless, her hands limp, her eyes blank and sightless, her wings half-opened beneath her like crumpled leaves.

'Tricked you!' Quern's gloating laughter resounded from the bulkheads. 'It is already dead! And so will you be, legionary, if you move!'

Keill turned slowly, painfully, as if his muscles were strangers to him. Quern stood towards the rear of the ship's interior, a beam-gun levelled at Keill.

The albino's red eyes drilled into him, the manic laughter slashing like a whip. At once within Keill the numbness of shock gave way to a volcanic flood of killing fury. He was on the point of launching himself at Quern's throat, whatever the energy gun did to him in the process.

But Quern saw the blazing rage in Keill's eyes and took a nervous step backwards. As he did so, the black metal case slung round his shoulder clanged against the bulkhead.

And that sound sliced through Keill's torrential rage, and reawakened his control.

A still rational fragment of his mind drew conclusions. Quern was still carrying the weapon's activating mechanism; and he was here, not on the shuttle. So there was a chance, for reasons he could not guess, that the weapon had not yet been used.

'Move away!' Quern screamed. 'Over by the controls!'

Keill moved as he was directed. The glaring mists of his

fury began to clear, and his balanced, cool alertness was restored. There *will* be a chance, he told himself. To avenge Glr and save the planet, at once, will make victory the sweeter.

Quern's gloating smile returned as he saw Keill apparently submissive. He stepped forward, positioning himself near the airlock, the gun held firm. 'Now take the ship up,' he ordered. 'Gently – no tricks with acceleration!'

Keill bent silently over the small body of Glr, lifting her with care into her special sling-seat, smoothing the limp, delicate wings. Then, obediently, he slid into his own sling-seat and lifted the ship up into the Cluster's yellow sky.

'Excellent,' Quern snarled. 'The Veynaans may well pursue us, but you will be able to enter Overlight before they become dangerous. Set a course to emerge in deep space beyond Veynaa, on its far side.'

Keill's hands moved over the controls.

'I was naturally reluctant to perform the final act of this drama without being on hand to watch it,' Quern went on. 'And it was good of you to provide me with a ship, when the Veynaans destroyed the second shuttle. I had thought for a moment that I might not personally have the pleasure of pressing the switches.'

Keill said nothing, but a fierce triumph leaped within him. The planet *was* still unharmed.

'Indeed, everything has worked out better than I dared hope.' The laughter was a vicious giggle. 'When the Veynaans attacked so suddenly I feared that I had lost you. But I might have known you would find a way out. With Shalet's help, no doubt?'

Still silent, Keill puzzled over the vague but ominous meaning of Quern's words. But at least the albino, enjoying what seemed to be his victory, was talking freely.

'I thought you wanted to lose me,' he said, letting his voice seem dull, defeated.

'So you have not become speechless?' Quern sniggered.

'Excellent. No, you are quite important to me. When we have watched my little show, we will journey awhile together – and I will seek more of your conversation.'

In the viewscreens, as Keill's ship left atmosphere, the distant flares of a squad of Veynaan fighters, racing in pursuit, slid into view against the background of starry vastness. But within seconds, the screens blurred – and the views of deep space were replaced by the blank and empty nothingness of Overlight.

'Then you can tell me more about yourself, legionary,' Quern continued, grinning like a skull. 'And about *that*. A telepathic alien – fascinating. Regrettable that it resisted me, and that my mind-force was too powerful for it. I might have learned many interesting things from it.'

'And made The One very pleased,' Keill added quietly.

There was a hiss of surprise from Quern. 'So your "wing of death" remark was not coincidence,' he said, his voice icily thoughtful. 'More and more fascinating. A legionary who has survived the death of his world, who comes posing as a wrecked space drifter but has a ship containing a telepathic alien – and who knows more of the Deathwing and its leader than he has any right to know.' The red eyes studied Keill like a specimen on a slide. 'This mystery will intrigue the Master himself. The One is already looking forward to prying out your secrets.'

Something odd in that last remark tried to force itself on Keill's attention. But he was concentrating instead on the disturbing information that Quern had already contacted the Deathwing's nameless leader, and had passed on information about Keill.

Still, it had to happen sometime, he thought. He had been lucky in his first meeting with one of the Deathwing, who had not communicated with his leader before he died at Keill's hands. And in any case it would not matter. He had no intention of remaining the docile prisoner of the maniac who had murdered Glr.

Around him the viewscreens shimmered. The welcome reality of space sprang to life on the screens as the ship emerged from Overlight. Putting the controls on manual, Keill rotated the ship slowly – until a small, bright spheroid that was the planet Veynaa was fixed in the centre of the forward screen.

As he did so, his eye caught a small flare in the distant black depths, and recognized the planetary drive of another ship.

Quern had spotted it too. 'Ah, my little fail-safe seems to be in position.'

Keill understood at once. 'The shuttle?'

'Precisely. On its way to the freighter, to stand by. If anything had happened to me—' Quern grinned maliciously at Keill '—they would activate the weapon directly. As it is, when I press the switches, they will know at once, and will have time to get clear.'

Quern reached down to the metal case slung round his shoulders and flipped open the lid, to reveal rows of multi-coloured switches.

Keill stirred, reaching for words, any words, to create a delay that might give him the opening he needed. 'What's going to happen, when you use those switches?'

The albino smirked. 'I wondered if you would be curious. And I am happy to enlighten you. Some of these switches will operate the freighter's controls, bringing it out of Overlight, altering its orbit. That will warn my fail-safe, to get clear. When the freighter is well into the Veynaan atmosphere, the container of the weapon will be opened – and its contents expelled. Then minute quantities of the radioactive substance will begin a reaction – sub-microscopic at first, accelerating at great speed into a chain reaction. It alters the very nature of the *air itself* – so that in moments the planet will be enveloped in a radioactivity that instantly and fatally enters the body of every air-breathing thing.' He giggled, horribly. 'As you will know, Randor, from having seen Moros.'

At the mention of his dead world's name, every scrap of

Keill's control was needed to keep him from leaping, suicidally, at Quern's throat. But he fought his fury again, and won. Coldly he said, 'What is this magical radioactivity? I know of no such substance.'

'If you did,' Quern tittered, 'you would be only the second in the galaxy to know – after myself.'

Keill blinked, taken aback by the implications. 'You mean that . . . *you* are. . .'

'The creator of the weapon, yes,' Quern announced, drawing himself up. 'I am a scientist, Randor, not a gunman. A *great* scientist. The radioactivity is my own discovery – and no one in the Deathwing, not the One, not the Master himself, can fathom the physics that led me to it. It is *mine*, legionary, mine alone!'

If that is true, Keill thought fiercely, then when you die, the secret of this monstrosity dies with you.

'Now,' Quern said, red eyes gleaming manically, 'let us proceed.'

Skeletal white fingers clawed over the switches. But the gun in the other hand did not quiver a millimetre. Desperately Keill sought a way to delay a moment longer, perhaps to make Quern forget himself, to make that gun muzzle waver – for just long enough.

'Are you really insane enough,' he asked harshly, 'to kill so many millions of people?'

Demonic anger flared in Quern's eyes. 'Insane? Small minds always see insanity when they look at a superior being!'

Keill shook his head. 'I have met superior beings, Quern. One of them lies there.' He gestured towards Glr's still form. 'Superior beings do not slaughter worlds. Only homicidal maniacs do.'

That, he knew, was the turning point, make or break. He was poised like a notched arrow, ready for the faintest opening that Quern might allow.

But Quern allowed none. Perhaps the prospect of destroying Veynaa gripped him too firmly to allow Keill's barbs to undermine his caution. The red eyes narrowed. Quern stepped away, his back to the airlock, putting more space between himself and Keill.

'I see,' he hissed. 'You wish to anger me, to make me careless. But you will not. I am ready for you, legionary.'

A bloodless finger curved over the gun's firing stud.

'Would you shoot me, Quern,' Keill said quickly, 'when the One wants me alive?'

'The Master's plan requires the destruction of Veynaa,' Quern snarled. 'Whatever secrets you might reveal are of secondary importance.'

Again, an oddness in the words nudged at Keill's awareness. But he could not focus on it. He was too overwhelmingly aware of the task he must perform.

Quern would not be diverted or thrown off balance. The gun remained rock-steady, and within seconds the switches would be thrown.

Keill knew that he would have to charge full into the muzzle of the gun – and would need all his speed and strength and will to stay alive long enough to get his hands on Quern.

And even then the planet would not be preserved – for Quern's 'fail-safe' in the shuttle would activate the weapon.

Even so, he thought grimly, it will be worth it. His death – and Glr's – would not be entirely meaningless. The Deathwing would not have a live Keill Randor to interrogate, putting the Overseers at risk. And the frightful weapon that was Quern's secret would be lost to the Warlord.

Quern was watching him coldly, the cruel smile twitching at his pale lips. 'Resign yourself, Randor. Be still, and watch the viewscreen. I only wish that I had time to bypass that strange barrier of yours – I would enjoy reading your inner reactions to what you are about to see.'

In the last instant before Keill flung himself suicidally at the albino, realization burst like a flare within him.

That was what had been so odd about those earlier remarks! Quern had spoken of prying out his secrets – and now of his 'barrier' – as if Keill's mind was still shielded!

Which could only mean . . .

But before he could complete the thought, Quern screamed.

He staggered backwards, screaming again, a thin shriek of pain. His face was contorted, the veins and cords of his neck jutting like ropes. The beam-gun dropped, harmlessly, and he clamped his hands as if in agony to his head.

Even before the gun landed, Keill was upon him.

He struck only once, with his fist. But every gram of his weight, every fraction of his towering fury, was released into that blow.

His fist crashed into the centre of Quern's white, screaming face. Bone splintered, blood spurted, masking the whiteness with red.

Quern's body was flung away, back against the inner door of the airlock. But – to Keill's astonishment – the door had opened, and the albino thudded limply into the airlock chamber.

Then the inner door closed – and before Keill could turn or move, the ship heeled violently to one side, throwing him off balance. The hiss of escaping air sounded unmistakeably from the opening of the airlock's outer door.

Then Keill righted himself and swung round – to be halted again, for a very different reason.

Glr was up, her great wings half-spread, her hands flickering over the ship's controls.

Above her, a viewscreen showed a glimpse of Quern's white, motionless body, drifting away into space, the activator dangling uselessly, trailed by the red, frozen crystals of his blood like a comet's tail.

Keill stared at Glr, speechless, as she turned to regard him with luminous round eyes.

'You were dead!' he whispered aloud.

Your thought is poorly formed, Glr said reprovingly. *Please stop gaping, and tell me what we must do next.*

chapter twelve

Keill slumped into his sling-seat, trying to focus his scrambled thoughts. *'Why did you let me think you were dead?'* he asked Glr, reproachfully.

I apologize for that, Glr said, sounding not at all apologetic. *But I could hardly lower my shields and reassure you.*

'You were shielding, all the time you were lying there, without Quern knowing?'

Certainly. My shielding, as I told you, seems too alien for human telepaths to recognize. They must see it as an absence of thought, a non-existence – easily confused with death.

As Keill shook his head, mystified as ever by the strange nature of telepathy, Glr went on to tell him what had happened.

Quern had arrived at Keill's ship only minutes after the Veynaan attack had begun. And as the albino had entered the ship, Glr had lowered her shields.

'Just like that?' Keill asked. *'When you knew how strong he was?'*

You had to be warned, Glr replied simply. *And he had to be stopped from lifting off, in your ship.*

But the moment that Glr's mind was open to him, Quern had hurled a ferocious psychic blast at her – then another and another. Under that terrible battering she knew that she could not survive for long, so she began rebuilding her mental shield – and Keill's – a little at a time.

To Quern it must have seemed that my mind was fading, dying, she said. *I let my wings flutter and droop, and when my shield was complete and my body still, he was sure he had killed me.*

'So was I,' Keill put in.

Your reaction made my portrayal all the more convincing, Glr said, with a smile in her voice. *Of course I left my eyes open, so I could see. And when it was plain that you were going to leap at Quern, despite his gun, I dropped my shield and struck him with the strongest mental blast I could muster.*

The images rose in Keill's mind – Quern's agonized screams, then the blood-masked body collapsing into the airlock . . .

An unpleasant death, Glr commented. *But well deserved.*

'It's not the end, though,' Keill said quickly.

As he told her about the others – Quern's fail-safe – he quickly scanned the viewscreens. The shuttle was out of visual range, but the sensors on the control panel revealed a tell-tale blip. The other ship was halfway round the planet from Keill's position.

It might already be at rendezvous with the freighter, he thought, and putting a stop to the huge ship's random dips in and out of Overlight. But there would still be time. Keill could hurl his own ship into Overlight, and arrive at the shuttle's present position in seconds.

He set the controls, and the viewscreens altered at once to the blank void of Overlight.

Can we stop them from activating the weapon? Glr asked.

'With luck,' Keill said. 'They're only on standby – they won't know Quern's dead, yet.'

They will know when you appear, Glr pointed out.

'But then,' Keill said fiercely, 'they won't have time to do anything about it.'

And do you know, Glr added, *who 'they' are?*

Keill's eyes darkened. 'I have a pretty good idea.'

As he spoke, the viewscreens shimmered. They were back in normal space – and ahead, outlined against the stars, was the dark cylinder of the ultrafreighter.

*

Keill slammed on full power, and his ship screamed down towards the huge ship. The shuttle had vanished, no doubt already within the freighter. But its occupants, not expecting to be pursued, had not altered the automatic action of the docking bay.

It slid obediently aside as Keill's ship approached, and he plunged into the opening, retros thundering, slamming his ship down jarringly on to the landing pad – next to the bulbous shape of the shuttle.

There was no sign around the pad of a human figure. For the necessary seconds Keill sat still, impatience struggling to overcome his control, while life support was restored in the freighter's stern compartment. At last his ship sensors showed that it was safe to go out. He sprang up, snatching another energy gun from his weapons store.

'*They'll be in the control room by now,*' he told Glr swiftly. '*Stay with the ship.*'

Keill . . . Glr began unhappily. But the airlock had opened, and he was gone.

Beyond the flame-scarred landing pad, one of the wheel-less, two-seater personnel carriers stood idle on the auto-magnetic strip. Keill leaped into it, slamming its starting lever ahead to send it forward. The carrier had only one forward speed – and impatience built to desperation within him as it trundled along with agonizing slowness.

He glanced over the edge of the trackway, down into the shadowy depths of the freighter. It was as empty as before, with a few work-robots still standing idle, arms drooping like the branches of dead trees.

It was likely, he thought, that one of the people from the shuttle would come back towards the launching pad, to investigate the arrival of a second ship. But there was only one way to come – along the suspended trackway of the vehicles which connected the landing pad and the control room.

Of course there was a flat hoist elevator at the landing pad, and another at the freighter's far end serving the control room, to give access to the deck of the cargo hold below. But no one would go down that way to investigate Keill's arrival. The trackway was too high, and an occupant of one of the carriers would be hidden from someone gazing upwards from the deck.

The small car slid onwards, passing through a doorway, automatically opened, in the first of the vast bulkheads that divided the freighter into sections. Ahead, the trackway remained empty, the hollow vault of the freighter silent. Then another bulkhead, another doorway . . .

And beyond, another of the carriers. On the parallel track next to Keill's, coming towards him, towards the landing pad.

Within it, the figure of a man – half-rising to his feet in alarm at the sight of Keill.

It was Fillon – pale and wide-eyed with startled panic, raising a hand that clutched the unmistakeable shape of an energy gun.

The gun in Fillon's hand crackled, but the beam flashed far over Keill's head.

The two cars trundled on towards each other.

'Fillon,' Keill shouted, 'Quern's dead – the rebellion is finished! It's over! Put the gun down!'

Fillon's answer was another wildly aimed shot, and another. Keill could see that the Clusterman's hand was shaking badly – yet the next shot bit into the trackway only half a metre from Keill's car, and the next sizzled not much farther away from Keill's right shoulder.

Keill crouched, eyes narrowed. The cars drew nearer, and still Fillon's gun blazed furiously, erratically but without pause.

As they drew closer, Keill knew that soon one of Fillon's blasts would be on target. His own gun flashed into his hand, and he snapped a shot without seeming to take aim.

But the beam struck just as he had intended, biting into Fillon's arm.

Fillon shrieked, lurching back. Yet somehow he did not drop the gun. He had been firing as he was hit, and the firing stud was still depressed as he fell back into the car, his injured arm jerking.

The lethal beam poured its power downwards, into the carrier Fillon was riding.

Keill heard the dull thud of an explosion within the machine. Then, like a blind, escaping animal, it veered suddenly to one side – and toppled over the edge of the trackway.

Fillon's thin, echoing scream was cut off when the carrier struck the metal deck of the freighter below, with a splintering, explosive crash.

Keill peered over the edge, as his own carrier neared the spot where Fillon had fallen. Below, what was left of Fillon's car lay in a heap of smoking, crumpled wreckage. It covered the lower half of Fillon's body – the upper half lying exposed, unmoving, eyes staring sightlessly upwards.

I wonder if you *were* a second Deathwing agent, Keill thought. Maybe I'll never know.

A moment more, and the carrier had reached its goal – a flat metal apron, as broad as the landing pad, outside the doorway that led to the control room in the freighter's nose.

Keill jerked the lever back, halting the carrier as it swung round into position for the return trip on the parallel magnetic strip.

Gun in hand, he sprang through the door.

The control room was narrow, cramped and unlovely, the metal coverings of the walls stained and dented with age. One of the meagre slits of the viewports was no longer clear plastiglass but a blank slab of metal – into which was set, like a plug, a shiny metal ovoid that Keill had seen before; in the container on the shuttle, during his secret visit to the roof of the Clusterhome.

The Deathwing weapon. The trailing hook-ups from one end of the ovoid now led into their connections within the freighter's control panel. The ovoid's other end would be jutting out through the port, ready, when activated, to spill its deadly capsules of radiation.

And at the control panel, across the open area from Keill, someone was standing. A small, slender figure in a bright Cluster coverall.

Joss.

As she turned to face Keill, she wore the same air of calm authority that she had shown on the first day they had met.

'I thought it would be you,' Keill said, just as calmly.

She studied him without expression. 'Fillon is dead?'

Keill nodded. 'And Quern as well.'

A frown creased the smooth brow, and anger flared in the dark eyes, quickly controlled. She glanced at the gun in Keill's hand. 'And are you going to kill me, too?'

'No.' Keill lowered the gun, returning it to his belt. 'But I'm not going to let you use the weapon, either.'

Joss backed away a step, leaning against the control panel. 'How will you stop me?'

'I hope you'll stop yourself,' Keill said. 'Think for a minute, Joss. I know how strongly you felt about the Cluster and its rebellion – but it's over now. The Veynaans have smashed the Home, and have probably taken the surviving Cluster-folk prisoner. There's nothing left!'

'Veynaa is left,' Joss said, her voice grating.

'But Veynaa means millions of innocent people,' Keill insisted. 'No matter how you feel, you can't commit murder on that scale, for revenge.'

'Quern told the Veynaans what would happen if they ignored our ultimatum,' Joss replied, determination drawing harsh lines on her face. 'Now it will happen!'

'Quern was insane,' Keill said sharply. 'He cared nothing for the Cluster. He belonged to an . . . an organization devoted to making war – and he was *using* you and the Clusterfolk. You can't use the weapon, Joss. That much evil makes everything it touches evil!'

To his surprise, Joss smiled. Not the warm, lovely smile he had seen so often before – but a thin, cold smile that held both mockery and triumph.

At the same moment, Keill felt a faint, throbbing vibration from the metal beneath his feet, heard a distant rumbling roar. The freighter's booster rockets, he realized, flaming into action to alter the giant ship's orbit.

'Joss . . .' he began, desperately casting about in his mind for the right words.

But she did not let him finish. With the speed that he had seen in her before, she swept her hand up towards him. It held a small, knobbled cylinder, covered with odd markings and tiny projections, like nothing Keill had seen before.

But he did not doubt that it was a weapon of some sort – and that Joss had caught him off-guard and flat-footed.

'Such a moving speech,' she smiled. 'But you have made it too late, legionary. And to the wrong person.'

She gestured with the cylinder. From behind him, Keill heard a slight grinding sound, almost muffled by the rumble of the boosters. He began to whirl.

But six powerful bands of shiny, flexible metal wrapped themselves round his body, pinning his arms to his sides.

chapter thirteen

Keill did not need to twist his head around to look. Another work-robot, he knew, with cold self-reproach. He had been too preoccupied with Joss to be properly alert, and the noise of the boosters had drowned the minimal noise of the robot's treads.

He tried to flex his arms, to seek some leverage within the steely grip. But the robot's six metal arms tightened round his body, and swung him up, off his feet. He was nearly immobilized, dangling as helpless as an animal awaiting slaughter.

Staring down into the cold and smoky eyes of Joss, seeing the demonic triumph that shone from her face, Keill wondered how he had ever thought her beautiful.

'You'll not smash this robot so easily,' she said, her mocking smile broadening.

'Then it was you – before – at the food tanks?' Keill spoke with difficulty as the robot's arms clamped ever tighter round his chest.

'Of course. You might have guessed. I told you I was a freighter pilot for the Cluster – and pilots learn to handle robots. With what Quern called a "delicate touch" – remember?'

Her laugh seemed almost metallic as she brandished the knobbly cylinder in her hand. And now Keill could guess its function – a remote manipulator for the robots.

He struggled again, lashing backwards with his boots. But he could not see, this time, the weak points to aim at, and his kicks glanced off the sturdy metal – while the unyielding bands around him tightened even further.

'I've set the robot controls to continue tightening its grip,' she said, still smiling. 'It will crush you to death in a few minutes. Meanwhile you may watch me complete the settings to activate the weapon – and then, when I've left you, you can pass the remaining time wondering which will kill you first – the robot or the radiation.'

'Can you kill ... so easily,' Keill gasped, 'so cold-bloodedly?'

Her eyes narrowed to icy slits. 'Easily?' she spat. 'I wanted you killed at the outset – I knew you would be a threat! But Quern would not hear of it. He insisted you were more valuable alive – he even reprimanded me for trying to kill you at the food tanks!' Her laugh was harsh, scornful. 'And now Quern is dead because he let you live – and I have been proved right. And when I have completed Quern's task, it will not be reprimands that I will receive!'

Keill stared down with chill horror at Joss's contorted, gleeful face, his mind half-numbed by the overwhelming truth that at last had been confirmed.

There *had* been a second Deathwing agent on the Cluster.

And he was looking at her.

He fought, in the robot's crushing grip, for breath enough to speak.

'Won't the One ... want me ... brought back for ... questioning?' he gasped.

Surprise and doubt flitted across Joss's face. 'How do you know so much?' she wondered, half to herself. 'Perhaps. . .' But then the look of cold determination returned. 'No – you will die. You have already disrupted the Master's plan enough, and you are too dangerous, as Quern found out.' A glint of anger flashed in her eyes. 'For that alone, the One himself would seek your death, if he were here. You have robbed the Master of his most valued weapon!'

That's something, at least, Keill thought, remembering

what Quern had revealed earlier, on the ship. No matter what happens now, the Warlord won't be murdering any more planets with that radiation. The secret of its making had died with Quern.

'Now our conversation must end,' Joss was saying. 'I have work to do – and soon the robot will crush your ribs, and put an end to your speeches.'

She turned away, laughing unpleasantly, towards the control panel.

Keill did not reply – but not because his ribs were crumbling under the robot's pressure. The increasing grip of the metal arms was painful, bruising the flesh of his arms and chest, but he pushed the pain to one side of his mind and ignored it, knowing that his bones could withstand stresses far more powerful than the robot could manage.

He calmed his mind, and formed the call. *'Glr – you'd better get up here. With a gun.'*

On my way, came the calm reply.

'No – wait!' An idea had sprung into Keill's mind – a way that he and Glr might thwart the Deathwing plan and still, with luck and speed, survive. *'Come in the ship! Burn your way through the bulkheads!'*

If you say so, Glr replied, with a faint note of puzzlement. *Are you aware that the orbit of the freighter is decaying?*

'I know,' Keill said quickly. *'How long before planetfall?'*

Your ship computer estimates four minutes.

And the weapon, Keill knew, would be activated before that – to release the radiation capsules into Veynaa's atmosphere, beginning the catastrophic chain reaction that would eventually leave nothing alive on the planet's surface.

'Then hurry!' Keill called, in silent desperation.

Two bulkheads remaining, Glr replied, as calm as ever.

Joss stepped away from the control panel, looking up at Keill, her eyes glittering. He let his body sag in the robot's grip, as if near death. And her smile was ugly – a distant echo of Quern's twisted gloating.

'If you can still hear me,' she said, 'it might brighten your final moments to know what is to happen. In about three minutes the container will open, and the radiation capsules will spill out.' She gestured towards the metal ovoid fixed in the viewport. 'But in one minute from now I will be back in the shuttle – or perhaps in *your* ship, if it is more suitable – and on my way to deep space. To watch Veynaa's death, and yours, from safety.'

She laughed mockingly, flung the robot control cylinder on to the control panel, and turned towards the door of the control room.

But then she paused. A new sound had begun to emerge from the bowels of the great freighter's shell. A crackling roar that was far louder and more powerful than the thrum of the boosters.

Glr – blasting her way through the nearest bulkhead with the energy guns of Keill's ship.

'What . . .' Joss muttered.

The roar outside grew to a bellow. Not of the guns now, but of the ship's retros. Keill twisted his head around, seeing the reflected orange flare of flame through the doorway as Glr swept the ship thunderously down on to the broad metal apron beyond the control room.

Paling, Joss whirled and sprang towards Keill, her hand clutching for the gun at his belt. But the robot's grip had pressed Keill's arm to his side covering the gun, and she could not work it loose.

Then Glr was in the room.

Wings booming, fangs bared, she seemed to fill the air above them, like some furious, blazing-eyed spirit of vengence.

Joss screamed and cowered away. And in one of Glr's small hands an energy gun flashed and crackled.

The beam struck into the centre of the robot's pyramidal body. Smoke gushed from the wrecked circuits, and the robot jerked, its arms straightening, flying uncontrollably apart.

Glr hovered overhead, as Keill, released, dropped to the floor on his feet, before the terrified woman.

For a flashing instant he locked eyes with her, the deadly weapons of his hands poised like blades.

Then, with an inner snarl at his own weakness, he flung her aside with a sweep of his arm. Her slim body slammed brutally against the solid metal of the robot's body. And she crumpled, half-unconscious, to the floor as the robot, out of control, flailed its arms crazily through the air above her.

Ignoring it and Joss, Keill sprang to the control panel. As he moved, his mind was forming words with rigid concentration.

'Glr, get back to the ship and get ready to lift off! I'm setting the freighter for Overlight in thirty seconds!'

But . . . Glr began.

'Don't argue – go!' Keill yelled.

The great wings swept once, and Glr vanished through the door. Keill's hands were blurs as he made the adjustments to the freighter controls.

Then a scream of manic rage from behind him made him whirl, poised to strike.

There was no need. Joss had recovered and regained her feet, and may have intended to hurl herself at Keill, to prevent him altering the control settings.

But she had been prevented.

Perhaps it was the impact of Joss's body that had restored at least a few of the connections in the robot's damaged circuits. Enough to reawaken it to its most recent instructions.

Its whipping, threshing, steely arms had found Joss as she had risen.

Instantly they had clamped round her body, as they had around Keill's, and jerked her up off her feet.

She hung, suspended, struggling faintly. The robot's instructions had included an order to increase its pressure – and mindlessly it was obeying. As Joss saw Keill spin to look at her, the fear and fury drained from her eyes. Only a desperate pleading remained in their dark depths.

'Keill . . .' she whispered. 'Please . . .'

He glanced at the cylindrical control mechanism, on the control panel where Joss had thrown it.

Within his mind, the time-count that he had begun, when the freighter's controls were set, ticked relentlessly ahead.

Twenty-four seconds left . . .

He looked back at Joss, his face expressionless. 'I don't know how to operate the robot,' he said stonily. 'And there's no time to learn.'

Her scream was little more than a whimper as he turned away towards the control room door.

Outside, his ship waited on the platform, airlock open. He dived through, sprang to his sling-seat.

Nineteen seconds . . .

The ship's drive thundered into life. It lifted slightly. '*Now*', he said fiercely to Glr, '*a way out*.'

The ship's forward guns blasted. On the side of the freighter, metal glowed, began to flow down the curving sweep of the hull.

Thirteen seconds . . .

A hole appeared in the hull. Through it he could see more flame flickering – from the heat of the freighter's entrance into Veynaa's atmosphere.

Even before the hole was wide enough, he slammed on full power.

Nine seconds . . .

The ship screamed forward, guns still blazing. Its blunt nose smashed into the gap in the hull. In a rending explosion of tormented, half-melted metal, it burst through, and clear.

Six seconds . . .

Brutally Keill dragged the ship howling upwards, curving it away from the plummeting freighter. The Overlight field, when it was operating, extended out around a ship. He had to get well away.

Three seconds . . .

He glanced at his viewscreens, his ship still at full power. Just about . . .

Now.

In the screen, the image of the freighter blurred, shimmered.

Then it was gone.

Keill. Glr's inner voice was soft, worried. *You know that entering Overlight so near a planet can distort the field. The freighter could emerge anywhere – with the weapon.*

'It won't,' Keill said bleakly. '*I didn't programme it to emerge at all.*'

And his ship climbed away towards deep space – while below, the planet Veynaa rolled peacefully on its axis, unheeding, unharmed.

Aftermath
chapter fourteen

In the distant, boundless expanses of deep space, in a sector of the Inhabited Galaxy where probably no one had ever heard of Veynaa or the Cluster, Keill's ship winked into existence out of Overlight.

At the controls, Keill ran his eyes again over the settings and computer data, confirming his course, then switched to automatic and leaned back, stretching luxuriously. Beside him, in her special seat, Glr also stretched, flaring her delicate wings.

Keill looked at her expectantly. She had been silent for a long time, reaching across the galaxy's distances to the minds of the Overseers in their hidden asteroid – reporting the final events over Veynaa, the ultimate defeat of the Warlord's plan.

Now awareness had returned to the bright round eyes that she fixed on Keill.

The Overseers are pleased, she announced. *All in all, they feel that we have been successful.*

'*All in all?*' Keill echoed, raising an eyebrow.

They do have certain regrets, Glr went on. *First, the Deathwing now knows that you exist, and that you are a threat to the Warlord's plans. Second, we have learned little more about the Deathwing, or its leader, or the Warlord himself.*

Keill snorted. '*I was a little short of time to have a long informative chat with Quern. Even if he would have told me anything.*'

I put that point to the Overseers – somewhat forcefully, Glr said. Quiet laughter curled for a moment around her silent voice. *They then reported that peace has returned to the Cluster. The*

Overseers have indirectly encouraged a rumour on Veynaa that the Cluster rebellion was the fault of one unscrupulous, power-hungry leader, who is now dead.

'Accurate enough, as far as it goes,' Keill put in.

As you say. But because of this, the Veynaans are not being vindictive. The Cluster survivors have begun to rebuild their Home, and Veynaa has agreed to hold talks about improving their conditions and giving them more control over their lives.

'If that had happened in the first place,' Keill said sourly, 'Quern would never have got a grip on the Cluster.'

Humans are renowned, said Glr, for perceiving the proper course of action when it is far too late to take it.

'But it's not too late,' Keill objected. 'Not for the survivors, or the Veynaans. It would have been too late only if that weapon had been used.'

Agreed, Glr replied. You will also be amused to know, from the Overseers, that the Veynaans are very pleased with themselves. They say that they were proved right – that the Cluster was bluffing, and did not dare to use such a weapon against an inhabited planet.

Keill shivered, remembering how close it had been, how few seconds had remained before those deadly capsules would have spilled out into Veynaa's atmosphere.

And that thought recalled another that had been troubling him.

'Glr, what about the weapon?' he asked. 'The radiation capsules were still set to be ejected, which means they'd leave the freighter in Overlight.'

There is no danger. The capsules, as Quern told you, would react only on air – so the chain reaction cannot begin in Overlight. The capsules will remain harmless, outside the freighter but within the Overlight field, for eternity.

Keill did not reply, silenced by the awesome weight of that last word. Eternity.

My race, the Ehrlil, Glr went on, has travelled longer and farther in Overlight than any humans, yet even we have fathomed only

a fragment of its nature. But we do know that a ship entering Over-
light has entered a nothingness all of its own. It no longer inhabits
'normal' reality – but also it cannot impinge even on other ships in
Overlight. In practical terms, the freighter simply no longer exists.
Nor does the weapon. She paused. *Nor does the woman.*

Keill nodded sombrely. '*I see that. Anyway, the robot's grip*
would have killed her before long.' His eyes grew dark. '*And I*
don't think I would have released her even if I'd known how.'

For a few moments they sat silent, each wrapped in separate
thoughts, not for communication. Then Glr stirred, shaking
out her wings, looking around at the viewscreens.

You still have not told me what course you have set, she said
brightly.

Keill responded to the change of mood, sitting up, glancing
again over the control panel. '*I'm keeping a promise to you.*'

A promise? Glr's eyes glowed. *About the place where you say*
there will be good flying – where I may stretch my wings at last?

'*I thought you'd remember,*' Keill smiled. '*We'll reach the*
system soon that contains the planet I'm thinking of. It has a very
small population in terms of land area – so there are huge tracts of it
still totally untouched. In those regions there are places where the sun
is warm, the turf is soft underfoot, and there are deep pools of the
clearest water you'll ever see.'

No doubt that would be of great interest, Glr said loftily, *to*
fishes and humans and other inferior species.

Keill laughed aloud. '*And beyond those pools,*' he continued,
'*are mountains that seem to reach up for ever, where strong winds*
blow all the time around the peaks, and the air is the freshest in the
galaxy.'

Perfection! Glr cried. Her wings thrummed, her round eyes
glistened. *Can you not get more speed out of this primitive craft of*
yours?

And her silent, bubbling laughter mingled with Keill's as
he reached towards the controls.

book three

Day of the Starwind

The mystery of Rilyn
prologue

Generations of peace had left the people of Jitrell unwary by nature. The planet was rich enough in resources to be nearly self-sufficient, yet not so rich as to attract the greedy or the violent from elsewhere among mankind's Inhabited Worlds. It was close enough to the main space lanes to profit from trade, when it needed to, yet remote enough to be untroubled by turmoil and upheaval on other worlds.

It was just about right, according to its first colonists, when man had been spreading himself among the stars in the centuries of the Scattering. Life was good on Jitrell; life was comfortable. Perhaps too comfortable . . .

Comfort was definitely uppermost in the minds of the space-port guards in Belinter, the premier city of Jitrell, in the middle of a balmy summer night. The guards were tending to lounge, to idle, to cluster in groups and exchange murmured jokes and easy chat. The port had not been busy for weeks, and was nearly empty – except for two or three freighter ships whose cargoes had already been forwarded on their long commercial journeys, and a few stacks of commodity containers behind the stout doors of storage depots. Nothing much worth stealing; nothing much worth guarding.

So the guards were totally unprepared for the sight of their command post, with all their outgoing communication systems, apparently beginning to collapse upon itself – as if struck by a giant, invisible club – and then exploding in a thunderburst of flame and flying debris.

The guards were ordinary men, with only basic training, and they reacted like ordinary men. They froze. Shock, bewilderment and fear blanked their minds, paralysed their limbs, for just long enough.

And the others were upon them.

They seemed to come from nowhere, as if the very shadows had given shape to them. Twenty or more men, in dark red, one-piece uniforms, moving in a perfectly co-ordinated attack that was all the more terrifying in its smooth speed and its eerie near-silence.

Some of the attackers rode light, two-man skimmers, hovering on a cushion of gases. Others were on foot, as swift as predators, and as deadly. They came at the guards in a rush, while those on the skimmers fanned out towards the dark shapes of the freighters and the storage depots.

In seconds both the ships and the depots were also crumpling in upon themselves before exploding in violent bursts of flame. But the Jitrellian guards did not see that happen. The guards were busy dying.

To their credit, one or two of the guards had overcome their panic soon enough to reach for their holstered weapons. But that merely meant that they were the first to die – in a storm of energy beams from the guns of the attackers.

Those slower guards who were not cut down by the searing beams fell soon enough. The attackers, closing in on their victims, used only their hands – with the easy, almost casual skill that a woodman might show lopping limbs from a tree with his axe.

At the precise instant that the last guard crumpled, a spaceship swept in low over the port, hovering for a landing. It was the shape of a semicircle, like half of a giant disc, with a dark, non-reflecting exterior and no visible insignia. As it landed the attackers moved towards it, with the same speed and co-ordination, their silence still unbroken. In seconds they were aboard, less than three minutes after their first appearance. The ship lifted swiftly, vanishing into the night sky.

On the ground of the spaceport the huddled forms of the

guards lay still, and a last small flame flickered and died within the shattered remains of a freighter.

The Jitrellians reacted to the news of the attack with a towering but useless rage, tinged with fear. Their rage was useless because there was not the smallest clue to the identity of the raiders, or their purposes. And their fear came from the fact that this was not the first such raid – though it was the most murderous – that had happened on Jitrell within the previous months.

All over the populated parts of the planet, units of the small armed forces were sent to reinforce the guards at spaceports and important industrial sites. And the Jitrellian authorities argued, debated, theorized, yet in the end came to the conclusion that they could come to no conclusion. There was no way of knowing *who*, or *why*.

It was pointless, they said. It was mindless.

But wiser, calmer heads, a long, long way away from Jitrell, studied the reports of the raids – which they gleaned from widespread monitoring devices that the rest of the galaxy did not dream existed. These wiser heads were sure that the raids were not pointless. And they were sure that they could recognize a mind – a very special mind – behind them.

chapter one

Like a spearhead with a rounded point, a small spaceship burst out of thick cloud cover, heat shields still glowing from its plunging dive through atmosphere. Its trajectory flattened as it curved down to skim the surface of the planet Rilyn, where the rust-coloured waters of a broad ocean moved sluggishly in slow, flat waves.

Billows of fog reached up to enfold the ship, which was a compact, one-person fighter. Within it the viewscreens showed only swirls of grey. But the man at the control panel – a lean, dark-haired young man in a grey uniform – did not alter his speed. The ship sensors and computer instrumentation gave him all the guidance data he needed. Leaning forward tautly in his slingseat, hands moving over the controls as if they had eyes of their own, he watched the data screens with tireless concentration.

He was Keill Randor, once a young officer in the celebrated Legions of the planet Moros. Now he was the galaxy's last legionary, the only survivor of the swift and terrible destruction of the Legions. But even though he was a man without a planet, without a people, he did not travel alone.

The other occupant of the small, hurtling ship was not human. It was a small, winged alien being, resting on an adapted slingseat that was nearly a perch. From the short body, with its soft leathery plates of skin, the seemingly delicate membranes of the wings extended like half-furled sails. The head was smooth and domed, and above a blunt muzzle two bright, round eyes stared at the control panel with a concentration equal to Keill's. The perch brought the alien's stubby legs and small feet within easy reach of the panel: and those feet, which were in fact hands – three fingers and an opposing thumb – fidgeted as if they too wanted to race over the controls.

The alien's name was Glr, a female of a race called the Ehrlil – from another galaxy, for man had found no other intelligent life in his own galaxy, when he had spread out to populate the Inhabited Worlds. The Ehrlil were a long-lived race, much given to roaming among the stars, and Glr's wanderings had brought her to man's galaxy. There she had eventually met and befriended Keill Randor, and had willingly joined him in the lonely and hazardous quest that had occupied him since the destruction of his world – a quest that had now brought them to the planet Rilyn.

Keill glanced up at the viewscreens as the fog thinned and fell away. The ship burst out into clear air beneath a dull, overcast sky, and swept over a shoreline where waves flopped heavily against reddish soil. The terrain beyond the shore was typical of Rilyn. It was uniformly flat and almost featureless – a reddish plain with outcrops of dark, bare rock, interrupted here and there by swathes of thick, greenish shrubbery that grew no higher than a few centimetres.

'Hard to imagine people ever wanting to live here,' Keill said idly.

It is usually hard to understand why humans want the things they want. Glr's silent reply formed itself in Keill's mind, for her race was telepathic. And while Keill was not, Glr was able to project her thoughts into his mind, and could pick up his surface thoughts when they were clearly formed. She had met only a few humans whose minds were clear enough for that kind of communication – which was one reason why Glr often claimed to hold a low opinion of mankind.

A smile tugged at the corner of Keill's mouth, but he left the remark unanswered. A smear of a darker red had appeared on the horizon, in the forward viewscreens.

'That's what we want.' His hands moved, and the ship

veered slightly, still skimming low over the empty land.

In moments the distant smear showed itself to be an upland region, where the land heaved itself into broad, rolling mounds and hummocks. Everywhere the dark rock thrust up out of the soil, as if striving to become hills – but without success. For the rock surfaces were flattened and razed, scarred with cracks and crevices, creased and pitted by erosion.

It looked almost as if some gigantic weight had settled crushingly on the land, and had then been dragged along to grind away any upthrust peak or rise. And that levelling image was reinforced by the abundance of crushed rock and cracked boulders scattered in the vales and gullies that lay between the flat-topped promontories.

There, too, the reddish soil lay heaped in drifts and dunes, as if it were light sand. Yet it was dense soil, Keill could see, held firmly by the tough green shrubbery and by a rich carpeting of flat vegetation like moss.

Nothing on Rilyn seemed to reach up, to grow vertically towards the light and the sky. The landscape seemed to cower, to prostrate itself, in its empty, silent bleakness.

Do you really hope to escape detection by flying so low? Glr asked, her mental voice sounding testy as the ship skimmed an outcropping.

Keill shrugged. 'Maybe – if whoever's here isn't being careful. There's no point in coming straight down on top of them.'

But if they are being careful, and their detectors are working?

'We'll take the chance,' Keill said.

As he spoke he slewed the ship around another shoulder of rock, and nodded at a broad expanse of open greenery ahead, like a shallow basin. 'We can set down here. If the co-ordinates are right, the place we're looking for isn't much of a walk from here.'

Walk? said Glr, spreading her wings, her tone implying that Keill had used a dirty word.

But before Keill could reply, he was flung to one side in his slingseat as the ship shuddered and bucked beneath him.

He heard Glr's mental yelp of surprise as his hands flashed over the controls. The power had cut out – the ship's energy drive had stopped. And the electronics were dead, the screens blank, the computer-guidance system silent.

What is it? Glr cried.

There was no time for a reply. The ship struck the ground with a grinding crash, torn shrubbery and red earth fountaining up around it.

But Keill had been flying low and had already begun to slow the ship with its retro rockets. So it struck the shallow basin flat, on its belly, without tumbling – skidding forward, ploughing a deep furrow across the basin's green surface.

At last friction halted the slide, and the ship came to rest. Keill and Glr, held safe in the slingseats, together expelled the breath they had been holding and looked at each other.

Not one of your better landings. The laughter in Glr's mental voice was slightly shaky.

Keill shook his head. 'It's some kind of force field, a suppressor. Whoever put it there wouldn't care much how we came down.'

Glr looked at the dead controls. *And what about getting up again?*

'We'll come to that,' Keill said. 'We'll go and find whoever owns the suppressor field – and convince him to turn it off.'

Glr's silent laughter rose as Keill reached for the fastenings of the slingseat. But he did not complete the motion.

The ship had started to move again.

The very ground where it had come to rest fell away, with a rumble of fracturing, collapsing rock. The ship lurched sideways, metal screeching against stone like a death-cry, and toppled with a slow finality into the yawning mouth of the pit that had opened beneath it.

chapter two

The ship's downward plunge halted in a few seconds, with a resonant crash. Keill waited a moment, listening, then carefully released himself from the slingseat. The ship had come to rest on its side, so the deck of its inner chamber was tilted steeply, but Keill moved easily up the incline towards the airlock.

Take a weapon, Glr said as she released herself from her perch. *It must be some form of trap.*

'Energy guns won't work,' Keill said. The suppressor field that had knocked out the ship's drive would also affect the guns that used an adapted form of the same power source. 'I'll just have a look – a careful look.'

The airlock had a manual failsafe that opened it readily even without power. Keill waited, sheltering within the lock, watching and listening, his body poised to meet any threat.

But no danger appeared. Only darkness, turned into twilight by the light from the opening in the rock where the ship had fallen through. And a tomb-like silence, save for a few trickles of crushed rock and gravel coming to rest around the ship. And the smell of dust, and of the musty dampness of very old stone.

Keill stepped forward, watchfully, to the edge of the lock, letting his eyes adjust to the dimness.

'It's a cave,' he said to Glr. 'The ship's weight simply broke through the roof of a cave.'

As he spoke he dropped lightly to the ground. Behind him Glr soared out of the airlock, swooping down on her wide wings to settle on Keill's shoulder.

I dislike caves, she said.

Keill nodded absently, intent on a survey of the ship's exterior. It seemed undamaged by the fall, as it should be: the niconium steel hull had survived far greater impacts in its time. He turned his attention to his surroundings.

It was a high-vaulted cave, not more than twenty metres wide but more than twice as long. There were patches of deeper black here and there in the curved walls that seemed to be niches, crevices, gouged into the rock. Keill stepped further away from the ship, and only then became aware that Glr's grip on his shoulder was unnecessarily fierce, and her wings were half-opening and closing with a nervous restlessness.

'*Glr . . .?*' He formed her name silently, in his mind, knowing that she could reach in and pick it up.

Keill, I cannot stay here. The words burst into Keill's mind rapidly, and with a quality that he had never sensed in Glr before. An edge of fear.

'*There's no danger,*' he replied soothingly.

But even as he formed the words, he was proved wrong – by the scratching, slithering noise behind him.

He whirled, into a fighting crouch, while Glr sprang away with a slap of wings. From the deeper darknesses of the crevices in the far wall of the cave, something – some*things* – were emerging.

The creatures seemed to be shaped like large inverted bowls, or perhaps helmets, the colour of the cave's dark stone. But as they pushed further out from their hiding places, Keill saw that the helmet shapes were only their heads – which tapered back into longer bodies, legless, like worms, but thick as a man's thigh. There were no recognizable features, nor did the creatures move threateningly. They had merely pushed their helmet-like heads out, as if waiting.

Keill stepped cautiously towards them. But his boot came down not on rock or gravel but on something soft, that gave beneath him. Reflexively he sprang sideways, staring down with some distaste.

This was a different sort of creature, squeezing out of a narrow crack in the cave floor. It was a dirty white in colour, and seemed to have no fixed shape as it oozed along the rocky surface – sometimes stretching out a long thin projection from itself, sometimes spreading out like a puddle of thick, viscous liquid.

It seemed anxious to get away from Keill, but its anxiety took it too near the wall. From beneath the bulky helmet-head of one of the creatures in the crevices, a long tendril lashed out – almost a filament, so thin that Keill might not have seen it in the dim light had it not been a bright orange.

The tip of the filament touched the oozing creature, and its motion stopped at once, its edges curling up like those of a dry fallen leaf. The tendril then withdrew, and the entire length of the creature slithered forward, down the wall, moving slowly towards its prey.

The tendril was a stinger of some sort, Keill realized, certainly lethal to the oozing thing. What the tendrils might do to humans was not something he was interested in finding out. As the helmet-head creature slid near, he turned, took two running steps, and sprang to grasp the lower edge of the ship's airlock. He swung himself up with acrobatic ease, and went into the ship to find Glr.

She was sitting in her slingperch, her round eyes fixed on the airlock as he came through. *Caves are unpleasant enough*, she said, still with that edge of fear in her inner voice. *But caves with slimy ground-crawlers* . . . A shudder rippled across her body to the tips of her wings.

Keill knew that she would have perceived some of what had happened, through his mind. 'They can't hurt us . . .' he began.

I do not fear them, Glr replied. *But caves . . . Keill, I am a creature of the air, the sky, openness and freedom. Most of my race have a horror of being underground. Caves, tunnels, pits, all such things are nightmares to me. I cannot control the feeling. I must get out.*

'Then let's get out,' Keill said with a smile. 'Take a lifeline up with you and fasten it so I can climb up. And I'll follow in a minute.'

Thank you, Glr said. She floated on half-spread wings to the airlock, where Keill detached one of the safety lines that could be fastened to a spacesuit if a pilot had to leave his ship in space. They were long strands of extremely tough artificial fibre – far longer than would be needed to reach from the surface down into the cave.

Glr took one end of the line, studiously not looking at the creatures that were still silently thrusting their heads out from the cave wall. *Climb carefully,* she said. And she rose in a sweep of wings towards the welcoming patch of light above.

Keill waited until a firm tug on the line showed that Glr had fastened her end safely, probably to some solid boulder nearby. Then he turned back inside the ship, to open the compartment that held his weaponry.

His eyes drifted across the assortment of beam-guns, useless to him now, and some of the other more sophisticated weapons. What could be used in a suppressor field? Knives and clubs? Pointless – his own barehanded combat skills were far more lethal. But ordinary, old-fashioned explosives . . .

He took up two small, flat oblongs of black plastic. They were one of the variety of grenades developed by the Legions. A flick of a finger could prime them, and they would explode powerfully enough to devastate a good-sized room. Yet they were designed to be clipped flat to a belt, where they seemed to be no more than innocent decorations or fastenings.

From another compartment he took a plain pouch, two handsbreadths wide, into which he stowed some wafers of food concentrate, a container of water and a basic medikit – the essential field pack of the legionary going into action. It too clipped neatly to his belt.

Now he was as ready as he could be. He stepped out of the airlock on to the tilted side of the ship, reaching for the lifeline. For a moment he glanced around at the cave, thinking how much it looked like a tomb, a place of burial. Then he shook himself, dismissing the morbid thought. Glr was right – caves were unhealthy places. Effortlessly he began his hand-over-hand climb towards the light, towards the purpose that had brought him to Rilyn.

That purpose was part of the larger purpose that had been the central driving force in Keill Randor's life – ever since the terrible day when he had returned to Moros, to learn that every man, woman and child of the Legions had been wiped out, murdered, before they could begin to defend themselves, by a mysterious, deadly radiation that had enveloped the planet.

Keill had begun a desperate, vengeful search through the Inhabited Worlds for the unknown murderer of his world. Yet he had realized that his search would probably fail, for he too had been lightly touched by the radiation. It had settled in his bones and was slowly, surely, killing him.

But a near-miracle had intervened. Keill's survival had been noted by a strange, secretive group of brilliant elderly scientists, whom he came to know as the Overseers. They had taken him to their hidden base, inside an uncharted asteroid. And there they had saved his life, astonishingly, by *replacing* all his diseased bones with an organic alloy – which, among other things, was virtually unbreakable.

From the Overseers Keill had at last learned why they had saved him, and why they lived in obsessive secrecy, so that Keill saw them only as robed and hooded figures, and was never to know the position of the asteroid. Their reasons had much to do with the murder of the Legions of Moros.

Before they had hidden themselves away, the Overseers had lived normal lives, deep in their different studies of events around the galaxy. But then, slowly, they began to detect a frightening *pattern* in many of those events. And that had led them to give up normal life, to set up their secret base, from which they sent out unique, nearly undetectable monitoring devices through the Inhabited Worlds.

The pattern they had found had to do with warfare among mankind's planets. It had become clear that more and more small, local wars were breaking out – but not in a random, accidental way. There was some guiding principle at work. Some force, some being, was *causing* them, spreading war like an infectious disease among the Worlds.

The Overseers had learned nothing of who or what this mysterious maker of wars might be, though they had given him a code name, for convenience – the Warlord. But they had no doubt about the Warlord's purpose. By spreading the infection of war wherever possible, he was working slowly towards creating a conflict that would involve the entire galaxy in an ultimate, all-consuming holocaust. And out of the ruins of that final calamity, the Warlord would surely emerge, to rule the galaxy unchallenged.

And the Warlord's methods could also be perceived. He sent out agents to various worlds, who would work their way into positions of power and influence, and then turn the local people towards war – using the human weaknesses of greed, or fear, or patriotic bigotry, or whatever else came to hand. So the infection was spread, and the Warlord's plans developed.

That was why, the Overseers told Keill, the Warlord had destroyed the Legions of Moros.

The people of Moros had learned to fight and to discipline themselves to survive the rigours of their harsh planet. Over the generations they had developed their fighting skills to an amazing degree – and had realized that those skills were the only real natural resource that Moros possessed. So they continued to develop, to train and discipline their children, until they became an almost legendary warrior race, with a matchless mastery of the arts of warfare. And they made that mastery available, for a price, to other worlds.

But the ethics of the Legions had insisted on one inflexible rule. They would not fight on the side of aggressors, exploiters, fanatics, any of the mad or greedy perpetrators of unjust wars. Most often in their history they had fought on the side of people *defending* themselves against aggression – no matter how high a price had been offered by the other side. And so the Warlord would have foreseen that the Legions could be a barrier to his master plan – and that one day, if they learned of his existence, they could even move against him directly.

So the day had come of the sneak attack, the strange radiation that had spread in seconds through the atmosphere, and the terrible death of Moros.

The Overseers then knew that only they could hope to block the Warlord's evil ambition. But they needed to know more about him. And they needed a way to thwart him here and there, to disrupt his plan and slow it down while they searched for the ultimate means of stopping him.

They had their far-flung monitors – and they also had Glr, who had found her way to them before they had fled to their asteroid. But they needed the aid of a human, one who could move freely around the Inhabited Worlds, and one who stood a chance of surviving the dangers he might meet.

They found what they needed in Keill Randor, the last legionary. And Keill needed little urging to join with the Overseers, and so pursue his own search for the murderer of Moros.

Keill, accompanied by Glr, had twice encountered agents of the Warlord since he had left the Overseers' base. He had learned that the best of these agents formed an élite force, called the *Deathwing* – led by the Warlord's chief lieutenant, known only as 'The One'. Deathwing agents were powerful, skilled and ruthlessly dedicated to the Warlord's purposes. They were also the most likely source of the information Keill needed to locate and identify the Warlord.

So despite the danger – and despite the fact that the Death-wing had soon learned of his existence and the threat he posed to them – Keill knew that he had to pursue these agents of his enemy, relentlessly, until either the Deathwing or he himself was finished.

Now, as he came to his feet above the pit where his ship lay, and stared across the desolate landscape of Rilyn, he felt the hairs on his neck lift and bristle. Intuitively, he knew what was out there.

Somewhere on Rilyn – somewhere near – the Deathwing waited for him.

chapter three

So you have come up for air at last.

The laughter in Glr's voice bubbled, with no trace of the nervousness that she had shown underground. Keill peered up at the overcast sky, and spotted her, a dark speck against the flat grey cloud, wheeling and dipping with the joy of stretching her wings.

'*Can you see anything?*' he asked her.

A great deal of ugly rock and green stuff, Glr said, *and something of a haze in the distance.*

Keill nodded to himself. The haze might be part of the heavy overcast, or a distortion caused by the suppressor field. It didn't matter. Whether or not Glr's bright eyes could see into the distance, it was a distance that Keill's earth-bound feet would have to cross.

He moved away at a jogging pace, settling into easy strides that he could maintain tirelessly for kilometre after kilometre. Both the moss-like plant growth and the bare red soil were firm underfoot, and the air was fresh and cool, full of the pleasantly acrid odour of the short-stemmed shrubbery that clung so closely to ground level. As he ran, only the light thudding of his boots interrupted the silence of the desolate land.

Animal life on this planet seems inclined to dwell underground, Glr said, distaste obvious in her voice. *You are the only moving thing I can see.*

'Be sure that you're not too visible,' he told Glr. 'Anyone watching will be put on guard by seeing a winged creature on this planet.'

Anyone watching on this planet, mudhead, Glr replied mockingly, *will have more sense than to look at the sky. They will be looking for a ground-crawler like you.*

Keill chuckled. '*Then reconnoitre ahead. Tell me what I'm going to ground-crawl into.*'

I am yours to command, Glr laughed. Keill glanced up without slackening his pace, and saw the dark speck soar away, dwindling to vanishing point.

He loped steadily onwards, picking his way through the more open areas that divided the flattened promontories of rock, moving in the same direction that his ship had been travelling in before the suppressor field had halted it.

If not for that field, and his intuitions, he would have been convinced that the planet was uninhabited. And everything he knew about the planet – from information supplied by the Overseers – said that it should have been. Yet humanity had colonized less hospitable worlds. At least Rilyn had a breathable atmosphere, and plant life that proved the presence of water, probably in underground wells and streams. This land mass had a mostly temperate climate – and Keill did not doubt that hard-working colonists could make the heavy red soil fertile, and perhaps find minerals in the seamed and ancient rocks.

Once, Keill knew, there had been a colony. During the centuries of the Scattering a starship reaching this solar system had been delighted to find *two* planets able to support human life. They named one Jitrell and one Rilyn, and planted colonies on both, which began to thrive.

The people of Rilyn even gloated a little when they heard tales of aggressive alien beasts that made life uncomfortable, at first, on Jitrell. Rilyn, its colonists boasted, was more kind. It kept all its animal life tucked safely away underground, in the caves and tunnels that honeycombed parts of the main land masses.

None of the colonists stopped to wonder *why* the creatures of Rilyn lived underground. In any case it was unlikely that they would have guessed – until the time came when the reason became clear, in a terrifying way.

The solar system of Rilyn and Jitrell also contained a small 'rogue' planet. This body had a highly erratic orbit, which swung it far out from the system's sun, and then back in – at irregular intervals, about every thirty years. And its path, as it approached the sun, brought it among the other planets of the system.

Most especially, its orbit brought it calamitously close to Rilyn.

It never came near enough to threaten a collision, even with its erratic orbit. But its passage, the presence of its gravitational field, was near enough to cause a slight wobble in Rilyn's movement round its axis. And that created an enormous turbulence in Rilyn's atmosphere. The turbulence, on the planet's surface, took the form of a wind – of titanic destructive force.

Many of the Inhabited Worlds had their share of hurricanes and tornadoes. But the wind that blew on Rilyn, every thirty years or so, made such storms seem like the gentlest of spring breezes.

So the time came when Rilyn's human colonists learned why the planet's animals had adapted to underground life. Why the plants grew low and flat, clinging to the soil with wide, sturdy root systems. And why the rocks were flattened, crushed and scoured bare.

The wind left almost nothing on the surface. The homes and buildings of the colonists were simply erased – their foundations filled in and smoothed over by the dense red soil and crushed rock driven by the wind as if it were powder. Most of the colonists themselves were never seen again. Even their starship – a huge, solid old veteran that had weathered every kind of storm and obstacle that deep space could throw at it – had been smashed into ten thousand fragments and scattered over half a continent.

When the rogue planet went on its way and the monstrous

wind subsided, the Jitrellians sent a ship. They found a hand-ful of human survivors – who had been sensible enough, as the wind rose, to seek refuge in deep caves. The Jitrellians took the survivors away, while their scientists went to work plotting the orbital path of the rogue planet. Soon Jitrell learned the dismal truth. Rilyn could never support human life, because it had to suffer regularly, every generation or so, the immeasurable force that people on Jitrell had begun to call the Starwind.

Since then Rilyn had remained uninhabited in all its barren bleakness. Or so it seemed – until the Overseers' monitors gathered some strange information from that solar system.

Reports of unexplained violence on Jitrell, culminating in a savage attack on the main spaceport, concerned the Overseers. Jitrell was a peaceful planet, which did not even have true armed forces – just a civil-control police force and a smaller militia with mostly ceremonial duties. The Overseers were disturbed that anyone should attack such a planet, and with such a high degree of military precision and skill.

As their suspicions grew, the Overseers sent out more monitoring devices – each self-propelled and equipped with the standard interplanetary drive called 'Overlight', that could leap across light-years in mere seconds. Soon the extra moni-tors detected something that should not have existed – the presence of technological activity, which meant a human presence, on Rilyn. The Overseers promptly passed on these facts, and their suspicions, to Glr – whose telepathic reach had no limits in space.

All of which had led to Keill Randor moving in an easy lope across Rilyn's rolling terrain, towards the area pinpointed by the Overseers as the centre of the mysterious activity.

But as he ran, Glr broke unexpectedly into his thoughts, every scrap of laughter erased from her inner voice. *Keill – move to your right and find cover. Quickly.*

Instantly Keill changed direction, increasing his speed,

running in a low crouch, finding a narrow path among the ragged rocks would hide him from anything except an observer in the air.

'*What is it?*' he asked tautly.

Two groups of armed humans. Widely separated, but on converging paths.

A mental image formed in Keill's mind, like a three-dimensional aerial photograph. Glr was projecting an image of the terrain as she was seeing it.

He saw the creased and flattened rocks, and himself moving among them like a scurrying insect. He saw, several kilometres away, a group of other insect-shapes, moving very slowly. And he saw a second group, moving much more swiftly in a direction that would have brought Keill face to face with them without Glr's warning.

The swift ones, Glr said, *are riding some sort of vehicle. How can that be, in a suppressor field?*

Another mental picture formed, and Keill recognized the shape of an old-fashioned skimmer – little more than a rounded platform, almost boat-shaped, with two open seats. It hovered on a down-draught of expelled gases, produced by a chemical combustion engine.

As he explained the skimmer to Glr, Keill let one hand stray across the flat plastic of the grenades at his belt. If the suppressor field allowed combustion, it would allow – as he had thought – other kinds of chemical explosion. He would not confront these strangers bare-handed.

But he would not confront them at all if he kept moving away from them. He stopped and turned.

What are you doing? came Glr's anxious voice. *The humans on the skimmers are less than a kilometre away. And they are sweeping back and forth, as if searching for something.*

'I want a look at them,' Keill said. 'To find out what they're up to.'

I can tell you that, Glr scolded. *They are no doubt searching for you, or for the ship. And they will certainly find you unless you move further away.*

Keill nodded, but even so doubled back along his previous route, slipping silently as a wraith among the rocks.

'If they're looking for the ship,' he told Glr, 'it means they don't have a fix on where it came down. Maybe the suppressor field distorts their detectors. And they aren't likely to find the ship, in a pit under a pile of rubble. Nor are they going to spot me. Tell me what you can see of them.'

Very well, Glr sighed. There are ten of them, on the vehicles, less than a kilometre away. They are male humans, fairly ordinary looking – if humans can ever be said to look ordinary. A ghost of a giggle, vanishing at once. They are wearing uniforms of some sort, and have hand weapons on their belts. Anything more?

'What about the others?' Keill asked.

There are eight of those, also male, also ordinary. They too wear uniforms, of a different sort, and carry weapons of the rifle type, and heavy packs on their backs. They are walking very slowly, and from their postures they are not enjoying themselves.

Keill smiled. 'Fine. We'll have a look at them later. How close are the ones on the skimmers?'

Too close, Glr scolded. When they see you, and shoot you, do not forget that I told you so.

Keill grinned. 'I'll remember to wave goodbye.'

He ran easily up a nearby slope, flung himself at full length and wedged his body into a narrow crevice from which he could peer with little more than an eye showing. Beyond his hiding place he could see a swathe of open ground, green with vegetation.

The skimmers moved into view with a mutter of engines, sweeping along in a disciplined, fan-shaped search pattern. Motionless, unblinking, Keill watched as they drew near.

The men on the skimmers all seemed young, well-built, athletic in their movements. Their uniforms were single-piece jump suits, of a dark and shiny red, as functional and plain as battledress – except for small insignia on their collars, like numbers, though Keill could not see them clearly. Aside from the holstered weapons at their hips, they were carrying nothing else – no provisions or forms of survival gear.

Which meant that they had come out from a base of some sort, and would return there when their search was completed.

Keill prepared his mind to inform Glr, so that she could follow the uniformed men, and examine their base. But the words were never formed.

The lead skimmer had curved near where Keill was lying, close enough for him to see the face of the driver. And what he saw nearly stopped his heart with shock.

It was a face he knew – but more than that.

It was the face of a legionary of Moros.

Miclas. A legendary figure in his own time, even on Moros. One who had become a Strike Group Overleader at the age of twenty. One who had been overall victor four times in succession at the Martial Games of Moros – a feat no other legionary had ever matched, not even Keill Randor, who had himself won the Games twice.

But what Keill had seen was impossible. Because Miclas had been of the same generation as Keill's *grandfather*. The last time Keill had seen him, he had seen an old man – still lean and straight of back, but with thinning white hair and a wrinkled, furrowed face.

While the red-uniformed man on the skimmer had a thatch of thick dark hair, a smooth brow, and could be no more than thirty years old.

chapter four

The shock that Keill felt, seeing the impossible, did not affect his trained legionary caution. Many moments went by before he slid stealthily from his hiding place. But the broad patch of green was empty – no outriders, no one swinging back on the searchers' path. Keill relaxed, and as Glr's questioning voice reached into his mind, told her what he had seen.

What can it mean? she wondered. *Did your Miclas have a son, or a son's son?*

'No,' Keill said. '*He had one daughter, who was killed in combat and who bore no children.*'

An enticing puzzle. Glr's voice was bright with curiosity.

'To be solved when we learn more,' Keill suggested. '*Can you keep watch on the skimmers, without being spotted? See where they go and what they do?*'

To hear is to obey, Glr teased. *While you no doubt will go and strive to be shot by the other humans.*

'Not exactly,' Keill said with a smile, as he loped away towards the area where she had spotted the second group of armed men.

The day was wearing on – with a slight darkening of the cloud cover and a gathering of light mist in the deeper gullies – by the time Keill settled himself behind an outcrop. The second group was rounding a rocky corner towards him, with almost no soldierly caution. Their boots clumped and grated on the rocks, metal rattled in their packs, and their voices had been audible nearly half a kilometre away – full of querulous grumbling, tinged with nervousness.

Keill shook his head. If this sloppy, undisciplined group

ran into those dangerous-looking men on the skimmers . . .

As Glr had said, there were eight of them, wearing sky blue uniforms decorated with white trim and plenty of bright insignia. They were very young, some barely into their twenties, all with the fresh-faced look of the entirely inexperienced. Keill smiled wryly as they straggled past, no more than three strides from him but totally oblivious to their surroundings. These youths were no danger to anyone but themselves – all the more so when the bulky laser rifles they carried would be useless in the suppressor field.

Calmly Keill stepped out from behind the rock, into full view.

The eight men whirled in unison, panic in their eyes. The two nearest to Keill swung their rifles towards him, thumbs jammed on to the firing studs.

Nothing, of course, happened. Except that Keill had in that instant crossed the space between them and grasped the muzzles of the two rifles. His wrists seemed to twist only slightly, yet the rifles were whipped from the astonished youths' grip and flung clatteringly away.

'Do you always shoot on sight and ask questions after?' he said sharply.

The two youths stepped back, alarmed and shaken. And another of the group shouldered between them to face Keill. He was short, stocky and round-faced, and there was a trace of anger as well as nervousness in his bright blue eyes.

'Who are you and what are you doing here?' he demanded, in a fair imitation of an officer's bark.

'Oddly,' Keill said, 'that was just what I was going to ask you.'

The blue eyes blazed, and the young man stepped to one side, gesturing to the others. 'Hold him and seek out his weapons,' he ordered. 'Do not hurt him too much.'

The seven moved purposefully towards Keill, who shook his head. 'You don't really want to do that,' he said quietly.

They ignored him, lunging forward, hands reaching out to grasp.

Not one of these hands reached its target. Swaying and twisting among the seven men, he struck each of them with such eye-baffling speed that it seemed as if all the blows landed at once. Yet they were all delicately judged – a half-weighted chop, a fingertip jab, a shoulder block, and so on – all aimed at fleshy areas where they would be briefly painful but not disabling.

The eighth man's blue eyes widened at the sight of the other seven suddenly sitting or lying on the ground clutching bruised bellies or shoulders, rubbing numb arms or legs.

Keill was still again, standing quietly relaxed. 'My name is Keill Randor,' he said, 'and I am here for good reasons that are my own. Your turn.'

The stocky youth looked around nervously, then drew himself up. 'I am Under-Commander Tamanaikl Re Saddeti of the Jitrellian Militia.'

Keill nodded encouragingly. 'And you are on Rilyn to find if the men who raided your spaceport are based here. But your ship came down when it hit a suppressor field, your guns and communications don't work, and you haven't the faintest idea what to do next.'

'Yes . . . no!' the boy scowled, confused. 'How do you know all that?'

Keill smiled. 'I'm not one of the raiders. Like you I'm here to find out who is on this planet.' He glanced at the other young men, getting to their feet with many angry mutterings and black looks. 'Under-Commander, if you can keep your young heroes from declaring war on me again, perhaps we can sit down somewhere and compare notes.'

The young man glowered. 'Why should we do that?'

'Because there is a force of men near by on skimmers,' Keill said firmly, 'who seem very much at home here, and very disciplined and dangerous. And it might be them, waiting for you, the next time you come blundering around a corner in these rocks.'

The under-commander's eyes dropped for an instant, and a trace of red appeared in his cheeks. 'Very well,' he said sheepishly. 'We will talk.'

Once settled in some comfort on a patch of soft moss, the young under-commander seemed more cheerful. Even his men lost some of their sourness when they were able to shed their heavy packs and take their ease – though most were still now and then rubbing furtively at their bruises.

The under-commander readily confirmed what Keill had said, and added a few details. After the raid on the spaceport the authorities on Jitrell were organizing every kind of search and investigation they could think of, including Jitrellian ships sweeping the planet's territorial space, and squads of militia sent on other ships to make low-level searches of all the other planets of the system.

The ship assigned to Rilyn had met the suppressor field, and crashed, killing the pilot. Since then the young militiamen had been wandering, in the desperate hope that somehow they might emerge from the suppressor field and get a message back to Jitrell.

Keill shook his head. 'I think the field stretches over most of this higher ground. And you were walking towards the centre of it.'

'Where the killers are? The raiders?'

'Most likely.'

'Then who or what *are* they?' the young man demanded.

But before Keill could speak, another of the Jitrellians interrupted, with a glare at Keill. 'We might better ask who this one is, who knows so much. Are we children, to take his word that he is no enemy?'

A babble of sullen agreement rose, subsiding slowly as the under-commander ordered them to silence. And Keill nodded quietly, aware that the young militiamen's bruises were nothing compared to the damage that had been done to their pride.

The young leader turned back to Keill. 'It is a point to be made. We must know more of why you are here, and where you have come from.'

'As to where I'm from,' Keill said evenly, 'the answer is nowhere in particular. But once I came from a planet called Moros.'

'Moros?' said the under-commander, frowning. 'I have heard the name . . .'

'Moros! Yes!' helped one of the others. 'The planet of the Legions!'

The under-commander looked startled. 'That is so. But the Legions are dead. Did not their planet blow up?'

'Moros was destroyed, yes,' Keill said in a voice empty of emotion. 'But not every legionary died. I survived . . . and there may be others.'

As he spoke he was seeing again the impossibly youthful face of Miclas, but none of the militiamen noticed the shadow that flitted across his eyes. Instead they were staring at Keill with saucer-wide eyes and expressions mingling awe and delight. All sullenness or anger now was gone: there was no shame in being overcome by a legionary of Moros.

'Will you tell us, sir,' said the under-commander, 'what brings a legionary to Rilyn?'

'It's a long story, under-commander,' Keill began, then paused. 'What is your name again?'

'Tamanaikl Re Saddeti,' the young man said proudly, then smiled. 'Everyone calls me Tam.'

'Tam, then,' Keill said. 'And you call me Keill – I'm not one of your officers.' Tam's grin grew even wider, but then his round face grew serious as Keill went on.

'You could say that I'm here because my world, Moros, was not destroyed in an accident. It was *murdered,* by . . . a very ruthless and deadly enemy. And I have good reason to think that the men on this planet, who are almost certainly your raiders, could also help to lead me to the murderer of my people.'

Tam gulped, and the other young men glanced nervously round at the gathering dusk. 'The enemy who destroyed the Legions?' Tam echoed shakily. 'Here?'

'Perhaps not that very person,' Keill said. 'But his agents.'

'Then why, sir . . . I mean, Keill,' stammered the young man, 'would such people concern themselves with Jitrell?'

'I don't know. There are many questions that need answers. And those men on skimmers may provide them.'

Tam set his jaw. 'Our strength is yours to command, sir . . . Keill,' he said, his stiff Jitrellian diction even more formal. A murmur of earnest agreement rose among the others.

'My thanks,' Keill said gravely. Just what I need, he thought to himself. Eight untrained amateurs stumbling about getting in each other's way. Yet they were willing and well-meaning, and there was a look of something near to hero-worship in their eyes. It would not be easy to leave them behind without both humiliating them and putting them at risk from the more dangerous men on the skimmers. Inwardly, Keill sighed at the problems people created for themselves.

But Tam saw none of that. 'The night approaches,' he announced, gazing round at the shadowed rocks. 'Should we not remain here tonight and make plans in the morning?'

'Good idea,' Keill said, trying not to smile as Tam beamed. 'We'll need to be rested – it's a fair march.'

'Have you knowledge of where the raiders are, sir?' asked one of the others.

'I managed to . . . fix the position of their base, from space,' Keill said. It was necessary, he reminded himself, to seem to be operating alone. Not the smallest hint about the Overseers could ever be allowed to slip out, to anyone.

Do you intend to mention me to these humans? Glr's voice entered his mind, sardonically. *Or am I to stay up here until I fall from hunger and exhaustion?*

'*I'm sorry,*' Keill replied to her, guiltily. '*Come down – but let me explain you, first.*'

Tam and the others had begun busily unpacking food stores and sleeping gear from their packs, but paused as Keill stood up. 'Don't be alarmed,' he said to them, 'but I have a . . . a companion. An unusual being, winged. She's about to join us.'

As he spoke, eight Jitrellian mouths fell open in unison. Silent on her widespread wings, Glr drifted out of the twilight, to alight as delicately as a puff of mist on Keill's shoulder.

The Jitrellians scrambled to their feet and stared. 'Some . . . some kind of alien creature?' Tam breathed, fascinated. 'It is native to Moros?'

'Not Moros,' Keill said. 'From . . . another world.'

'A pet, could it be, sir?' asked one of the others.

'A pet?' He saw no point in burdening the Jitrellians with too much information. There was no knowing who might be interrogating them, in the next few days. 'Yes . . . something like that.'

And then he had to duck with all his reflexive speed as Glr's sharp little fangs snapped within a centimetre of his ear.

A pet? Glr repeated, laughter bubbling behind her mock anger. *One day, insensitive human, I will take you to my world and let the Ehrlil decide who is the pet!*

Smiling wryly, Keill moved slightly away from the group of Jitrellians. He found a comfortable patch of moss, with a solid boulder at his back, and reached into his belt pouch for his food concentrates. Glr took her share – her wordless distaste echoing in his mind – and hopped up to perch on the boulder.

'*Tell me about the men on the skimmers,*' Keill said to her as they ate.

Your faithful servant watched them as ordered, Glr replied. *They*

*did not locate our ship — but they did come upon the wreckage of
another one. No doubt it belonged to these humans.* Keill nodded,
and Glr continued. *That may have satisfied them, for as darkness
began to fall they turned back the way they had come. They passed by a
safe distance from here, but then the darkness and mist hid them. I
have, however, noted the direction.*

'Then you can point me in that direction,' Keill said, '*after first
light.*'

I will. The humour had drained from Glr's inner voice.
*And I wish it could be sooner, and that everything here could be
finished swiftly.*

Keill stared up at her. '*Why the urgency?*'

*Because while I was watching the humans I contacted the Overseers.
They told me we have only some days to do what must be done here.
Though even they cannot yet tell exactly how long.*

'What is it?' Keill asked, half-knowing what the answer
would be.

The Overseers' monitors, Glr said darkly, *show that the rogue
planet of this system has reappeared. Very soon, Keill, this planet will
once again be overwhelmed by what the humans call the Starwind.*

Deathwing Legion
chapter five

The next morning Keill led the young Jitrellians along the route plotted for him mentally by Glr. She ranged ahead, again flying high enough to be almost invisible against the full overcast sky. And not for the first time Keill found himself envying those sweeping wings.

It seemed that if a single rock or furrow or shrub lay in the way, the heavy feet of the Jitrellians would find it. So their progress was painfully slow, punctuated by stumblings, muffled curses, heavy panting and much rattling of equipment. Keill kept his face and his voice expressionless, knowing that if he urged the young men on he would merely make them more anxious, and therefore more awkward. But inwardly he was chafing. Glr had not yet seen the strangers' base through the distant haze. It was possible that it could be several days' march away, at this plodding pace. And Keill did not have several days to waste – not when the rogue planet was again threatening Rilyn with the Starwind.

That thought led to another. Did Tam and his troop know how near they were to the cataclysm? During the midday break, he casually mentioned the subject.

'The Starwind?' Tam nodded knowingly. 'Yes, soon, our scientists say. But who can know exactly? Not until the planet Qualthorn, the intruder, appears in the night sky. Then we know.'

So, Keill mused, the rogue planet – the 'intruder' – hadn't been detected by the Jitrellians before Tam left his planet. Yet how could he tell them that the planet had now appeared, without having to explain how he knew?

'What if the wind rose,' Keill asked, 'while you – *we* – were still here?'

'We would find a deep cave, and hide.' Tam waved a hand at the rocks around them. 'Here the land is riddled with caves and tunnels, where the creatures of Rilyn have lived and dug for centuries.'

'And what of the creatures?' asked another Jitrellian. 'Do we hide from the Starwind only to be killed by the stone-whips?'

Tam glowered at the speaker, then turned to Keill. 'Our briefing for this mission told us of cave beasts . . .'

'I've seen them,' Keill broke in. 'You've named them well. They have stingers like whips – but they themselves don't move much faster than stones.' He smiled drily. 'I'm told the Starwind moves faster.'

A ripple of laughter moved through the troop, and the good humour lasted through the task of restoring their packs and resuming their trudging march.

But Keill's mood grew steadily darker. It was all very well to plan on finding a safe and cosy cave when the Starwind struck. But would the strangers do the same? Their base might be underground – it would be the logical way to build, on Rilyn. But when the wind rose, what if they simply went elsewhere? What if their stay on Rilyn had been planned to end when the Starwind appeared?

Too many questions. And too slow a progress towards the answers.

Glr's clear inner voice broke into his thoughts.

Keill, I can see a shape ahead that may be a structure. Shall I go closer – or shall I attend to the group of armed humans on vehicles directly below me?

'How far are they from here?' Keill asked quickly.

Glr's projected map appeared again in Keill's mind, show-ing moving dots representing men on skimmers, a few kilometres away. But their course looked like it would bring them directly upon Keill and the Jitrellians.

They are not moving swiftly, Glr said, *so I assume they are not aware of you.*

'I'll get this group into cover somehow,' Keill replied, 'and have another look at them – while you might go closer to the structure.'

Your pet obeys, master, Glr teased, before breaking contact.

Keill grinned wryly to himself, knowing that it would be a long time before Glr would let him forget that fatal three-letter word. He glanced round for a possible hiding place, and spotted a likely-looking gully to one side. But he let the terrain disguise his change of direction, so the Jitrellians suspected nothing.

Soon, to his relief, the gully deepened and narrowed into a ravine, where the shrubbery grew densely at the edges, providing extra cover. There he halted the troop.

'I'm wondering about those other men,' he told them quietly. 'We don't want to walk into a trap. I'm going to scout ahead for a while.'

'I will come with you,' Tam said at once.

'One man alone runs less risk of being spotted,' Keill said. *And can move faster,* he added privately. 'Keep your men here, and keep them out of sight – in case the others are out there somewhere.'

Tam agreed, reluctantly, and his men began shedding their packs as Keill moved away. Out of the ravine, he angled back towards the direction that they had been following before. At once he settled again into the loping run that devoured the distance – while shunning the more open areas, winding his way through the sheltering outcrops of rock with all the instinctive stealth of a wild creature.

After a few moments Glr's inner voice returned. *I can see the structure more clearly now. It seems to be a substantial tower, rising from a level plateau. It has few external features that I could see, through the haze that seems to surround it – but there is a semi-circular shape on the very top of it that I am sure is a spacecraft.*

A tower? Keill nodded sourly to himself. If anything spelled the presence of the Deathwing, it was the brazen arrogance of building a tower on the planet of the Starwind. It was just the Deathwing style.

But the fact that the strangers' base was a tower could also mean just what he feared – that the occupants might leave Rilyn before the Starwind struck, especially if they had a ship waiting. Would there be time for him to learn what he needed to know?

'*Stay there and see what else you can find out,*' he said to Glr. '*I'm coming up to the men on skimmers now.*'

But he was wrong. His sense of direction and of terrain had brought him almost to the point where he should intersect the route of the others. But he could hear no hint of the muttering rumble of skimmers.

Uneasiness began to gnaw at him as he changed direction, changed again, casting back and forth like a hunting animal searching for spoor, stopping now and then and straining his ears to pick up the sound of engines.

Nothing. Then where were they?

Maybe they had stopped, he thought. Glr had said they were moving slowly, so they might be still a kilometre away, idling over a delayed midday meal.

But they might well have unpredictably veered aside from their original path. If so, he would need Glr to come and spot them again from the air. And he would need to hope that they would not come upon the Jitrellians first.

His uneasiness grew. I hope they keep their foolish heads down, he thought.

He changed direction again, retracing his steps back towards the ravine where he had left the Jitrellians. Though he still kept carefully within the cover of the rugged, broken terrain, he speeded his pace, driven by the strengthening feeling that something had gone wrong.

The ravine was a good hiding place: only wild chance would bring the others close enough to spot Tam and his troop. Unless someone among those inexperienced youths did something foolish, or clumsy, and exposed them . . .

Soon the ravine was in sight, and Keill was moving towards its entrance, crouched low, boots silent on the moss. All his highly tuned senses were picking up a feeling of tension around the place, an unnatural quiet – as if the plants, the rocks, the very air itself were holding still in the presence of danger.

Keill drifted soundlessly forward, his eyes sweeping over the shrub-clad slopes that formed the sides of the ravine. Perhaps it had once been the bed of a stream, for it curved and twisted as only the path of moving water will do. And around one of those curves Keill found what he had most dreaded.

The bodies of five of the Jitrellian youths lay sprawled, sightless eyes staring up at the indifferent Rilyn sky.

Keill knelt beside each, his soldier's mind noting the positions of the corpses, assessing the gaping, bloody wounds in their bodies. They had been killed by some sort of projectiles – bullets fired from guns by controlled explosion, which would not be affected by the suppressor field.

His eye caught the gleam of metal in a thicket of nearby shrubbery, and there he found two more Jitrellian bodies – two who must have been quick enough to try to dive to safety into the dense greenery, but not quick enough to escape the bullets of their attackers.

Keill had fought in too many battles to be disturbed by death alone. But this had not been war – not against young, inept and totally defenceless young men. This had been savage and evil murder.

Anger swelled within him – the controlled anger of a legionary, hard as a diamond, cold as space, fuelling the readiness for combat. A readiness that was complete when the two red-uniformed men came round a curve in the ravine.

One had the face of the legendary Miclas. But he was *not* the man Keill had seen before. This version of Miclas was even younger – in his early twenties.

So was the other man moving towards Keill. And he had the face and the tall, broad-shouldered body of another famous legionary of Moros – the great Callor.

Who had died of old age two *years* before the Legions had been destroyed.

Keill straightened, neither his anger nor the shock he felt at the others' appearance showing in his face as he stepped easily forward.

The two men carried guns – projectile weapons, as Keill had guessed – holstered at their hips. But they did not reach for their guns. So they weren't seeking to kill him at once, he realized, nor even to capture him at gunpoint. What, then? Did they think they could take him barehanded?

He was happy to let them try.

Their attack began without warning. And even though Keill had been expecting it, he was surprised – when one of them, with the Miclas-face, suddenly dropped to one side and swung a scything leg at Keill's ankles while the other leaped into the air, a blur of red, and drove a flashing, venomous kick at Keill's face.

They were ferociously fast and skilled. And Keill knew that he had a very dangerous fight on his hands.

But even before the knowledge had formed, he had responded, his own skills and reflexes doing what they had been trained to do from the cradle. He seemed to leap and to drop, both in the same instant, so that he was flying sideways, horizontally in the air, while one kick swept beneath him and the other lashed harmlessly above. Then his left hand struck the ground to brace him, and his own boot lashed out at the knee of the man with the Callor-face.

The kick would have shattered bone, but it did not land. Callor-face parried, and dodged away. Then Miclas-face was up, circling, so that the two were on either side of Keill as he came to his feet.

They sprang at the same moment, but Keill had expected

that. He feinted a counter-punch at one, swivelled to meet the other. His forearm blocked a chop at his throat, but his own elbow-smash was parried, and then he had to twist aside from a brutal drop-kick that grazed his tunic at kidney-height.

Again they attacked together, from opposite sides. Again Keill feinted towards one – but it was also a feint when he turned to the other. A boot glanced off his thigh as he leaped away – leaped *backwards*, into a bruising but balanced collision with the attacker behind him. His hands instantly found the grip for a throw – but the other had shifted, twisting into a new leverage. And it was Keill who was flung off his feet in a perfectly executed counter-throw.

But he had anticipated it – and in fact had planned it. As the other, Callor-face, had made the throw, Keill's hand had snatched with perfect timing and speed at the butt of the holstered gun. He struck the ground in a neat roll that took the impact, and came acrobatically to his feet with the gun levelled at the others.

The two halted in their tracks, faces showing anger and amazement. Keill began to step towards them, but the motion was not completed.

'Drop the gun!'

The harsh voice struck like an explosion through the ravine. Keill looked slowly around, then opened his hand and let the gun fall.

The man Keill had seen before – the thirty-year-old with the face of Miclas – had stepped into view, with a gun in his hand. But he was not aiming it at Keill. It was pointed at the head of a limp body that the gunman gripped by the collar.

Despite dirt and encrusted blood, Keill had no difficulty recognizing Tam.

'This one is still alive,' snarled the man with the gun. 'Keep still, or he won't be.'

Keill turned to face him, half-raising his hands, calm and watchful.

'Excellent.' The gunman glowered at him for a moment, then turned the look towards the two younger red-uniformed men.

'Now perhaps you believe me,' he snapped, 'that you still have things to learn.'

'He was lucky,' the young man with the Callor-face said sulkily. 'We could take him, any time.'

'Your chance may come,' said the gunman coldly. He turned back to Keill with an ugly grin. 'Impetuous youth. Like your young men.' He gestured with the gun towards the fallen Jitrellians. 'No doubt you ordered them to remain hidden – but one of them had to come up for a look around. We saw him before he saw us, and it was his last look at anything.'

He paused, but Keill said nothing, merely gazing steadily at the other.

'Silent and wary, like a true legionary,' the gunman said, with a grating, humourless laugh. 'And I should know, should I not? For I too am a legionary. We are all legionaries here.'

He took a step forward, and his next words struck Keill like daggers of ice.

'You may be the last legionary of Moros, Keill Randor. But here is a new legion – the Legion of Rilyn!'

chapter six

Keill sat silently in the forward seat of the skimmer, his hands resting on the sides in full view, as he had been instructed. Around him the other skimmers clustered, as closely as the terrain allowed, as they moved steadily on a route that Keill knew would lead to the tower Glr had spotted. He seemed as calm and controlled as ever, yet within his mind he was frozen with shock and revulsion at the ugliness of what he had learned.

When the gun of the red-uniformed leader had urged him further along the ravine, he had found that this group was ten in number, as had been the other that he had watched from hiding the day before. But they were *not* ten different individuals.

Five of them were exactly alike, in every detail – and the details were those of Miclas, as he must have been when a young man.

Three more of them, also exactly like one another, also young, were the images of Callor.

And the remaining two, as youthful as the others, but slightly shorter and bulkier, were precise replicas of another great legionary from the past of Moros – Osrid, the space captain, who had died of a degenerative illness a month before Keill himself had left Moros for the last time.

It needed no great effort of deduction for Keill to realize what they were.

They had to be clones.

Somehow living cells had been taken from the real Miclas, Callor and Osrid, to be bred and developed into these youthful duplicates.

It was chilling enough for Keill to be seeing young versions of legionaries who had been old and venerated when Keill was a boy. It was more chilling to know that the cloning process, the growth of the duplicates, had to have been going on for more than twenty years.

If it was a Deathwing operation – and Keill felt no doubt now that it was – it showed how long the Warlord's plans had been taking shape. And how long the Legions had had an evil, deadly enemy without having an inkling of his existence.

But *why*, Keill asked himself, had the Deathwing cloned legionaries, and obviously trained them to a high level of martial skill? What purposes had the 'Legion of Rilyn' been created for?

And – more immediately – how had the clones' leader *known Keill's name?*

It was almost as if they had been expecting him . . .

The clone driver of the skimmer ahead of Keill glanced round, ensuring that the prisoner had not changed position. And Keill knew grimly that he would have little chance if he did so. All the clones, even the drivers, were holding their drawn guns in readiness – and their leader, the older Miclas clone, had ordered them to shoot at the first sign of a threat.

They had been told merely to injure Keill – again, an indication that they were keeping him alive for some reason. But they had been told to kill young Tam – who was slumped in one of the other skimmers, still unconscious, from a head wound caused by a bullet that had grazed his skull.

Against that double threat, Keill had no choice but to remain still. The odds had been lessened slightly, when the two clones with whom he had fought had been sent back to their base on foot – as a punishment for their defeat, and to make room in the skimmers for Keill and Tam. But they were still odds that only a fool would oppose. And Keill felt that he had been fool enough already that day.

He could still see, in his anguished mind's eye, the sprawled bodies of the young Jitrellians. But the pain and sorrow that rose within him was matched by his deep-rooted, icy anger. Sorrow could not bring the young men back to life, nor could the guilt he felt for leaving them alone in their clumsy inexperience. But anger might avenge them – and also avenge the insult, the desecration, that had been done to the memory of three revered legionaries of Moros.

There would come a time when that anger could be released. But not yet. And at least the skimmers were taking him where he wanted to go, towards the clones' tower. That was where the answers would be found to the questions and mysteries that had gathered around him on Rilyn – answers that he needed, before he launched any sort of action.

He did not even consider the idea that action might be impossible. To a legionary, no position was totally hopeless while life remained. He had some advantage in the fact that the clones' leader wanted to keep him alive. Also, none of his captors had spotted the two well-disguised grenades at his belt.

And finally, there was a small winged alien high in the dull sky, no doubt watching everything.

Glr's inner voice spoke, perfectly on cue.

Keill, are you intending to stay in that unpleasant cavalcade?

Quickly Keill recounted what had happened, knowing that Glr would soon pass on the information about the clones to the Overseers. Then he explained why he was remaining passive for a while.

I do not like the idea of you being in that tower, Glr demurred. *Should you not free yourself, and choose your own time to approach the tower?*

'I'd prefer that,' Keill replied. '*But right now my chances are poor.*'

Then I shall improve them, Glr said blithely.

'*How?*' Keill asked, concern colouring the mental words.

'There are eight guns here!'

My friend, Glr said, her laughter rising, *if I am not to expose myself to risk, why am I on this dreary planet at all? Watch and wait.*

Her voice withdrew, ignoring Keill's urgent attempt to recall her.

Worry tugged at his mind, as he tried to imagine what Glr might be planning. But at the same time his trained self-discipline resisted the pointlessness of tension. Glr had said 'wait,' so he waited – relaxed and still, as only a legionary can be when waiting is necessary. But at the core of his stillness was a fiercely concentrated alertness – which could blaze into instant, lethal action at the first glimpse of a chance.

And eventually, his chance came.

A small dark shape appeared in the dull sky, ahead of the skimmers. Descending, it revealed itself as the form of Glr, soaring on the wide sails of her wings.

The clones saw her at once. The leader snapped an order, and the skimmers slowed, while their occupants stared upwards. Yet even then their discipline held: the gun muzzles did not waver a millimetre away from Keill.

Except for their leader. 'What in space is that?' came his harsh voice from a skimmer behind Keill.

Glr wheeled above them, curving away as if she were a wild creature seeking safety.

'There are no winged beasts on Rilyn!' the leader shouted. 'Is this something to do with you, Randor?'

'I know nothing of this planet's wild life,' Keill said flatly.

At the same time his mind was desperately shouting at Glr. *'You're too low – they'll pick you off!'*

I presume that burst of mudheaded thought was some form of warning, Glr said acidly. *I know what I am doing.*

Keill concentrated, to form his thoughts more clearly. But he was distracted, his heart jumping within him, when the clone leader's gun crashed without warning.

Glr's wings beat furiously as she sought to gain height.

'Knock it down, men!' the harsh voice ordered. 'I want a look at that thing!'

Other guns boomed around Keill. Not all of them, for at least three remained steady on him. But he hardly noticed them, his eyes fixed on Glr's frantic ascent.

The guns crashed again. And Keill watched in horror as Glr seemed to veer suddenly, one wing drooping to her side.

The other wing flailed weakly as she began a slow agonizing spiral, down, down ... till she vanished from sight beyond a rocky promontory.

'Got it!' Miclas yelled. 'Let's go pick it up. But spread out – it may be still alive, trying to get away.'

He pointed at the two clones on the skimmers carrying Keill and Tam. 'You two, stay and watch Randor. Don't take your eyes off him – and shoot if he moves a finger.'

At his gesture, the other skimmers swung round and moved away.

But Keill was scarcely aware of them. Inside his mind he was screaming, '*Glr! GLR!*'

The silent voice that replied was vibrating with excitement as well as laughter. *A convincing performance, was it not?*

Relief flooded through Keill. '*Are you hit?*'

I very nearly had wing perforations, Glr laughed. *But shooting upwards is never certain, with hand guns.*

'*Where are you now?*'

A long way from where I seemed to fall. They will surely search for me a while – so if you plan to do anything, I suggest you begin soon.

'*I intend to,*' Keill said fiercely.

Slowly, cautiously, he turned his head. His two guards might have shot without warning, he knew – but he was relying on the fact that they were young men full of self-esteem who would feel even more bravado when holding guns over an unarmed and apparently defeated captive.

'Stop it there,' said the clone in the seat behind him.

He halted his movement as soon as the clone spoke. But he had turned far enough to take in the details he needed, in his peripheral vision.

When he had been taken at gunpoint to the skimmers, he had learned that only the older leader of the clones was called by the full name of Miclas. The others bore shortened forms of their names, along with identifying numbers corresponding to the numbers worn like insignia on their uniform collars. Keill had heard the leader use the names Mic-4, Cal-31, Os-15, and so on – and the leader had named Mic-12 and Os-9 as the drivers of the skimmers carrying himself and Tam, and now as his guards.

But he was not interested in their names, nor their appearance – only their positions. The clone called Mic-12 was in the seat behind him, gun resting lightly on the top of the skimmer between the two seats. The second clone, Os-9, was in the rear seat of a skimmer to Keill's left and slightly behind him, with Tam still slumped silently in the forward seat.

But even as he looked, he saw Tam's eyelids flicker and open. His body twitched, and one hand reached up to the wound on his head.

For an instant both clones shifted their gaze towards Tam. 'Keep still or you're dead!' snarled Os-9 as Tam swung slowly around to stare at him.

Tam settled back, frowning, glancing towards Keill. 'What are they . . .' he began.

'Shut it!' Os-9 hissed, raising the gun menacingly.

Tam subsided nervously, and both clones returned their watchful gaze to Keill. He appeared not to have moved a muscle. But in that brief time he had minutely shifted position.

His body was now inclined slightly towards the left; his right leg was solidly braced. Moving at speed out of the skimmer seat would still be difficult – especially with two guns waiting. But he was far more ready than before.

'I almost wish he would try something,' said Os-9. There

was a brittle edge to his voice that told Keill of taut nerves, tense anticipation. 'The brothers were right – he did get lucky, before.'

'That right, Randor?' asked the other clone, Mic-12, lounging in the seat behind Keill. 'Just luck?'

'Put your guns down,' Keill said quietly, 'and try for yourselves.'

The fact that those were the first words he had spoken since his capture – and that they were spoken with a deadly edge wholly different from his apparent placidity – seemed to disturb the two clones. They both laughed aloud, but there was more tension now, in both voices.

'No chance,' said Mic-12. 'We'll just sit here, peacefully, till we get you back to the boss.'

Keill wondered at that. 'You mean when the *boss* gets back,' he said casually, 'from his little hunt.'

'Miclas? He's just the captain, and a brother,' said Os-9, with a snicker. 'The boss is something else. He'll turn you sick-scared, Randor. Wait'll you see his . . .'

'Brother, you talk too much,' Mic-12 broke in sharply. 'Shut your mouth and mind your trigger.'

Os-9's face flamed red and his mouth closed with a snap. In the silence, Keill weighed this new information.

The clones had another leader, the 'boss', back at the tower. And apparently that person was not another clone – not a 'brother', like Miclas the captain.

It added up beyond any doubt. At the tower, at the head of this curious force of clones, was an agent of the Deathwing.

Keill wondered briefly if he should after all let the clones take him in, to face this mysterious leader. But in the end it still seemed wiser to free himself, now that Glr had created the diversion. And then, too, there was Tam to consider.

'What about having a look at my friend's wound?' he said. 'It's still bleeding.'

'Let it . . .' Mic-12 began. But he was interrupted by Tam

himself, as perfectly timed as Keill could have wished. Involuntarily the young man had started, and his hand had reached up again to his injury. The movement drew the gaze of both clones, for an instant. And Os-9, behind Tam, even made the mistake of swinging his gun muzzle towards the Jitrellian.

He had barely begun that move when Keill had finished his.

His hands flashed with the speed of thought across the narrow space between the skimmer seats. His right hand reached towards Mic-12 – while his left hand clamped like a band of steel round the barrel of the clone's gun, the heel of the hand jammed against the muzzle.

Mic-12 had felt rather than seen Keill's blurring movement. Reflexively he pulled the trigger. The bullet should have ripped away most of Keill's left hand, leaving the rest a shapeless, useless mass of bone splinters, torn flesh and dripping blood.

But the substance that the Overseers had used to replace Keill's entire skeleton could withstand even that force.

The bullet merely gouged a painful furrow in the flesh of Keill's hand, as it struck that unbreakable bone and ricocheted away.

And by that time Keill had grasped the front of the clone's uniform and dragged him forward – to make him a shield against the gun of the other clone.

Mic-12 tried instinctively to jerk away from Keill's grip. But Keill did not resist the movement. He let the clone pull back, and went with him – using the momentum to vault smoothly out of the skimmer, towards Os-9.

That was a moment of danger – when Os-9 might have been quick enough, and clear-headed enough, to stop Keill in his tracks by threatening Tam.

But Os-9 panicked at the explosion of movement that he had not even been able to follow properly. He clenched his finger on his trigger, and his gun blasted three times.

One bullet whined over Keill's head. And the other two slammed with finality into the body of Mic-12, who was still stumbling backwards, trying to free himself from Keill's hands.

At the instant Keill felt the impact of the bullets on the man who was his shield, he flung the dying clone away with all his power. The body hurtled backwards, crashing in a flail of limp arms into Os-9, who was leaping from his skimmer for a clear shot at Keill.

Before Os-9 could regain his balance, Keill had hurdled the body of the dead clone in a long, raking leap, one booted foot driving forward in a murderous kick that smashed against the side of Os-9's jaw.

Keill dropped smoothly from the kick into a balanced crouch, but there was no need for a follow-up. Os-9 sprawled on the moss like a stringless puppet, his broken jaw askew and his head twisted in a manner that showed how cleanly his neck had been snapped.

'Keill, that was . . .' Tam's voice was choked with awe. 'I could never have believed . . .'

'Later,' Keill said curtly. 'Stay where you are – we're getting out of here.'

He tore at the uniform of Os-9, ripping away a long strip of the light material and binding it tightly round his left hand in a makeshift bandage. Then he took the clone's gun and turned towards the other skimmer, pumping the remaining bullets into the vehicle's engine till it was an unrecognizable clump of shattered metal.

Flinging the empty gun aside, he gathered up the gun of Mic-12, which had fired only the one shot, and jammed it into his belt before leaping into the skimmer seat behind Tam.

'Hold tight!' he ordered the wide-eyed youth.

The engine throbbed into life, and the skimmer shot away at full speed, as if the machine itself were some wild, hunted beast fleeing from deadly danger.

chapter seven

The skimmer was a simple mechanism, steered by foot pedals and with a hand-held accelerator. It was speedy and manoeuvrable – and it needed to be, as Keill flung it into a winding, torturous route among the rocks, at top speed even round blind corners or on the edges of deep ravines.

Several times a yell of fear burst from Tam when the skimmer seemed certain to flip over on a careering turn, or to slam lethally into a wall of rock. But always Keill's reflexes dragged them out of danger, so that after several kilometres – though Tam had been sure at least five times that they would be killed – there was not the smallest scratch on the skimmer's shiny hull.

Keill knew that the other clones, alerted by the gunshots, would be after him by now. Even so, he guided the skimmer in the same direction they had been taking before. It was all the more urgent to have a close look at the tower that was the clones' headquarters, before working out what he was going to do next.

The skimmer engine strained as he swung it over a projecting spur of rock, at once swerving it in nearly a right-angled turn to avoid another outcrop. In the seat ahead, Tam moaned, covering his eyes.

'Keill, may we slow the speed?' he called plaintively above the engine noise. 'My head hurts, and my stomach grows sick.'

'You'll feel worse if they catch us!' Keill shouted back, accelerating across a patch of moss.

Tam groaned and leaned back, eyes closed. But Keill ignored him, forming a call to Glr, who he knew would now be aloft again, keeping watch with her keen vision.

'How far is the tower now?' he asked.

About three kilometres, as the Ehrlil flies, Glr replied with the ghost of a laugh. *But the other humans are nearer than that to you – and they are on your course, as if they have guessed that you will move towards the tower.*

Keill's mouth tightened. He had hoped that the clones would think that route the most unlikely one for him to take. But their captain was clever, a good officer. And a dangerous opponent.

He forced every scrap of speed out of the skimmer's throbbing engine. The ground seemed to be levelling off, he noticed – the rocks becoming even flatter, with broader and smoother open spaces among them. It made travelling easier – though it also made his skimmer more visible to searching eyes. But Glr was watching, and would know the instant that he was in danger of being spotted. And meanwhile the tower must be growing closer every moment . . .

Then he glimpsed it, like a spike of metal rearing up in the middle distance. A short distance away he found a vantage point, and halted the skimmer, letting its engine idle as he studied the flat, open plateau before him.

The tower thrust up towards the dull sky of Rilyn, nearly two hundred metres of darkly gleaming metal, flat-sided and square-cornered. There were no apparent breaks or openings in the smooth outer walls – except for two vertical grooves, or channels, nearly as wide as the height of a man, running from top to bottom of the wall facing Keill. If the tower had windows, Keill thought, they would be flush with the walls, and polarized somehow to appear part of the smooth metal, with no edge or seam visible.

But he could see a faint seam at the base of the tower, that might mark the outline of a sizeable doorway. Yet it was hard to be certain. The tower's details were not sharply defined – as if the haze that Glr had mentioned was somehow clinging to it, slightly blurring its edges.

Tam noticed it as well. 'My wound has affected my vision,'

he said worriedly. 'The building seems misty.'

'It's not your eyes,' Keill replied, as the answer came to him. 'It must be a force field. The whole tower is completely enclosed.'

And that, he realized, was what lay behind the arrogance of building a tower on Rilyn. Deathwing technology must have adapted the known forms of force field to create an immovable barrier that would withstand even the power of the Starwind.

He looked again at the base of the tower, where the haziness seemed more dense. That, he guessed, would come from the interface of the vertical force field and the horizontal suppressor field, which also had its centre at the tower.

Keill could think of nothing that could breach those defences. Of course the force field would be shut off, he knew, to let clones out or to let the spacecraft, on top of the tower, lift off. But even then the building would be heavily guarded. From the numbered names of the clones that he had overheard, there would be more than thirty men in each of the three duplicated groups – making at least one hundred men occupying the tower.

For now, he thought sourly, he would have to stay out among the rocks, and reduce the odds by picking off pursuers a few at a time.

As if in direct response to that thought, the tower's hazy surround seemed to flicker, then faded – showing Keill not only that it *was* a force field, but that it had just been shut off. Now he could clearly see the seam of the wide doorway at the base.

As he watched, it opened. Out slid twenty of the two-man skimmers – forty men, in squads of ten men each. They spread out in a semi-circular formation, and began to sweep across the plateau, while behind them the haziness of the force field sprang back into life.

Keill swung his own skimmer around, back among the rocks. So Miclas, the clone captain, was getting reinforcements. It would give Keill that many more to set up ambushes for – but first he had to find a safe place to leave Tam during the dangerous game of hide and seek.

As their skimmer sped among the rocks, he raised his voice to explain to Tam what was to happen.

'But I wish not to hide!' Tam protested. 'I would come with you, and fight! I have no fear of them!'

'Your courage isn't the question,' Keill replied. 'I know about this kind of fighting – you don't. We'll both be safer if you're out of it.'

Tam nodded sadly. 'I see it. I would hamper you.'

'Something like that,' Keill said. 'Don't worry. You may yet get your chance to fight.'

'You will see,' Tam said, eyes glowing. 'I will prove worthy.'

Keill didn't reply, because he had spotted what he had been searching for. A black smear of shadow, at the base of a low wall of rock, had to be the mouth of one of the caves that honeycombed the region. He cut power at once, sliding the skimmer to a halt.

'There's your hiding place,' he told Tam, pointing to the cave mouth. 'Stay inside, and if you hear skimmer engines, get as far into the cave as you can.' He grinned tightly. 'With a little luck, we'll both survive.'

Tam stepped out of the skimmer, looking dubiously at the cave. 'What of the stonewhips?'

'I told you before – they're slow-moving creatures. Just stay out of their way. Stay out of the way of everything.'

He unfastened his belt pouch and took out a vial of clear liquid from the medikit. Peeling away the ragged red cloth from his injured hand, he dabbed some of the liquid on to the angry gash. At once the throbbing pain – which he had not let himself acknowledge, during the wild flight through the rocks – eased to a distant ache. He flexed his fingers, to be sure he had full use of the hand, then rewrapped the bandage before passing the vial to Tam.

'Smear some of that on your head wound. It'll stop the pain and the swelling.'

Tam was staring at him wonderingly. 'Your hand is not smashed? How . . .'

'Just luck,' Keill said lightly. To change the subject, he handed Tam his belt pouch, and the gun that he had taken from the clone. 'There's food concentrates and water to keep you going. And if our friends in red find you, get some good use from the gun.'

Tam hefted the weapon, looking worried. 'What will you do, unarmed?'

'I'll get another,' Keill said quietly, 'the way I got that one.'

And he gunned the skimmer away.

In my opinion, Glr said, *you are in trouble.*

Wordlessly, Keill agreed. In the half-hour since he had left Tam, he had been doing little but running and hiding. He had tried to swing out to the right, hoping to get behind the wide arc of skimmers that had come from the tower. But the first six clones, led by Miclas, had changed direction – and Glr had warned him only just in time before he had driven straight into them.

Now they were close behind him, like predators on a blood-trail. And their forty 'brothers' had tightened their arc, and were closing from the other direction.

Too many to fight, and too many to run from, Keill thought to himself. But maybe not too many to deceive.

'*Can you see a deep gully or ravine near by?*' he asked Glr.

For a moment Glr was silent. *About thirty degrees to your left, not far,* she said at last. *What are you planning?*

'*I'm going to kill myself,*' Keill replied. '*It might slow them up a little.*'

Keill . . . Glr said worriedly. But by then he had seen the gully that she had located – a narrow, deep ditch gouged in the rock, within a profusion of the tough shrubbery.

He pointed the skimmer towards it, gauging distances and timing. At the last instant before the machine plunged over the edge, he flung himself clear in a low, flat dive, tucking into a forward shoulder roll and coming to his feet.

The skimmer crashed into the gully in a crunch of metal, followed by a heavier explosion as the fuel blew up in a fountain of flame and metallic fragments. That explosion was a nice touch that he hadn't counted on. The searchers might be all the more likely to think that he had crashed the skimmer and died – and would waste valuable time examining the wreckage for his charred body.

Now what he needed was a cave of his own, where he could stay hidden until nightfall. If the search continued after dark, he would have all the cover he needed to start reducing their numbers. And he wouldn't have long to wait, for the daylight was already beginning to fade a little.

On impulse he turned back to the edge of the gully. The tough shrubbery was dry enough to burn, and much of it was merrily blazing where the skimmer had exploded. Keill ripped up an armful of the greenery, and with it a substantial bunch that was already aflame. Then he sprang away, running surefootedly through the crumbled, uneven rock.

From a distance, as the light waned, he could not easily tell whether shadowed areas in the rocks were only clefts or wrinkles, or actual openings. Over there, for instance – could that narrow strip of darkness be a cave mouth?

He found that it could, and was. Inside, the flame in the handful of shrubbery flickered enough to show him that the cave was low-ceilinged, and apparently cut deep into the rock. He moved deeper, glad to see no sign of the stonewhip creatures. Then he halted abruptly.

An odd feeling – like a current of air. And moving *towards* him – out of the dark interior of the cave.

He moved forward again, guarding the flame, and saw that the cave extended itself to become a tunnel – low, narrow, but roomy enough for him to move along.

Keill, beware. Glr's voice was anxious in his mind. *A skimmer has stopped outside the cave you entered. One of the humans is looking in, with some sort of flame-lamp in his hand.*

The clones were good trackers, he thought with annoyance. And, of course, they would have torches not affected by the suppressor field.

An idea struck him. '*Glr, can you keep a mental fix on my position, and look for another opening out of this tunnel that you can guide me to?*'

I will try. The nervousness in her voice was stronger. *But I cannot stay in your mind for long. I can sense the darkness, the stone around you – it is like being in a cave myself.*

'*No matter,*' Keill said reassuringly, remembering her over-powering fear in the cave before. '*Just make quick contact every few minutes, in and out. And look for an exit.*'

As Glr hastily withdrew, he moved on, carefully setting a fresh portion of the shrub alight from the first one, now nearly burned away. The tunnel curved and twisted as it progressed, and now and then there were smaller tunnels branching off to the side. But Keill kept to the main passage, still led by the faint movement of air that he could feel. It had to come from an opening; he only hoped it would be large enough to let him through.

He moved as swiftly as he could, his flickering flame cupped behind one hand. At times, in the smaller side tunnels or in crevices carved into the walls, he caught sight of faint, obscure movement. They could only be lurking stonewhips – but he was past each hiding place before any of the ugly helmet-heads thrust itself out into view.

He did not let himself think about what might happen if all his store of shrubbery had burned before he had found a way out of the tunnel.

Keill, I have not yet seen another opening. Glr's voice was tense and strained. *But you are now moving under the plateau where the tower stands – almost directly towards it.*

'I'm not sure if that's good or bad,' Keill said dourly.

And the human who entered the cave behind you has not emerged, Glr added. *He may be following you.*

Again her mind withdrew. Keill glanced back, but there was no sign of light or movement in the blackness behind him. Knowing there was no choice, he strode on.

The tunnel seemed unchanging. It did not widen or narrow to any great extent, nor did its level alter. The faint waft of air was no stronger or weaker. The almost inaudible slither of stonewhips still came from crevices here and there. Only his supply of the dry shrubbery changed – dwindling steadily as he walked on.

Soon he was lighting the last fragment of it, with no end in sight to the tunnel yawning in front of him. And the fragment seemed to last only a few steps before it had burnt down to a stub, scorching his fingers. When he let it drop, the blackness reached out and swallowed him.

Gritting his teeth, he kept moving. But now his advance was heartbreakingly slow – one step at a time, his right hand thrust out ahead to keep him from walking into solid rock if the tunnel curved in the impenetrable dark. He blocked out of his mind the skin-crawling thought of the stonewhips that might be lining the walls, invisibly, waiting to strike out. Grimly, steadily, he moved on.

His out-thrust hand brushed against cold stone, and he drew it back sharply. The tunnel had begun another curve. Even more cautiously, he groped forward. Again his hand touched stone – a projecting bulge of rock, rough and seamed . . .

Under his hand, the bulge moved.

He flung himself forward, stifling a yell, hearing the hiss as the stonewhip's sting lashed out. He had no idea how near it had come – or how many others were gathering . . .

And then, around the tunnel's curve, his unbelieving eyes saw a faint gleam of light.

Not from behind him, where the pursuing clone might be.

From *ahead*. And a dull, reddish light, not the yellow glow of flame.

As he moved closer the shape of the tunnel regained vague form in the blackness. Rapidly he covered the remaining metres, until he reached the source of the reddish light.

The realization was crushing.

The tunnel had opened out, into a broad and high-roofed cavern. But the far side of it, where the hazy redness gleamed, was a wall of smooth, polished metal.

The tunnel had led to the foundations of the tower itself. And the reddish light was obviously from the force field, being emitted directly from the walls themselves, even below ground.

It was a dead end. All the more so when he saw a tiny patch of grey in the high vault of the cavern, and recognised it as a small slit opening in the rock. That was the source of the current of air that he had detected – but it was far too narrow to let him out.

For a moment his mind went as blank as the smooth metal of the tower, as he stared at it, wildly trying to think of a way out of the trap.

And then he saw his own shadow flung large against the metal by a glow of yellow light behind him.

He whirled – to confront a red-uniformed clone with a flaming torch in one hand and an unwavering gun in the other.

But not just any clone. Peering past the brightness of the torch, Keill saw that it was the captain – the older Miclas-clone.

'You make a fine quarry, Randor,' Miclas said with an ugly grin. 'Good training for the young ones. But I'm too wise a head to be fooled by a crashed skimmer – and too good a tracker to miss the signs you left.'

As before, Keill remained silent and watchful, idly hooking his thumbs into his belt – where his fingers trailed over the flat plastic of the grenades.

'I'm not taking any more chances with you,' Miclas went on. 'You get to stay alive – but a bullet in the leg will take the fight out of you.'

Keill saw the tightening of the clone's forefinger on the gun's trigger. At the same time he saw another faint motion, on the cavern wall near Miclas's elbow.

'Do you know,' he asked idly, 'what effect the sting of a stonewhip has on a man?'

Miclas frowned. 'It's too late for your tricks now, legionary,' he growled.

The knuckle of his trigger finger whitened as it put on the final pressure. And then several things happened at once.

Keill plucked a grenade from his belt and flung it, with a blurring snap of his wrist. With almost the same speed, the stonewhip that Keill had seen in the wall beside Miclas lashed out, the tendril stabbing at the clone's gun hand.

Miclas screamed shrilly as he fired, but his injured hand jerked aside, and the bullet sang harmlessly away into the darkness.

A fraction of a second later, the clone vanished in an eruption of dust and rock as the grenade exploded at his feet.

And then, as Keill desperately leaped for the tunnel, the roof of the cave fell in.

chapter eight

A vast weight, which seemed to have a polished metal surface, was pressing down upon him, crushingly, irresistibly. He felt no pain – only a deathly numbness, a near-paralysis, so that his arms and legs moved as if held by thick, clinging glue. Yet still he tried to struggle against the pressure that was seeking to kill him. Somewhere near by a reedy, nasal voice was muttering, the words not clear. With a supreme effort he pushed upwards at the monstrous weight – and miraculously it lifted, as if plucked away by some godlike hand. And now the words of the reedy voice were plainer . . .

'We'll know soon,' it was saying. 'The knife will tell.'

Keill opened his eyes, coming out of the dream into immediate full alertness. Yet it seemed that not all of the dream had been left behind. The gluey restriction still held his body, so that it was an effort even to move his eyes.

He was lying on a hard, narrow bed. His uniform and boots had been removed, and he was wearing only a thigh-length bed-kilt of a light material. There were synthaskin bandages on his injured left hand, and elsewhere on his body – where the rock fall must have gashed his flesh. And around him was a medical clinic of some sort, with banks of high-technology equipment lining the sterile white walls.

He tried to move, to lift himself, but without success. Every cell of his body seemed to ache, as if his body were one oversize bruise. And the feeling of being immersed in glue impaired every movement. He wondered miserably if the rock fall had damaged his nervous system, left him paralysed . . .

With a huge effort he shifted his eyes further to one side

and saw the owner of the reedy voice. A medic, in the usual white tunic – a narrow, bony man whose eyes and teeth protruded just as his hair and chin receded. The medic was making adjustments to a laser scalpel, and Keill remembered the words he had heard upon waking.

'If you touch me with that,' Keill said evenly, 'you'll regret it.' His words sounded slow and far away in his own ears.

The medic jerked his head up, eyes bulging further. 'Ha! Awake? Sooner than you should.' The thin voice and staccato speech seemed designed to grate on the nerves, Keill thought. 'But you can't threaten. The injection will hold for hours.'

Injection? With some relief Keill realized that his body seemed half-paralysed because he had been drugged. The medic read the look in his eyes and nodded, with an unsettling titter. 'Nerve relaxant. Blocks the brain's messages. Slows you down, holds you back, keeps you quiet.'

'While you cut me open?'

The medic glanced at the scalpel in his hand, and set it down with another titter. 'A small incision. Exploratory. You're very strange. Dragged out from under half a ton of rock – should have smashed you like an egg. Like poor Miclas. But you – abrasions and contusions. Not so much as a finger broken.'

'Lucky for me,' Keill said ironically.

'More than luck. Freak bones, maybe. A mutant?' A bony finger prodded Keill's ribs. 'The knife would tell me. But there will be time later. No shortage of time.'

You're wrong about that, too, Keill thought. 'How long have I been here?'

'Brought in last night. Now it's tonight.' The titter rose again as the medic moved away, busying himself at one of the machines, then bustling out of the room.

Unconscious for a whole day? Frustration and anger swept through Keill, and he sought to lunge up from the bed. But the gluey feeling held him. His body moved only slightly, in a terrible slow motion, and pain lanced through his stiff and aching muscles.

He sagged back, fighting down rage and desperation, gathering his thoughts – and finding that not all the thoughts were his own.

You are awake at last. Glr's inner voice held equal mixtures of relief and anxiety. *I feared you might be in coma. What is happening to you?*

Keill explained about the drug, and then told her what had happened, since the explosion in the cave, as far as he knew. 'They're probably going to interrogate me,' he concluded, 'and in the end they'll get round to killing me.'

What can I do? Glr asked.

'Right now I have no idea,' Keill said sourly. 'There's no way you can get in here past the force field.'

Glr was silent for a moment. *I have to tell you*, she said at last, *the clones found Tam, earlier today. He tried to fight them, bravely, but he had no chance. They took him away – still alive – to the tower. I can detect his mind on the same level as you – halfway up the tower.*

Keill ground his teeth with rage. If there were to be any kind of chance that he might escape, it would be even slimmer if he had to worry about Tam as well.

He is a well-meaning young human, Glr added. *I visited him last night briefly – and he was surprised, but friendly and kind, even sharing some food with me.*

'I know what you're saying,' Keill said wryly. 'Don't worry – if there's any chance at all, I'll try to get him out. But I can't do anything lying here like a corpse.'

You will find a way, Glr said confidently, as her mind withdrew.

Then it's time to start looking, Keill said to himself. He lay perfectly still for a moment, breathing deeply, gathering his concentration and strength as his training had taught him. Then he began to do battle with the drug.

Sweat burst from his skin, and his bruised flesh screamed, but he clenched his teeth and fought to move. Left arm first – bring it across the body. Slowly, maddeningly, as if it were not truly attached to him, the arm lifted, dragging itself over on to his chest. In the same cruel mockery of movement, his left leg bent at the knee, raising itself from the bed. And after what seemed an hour of gruelling, exhausting concentration, he had managed to roll halfway over.

Then he let himself roll back to his original position, feeling the sweat dry as he rested. Some achievement, he thought dourly. At this rate it will take me a year to cross the room.

He was gathering himself for another effort when the medic returned. The bulging eyes glanced over Keill, 'Good, good. Still and quiet.' The narrow head nodded several times with satisfaction. 'Injection will hold a while yet. Then another, and sleep again.'

He tittered as before and moved away. But a trace of satisfaction spread through Keill as well, among the frustration and urgency.

The medic believed that he should still be wholly unable to move. So it seemed that the drug was wearing off more quickly than was normal.

But then legionaries were *not* normal. Their training demanded a peak of health, physical condition and body control far beyond the ordinary. And that had always meant that a legionary was far more resistant to disease – *and* to the effects of drugs – than most people. Keill remembered the surprise even of the Overseers, after they had saved his life, when he had regained consciousness days sooner than they had expected.

It wouldn't give him much of an advantage, he knew – not in this position, and not with another injection due before long. But it was all he had.

Cautiously he struggled to turn his head a fraction. The medic had apparently gone through another door, probably leading to an adjoining room. Keill wondered if that might be where they were keeping Tam. More immediately he wondered if he might chance another effort to loosen himself further from the relaxant drug.

That chance did not come. The medic scuttled back into view, still fussing with some equipment against the wall. And then he halted, jumping as if stabbed, as a voice spoke from the other side of the room.

'Has he regained consciousness?'

It was a carrying voice, though hollow and flat, totally lacking in resonance or richness. Keill could not see its owner, but a chill brushed his spine at the mere sound.

Then the speaker stepped into his view, and the chill deepened.

At first glance the person looking down at him was beautiful, in an inhuman way. A tall, broad-shouldered, imposing figure that seemed to have been carved from gold – or from some smooth and burnished metal that was the colour of gold. It might have been a sculpture of some mighty ancient god. Yet it moved – the flexible seams at the joints hair-thin and almost invisible. For an instant Keill thought the golden figure was a robot, but then he saw the face more clearly, and knew otherwise – sickeningly otherwise.

If the metallic body was that of a god, the face was that of a devil. A devil made of flesh, human flesh, and revoltingly ugly. The skin was a sickly grey, puffy and mottled. And the features were small, clustered in the centre of the grey face – close-set eyes that lacked brows or lashes, a nose not much more than two gaping slits, a small blubbery mouth held partly open to reveal tiny, blackened teeth.

A cyborg, Keill decided, staring at the being. A cybernetic robot body, with the organic human flesh of the face – and behind it, no doubt, a human brain – linked and melded perfectly into the smooth golden hood that formed its head.

The medic sidled forward anxiously. 'He is conscious. But no movement yet.'

'Are you certain?' The small eyes fastened unblinkingly on Keill. 'He is a man of many talents and resources. Watch him carefully.'

The medic jerked his head in a half-bow and scuttled away. Keill and the golden giant studied each other silently for a moment. Flat on his back and barely able to move, Keill had never felt so vulnerable in his life.

'I am Altern.' The hollow, eerie voice was as expressionless as before.

'And you're the boss here, from the Deathwing,' Keill said, striving to make the muscles of his mouth move properly.

A broad golden hand moved as if brushing the word aside. 'I am aware that you know that name. I am aware that you have many pieces of information about the Deathwing that you should not have. I intend to learn what else you know – and above all how you came to learn what you know.'

Keill was silent a moment, remembering. In his most recent clash with a Deathwing agent, on the Cluster near the planet Veynaa, his enemy had been surprised that Keill knew anything at all about the Deathwing. It was inevitable that the facts of Keill's knowledge – of his very existence – would have been relayed back to the Deathwing leader, who was never called anything but The One.

'I learned it easily enough,' he said at last, mockery in his slow voice. 'I made a vid-call to The One, and asked him.'

Altern's puffy grey face did not flicker. 'That you did not. Equally, you did not learn what you know by your own devices. You are not so clever.'

'No?' Keill replied. 'Then maybe I'm just lucky.'

The hollow voice deepened slightly, sounding even more as if it came from beyond the grave. 'You survived the destruction of your world, though no others did. Twice you found your way to Deathwing operations on other planets, and twice you thwarted us. No one is so lucky. You have been *aided*, Keill Randor. And you will tell me how, and by whom.'

'No,' Keill said quietly, 'I won't.'

The slit nostrils flared. 'In a nearby room lies the Jitrellian officer. I can have him brought here and allow Doctor Rensik to operate on him in unbearably painful ways. The doctor enjoys the use of the scalpel.'

Keill kept his face blank, his voice level. 'I met the boy only a short while ago. He is clumsy, stupid and undisciplined. Do you really think that concern for him would make me say anything to one of the killers who murdered Moros?'

It was a bluff – but Keill had delivered it with an icy, convincing calm. The golden giant studied him a moment, then again gestured dismissively. 'Indeed. The boy is unimportant. And you seem to have rid yourself of some of the Legion scruples, since your planet died. I may find it even easier to make use of you.'

'Use of me?'

'The Deathwing is not wasteful.' Altern's puffy lips twitched in something that might have been a smile. 'Some thought that you should be pursued and killed outright. But I believed that you might one day find your way here, to this operation – which would have peculiar interest to a legionary. And I felt that the last of the Legions of Moros would have much to contribute here, which would be a satisfactory way to put an end to your meddling. My opinion . . . prevailed.'

'So you *were* expecting me,' Keill said coldly.

'When our training programme extended to off-planet manoeuvres, computer predictions gave an eighty-eight per cent probability that you would learn about them.' The small eyes glinted. 'Yes, I have been waiting for you.'

'Training?' Keill spat the word. 'That murderous raid on the Jitrell spaceport was *training*?'

'Quite so. And results were most satisfactory.' Again the mockery of a smile.

'And you really think,' Keill said bitterly, 'that you can somehow force me to work for the Warlord?'

'Warlord?' Altern said, as if tasting the name. 'That is what you name the Master? How suitable . . . But yes, Randor, I can. This operation is one of the . . . Warlord's . . . central plans. The creation of an élite fighting force, as skilled as the legionaries from whom they were cloned. They have been created to fight – whether as special task forces, assassination squads, even mercenaries like your Legions. But always they will serve the Master's purpose. And in the end they will spearhead the final assaults – they and more like them, soon to be developed – that will bring the Master to victory over the galaxy.'

Keill snorted. 'And I'm supposed to come along, carrying the flag?'

'You will fight at their head, Randor, after putting the final touches to their training. Especially now that you have caused the death of their captain – Miclas, who was bred and trained first, to aid me in setting up the operation and carrying it through.' The evil little eyes grew cold. 'I intend to plumb your mind for what it knows – and *how* it knows – about the Master. Then I will empty your mind entirely, of identity, personality, will. And I will *reprogramme* you, Randor, and put your legionary skills to my use.'

Keill bared his teeth, straining to lift himself. 'You'll never do it! If I can't kill you first, I'll die first!'

'You will do neither.' The smooth golden head swivelled towards the door. 'Rensik!'

The skinny medic hurried near, twitching nervously.

'Set up the equipment for a full mind-wipe,' Altern ordered. 'But first prepare the drug that will make Randor answer questions freely, and bring it and him to me tomorrow. Until then, keep him immobilized.'

The medic nodded. 'Next injection is due soon . . .'

'Administer it now. Take no chances with this man.'

Rensik nodded again, and scuttled to one side, reaching for a compressor syringe on a nearby cabinet. He hurried to the bed, and before Keill could move within the gluey constriction of his body, the syringe hissed. The heavy numbness at once increased as the new dose of nerve relaxant entered Keill's system.

The golden giant stared down, again wearing the chillingly evil half-smile. 'You should be grateful, Randor. I will be freeing you from unpleasant memories, and giving you a chance to be a legionary again, on a winning side. A legionary of the Deathwing.'

The many and the One
chapter nine

As before, Keill rose out of sleep with the cloudy shapes of dreams scattering from his mind – dominated this time by the image of a giant golden hand that closed crushingly on his helpless body. Also as before, he was fully alert the instant that he forced his eyes slowly open.

Little had changed, except that much of the physical pain from his battered body had subsided. The prolonged sleep, and presumably ministrations by the medic – for many of the synthaskin bandages had been removed – had obviously aided his own remarkable resilience and speed of healing.

Yet his improved condition would be of small use unless he could free himself from the nerve relaxant. And he could tell, by the effort of opening his eyes, that he was as firmly held by it as he had been upon awakening before.

He strained to turn his head, enough to see that he was alone in the room. And to see a new piece of equipment against the far wall – something that made his stomach lurch.

A complicated console of machinery, focusing on a spray of long electrodes, emerging like tentacles, each fining down to a thread of metal that was nearly a monofilament. Electrodes that would soon be implanted in his brain . . .

It was the equipment for the full mind-wipe ordered by Altern – to destroy his personality, to put an end to the man that was Keill Randor and create in its place a Deathwing slave.

Now he had no choice. He had to move, had to get to his feet. He had no illusions that he could win – but he intended to fight so that they would have to kill him. At least then he would not give away the Overseers' secrets, and would not go helplessly into the service of his enemy.

His mind formed Glr's name, and when she responded told her swiftly about the golden giant, and what he was going to do about the cyborg's plans for him.

'*We can't help each other now,*' he went on. '*Just hope that they shut off the suppressor field so you can get off the planet.*'

There must be a way, Glr said, her voice anguished.

'*There isn't,*' Keill said quietly. '*I can fight some of the effects of the nerve relaxant, but even then I'll still be moving like a tired old man.*'

If you were a telepath, Glr cried, *I could blast you free of the drug with a psychic shock.*

'*But I'm not,*' Keill said. '*So . . .*'

He paused. A shock – jolting his nervous system back into full operation? It could work. And there were other kinds of shock, besides telepathic.

Hope rising within him, he quickly outlined to Glr what he was planning.

Can it be done? she asked worriedly. *It could kill you . . .*

'*Either way,*' Keill said with a grim silent laugh, '*I win – and the Deathwing loses.*'

As Glr withdrew in a mental cloud of anxiety, Keill readied himself. If his concentration and inner strength had been powerful, during his attempt to move the day before, now it was total. He was no longer merely experimenting. He was battling for survival – his determination, his will, his courage, every portion of his being focused in a final supreme effort. He did not consider the possibility of failure or defeat; they were not in the vocabulary of the Legions. For a trapped legionary, there were only two alternatives. Win through – or die.

Time slid past as Keill fought his tireless, relentless battle against the drug. Once again he forced himself to roll to one side, to draw up his legs. A centimetre at a time, he dragged his legs past the edge of the bed, letting them trail while he concentrated on his upper body. Time and again he felt himself slump back, as the gluey constriction clung to his muscles. Time and again he gritted his teeth and struggled. Until at last he was half-sitting on the edge of the bed, allowing himself to slide in an awkward crumple to the floor.

He paused there, relaxing for a moment, breathing deeply, listening for a movement from outside the room, in case the sound of his fall might bring Rensik or some of the clones to investigate. But no one came – and he gathered his resources for the next stage in the battle.

Half-crawling, half-sliding, he pushed his way across the floor. His progress was no faster – an agonizing centimetre at a time. Yet it began to seem microscopically less difficult as time went on. Was the very fact of his battle helping his resistance – speeding the moment when his body would throw off the effect of the drug? Hope surged, but he put it aside, pouring his concentration with increasing ferocity into his unwilling muscles.

And at last he reached his goal. The nearest bank of medical equipment – some form of diagnostic machine, fed from the same power source that, overall, operated the tower's life support within the force field.

He reached out a hand. There was no doubt now: he *was* moving ever so slightly faster, more easily. But it would still be some time before all of the drug had worn off naturally. And too much time had already passed. The medic might be back in the room any moment. His desperate plan had to be carried through.

The machine's power lead pulled away from the wall, with a faint snap of a spark. With slow, fumbling fingers, Keill peeled the insulation further back from the thick cable. Then he took a grip on the bare wire – and without hesitation plunged it firmly back into the power socket.

It was a livid blaze of white fire blasting into him – through every cell, along every nerve. His mouth opened in a soundless scream, his body arched and leaped in a giant convulsion, stiffening, jerking, contorting. But the terrifying spasm lasted only a second – for as his body flailed, the cable that he gripped was torn free of the socket.

Released from the agony, he collapsed limply to the floor, half-unconscious. His heart was battering against his rib-cage; his lungs were unwilling to accept air; every muscle seemed to have turned to water. But the centre of his being, where his discipline and will existed, fought the weakness and coldly dragged him back to consciousness. He forced his eyes open, gasping with deep, ragged breaths, and raised his hand feebly to wipe the streaming sweat from his eyes.

And a surge of elation swept him – swept aside the weakness and pain, even the agony of his fingers where the wire had scorched the skin.

The hand that he had raised to his head had moved easily, normally.

The shock had done its job. His nervous system was free of the drug.

The elation, and his limitless determination, raised him from the floor. Unwilling to risk standing, he crawled back towards the bed and struggled to lift himself into it. Only then did he allow himself to relax, to slump on to the hard mattress and let weariness and reaction claim him.

Rest was all he needed, he knew. The effects of the fearsome shock would not last long – his astonishing physical fitness would soon reassert itself, bringing his heartbeat back to normal, restoring strength to his body. He would lie still, regathering and readying himself. Anyone who came in now would assume he was still drugged – and he could carry on the pretence as long as necessary.

But soon he would be himself again – with all his faculties and skills, awaiting their moment.

Glr entered his mind with a cry of delight as she sensed what had happened. *And now?* she asked.

'I'll stay quiet awhile,' Keill told her. 'But I won't wait around for Altern to use his truth drug, and the mind-wipe.'

Please do not, Glr said. *There is another reason why you must act soon. Last night, while I sat sleepless among these miserable rocks, I glimpsed the stars through gaps in the cloud.*

For a moment Keill was puzzled by the triviality of the remark. Then he grasped her meaning, just as her inner voice sombrely confirmed it.

Correct. During the night, quite a stiff breeze sprang up out here.

Urgency nearly disrupted the clarity of Keill's mental reply. 'Glr, if the Starwind's rising, you'll have to find cover. Get back to the ship, in that cave.'

Not yet, she said firmly. *There still might be a way I can aid you. And at the moment it is merely a windy day.*

'Glr . . .!' he began. But then he was aware that she had left his mind, to prevent further argument. And in any case there was no more time for talk – or for rest.

Four armed clones had entered the room. They were three Callors and a Miclas – but Keill was less interested in their faces than in their hands.

The guns they carried were not projectile pistols, but up-to-date energy beam-guns – which, of course, would operate inside the force field, just like all the other powered equipment. Clearly Altern was taking no chances, even though Keill was supposed to be drugged and immobile.

He allowed his body to remain limp, apparently helpless, as two of the clones lifted him roughly from the bed. While the other two held their guns fixed on him, he was deposited in a special chair standing against a wall near by – on wheels, sturdy and metal-framed, with a high back and an adjustable leg support. Keill slumped in the chair, letting himself sag to one side, as the four guards wheeled him from the room.

The door opened on to a broad, circular area, giving Keill his first glimpse of the layout of the tower. At the centre of the open area were elevator shafts – tubes of energized metal, with flat metal discs sliding up or down within them, riding on some form of magnetic force. Each disc was large enough to hold six persons, clustered tightly together – and there were four of the shafts within the circular area, one pair back to back with the other. And around the area, solid doors gave access to every room on that level.

Within the elevators themselves, the discs never stopped, but moved steadily at three-metre intervals. It was a familiar enough design, so that Keill knew that a disc reaching the top would slide over to enter a descending shaft, and those at the bottom would move to a rising one. He also knew that the walls of the shafts would be solid except at the level of each floor, where an opening allowed passengers to step on or off the moving discs. Doing so would not be difficult for a normally mobile person, but there was a heavy thump and jerk as the guards dragged Keill's chair on to a disc.

As they did so, one of them misjudged the weight of Keill's sagging body, and a corner of the metal chair scraped against the wall of the elevator shaft.

'Watch it!' yelled another clone, dragging the chair hastily back. 'You trying to disrupt the power?'

'Right,' said a third clone with a snicker. 'We're supposed to go up, not down.'

There was a general laugh, which subsided as the disc rose steadily up the shaft. But Keill had filed away that scrap of information. The discs were powered directly from the walls of the shaft – and that power seemed easily vulnerable to disruption.

If he was ever going to make a break, he knew he would need all the disruption he could get.

Carefully he noted all the other details he could see, as the smooth ascent continued. Each level of the tower was more than three metres high, floor to ceiling, and the floors were thick – leaving a space of several seconds when the disc was fully enclosed, between the various openings in the shaft on each floor.

And every level seemed to be laid out alike – the circular area around the elevators, doors opening from it to give access to the various rooms. And of course the rooms would have interconnecting doors, as the clinic had.

It was a simple and functional layout. And it meant that there was no way to leave the building, or to move up and down within it, except by the elevators. Not very encouraging, Keill thought, for anyone planning to escape. Especially not when he would also need to find Tam, and take him along. Yet he calmly went on studying the surroundings, probing for something that might offer him the edge of a chance . . .

Finally, on a higher level, the clones heaved the chair off the elevator disc and wheeled it in through the nearest door. It led to a remarkable room. An office, or a control centre, extending the full width of the tower, it was filled with complex hardware of every sort. A variety of computer and data storage consoles, serving many different purposes, mingled with communications devices of every shape and size. Keill stared at it longingly. Somewhere in that bulk of machinery might be a communications link leading directly to the headquarters of the Deathwing. Only a few metres away from him – but it might as well have been light years.

The golden figure of Altern was standing at a long metal table, itself bearing tidy piles of machinery and material – smaller communication devices and calculators, sheaves of the thin plastic wafers of computer printouts, star charts, and more. But Keill's eye was caught by the expanse of window behind the golden giant. He saw the sky of Rilyn – with torn rags of cloud scudding across it, patches of sun-bright pale sky shining through.

Altern followed his gaze.

'This planet's regular storm has begun to build,' he said in his empty, hollow voice. 'It is, of course, why we chose this planet – because it is almost never visited.'

'I would have thought,' Keill replied, moving his mouth slowly as he had when drugged, 'that you'd have the sense to build an underground base.'

'The Deathwing does not hide in caves. The force field will easily withstand the windstorm. It is a symbol, if you like – of how the Master will meet force with greater force, and defeat it.'

There it was again, Keill thought. That eternal arrogance, the smug pride and self-satisfaction that the Deathwing always showed – as if belonging to it bred a conviction of superiority in its members. In past encounters, Keill had turned that arrogance to his own advantage. And now he might be able to do so again.

'Let's hope you have a power failure,' he muttered.

'We will not,' said Altern. 'And it would not help you if we did.' The smooth golden head turned. 'Rensik!'

From a corner of the room that Keill had not yet looked towards, the skinny medic hurried forward.

'Inject the truth drug,' Altern ordered.

Still slumped as if helpless in the chair, Keill remained relaxed and motionless. He was aware that Rensik was fussing with another compressor syringe. And he was aware that Altern had snapped an order at the clones, so that two of them turned smartly and marched from the room, while the other two took up positions behind Keill's chair, one on either side.

But most of his awareness was turned inward. It was assessing his physical condition, noting that his heartbeat and breathing had returned to normal, that strength and vitality were flowing back into his body. And again he was gathering that strength, directing it, letting it build and swell within his control, the way a river will build its awesome pressure behind the controlling barrier of a dam.

Then the medic bustled forward, syringe at the ready. And the dam burst.

Keill exploded into action.

chapter ten

Keill powered his body into a backward roll, using the inclined chair for leverage as he swung his legs up and over. The whiplash movement was so swift that the two clone guards had barely begun to register it when Keill's feet sledgehammered into their faces and flung them into crumpled heaps across the room.

The impact had not slowed Keill's movement. The back roll brought him smoothly over on to his feet, facing the table where Altern stood. Rensik still had not moved, though his jaw had begun to drop – but the golden giant was quick enough to reach one huge hand towards a beam-gun resting on the corner of the table. Effortlessly Keill swept up the chair where he had sat and flung it at Altern, sending him reeling backwards. Then Keill turned and sprang for the door.

He rose in the air in a leaping kick, his foot driving forward at precisely the centre point of the door's mass. The door did not merely open; it was blasted off its hinges by the force of the kick – and took with it the two other clone guards, who had been posted outside, and who had started to enter the room at the sound of the burst of violence from within.

Hardly pausing in his smooth flowing movement, Keill reached down to wrench the energy guns from the fallen guards' holsters. The circular area was deserted, but as he leaped towards the nearest elevator, a beam of energy sizzled past his shoulder – from inside the room, where Altern had recovered his balance. But then Keill was on a downward elevator disc, hidden within the solid walls of the shaft.

He knew exactly how many levels he and his guards had

risen – and leaped from the disc at the floor where the clinic was. The area around it was empty, for the tower's other clones would only now be receiving the alarm from Altern. Soon enough, though, they would be storming through the tower looking for him. Every second would count from now on. But Glr had said that Tam was also on the clinic level – and he was not leaving Tam behind.

He burst in through the clinic door, gun ready, but the room was empty. Near the bed where he had lain, he saw a locker, and inside it found his uniform and boots. He pulled the clothing on without a wasted motion, and almost laughed aloud. Altern had made another mistake. The square of plastic that was his second grenade had not been recognized: it was still on his belt.

He went through the nearest door at a dead run, hoping to find Tam. But there was no one, again, in the room he had entered.

Instead, there was something that brought him to an abrupt halt.

He was in a laboratory. It was nearly the size of Altern's control centre, and nearly as full of computer hardware and other complex equipment. But the main purpose of the laboratory seemed biological, or biochemical. Large containers of chemicals and viscous liquids lined the solid metal counters. There were oversized electron miscroscopes, vacuum chambers, heating devices and more.

Keill felt an icy chill as he guessed where he was. Here was the scientific heart of the entire operation on Rilyn. Here was the birthplace of the clones – where the original cells from the three legionaries were induced to grow and reproduce, and form their youthful duplicates.

He moved towards the nearest counter for a closer look – but then whirled and crouched as a tiny rustle at the doorway alerted him. Even as he registered the presence of two clones, one on either side of a frightened Doctor Rensik, his guns were flaming. The clones dropped in their tracks, before they could fire, smoke trailing from their uniforms where the lethal beams had struck.

'Don't, don't,' Rensik babbled. 'Don't kill me!'

Keill straightened, gesturing around him. 'Are the original cells here?'

'Original? Oh – yes, yes, here,' Rensik quavered.

'Show me. Carefully.'

The medic scurried past Keill, and opened the heavy door of a metal cabinet. A gush of refrigerated air swept out. 'They are here,' Rensik chattered. 'Soon we begin again – another batch. Another Legion.'

'No,' Keill said harshly. 'You don't.'

He moved forward, staring into the cabinet at the tiny vials that held in suspension all that remained besides Keill himself of the Legions of Moros.

'No,' he repeated, half to himself. 'They deserve a better death than this.'

He sensed the movement even as Rensik began it. The medic had snatched up his favourite implement, the laser-scalpel, but he had no chance against the speed of Keill's turn. The axe-edge of Keill's hand smashed against his wrist, and the scalpel twisted around just as Rensik pressed the stud. The needle-point beam swept in a compact arc, opening the medic's skinny throat from ear to ear.

Keill sprang back as the corpse slid to the floor, blood fountaining. Again his eyes sought the cabinet where the original cells lay. A diversion, he thought, to take some of the clones away from the hunt. And to put a final end to this ghoulishness.

He slipped his one remaining grenade from his belt and tossed it, almost gently, into the refrigeration cabinet. 'Rest in peace,' he said quietly. Then he turned and ran.

He was halfway across the adjoining room when the laboratory erupted in a thunder of smoke and flame. The shock of the blast struck him like a giant hand, but he rode the impact, using its impetus to hurl him against the inter-connecting door to another room, slamming through it at top speed, balanced and ready.

A room like the one where he had lain – and a bed, in which he saw Tam, staring wide-eyed towards him. And one clone guard at the foot of the bed, whose gun fired harmlessly wide as the beam from Keill's gun blazed a gaping hole in his chest.

'Keill!' Tam gasped. 'Where did . . . what is . . .'

'Don't talk,' Keill grated, crossing to the bed. 'Can you move?'

'I was drugged,' Tam said weakly, 'but it has nearly worn off.' He sat up, swung his legs to the floor, his face contorted with effort. He too was wearing only a thigh-length bed-kilt.

'My clothes . . .' he said, looking hopefully at Keill.

Keill moved swiftly to a nearby cabinet, chafing at the loss of precious seconds. He could hear the crackle of flame in the ruined laboratory, but he knew that even that destruction would not divert every clone . . .

And he knew it all the more when a different crackle heralded the energy beam that bit into the cabinet beside his hand.

'Don't move,' said a voice, 'or the next one kills your friend.'

He froze, poising himself.

'Throw the guns away, very slowly,' the voice went on.

Gritting his teeth, Keill let his energy guns drop to the floor, and carefully, slowly, turned.

Ten red-uniformed men – a full squad of clones – clustered in the doorway, guns fixed on himself and Tam.

The one who had spoken, a Callor wearing a number three, stepped easily towards Keill. 'The boss predicted you'd come this way,' he said scornfully. 'It's too easy.'

Keill said nothing, but watched in surprise as Cal-3 slid his gun back into his holster, and his nine men, grinning, did the same.

'Altern wants you back in one piece,' Cal-3 said. 'But he

won't mind if you've got some new bruises.'

None of Keill's astonishment showed in his face. They were going to try to take him alive – since Altern obviously still wanted to carry through his plans.

'You're good, Randor,' Cal-3 went on arrogantly, 'but not that good. It's time you learned that we're legionaries too.'

No, Keill said silently, you're not. You only have the bodies, and some of the skills. A great deal of skill, there was no doubt about that. But the clones knew nothing of the true Moros training, from infancy. They knew nothing of the background, the traditions, the example of generations, that motivated each legionary to strive to perfect himself or herself.

There was no way that the clones could have become legionaries *inside*, where it mattered. In the heart and the mind and the will – in the discipline and self-mastery.

And in any case, Keill had fought legionaries – in the un-inhibited, exhilarating violence of the Martial Games of Moros. Where legionaries tested themselves against one another in every form of competition, including hand-to-hand combat, and only the light regulation padding saved the losers from crippling injury, or death. The first year Keill had reached the final round, he had confronted five other legionaries, in an all-in free-for-all. Afterwards it had taken more than a month for his injuries to mend – but he had won. And the following year he had won again.

No, the clones could have no conception of what it really meant to be a legionary. They were mockeries, travesties, skin-deep imitations. And he was ready for them. All the coldly burning anger that had been born within him when he first discovered what they were – all the vengeful determination to erase this ultimate Deathwing outrage against the memory of Moros – flared within him, feeding and strengthening his readiness.

'If you really were legionaries,' he said to them, his tone biting like a whip, 'you wouldn't have to boast about it.'

As he expected, fury blazed in the eyes of Cal-3. In a blur of movement he feinted a blow with one fist, and lashed a brutal kick at Keill's groin.

But even before the kick was fully under way, Keill had read it and countered. He stepped inside it, and struck upwards with a short, perfectly judged elbow smash that drove deep into Cal-3's lower ribs. Air whistled from the clone's sagging mouth as he was lifted off his feet by the power of the blow. Then he crumpled, face purpling as he strove to breathe, lips flecked with blood as fragments of his crushed ribs stabbed into his lungs.

Keill stepped away, almost casual in his relaxed calm. The other clones looked at each other grimly, then began to edge forward, some sidling away so that their movement brought all nine of them in a circle surrounding Keill. Still they did not reach for their guns: pride, and the order to cause no permanent injury to Keill, held them back.

Within the circle Keill tuned his awareness to its highest pitch – alert to every intake of breath, every rustle of clothing, from the clones behind him. As if he could see backwards, he knew where each of them stood, how each was positioned. And the slide of a boot on the floor was all the warning he needed, to let him drop into a crouch, perfectly balanced, and without looking drive a precisely aimed, ferocious kick backwards, at the knee of the clone trying to spring on him from behind.

The crack of splintering bone was audible above the clone's shriek, before he collapsed, fainting from the agony. Still Keill did not look round, but straightened – the entire movement having been so swift that the other eight had only begun to tense themselves to react.

But they were going to move any second, Keill knew – and this time there would be no one-man bravado. This time they would all attack at once.

No point, Keill thought, in letting them take the upper hand.

With not the slightest warning, without seeming to set himself in any way, Keill leaped – a standing jump that became a mid-air twist, ending with the meaty sound of his boot striking the solidity of a skull.

But as the owner of the skull toppled, the other clones were upon him.

They were strong and quick, and fought well as a team. Chopping blades of hands, battering fists, crushing kicks rained in on Keill from all sides.

Yet it seemed that they were trying to hit a wraith, a spinning, dodging will-o'-the-wisp – and one that had also apparently grown extra limbs and joints. However swiftly a clone struck, whatever unexpected angle the blow came from, Keill always seemed to have an extra millisecond to block or parry, to weave aside or slip beneath.

And every defensive evasion became in the same flowing motion a counter-attack. A forearm block by Keill, halting a chop at his throat, would smoothly extend itself into a savage hooked punch at a clone's face. A twist of Keill's body away from a kick led to a wrenching grip on the clone's leg, hurling him full into the leaping rush of another.

In one instant Keill was gripping the shoulder of a clone, swinging him around off-balance, so that the clone took a murderous punch aimed at Keill. In another instant Keill was falling backwards away from a lashing kick, turning the fall into a perfect backspring that slammed his boots into a clone's face on the way.

Yet the clones were not amateurs, not untrained, clumsy brawlers. They too could dodge and parry and counterpunch. Often their vicious attacks broke through Keill's defences, and though even then he could ride the blows, and so lessen their force, he was battered and bruised within seconds of the first onslaught.

Yet he realized in the first of those seconds that the clones' orders were still holding them. They were seeking only to *disable* him. And their training was very properly directing their most punishing blows to crack a rib, smash a knee, splinter a forearm.

The clones could not have known the impossibility of breaking any bone in Keill Randor's body. But they did learn, quickly – though for them too late – that the controlled and deadly battle fury of a legionary, fighting for his life against heavy odds, shows no mercy and pulls no punches. When Keill landed *his* most punishing blows, with precision and perfect timing, the clones that were their targets simply never got up again.

And all of this, all of the combat that stormed and raged ruinously through the confines of the room, happened at the speed of instantaneous reflex and reaction, so that few eyes could have followed the separate incidents within the furious, shadowy blur of battle.

It seemed that one moment Keill was hardly visible under the onslaught of eight red-uniformed men. And almost the next moment, he was standing among seven fallen bodies, while the eighth clone, taken in an intricate one-handed throw, sailed gracefully over his head and crashed with finality against the wall.

Brushing an ooze of blood from his cheekbone, where a fist had slashed his flesh, Keill turned back towards Tam – and froze. The clone whose knee he had smashed, lying on the floor with his face grimacing in agony, had nonetheless managed to drag out his beam-gun. Keill knew he had no chance to reach him before he fired.

But it was another beam-gun that flashed, and it was the clone whose body jerked with the impact of the deadly energy. Young Tam had picked up one of Keill's guns, during the brief seconds of the combat, and had used it in time.

Keill grinned at him savagely. 'Couldn't have done better myself.'

Tam's face was deathly pale, but he managed an answering smile. 'I thought they would kill you.'

'They might have,' Keill said, 'if whoever trained them had

cured them of over-confidence.' He glanced round swiftly. 'Now we have to get out of here. There'll be more along soon.'

'Have we a chance?' Tam asked.

'Always a chance,' Keill grinned. He glanced towards the cabinet that held Tam's clothing, but then a better idea struck him. Quickly he stooped and began dragging the red uniform off one of the fallen clones. 'Here you are,' he told Tam. 'You're going to be a brother.'

Tam looked bewildered, but pulled on the uniform at Keill's urging.

'Now look outside, and see if we have company,' Keill told him.

Tam obeyed, then beckoned to Keill. The open area beyond the door, round the elevators, was clear. Obviously the laboratory fire was occupying many of the clones. And no doubt they all imagined that the squad of ten sent by Altern would have no trouble subduing one man.

Thrusting a beam-gun into his belt at the back, Keill hurried Tam towards the nearest elevator shaft, handing another gun to the Jitrellian.

'Stand with your back to the elevator opening,' he said, 'holding the gun on me. Anyone on the other levels will see me under guard, by someone in a red uniform. We just might get away with it.'

Tam looked dubious, as they stepped together on to the next disc. But he took his position as instructed, while Keill stood opposite him, hands raised, wearing a glum, defeated look.

The energized metal walls of the shaft slid past as they descended. On the next level, clones about to step on to a rising disc whirled, guns ready, but paused with puzzled looks as Keill and his 'guard' went down past them. On the next level and the next the pattern was repeated, as clones waiting to ascend watched them pass without challenging them.

But as another level approached, before their disc reached floor level, one clone jumped towards the shaft. 'Move, brother,' he shouted. And Tam had the presence of mind to step forward just in time as the other man crowded on to the disc behind him.

The disc slid steadily down. The newcomer, an Osrid with the number twenty, hardly glanced at Tam, who was anxiously trying to keep his face hidden, but stared curiously at Keill.

'Shouldn't you be taking him up to the boss?' he said at last.

Tam shook his head – but Keill could see that the young Jitrellian was close to panic, knowing that he would be exposed at any second. Then the memory of his earlier ride on the elevator stirred in his mind.

Before anyone could speak again, Keill said idly, 'Something wrong with the power? This thing's slowing down.'

Os-20 glanced round at the shaft, then laughed. 'Not likely, legionary. These elevators don't change speed unless the walls get damaged somehow.'

'That's what I hoped you'd say,' Keill replied. His hand seemed only to twitch, but then there was a beam-gun in it. Slowly Os-20's jaw fell open.

'Cover him, Tam,' Keill snapped – and turned, firing the gun in a sweeping downward arc against the walls of the elevator shaft.

Energy hissed and crackled as the metal split, molten globules running down its surface. And beneath their feet the disc leaped and bucked, as the magnetic support from the shaft walls was disrupted.

'You'll kill us!' wailed Os-20, stumbling to his knees.

But then it was too late. The disc jerked again, as – though Keill did not know it – did all the other discs in the linked pattern of descent down the shaft. Then the disc tilted slightly under their feet, and began to accelerate downwards in a plunging fall.

chapter eleven

Keill fought to keep his balance as the disc tilted in its crazy plunge. If he had guessed wrongly about the nature of the magnetic power in the walls, he knew that it would be his last guess of any sort. There was a long way to fall . . .

But he had not been wrong. Within seconds the disc settled and began to slow, as the magnetic grip of the walls reasserted itself. Yet as it did so, the restored disc slid down to one of the floor-level openings in the shaft – into full view of two clones with guns in their hands.

They were ready and they were quick. Their guns flashed at the very instant that Keill fired. But none of the beams hit their targets. Os-20, half-dazed with fear, had lurched to his feet at just the wrong moment, blocking much of the opening. All three beams blasted into him, and he was dead before he began to fall.

By then the disc had slid away, down into the solid shaft before the next level. Ignoring Tam's white-faced look of alarm, Keill swung his gun and fired once more into the wall.

As before, the disc jerked, and began to fall at an accelerating speed – whisking past the next level's opening. As before, it slowed and righted itself within seconds – only to be accelerated again by a blast from Keill's gun.

On they fell, speeding and slowing, while the levels slid by. Keill could not be sure how far they were now from ground level, but guessed that it must be near. There seemed to be fewer clones as they descended: obviously most of them had hurried to the higher levels, where the action was. But he knew it would not be long before they were moving as rapidly downwards, after him.

Then the disc struck bottom, and as it slid sideways to take its place in the ascending shaft, Keill leaped off, dragging Tam with him. A quick glance around showed no sign of clones on this level. Turning, he swept the lowest section of the elevator with the deadly beam from his gun – and in a flaring shower of sparks the disc came to rest, the shaft's magnetic energy collapsing finally upon itself.

One set of elevators out of action, he thought. That might slow them down a little.

On this lowest level, he saw as he looked more carefully around, there were no room partitions. The whole area was open, the entire breadth of the tower. Part of it seemed to be used for storage: containers, spare skimmers and other objects were stacked at the far end. On one side of the elevator shafts, a wide ramp led upwards, presumably used by skimmers as well as men. But what lay nearer the elevator caught Keill's attention especially.

A broad, squat shape of metal – large as one of the rooms on the upper levels, but an apparently solid casing of matt-black metal fixed immovably to the floor. From within the casing Keill could hear the hum and rumble of mighty machinery.

He knew what he had found – he was sure of it. The power source of the tower's force field.

As he studied the metal casing, Tam moved wearily up beside him. 'It is a surprise to me,' he said in his stiff Jitrellian diction, 'that we still live.'

'We're not out yet,' Keill said. As he spoke he was reaching for the gun in the holster of Os-20, whose body still lay in the elevator shaft. Then Keill leaped towards the great bulk of humming machinery, his fingers swiftly disassembling the guns, freeing their energy charges.

Tam watched, horrified. 'Keill – if you remove the control caps, the charges will go critical! They will explode!'

'That's the idea,' Keill snapped, bending to press the freed energy charges against the base of the metal casing. 'Just hope it'll be enough. Now – run!'

They fled up the ramp, flinging their weight against the heavy metal door at the top. It opened on to a broad but short sweep of corridor – the entrance-way of the tower, and as deserted as the lower level. At the near end Keill saw the seams in the metal where the wide outer doorway would open. At the far end, the remaining elevators rose and fell, with no one on the discs. But there soon would be, Keill knew.

Then beneath his feet the floor shuddered, and the heavy door leading to the ramp trembled and boomed, as the energy blast exploded. Keill leaped to the controls that opened the tower's great door, and felt a fierce delight as it swung ponderously open.

There was no sign of a red haze. The force field no longer existed.

But as he and Tam rushed through the opening, delight turned to dismay. A sweep of choking dust struck them, borne on a blast of air that made them reel.

The Starwind was reaching gale force – and still rising.

You seem to have won the war, Glr's inner voice said joyfully.

'*Only a battle,*' Keill said. '*The clones will soon be pouring down here.*'

What can I do?

'*Protect yourself,*' Keill said sharply. '*Why didn't you tell me the wind was this strong? I'm sending Tam out – you and he can find a cave somewhere.*'

Not I, Glr replied. *I told you earlier – I would rather face the Starwind at its worst than lose my sanity under the ground.*

'*Then try to reach the ship!*' Keill said. '*The suppressor field will be off as well as the force field.*'

Should I not join you in the tower? Glr asked dubiously.

'*The tower won't be standing much longer,*' Keill said desperately. '*I've got to be out of here by then. I could never reach the ship in time, on foot, but you could – and come back for me.*'

If you survive that long.

'*I will,*' Keill insisted. '*And when you bring the ship, you might also do something about that spacecraft on top of the tower.*'

Glr paused for a moment. *I had almost forgotten that. We cannot let the metal one escape, can we?* Her laughter was bright. *Very well – I will bring the ship. Stay alive.*

'You too,' Keill said softly, aloud. But the Starwind seemed to snatch the words from his mouth, as if mocking the idea that a small winged being could expect to survive the growing power of the storm.

Tam had turned questioningly when he spoke, but Keill silenced him with a gesture. 'Get out of here,' he ordered. 'Find a cave, as deep as you can.'

'And you?' Tam asked doubtfully.

'I'm staying awhile. The Starwind will flatten the tower before long – but first I want to find a way to get at the leader of all this.'

Tam blinked solemnly. 'I will stay and fight at your side.'

'You've fought enough today, and fought well,' Keill said. 'It's no longer your fight. You'll take cover, and let me do what I'm here for.'

The young Jitrellian straightened. 'If that is your wish. I would not want to impede you. And my world will always remember you with honour.'

'Don't plan my funeral just yet,' Keill said wryly. 'Now go!'

He watched Tam hurry out into the grip of the wind, vanishing into the swirls of dust almost at once. Then he turned, glancing up at the blank ceiling as if wishing his eyes could pierce the metal.

If only there were some other way to reach the upper levels. He gazed longingly at the elevators, but knew he could not risk that route again . . .

And as he gazed, a descending disc slid down into his view, crowded with armed clones.

They began firing wildly as soon as they spotted him. He

snapped a shot towards them, heard a cry of pain, but the others' beams were sizzling too close around him. And the next disc, he knew, would be bringing more.

He wheeled and sprinted away, into the teeth of the Starwind.

The blast of wind struck at Keill like a furious, gigantic beast – a beast that deafened him with its roaring as it tried to hurl him off his feet. Half-blinded by the dust, he stumbled away from the doorway, angling sideways so that he soon came to the smooth metal wall of the tower. He glanced back – but if the clones had followed him into the storm, they were not visible in the rage of dust and wind.

One arm flung across his face, Keill pushed forward, hugging the tower wall. There the wind eddied and gusted, twisting back upon itself as the expanse of smooth metal blocked its forward sweep. And like a deeper bass note beneath the howl of the wind, Keill could hear the tower creak and groan under the assault.

Altern had relied too much on his force field, not conceiving of the possibility that someone might shut it off. So there was no failsafe – and the tower would crumble and be swept away, before this day was over, just as the first human structures on Rilyn had been swept away so long before. The only question was whether Altern would escape the tower's fall.

Or, Keill thought, if anyone would – including himself. The wind's force seemed to have grown even in the short time he had been outside. Worriedly he shaped a questioning call in his mind.

There was no reply.

Of course he could not speak to Glr unless she reached with her mind into his. And she would be concentrating more on survival, as her membranous wings did battle with the Starwind. That's why she doesn't reply, he told himself. That has to be why . . .

At his shoulder the tower wall suddenly ended in a sharp corner. He had come to one of the vertical grooves that ran up the full height of the wall. It was about a metre and a half wide and about a metre deep, probably providing extra support for the high sweep of metal. But this groove, he found, also had another function.

There was a flat, oblong platform of thick metal, fitting neatly within the groove at the height of Keill's chest. Beneath it was a metal casing that seemed to contain the machinery of some kind of energizing magnetism.

For whatever reason – to carry cargo down from the spaceship, or for maintenance on the outer wall – the tower had offered another way it could be ascended.

An *external* elevator.

Through choking flurries of dust he located the controls, on the wall beneath the platform. He slammed his hand against the activating stud, then vaulted on to the platform as it began to rise, without haste, along the vertical groove.

Crouched at its edge, Keill looked down, gripping the platform as the wind tried to drag him from his perch. By the time he had risen to the first level, he could no longer clearly see the ground, in the sweep of windborne dust. Equally he would not be visible to searching clones – and perhaps none of them would think of the external elevator.

So Keill fed his hope as the elevator carried him up the tower, which was groaning ever more painfully as the Starwind's violence swelled.

And then hope faltered. The elevator platform shuddered, slowed and came to a halt. There it rested, as if it had become welded to the metal sides of the groove.

Keill moved towards the edge, but jerked back as an energy beam sliced into the metal. The clones had found him – and he was neatly trapped, to be picked off at their leisure.

He snapped a quick shot downwards, not sure if he had hit anything, but knowing that the threat of his gun might hold them back briefly. Then he glanced round, his mind racing, while the Starwind howled like a thousand devils, gleeful at the prospect of victory.

Around him the tower seemed now to be vibrating slightly under the wind's onslaught. But Keill kept his balance, and leaned forward slightly to peer at the expanse of smooth metal wall on either side of the groove. There ought to be windows on every level of the tower, he knew, even if they were so polarized that they could not be distinguished from the metal, to an outside observer. Not even one as close as he was – not in that storm of blinding dust.

He slid his hand along the wall. Smooth metal, for half a metre – that would be the solid vertical supports at each side of the grooves. But then . . . the slight, almost indetectable line of a seam, under his fingers. The kind of seam that even Deathwing technology would have to leave, between the metal of the wall support and the polarized plastiglass of a window.

At once he swept his gun's blast of energy along the line where he thought the seam might be. And instead of an eruption of molten metal, there was the splintering crash – almost inaudible in the wind – of collapsing glass. He had an entrance, back into the tower.

He accepted the offer without hesitation. Though the devil-voice of the Starwind shrieked in anticipation, he tucked the gun away and leaned out into the full force of the blast, reaching with one hand to clutch the lower edge of the window-frame, where the plastiglass had fallen away. Then he swung out – dangling for a breathless instant with only the strength of one hand, and the strength of sheer determined will, keeping him from being plucked away like a leaf from a tree by the raging wind.

But his other hand at once reached up and found its hold, and then he was raising himself with acrobatic smoothness, up and over the edge of the window.

In the room, he did fractionally hesitate – with astonishment. Luck, or fate, had stopped the elevator beside the window of the room where he had been interrogated – the control centre of Altern.

But there was no one inside. Only the array of complex equipment that Keill had noted before, along with a cloud of hurtling sheets of paper and plastic, swept from the broad table by the wind that stormed in, a beast robbed of its prey, through the shattered window.

Keill moved towards the door, then paused. He wanted to hurry to the roof of the tower, in case Altern was seeking to escape on the spacecraft. But he also knew that the ranged rows of technology might hold some information, some clue or hint, that could reveal the whereabouts of the Deathwing leader, The One – or even the Warlord himself.

With feverish speed, he moved to the banks of equipment, scanning the computer and data storage consoles, fingers stabbing at their keys. Display screens flashed up data, but it was disjointed, meaningless. He needed time to make sense of it – time he did not have.

Yet he worked on, forcing himself not to think of how the tower would be shuddering and creaking under the Starwind's relentless assault. And especially not to think of how Glr, too, would be running out of time, as the ravaging wind grew more terrible every moment.

His eyes blurred as the wind hurled dust like needles through the air. Even the computer's clatter was nearly drowned by the mad howling of the wind. So it was not a sound that alerted him. It was some instinct, bred of his unbelievably tuned awareness, that gave his reflexes their warning. It gave him just a microsecond to begin to whirl and crouch.

But that was not quite enough to take him clear of the savage, clubbing blow to the side of his head – from a giant, golden fist.

The glancing blow flung Keill off his feet, slamming him into the row of computers. He sagged to the floor, battling to retain consciousness, as Altern reached down to pluck the beam-gun from his belt and fling it out of sight across the room.

The puffy face, contorted and even more mottled with fury, drew close.

'I am going to kill you, Randor – painfully and slowly. You have destroyed a key element in the Master's plan. You are of no further use to me.'

'The One won't be pleased with you,' Keill said, trying to gain time while his head cleared from the effects of the blow.

The thick lips twisted scornfully. 'You are a fool. Do you think the Master would entrust this operation to *any* agent? Here I have used a name, for convenience – but among the Deathwing I have another name, that is no name.' The eerie voice seemed to slice effortlessly through the rage of the wind. 'Randor – I *am* The One!'

chapter twelve

The words that Keill could scarcely believe he had heard seemed to whirl round the room, as a huge gust of wind, slicing in through the window, echoed and amplified them into a demonic howl.

Altern . . . The One. The great golden cyborg was not merely another powerful agent of the Warlord. He was the mysterious head of the Deathwing himself – the Warlord's principal aide.

For a blinding second Keill's mind reeled at the thought of what he might have done with that information, if he were not trapped and disarmed within a tower that would soon be like flimsy paper in the swelling might of the wind.

But in the same instant he recovered his control. If the words of The One had been intended to freeze him with shock and terror, they failed. Instead, they galvanized him. The effects of The One's attack were swept away, as adrenalin surged through his body, fuelling his battle readiness.

And just in time, for the golden giant was carrying out his threat to kill him.

The One's huge metal foot stamped down crushingly towards Keill's groin. But Keill wrenched his body aside in a twisting roll – and rolled again as The One struck out a second time in a sweeping kick. It missed Keill by centimetres, slashing past him to crumple the front of a computer as if it were made of cloth.

As it did so Keill came to his feet, backing away swiftly, ducking under another clubbing swing of a great golden fist. Before the giant could strike again, Keill had lashed a kick of his own, hammering his boot with concentrated power into the golden metal midriff.

At once he was spinning away, out of reach, and his mind too was spinning. Such a kick would have crushed bone, splintered wood, at least dented heavy sheet metal. And Keill had expected that the complex mechanisms of the cyborg's body would not withstand that kind of impact.

But though The One had been briefly jolted, the unique golden metal of his torso showed not the slightest mark or blemish. And he was advancing as menacingly as before.

Keill backed away, poised and watchful. The One seemed to have no special combat skills – but clearly he did not need them, with that metal body to protect him. Of course the puffy grey face was mere flesh. The One carried his great hands high, as if aware that his face must be guarded. But even so . . .

Keill sensed the presence of the broad metal table behind him, and without warning dived towards it, with a half-turn, his hand slapping on to its surface as if he intended to vault over it. But instead he swung his body round in a full circle, on the rigid pivot of his arm, driving both feet together like a battering ram at The One's head.

The giant staggered back, but he had flung up his huge hands in time against the blow, and the inhuman strength of those hands blocked and absorbed its force. At once Keill found his balance, and this time did dive smoothly across the table, regaining his feet to face The One across the breadth of metal.

But the giant simply took hold of the table and lifted it – nearly half a ton of metal, lifted as an ordinary man might pick up a light board. Then he flung the massive weight of it at Keill.

Instantly Keill dropped to the floor, and the table sailed over him, plunging with a shattering burst of fragments through what was left of the window. The Starwind burst through the enlarged opening with even greater power, howling its fury. And even The One was halted, driven backwards a stumbling step or two, by the awesome blast.

Keill came swiftly to his feet, pressing the advantage. He closed on the giant, feinting with stabbing fingers towards the face, then dropping away to drive a lightning kick against the knee, hoping that the need for flexibility at the joints might have reduced the strength of the metal seams.

But his guess was wrong. The huge leg barely moved under the impact. And this time The One was quick enough to deliver a counterblow of his own, kicking savagely at Keill as he twisted away.

The kick glanced off his ribs, and he felt his tunic rip, felt the blaze of pain from tormented flesh, and knew that any bones but his would have been snapped by that kick. As he came to his feet again, fighting for balance and vision in the dust-laden storm of wind, he wondered if he could use the secret of his bones to his advantage – as he had done before, in hand-to-hand combat with Deathwing agents. But to do so he would have to give The One an opening – and there were too many parts of his body that were *not* unbreakable, if they came into those inhuman golden hands.

Much better, he thought as the giant lunged towards him, to find the beam-gun that had been flung so arrogantly aside.

He slid under The One's reaching hand and sliced up at the face with a lethal chop. But the other giant hand was there to block, clamping on to Keill's wrist and wrenching it with ferocious strength. For an instant they were almost face to face – close enough for Keill to see the look of surprise in the tiny eyes as Keill used the impetus of the wrenching twist to complete a forward half-roll that gave him leverage enough to drag his wrist free from the terrible grasp.

We could go on like this for ever, he thought, backing away. But the tower isn't going to be standing much longer. Where is that gun?

Even as he completed the thought, he saw it. Just a glimpse of it, lying near the far wall, almost invisible in the driving torment of the dust. But The One was standing in the way.

Cautiously Keill began to circle, edging nearer to his goal. The golden giant seemed unaware of Keill's purpose, single-mindedly, fanatically intent on savage murder. He lunged forward again, but Keill dodged and slid away, a step or two closer. Again the giant stepped near, huge fist lashing out. And as Keill surged aside he saw an opening, and struck fiercely upwards with his own fist.

It took The One just at the junction of the golden hood and the grey flesh of the face – and though Keill's fist had travelled less than half a metre, it was delivered with a focused balanced power that had Keill's entire weight behind it.

The giant staggered back and half-fell, the blubbery lips opening in an inaudible cry. And Keill turned and dived towards the place where he had seen the gun.

But it was no longer there.

A sheaf of plastic computer printouts had scudded across the floor before being snatched up and flattened against the wall by the wind. And it had slid into the gun, sweeping it away.

Keill stared around frantically, and saw it again, only a few strides away, against the wall. But The One had regained his balance and was plunging towards him, fingers curved to grasp like great golden claws, dark blood oozing from the side of the puffy face.

Poising himself, Keill waited for half a second's space, then moved forward – straight into the giant's grasp.

His hands flicked up, thrusting the clutching hands aside, and in the same motion gripping the huge wrists. Then Keill flung himself backwards, back and down to the floor. The momentum of The One and Keill's grip on his wrists brought the golden body hurtling forward. And Keill swung his legs up, his boots taking the giant in the middle of his torso and lifting him up and over in a smooth, curving arc – towards the gaping space that had been the window.

If The One had been only a few kilogrammes lighter, he

might have hurtled out through that gap into the raging grip of the Starwind. But even Keill had barely managed the throw, despite his finely judged leverage and timing, with the awesome weight of that metal body. And The One crashed against the wall just below the empty window frame, with an echoing metallic thunder that not even the wind's bestial roar could completely drown.

At once The One was clambering to his feet. The golden body seemed twisted slightly, one leg slightly askew, as if the impact of the fall had dislodged some of the cybernetic circuits within. But there was no doubt that he was still functioning well enough to continue the murderous combat.

Except that as he began his charge, an irresistible, blasting gust of wind burst through the window. It swept Keill off his feet, for all his uncanny balance, sprawling him full length on the floor. And it staggered the great bulk of The One, so that he too lurched away to one side, slamming against the same wall.

With all his prodigious metallic power he fought to recover, to resume the attack. But then it was too late.

That wild gust of wind had hurled Keill directly on top of the beam-gun that he had been seeking. And he simply snatched it up and blasted a fist-sized molten hole through the precise centre of The One's golden torso.

For a moment Keill waited – but there was no sign of movement or life in the fallen metal body. At last he thrust the gun into his belt and moved to the door, dragging it open a crack against the huge pressure of the wind, and peered out. There was another, smaller room beyond, which seemed deserted.

But just as he was about to move into it, a door at the other end of the smaller room began to move – and he caught a glimpse of dark-red uniforms.

Quickly he let his own door close. So there were clones still in the tower. Their training, he thought, must have included a high degree of blind loyalty, if they were so ready to risk their own lives to seek out The One. For they must have known that there would be no room for them in the small spacecraft on the tower's roof.

He heaved at a computer console next to the door, toppling it in a burst of sparks across the doorway. That and the force of the Starwind would hold the clones back awhile. Long enough for him to take the only chance he had left.

He slid towards the window, barely glancing at the golden form of The One, huddled face down and motionless against the wall. For a moment he paused, crouching low beneath the window, while the wind pounded and screamed through the room. He was aware, separately, of all the different wounds and bruises that throbbed in his body, and how much the savage battles of that day had taken out of him.

He also knew that what he was planning would have been difficult enough on a calm, still day when he was wholly fit and rested.

His mouth twisted in a wry half-smile. As his training captain had liked to say, only a dead legionary gives up.

He used another fraction of a second forming Glr's name in his mind. But again there was no reply. For a moment his shoulders sagged – because he knew that if she had reached the ship, she would respond. And if she had not reached it by now . . . then she never would.

Outside the tower, the Starwind was reaching hurricane force. And not even Glr could fly in that shrieking, dust-laden hell.

Then he straightened, his expression cold and determined. There was still the spaceship on the tower, and somehow he would find the strength to reach it. Somehow he would survive, to avenge Glr – by finding the Warlord.

He reached up and took a firm grip on the edge of the window-frame. Then he slid up, and over, swinging out into the monstrous grasp of the storm.

chapter thirteen

As he hung from the window edge, the Starwind bellowed and clawed at him, flailing his body against the wall as if he were a dangling strip of cloth. Pouring every scrap of his strength and will into the steely grip of his hands, he braced himself for the nearly impossible – when he would release one hand and try to swing sideways, back on to the platform of the external elevator.

He gathered himself, and let his right hand go. And in that fraction of time the Starwind seemed to whirl back upon itself. A gigantic gust struck Keill's swinging body, scooped him up and hurled him past the corner of the vertical groove, down on to the solid metal rectangle of the elevator.

'That's the second time you've helped me,' Keill said aloud into the wind, remembering the gust that had staggered The One. 'Are you on my side now?'

It almost seemed that it was. The wind no longer threatened to sweep Keill off the elevator at any second. Instead, its titanic gusts were plastering him, almost to immobility, against the inside of the vertical groove.

He glanced up. It was a long way to go, and very little chance he would get there. The tower was now not merely trembling, but vibrating enormously, like a vast tuning-fork. And the structure seemed to have taken on a definite sideways lean. Time was running out, for anything above ground on Rilyn.

He set his jaw, fought his way to a sitting position across the groove, his left side towards its inner wall. He was just tall enough so that his shoulders pressed against one of the side walls of the groove, while the soles of his boots touched the other.

Much of a legionary's training took place in the harsh, unforgiving terrain of the Iron Mountains of Moros. So the techniques of the climber were second nature to Keill, including the method of ascending a wide crack in the rock – a fissure or 'chimney'. He had to brace his back against one side and his feet against the other, and move up step by sliding step, using friction and the strength of his legs to keep position.

Keill had done it many times. But not on a wall of smooth metal, in the midst of the most terrible windstorm in the galaxy.

Nevertheless, he began to climb.

All of his ferocious concentration gathered to focus and direct his strength. His legs were like bars of rigid steel, their lateral force keeping him braced within the groove. Pushing with his hands beneath himself, he slid his back upwards a centimetre or two. Then one foot moved up; then the other. Then the process was repeated – only a tiny advance each time, so that there could be no chance of a hand or foot slipping, toppling him back where he began.

Sweat burst from his body, as the wind swirled and stormed within the groove, trying to fling him upwards, slamming at his body as if it would break him in two. His lungs laboured to draw breath as the air was snatched from his gasping mouth by the wind. Pain grew in his legs as the cruel pressure took its toll on his muscles.

He felt all these things, but locked them away behind the diamond-hard barrier of his concentration.

With agonizing slowness, but without pause or let-up, he climbed the tower.

All sense of time drifted away, so that he could have been climbing for minutes or days. All sense of other dangers was put aside, so that if the tower had toppled at that moment,

Keill would have maintained his position until he struck the ground. Even the overwhelming, demented fury of the wind receded from his awareness, till it seemed no more than a distant roaring in his ears. He did not look up, or down; his eyes saw nothing but the wall of the groove ahead of him. And he climbed.

Slide the back up a centimetre or two. Then one foot up; then the other. Repeat the process. Repeat it again. Again. Again...

A century seemed to drift past. A millennium – an eternity. A small area of Keill's mind began to inform him, in cold, rational tones, that even a legionary's strength and determination had its limits – and that he had reached his. He continued to climb.

The small area of his mind told him that the tower was now leaning more severely, that metal supports were bending and cracking, with huge rumbling crashes of tortured metal, that it was an interesting question whether his strength or the tower's would give out first. He continued to climb.

The small, rational area of his mind went silent, and prepared itself for death.

Then his upper back slid painfully across a sharp edge of metal. Reflex flung his left arm out, and miraculously the clutching fingers found a grip, and held. There was no inner wall to the groove any more; there were no side walls.

He was at the top.

With the last desperate remnants of his strength he dragged himself sideways, on to a flat surface of metal, and rolled. For an instant the wind crushed him motionless to the metal surface where he was lying – then flicked him away, almost contemptuously. He rolled again – and fell.

The roof of the tower had been constructed some three metres below the top of its thick walls, so that it formed a broad well. Keill had rolled across the thickness of the wall, and had toppled down on to the roof.

Even then his legionary instinct twisted him as he fell, so that he landed on hands and feet, absorbing the impact, before sprawling full length in an exhausted heap.

It seemed the most pure and delicious pleasure – to lie there, letting the agony of his tormented muscles drain and fade as they relaxed, gulping deep breaths in the relative protection of the roof-well. He wanted to lie there for ever, just resting and breathing.

But then he forced his head up, to look around. And what he saw on the far side of the roof wrenched him, cold with shock and disbelief, up into a half-crouch.

The semicircular shape of the spacecraft was still there, also protected by the roof-well, and held fast by solid clamps on its landing pad. Even so, it was quivering and heaving under the impact of the wind, as if it were about to leap into the sky of its own accord.

But it was not the ship that froze Keill with horror. Nor the sight of two armed clones, also crouched low to avoid the full monstrosity of the wind. Instead it was an object lying on the roof just beside the spaceship's open airlock.

A giant human shape of golden metal.

Keill's mind blurred under the impact of the unthinkable. The One could not have survived, to reach the roof. That blast of energy exploding into the golden body would have permanently destroyed all the complex mechanisms of even the most advanced cyborg. The One must have been killed . . .

Then Keill looked more closely, and the sickening, ghastly realization struck him.

The smooth golden hood of The One's body was empty, faceless. And a seam had been opened across the metal shoulders and down the chest. Something . . . had emerged.

The One was not a cyborg, not a being in which mechanism and organism were *permanently* united. The metal body was simply an exo-skeleton – like a vastly complicated suit of golden armour, containing a myriad of high-technology servo-mechanisms, that operated the body at the command of the wearer.

Keill had killed the vehicle – but not the passenger.

The loyal clones had obviously carried The One up to the roof, and freed him from the wrecked metal body so that he could make his escape.

And then, revealed for an instant within the spaceship's airlock, Keill saw The One as he truly was.

A tiny, twisted, deformed shape, scarcely human, of mottled grey flesh. Unable even to walk, it wriggled and dragged itself with short, spindly arms, while legs that were little more than twisted tentacles trailed behind it. The head was out of proportion, huge on the grotesque body – and Keill caught a final glimpse, as it half-turned, of the puffy face, the blubbery lips contorted with effort.

Then the creature had wriggled out of sight. The airlock slammed, the heavy clamps fell away from the ship as its energy drive bellowed into life.

With a raging yell of his own, Keill sprang up, his gun flashing into his hand. But the ship lifted at once, yawing and swerving as the wind's fury struck it, and Keill's beam merely flamed harmlessly against a jutting portion of undercarriage. He fired again, begging the wind to strike the ship down – but the wind seemed to sweep it upwards, aiding its flight, flinging it so rapidly that Keill's shots flashed through empty air.

And then Keill had to throw himself flat on the roof, for energy beams were slashing dangerously around him. The two clones – mindlessly loyal even after their leader had left them behind to die – had spotted him, and were firing furiously.

Keill raised his gun to fire back, as the clones crept determinedly towards him. But the gun only flared weakly in his hand. The energy charge was spent.

He flung it aside and gathered himself for a final rush. So he had made that agonized, suicidal climb only to watch The One flee to safety, while he met his death under the clones' guns. Very well, he thought, let it come. It had been a good fight, a good try.

The clones' guns came up, and Keill leaped towards them, knowing they were too far away, knowing that they would cut him down before he was halfway to them.

An energy gun blazed, its beam crackling as it lanced out. But the clones had not fired.

It was a beam striking from the sky. And the two clones were hurled backwards as molten metal erupted where the beam sliced into the roof.

Then they were both flung into oblivion as a gout of rocket-flame swept the roof clear.

Retro-rockets. The retros of Keill's ship, plunging through the titanic frenzy of the Starwind towards the tower.

And a wild, wordless, telepathic battlecry filled Keill's mind. A cry that was not his own.

'*Glr!*' His own heart-stopping exultation could not prevent him from knowing what had to be done, or from forming the mental shout with care. '*Get that other spaceship!*'

Keill, the tower is falling! It will be down in seconds!

'*Get the ship!*' Keill yelled. '*Destroy it!*'

He watched his ship pull up, its drive howling as it fought both the force of the turn and the hurricane power of the Starwind. But Glr was a pilot to be reckoned with – and hope surged within Keill as his ship arrowed away, vanishing in seconds into the darkened maelstrom of the sky.

Beneath him the roof tilted. Metal screeched and buckled – and a deep, widening crack split open the tower wall at one corner, running across the roof like a terrified living thing.

Keill was flung to his hands and knees. He waited there, unmoving, watching the final torment of the tower that would bring him his death.

The Starwind shrieked, proclaiming its final, ultimate victory.

And then its shriek was joined by the thunder of a spaceship's drive. Keill again heard the roar of retros, felt the blistering heat of their flame surging above his head.

Lifeline! Glr screamed in his mind. *Take it!*

He glanced up and saw the slender thread of the lifeline, swinging towards him from the open airlock as the ship flashed past above him. Glr's skill had timed the sweep perfectly. The lifeline slapped across his chest, and his reflexes were swift enough. He clutched it, and was yanked instantly off his feet.

From somewhere he found the strength to hang on to the line, and the extra strength to form the most urgent thought of all.

'The ship – what happened?'

Gone, Glr said swiftly. *Into Overlight as soon as it reached deep space – before I could get near.*

Keill's heart sagged. So The One had made good his escape, vanishing into the faster-than-light drive where he could not be pursued. For an instant the taste of failure struck at his will, sought to loosen the grip that was nearly tearing his arms from his shoulders as the ship curved up and away, and as the colossal force of the Starwind struck at him in a final desperate fury.

But then the line was being automatically reeled in, the safety of the airlock growing closer. While beneath him the tower came apart in a rending, grinding thunder, a blossoming orange-red explosion, vast metal fragments crashing and crumpling towards the ground, only for the Starwind to gather them up again, and fling them away into the sky like a flurry of dry leaves.

Aftermath
chapter fourteen

Keill's spaceship hurtled upwards, out of the atmosphere of the planet Jitrell, the forward viewscreens displaying the welcoming expanses of deep space.

'A friendly people,' he said idly, speaking aloud, his fingers making final adjustments at the controls.

Mudheads, every one, Glr replied. *But generous enough with their food.*

Keill laughed. 'Generous with most things.'

True, Glr said, her own laughter bubbling. *I shall always enjoy remembering your embarrassment when Tam was determined that you should have his medal.*

Keill shook his head ruefully. 'I think he was secretly relieved when I wouldn't take it. Anyway, he deserved it.'

And I? Glr teased. *Did I not deserve some official honour?*

'They couldn't have stopped you eating long enough to present it,' Keill grinned.

But the grin faded as he remembered just how much Glr deserved, for what she had been through. She had given him only the barest outline of her harrowing fight through the Starwind. But he had understood that her struggle had been a terrifying counterpart of his own climb up the tower. She, too, had fought to advance and to survive for what had seemed eternities – while with every wing-beat the wind had threatened to dash her down against the rocks or snatch her up impossibly high, to suffocate in the upper atmosphere.

But in the end, by some miracle of determination and direction-finding, she had reached the cave where the ship lay. And then, she told him with a note of shame, she had collapsed into unconsciousness as soon as the airlock had closed behind her. When she had finally awakened, and found strength enough to move, she had been unable to tell how much time had passed. She had blasted the ship into the sky, using both the drive and the forward guns to free it, in terror that she would reach Keill and the tower too late.

'You nearly did,' Keill had said lightly when she had finished her story. And then he had a further glimpse of the suffering that she had undergone – because for once Glr had had no light-hearted reply to make. Instead, a shudder had rippled through the small body, and a cloud had seemed to sweep across the brightness of her round eyes.

That had been just after they had fled the collapsing tower, to the safety of deep space. There they had waited out the storm of the Starwind, watching as the planet's atmosphere became like a monstrous living thing, in the writhing contortions of a final agony. Even after they had fled, the wind continued to rise, so that it seemed as if the very solidity of Rilyn would be split and shattered. But at last it reached its peak, and began to fade, as the rogue planet that was its cause swung further away from Rilyn.

When the storm was spent Keill and Glr plunged back down, landing near the spot where the tower had stood. Hardly a sign was left that any structure had ever stood on the plateau – only a riven hole in the earth, and a few enormous shards of metal from the tower walls, driven like gigantic knives deep into the very rock itself. The surface of Rilyn was as silent as before, scoured and desolate, with almost no trace of the tough shrubbery or the green carpet of moss. They would need many years before the remaining few fragments of roots could grow and sprout and spread again.

Keill had used his communicator to contact the Jitrellian authorities and explain some of what had happened, then had begun his own search for Tam. In the end it had been Glr who spotted him, from the air, lying half-dead at the mouth of a cave, having crawled out when the wind had dropped.

But he had revived quickly in his delight at seeing Keill alive – and when a substantial force of armed Jitrellians had landed, Tam had insisted on joining them, and Keill, in a thorough combing of the surrounding terrain, in case any of the clones had also survived.

They had come upon several battered bodies, pulped beyond recognition, in caves that had been too open, or shallow. And then in the bowels of a deeper cave they found two clones who had managed to stay alive. Even then their stony loyalty to the Deathwing could not be put aside: they resisted, injuring three Jitrellians before the combined laserifles of the rest of the force cut them down.

Then the Jitrellians thankfully left the desolate destruction on Rilyn and swept back to their home world, bearing Keill and Glr and the delighted Tam to be greeted as conquering heroes. Tam told his story over and over, to the authorities, to the media, to anyone who would listen. But Keill stayed as far out of the limelight as he could, making no mention of the word Deathwing or of a golden, metallic giant.

During his captivity in the tower Tam had decided that the clones were a new variety of space pirates who had set up a base on Rilyn. And Keill did not contradict the story, which became the official version. Then, as soon as he could without hurting Jitrellian feelings, he had escaped from the ceremonies and the celebrations, and had taken Glr and himself off-planet, into the peaceful anonymity of space.

As the ship left Jitrell's atmosphere, Keill released control to the computer guidance system and let himself sag back into the slingseat. He and Glr would now drift awhile, resting and recuperating from the injuries and the batterings that they both had suffered. But he knew that this time of peace would not last long. The Warlord had suffered a major setback – but he was far from defeated. There was no telling how soon, or where, the next battlefield would present itself.

He glanced towards Glr, whose round eyes were staring into space as if she were again reliving that final, hideous day of the Starwind.

'You must have contacted the Overseers by now,' he said, a wry irony in his voice. 'I suppose they complained that I let The One get away.'

Not in so many words. They were too delighted about knowing who and what he is. They believe that, with luck, they might be able to locate such a creature, if he comes within reach of their monitors.

'Maybe they will,' Keill said. 'Because I have a feeling that The One and I are going to meet again.' His voice grew steely-cold. 'And next time only one of us will walk away alive.'

book four

Planet of the Warlord

Prisoner of the Deathwing
chapter one

The lean, dark-haired young man was the last to enter the arena. The heat of Banthei's giant sun met him like a wall – made to seem even more solid by the unbelievable noise. More than a hundred thousand Bantheins, in steeply banked tiers rising high above the oval arena, roared their welcome to the fourteen combatants.

Within that avalanche of sound, the young man could hear his own name being chanted by a section of the crowd that was clearly backing him to win.

'Ran-dor! Ran-dor! Ran-dor!'

As the Banthei officials began the opening ceremony, the young man moved into the shade cast by the three-metre height of the arena's containing wall, and stood relaxed, his arms loosely folded. He was slightly above average height, well-muscled, with the balanced litheness of the trained athlete. His dark-grey trousers and boots might have been part of a uniform, but with them he wore only a light, loose-fitting shirt that left his arms bare from the shoulders. In that arena, among the mostly hulking and often misshapen forms of the other combatants, he seemed slight, and unimpressive.

He was also the only one of the fourteen who was empty-handed.

Two voices reached him, over the crowd's uproar, from near the edge of the arena.

'I tell y', he's got t' be,' one voice was saying. 'Y' seen him fight. An' somebody seen him dressed, with th' thing on his tunic – y' know, insignia.'

'Sun's got t' y', the second voice scoffed. 'They're all dead, ev'body knows it. Planet blew up, or somethin'.'

The young man in the arena glanced round and saw two flashily dressed Banthein gamblers staring down at him. He turned away again, his face showing nothing of the grim satisfaction that he felt.

The rumours had been spreading fast. Most of the crowd had quickly learned that Keill Randor was the name of the young man who, for four days, had been barehandedly sweeping aside some of the galaxy's finest warriors. Now they were beginning to learn the rest of the story – that Keill Randor was said to be the last known survivor of the Legions of Moros, the renowned martial race that had been wiped out when their planet was mysteriously destroyed.

Not many of the crowd were aware that the planet Moros and the Legions had in fact been murdered, in a monstrous sneak attack by an unknown enemy.

And not one of the crowd would ever know the real reason why Keill Randor, the last legionary, had abandoned the Legion principles of discretion, of keeping yourself to yourself, and had come to compete in the individual combat section of the galaxy's most popular and exciting entertainment event – the annual Battle Rites of Banthei.

The crowd was growing even more feverish as the voices of the officials droned on. Keill let his eyes stray over a section of the huge throng. He knew it was unlikely that he would spot anything in that mass of people. But he also knew that someone else was studying the crowd, on his behalf.

As if on cue, a voice spoke to him – not aloud, but in a silent mind-to-mind communication.

I have never known so many humans cling to one state of mind for so long, the voice said, with a hint of bubbling laughter.

It was the voice of Keill Randor's friend and companion, Glr – an alien being from another galaxy, small, female, winged, and telepathic. She was high above the arena, riding the thermals on her broad, membranous wings, invisible against the sun. And from there she was using her telepathic powers to scan, as best she could, a hundred thousand human minds.

Keill knew that Glr could project with ease, but found most human minds too alien and clouded to be read clearly or in depth. She could take thoughts from his mind, perhaps because the self-discipline bred into every legionary made his mind especially clear. But even then, Keill had to form his mental words with care, as if projecting them on an inner screen for Glr to read.

'We're a bloodthirsty species, I suppose,' he replied, grinning inwardly at Glr's oft-repeated, mocking disdain for human-kind.

Children, Glr agreed. *Primitive children. But at least no one in that mob seems to be planning to spill any blood. Just to watch it being spilled.*

'Keep scanning,' Keill said.

I will. Glr's mental voice took on a tinge of severity. *I will expect a great deal of gratitude from you when this is over. Studying human minds in the mass is very like flying at speed into a mountain of mud.*

Keill laughed to himself as Glr's voice withdrew. But laughter faded as he caught the words of the official oration, and knew that the opening ceremony was about to end. He began to ready himself – gathering his balance, deepening his breathing, building his concentration and alertness.

Anyone watching would have seen no change in his easy, relaxed stance. But inside, Keill was marshalling and focusing all the power, the speed, the supremely controlled combat readiness of a legionary of Moros.

The other thirteen combatants were also readying themselves in their own way, which in most cases meant paying attention to their weaponry. Keill surveyed them carefully, for they were winners like himself, whose strength and skills had got them through the eliminating rounds of the first four days. Today would be the two final eliminations – and by the end there would be only two combatants left, to meet in the climactic fight of the sixth day of the Battle Rites.

The Rites had a long history, reaching back to a time soon after the planet Banthei had been colonized, during the centuries of mankind's Scattering throughout the galaxy. The Bantheins had turned out to be an unusually violent, aggressive group, much given to duelling, feuding and, as the colony grew and developed, localized warring. Some wise ruler had decided that it would be better to turn that tendency into a ritual, before the colonists could wipe themselves out.

Over the centuries the Battle Rites had developed into a gigantic, highly commercialized entertainment, drawing visitors and contestants from all over the Inhabited Worlds. At this very moment, Keill knew, elsewhere on Banthei armies of men were marching against one another, guided by intricate battle plans, where victory would be won by the most skilful strategist, without a single shot being fired. On another battlefield, huge high-technology war machines, robot-controlled, were fighting thunderous, earth-shaking battles on land and at sea. Above them, fleets of robot aircraft wove intricate patterns in the skies and blew each other to bits. And even above them, squadrons of robot spaceships clashed at terrifying speeds and with more terrifying weapons.

All these battles would be watched by millions of avid spectators, on giant viewscreens around the planet – and by many millions more throughout the Inhabited Worlds, on vid-tapes. But for all those hundreds of millions of viewers, the main attraction was the individual combat section, when for five days groups of fighting men and women, fourteen at a time, entered the oval arena and fought with bloody fury until only one from each group remained standing.

The winner of the final combat would be, for a while, one of the most famous and admired people in the galaxy. Even the names of the runners-up – those who survived till the fifth day – would be on the lips of humans on nearly every Inhabited World. So already there would be few people in mankind's galaxy who had not heard that one of those survivors was Keill Randor, the last legionary of Moros.

But for Keill himself, it mattered only that *one* person, out of all the billions, knew of his presence on Banthei.

The official oration wound down, the ceremony came to an end. And the crowd screamed expectantly as the combatants began to move, seeking favourable positions, sizing up their opponents.

Keill stood as quietly relaxed as ever, lowering his hands to his sides. In front of him, a bulky figure wearing a light kilt of metallic cloth turned and glared towards him.

Many of the best fighters in the Rites came from the Altered Worlds – planets where the environment, over generations, had wreaked changes on the basic human form. The man now sidling towards Keill was one such – squat and inhumanly broad, with leathery reddish skin, his small hairless head set low in the midst of massive, humped shoulder muscles. In one huge paw he held a weapon that was both a bludgeon and a short sword – a heavy, gnarled club with a razor-sharp blade set edgeways along its length.

There were only two rules governing the individual combat of the Battle Rites. First, quite simply, there was to be no killing. A combatant could wound, maim and disable opponents as much as he liked. But if anyone was killed, even accidentally, the killer would at once be disqualified, fined, and forbidden ever to compete again. Which, it had seemed to Keill, would not be much comfort to the victim . . . But it was the rule.

The second rule banned all high-technology weapons. Competitors could use only primitive, traditional weapons, and a team of inspectors made sure that this rule was strictly observed.

Keill Randor was the first man for twenty years to fight in the Battle Rites using only his bare hands.

The arena began to echo with the yells and grunts of furious combat, the clash of weapons, as the club-wielder edged warily closer to Keill. Still Keill had not moved. Then the other man's eyes glittered, and he lunged forward, the bladed club slashing with surprising speed towards Keill's legs.

But Keill was no longer there. Without apparently gathering or bracing himself, he had leaped – not just above the weapon, but high in the air, above the very head of the squat club-wielder.

The man had perhaps only just noticed that his opponent was somehow in the air above him, when Keill's boot slammed down with measured precision on the top of the hairless pate.

The impact drove the squat man face-down and unconscious on to the artificial turf that was the arena's floor. By then, using the club-wielder's head as a springboard, Keill had flung himself into a controlled, headlong dive at two other combatants.

One was a heavily built woman, wearing a decorated helmet and body armour, swinging a long two-handed sword. She was facing a tall, powerful man whose body was entirely covered with a pelt of thick white fur, and who was defending himself with a short stabbing spear, a wickedly barbed metal head on a wooden shaft. Neither of them was aware of Keill until he crashed down upon them, all three tumbling to the ground in a tangle of flailing limbs and weapons.

Few eyes in the crowd could have been quick enough to see the movement of Keill's fist. The blow travelled only a few centimetres, but Keill had instantly found the balance he needed to put all his power behind it. As he came to his feet to confront the fur-covered warrior, the woman remained down, gasping and retching weakly, with a deep, fist-sized dent in her armour directly over the pit of her stomach.

The crowd whooped as the furred man feinted at Keill, and then stabbed towards him, lightning-quick, with the short spear. But the point struck only empty air. Keill had spun inside the blow, close to the furred body, with his back to his opponent. As he did so, the edge of his right hand chopped down at the thick haft of the spear, slicing through it as cleanly as if he had used an axe. And in the same instant his left elbow drove backwards in a precise smash against the edge of the white-furred jaw.

He had carefully weighted the blow, mindful of the rules. So it was only the jaw that broke, and not the neck, as the furred man crashed to the ground. The crowd screamed with delirious joy. It screamed again as Keill leaped without pause towards the other competitors.

The untrained observer might have seen them as a tangled and confused mêlée, a wild jumble of heaving, flailing, surging bodies and weapons. But as Keill plunged among them, the combat computer that was the mind of a fighting legionary was sorting all the movements within the tangle, and directing his own movements at incomparable speed. In slow motion it might have looked like a finely controlled and smoothly flowing ballet, as Keill spun, twisted, swivelled and leaped in the midst of the others.

But ballet dancers do not include, in their repertoire, bone-crushing blows of fist or boot. Every eye-baffling move of Keill's brought a moment when an opponent collapsed – into glazed unconsciousness, or with a cracked bone, or with a nerve centre disabled with pain.

Until finally there was only one left, backing warily from the lean figure of the legionary who stood calmly amid the heap of fallen bodies.

The crowd went berserk with joy.

Then the sound faded to a tense, expectant rumble, as the two men considered each other. And in the lull Glr's voice reached tentatively into Keill's mind.

Keill, I have picked up a trace. Some mind down there is very nervous, very on edge. And I glimpsed the mental image of an energy rifle.

'Can you pinpoint him?' Keill asked.

You seek miracles, Glr replied testily. *One individual in this ocean of crazy mudheads for whom you are showing off?*

'Try,' Keill said, smiling inwardly. 'While I get back to . . . showing off.'

355

Glr withdrew, laughing, and Keill turned his full attention back to his last opponent. He was a broad-shouldered man, a head taller than Keill, wearing a leather tabard of deep blue that might have seemed black, had it not rested against the pure and total black of the man's skin. The skin gleamed and shone as if the man were carved in obsidian, and Keill knew that it was nearly as hard – a mutated substance like the chitin of an insect's carapace.

Keill also knew, from the previous days, about the man's weapon – a long steel staff with a heavy club-head at each end. From each club-head bristled slender spikes, like thick hairs, which carried a substance that caused instant, if temporary, paralysis.

Keill stepped forward, his balance precise, his concentration total. The black man also moved forward, spinning his strange weapon as he did so. The spin grew faster as the weapon moved from one hand to the other in a bewildering blur, creating an eerie, menacing howl, forming an almost unchallengeable shield in front of its wielder.

But the skilful spin weaved a pattern, and patterns repeat themselves. It proved to be a serious mistake. Keill's eye was quick enough to detect the pattern – and to interrupt it.

Moving at a speed that made it invisible, his hand clamped on to the long steel staff, halting its spin with a grip that was no less steely. And before either the black warrior or the crowd had fully registered what had happened, Keill struck. Three times, with fist, knee and boot, so swiftly that the blows seemed to be simultaneous, to elbow, kneecap and solar plexus.

The black man hurtled backwards, an arm and a leg numbed, breath driven from his lungs, muscles turned to jelly. He struck the ground heavily, landing in a foolish half-seated position – leaving Keill standing with the two-headed weapon in his grasp.

The crowd shrieked with ecstasy, and then fell silent again as Keill shifted his grip on the weapon. Careful of the poisoned spikes, he slid his hands along the thick rod so that he was gripping it near each club-head, holding it before him. For an instant he was still, focusing his power. Then slabs of hard muscle leaped into corded, sculptured relief on his arms and upper body. Slowly, steadily, as he exerted pressure, the heavy steel rod bent double, until it was a perfect inverted U.

The crowd's thunderous rapture reached new heights, and then rose even higher when Keill turned and casually, as if with distaste, tossed the bent weapon aside. But it had been a studied throw – and the U-shape of metal looped through the air towards the still half-seated form of its owner. The club-heads missed his head, but the inner curve of the U caught him neatly across the throat, so that he toppled backwards wearing his own weapon like an ungainly collar.

And a hundred thousand people were on their feet, howling the name of the man standing alone in the centre of the arena.

'Ran-dor! Ran-dor! RAN-DOR!'

Feeling slightly foolish, Keill did what was called for – raising one hand in a sweeping gesture of acknowledgement. And the entire stadium seemed in danger of collapse as the crowd stamped and shrieked its tumultuous applause.

Glr is right about showing off, Keill thought ruefully. But there's no point in making yourself bait, if the fish doesn't notice you.

If that thought was directed at me, mudhead, Glr's inner voice said sharply, kindly form it again, more clearly.

'It was nothing,' Keill replied, as he began to walk towards the combatants' exit from the arena, stepping round the medics who were coming out to gather up the losers. 'What about that rifleman?'

As yet . . . Glr began. But then her silent voice rose into an urgent shout. Keill – MOVE!

With a legionary's unhesitating reflexes, Keill hurled himself into a shallow sideways dive while Glr's warning cry was still forming in his mind.

As he did so, the unmistakable crackling hiss of an energy beam sliced through the air above him.

chapter two

Keill's swift dive ended in an athletic shoulder roll, that brought him smoothly to his feet. At once he was up and running, as Glr's voice sounded again in his mind.

I see him! Across the arena from you – near the top! Bright green tunic – and the rifle . . !

But the rifle was making its own presence known. Twice more, as Keill sprinted in the direction Glr had indicated, an energy beam crackled dangerously near to him. Then Keill was at the wall of the arena, leaping to catch the top of it, pulling himself effortlessly up and over.

He's turning, running! Glr cried.

So were quite a few thousand people. The shots, the attempted killing, had sent the section of the crowd around the gunman into a screaming panic. Ahead of Keill, the steep ramp that offered passage between the tiers of seats was thronged with terrified, milling people. And among them, near the upper end of the ramp, Keill caught a glimpse of bright green, saw the glint of metal as the rifle was used like a club to clear the gunman's path.

Keill flashed up the ramp, using his reflexes to cleave through the frantic mob. Once again he glimpsed bright green, disappearing into the surging horde who were all trying to get out of the exit at once. In a few strides Keill too was at the exit, battling his way through.

He is moving towards the spaceport complex, Glr's voice came again. *Towards our pad!*

The stadium containing the arena was the centre of a huge, linked complex of buildings, all devoted to the administration of the Battle Rites. On the tops of some of the buildings special landing pads for spacecraft had been built, reserved for those off-world combatants who, like Keill, arrived in their own ships.

In moments Keill, guided by Glr, was bursting in through the door of one of the buildings, and hurtling up the moving walkway that spiralled through all the levels. There was no doubt that his quarry was still ahead of him. Most of the people on the walkway had drawn aside to its edges, and were staring up with expressions of surprise or fear – as people would do if they had just been thrust aside by a running man carrying an energy rifle.

Keill's headlong rush did not slow. At the topmost level of the building, there was usually a Banthein guard on duty, to protect the landing pad and the privacy of the off-world competitors. But again it was clear that the rifleman had passed this way, for the guard lay inert and bleeding by the entrance.

Keill sprang out on to the open surface of the pad, veering side-ways into cover behind the nearest ship. There he waited, listening. The sun's heat was ferocious, intensified by reflection from the plasticrete of the pad, and from the gleaming surfaces of the half-dozen spacecraft, dispersed across the pad's broad expanse.

He came out on to the pad, Glr announced, *but he vanished into the ship with green markings. Near ours, at the centre.*

Warily Keill edged forward, towards the blunt wedge-shape of his own ship, its sky-blue Legion circlet glistening. In the space nearest it was an angular, green-decorated vessel, bulging with exterior hardware. Keill crouched low as he drew closer. But the landing pad was silent in the sun's furnace blast. No energy rifle spat its deadliness towards him; no figure in bright green could be seen.

He has gone to ground, Glr said, excitement in her voice. Keill glanced up, smiling, as she swooped down towards him with a thrum of wings.

Between the broad, delicate membranes of the wings Glr's body was slight, less than half Keill's height, covered with overlapping plates of thick, soft skin. Her head was high-domed, with a snubbed muzzle and two perfectly round, clear, bright eyes. Her feet, tucked up beneath her, were in fact hands, small but sturdy and capable.

'Don't come too close,' Keill warned. 'That gunman could pick you off.'

As he could have picked you off, Glr said sharply, while you postured in the arena. And you assured me that they would not be likely to kill you!

'I don't think he was trying to,' Keill said soothingly. 'No assassin would miss by so much, so often.'

Then what was he doing? Glr demanded.

'When we find him,' Keill said reasonably, 'we'll ask him.'

And how do we find him?

Keill smiled. 'I go into his ship, and invite him out.'

Glr was silent for a moment, and then her laughter rose, almost reluctantly. Try not to get shot. Think of how disappointed all the millions of your admirers would be.

'I wouldn't dream of it.' Keill grinned. 'Keep watch a moment while I get a gun. He might have some friends in there.'

As Glr wafted upwards again, Keill moved to his own ship – which, like many other competitors, he used as a dwelling while on Banthei. Once inside, he reached for the tunic of his uniform, which also bore the blue Legion circlet. Despite the heat, he always felt uncomfortable out of uniform for too long.

He did not see the tiny capsule tucked undetectably in the tunic's folds. Not till it burst, with a sound like a muffled sneeze, and enveloped him in a clinging cloud of grey vapour.

Gas, his mind told him, as his vision began to fade and his legs became unwilling to support him. He had time to feel a slight surprise, that anyone had had the technological skill to penetrate the locking devices of a Legion ship. And he even had time, as the greyness drew him down into unconsciousness, to feel a mild regret that he would not after all be taking part in the climax of the Battle Rites of Banthei.

❖

He awoke as always into full alertness, registering that he was naked but unharmed, save for a distant headache and a bitter taste in his mouth. When he opened his eyes, a sweeping glance showed him an empty, indirectly lit room, with totally featureless matt-grey walls, floor and ceiling – the whole room not more than six metres long, about three metres wide. He was alone, lying on a narrow bed that resembled a spaceman's bunk, bonded solidly to wall and floor. At the end of the bed lay his clothes – his full uniform, but without weapons.

He came to his feet, letting his inner control deal with the surge of nausea, and dressed swiftly, then began a careful examination of the room.

Artificial light emerged from a source at the junction of wall and ceiling, where there were also small vents admitting conditioned air. In one corner were minimal plumbing facilities, and on the floor nearby were containers of water and food concentrates.

Everything that the well-furnished cage needs, he thought wryly.

In one end wall was the door, tightly sealed with an almost invisible seam. Keill ran his fingers over the cool, metallic surface. Then he stepped back, breathing deeply, gathering himself – and launched himself explosively forward. One leg swung up as if he were hurdling some low barrier, and his booted foot smashed against the edge of the door like a battering ram.

Very few kinds of sheet metal would have withstood that powered assault. But this room proved to be clad in a substance that Keill had not encountered before. What had seemed to his fingers to be hard and metallic became, under the impact, soft and yielding, absorbing the power of the kick, as if that very impact had somehow changed the essential nature of the metal. Yet immediately afterwards it was as before – cool and seemingly hard to the touch of a finger, the matt-grey surface unmarked.

He nodded to himself once, acknowledging defeat, and went

calmly back to the bed, sitting quietly on its edge. Knowing that he could not break out left him no option but to wait, until something happened to change his circumstances. So he waited, relaxed and still, without the anger or fretful anxiety that would burn away his inner stamina.

Time passed emptily, but his relaxed patience did not fray. At times he rose to rinse his mouth out with water, to chew a few mouthfuls of food concentrates. And eventually, a change occurred. An eerie sensation floated through him, like an inner displacement, as if some unseen force was trying to rearrange the cells of his body.

He was not disturbed, for he knew the feeling. And it confirmed his guess – that he was a prisoner on a spaceship. The odd sensation was the effect of a ship entering or leaving Overlight – the mysterious field that allowed a ship to bypass real space and time, and to leap across the empty immensities between the stars.

Almost at once Glr's voice slipped into his mind. *Welcome back.*

Keill had expected her, knowing that while Glr's telepathic powers had no limits in space, she could not locate him when he was moving in Overlight. Which meant that the ship carrying him had just re-entered normal space.

'*Not much welcome here,*' he replied flatly, and described his situation. '*Can you tell me what happened, and where I am?*'

Swiftly, Glr told him. Back at the launching pad she had had to watch, unarmed and outnumbered, as men in uniforms like the rifleman had rushed from the green-marked ship towards Keill's, reappearing shortly with Keill's inert body. They had re-entered their vessel, which had lifted off almost at once. Glr had quickly taken Keill's ship up in pursuit. But of course she had lost them when their ship, reaching deep space, had vanished into the pathless void of Overlight, where they could not be tracked.

Clearly you were right, Glr added. *The one with the rifle was not trying to kill you – just to draw you out of the arena.*

Keill agreed. '*If they are who we think they are, they'll have special plans for me. Now – can you tell me where I am?*'

As I have told you before, Glr replied, *I can pinpoint the location of your mind across the galaxy. Unfortunately, that is almost how far apart we are. You have been most of a day in Overlight – and it will take me that long to catch up with you. The ship you are on is approaching a distant solar system that, according to your star charts, contains one planet inhabited by humans. A world called Golvic.*

Keill felt none the wiser, for he had never heard of Golvic. But behind the barrier of his rigid self-control, he felt a keen anticipation. He had gone to Banthei for the single purpose of exposing himself, making himself bait in hope of bringing a fearsome enemy out of hiding. There could be little doubt that the plan had worked.

Now Keill was sure that the planet called Golvic would provide some new developments in the deadly search that had occupied him for so long.

It was a search that had begun for Keill Randor on the terrible day when he returned to his planet, Moros, and found a dead world, enveloped in a strange radiation that had wiped out all life. Keill himself had come close enough to be touched by the edge of the radiation, and afterwards found that the radiation had entered his bones, and was slowly killing him.

In the time he had left, Keill had gone out among the Inhabited Worlds on a relentless quest for some clue to the identity of the murderer of Moros. But it had seemed hopeless. No one had any information, and his time was running out. Yet, meanwhile, others had been seeking him.

He had been gathered up by a group of mysterious brilliant scientists, whom he came to know as the Overseers. And with their amazing skills and knowledge, they had healed him – by *replacing* his radiated bones. They gave him a new skeletal structure, made of a unique organic alloy – with a special side-effect. The material was virtually unbreakable.

If that had astonished Keill, he was astonished even more by the story that the Overseers had told him, through their elderly leader, Talis. Keill learned that the Overseers too were seeking the murderer of Moros, and had been doing so for some time before the attack on the Legions.

Talis told him that they had become aware of an evil force at work among the Inhabited Worlds. They had been unable to learn who or what it might be, or where it was located. But its intentions were plain to the Overseers, in their wide-ranging study of galactic events.

The force, or being, was dedicated to stirring up the horror of war wherever possible among mankind's worlds. So the Overseers had given that unknown being a suitable name. They called him . . . the Warlord.

The Warlord seemed to be using the old human failings – greed, fear, bigotry, power hunger – to turn people towards war, to set race against race, planet against planet. It became clear that his ultimate aim was to spread the infection so widely that the whole galaxy would be plunged into conflict. And out of the ruins of that final holocaust, the Warlord would emerge – to rule supreme over what was left of the Inhabited Worlds.

When the Overseers first understood the Warlord's existence, and the nature of his plans, they had left the separate, peaceful lives that they were leading, and had retired to a secret base, built within the interior of an uncharted asteroid. From there they kept up their investigation, sending out a host of unique monitoring devices to scan as many of the Inhabited Worlds as possible. So they hoped to learn more about the Warlord, and how to oppose him.

But they found that he was as secretive and well-hidden as themselves. He operated through agents, who did his work on other planets, sowing the seeds of war, but who had no direct contact with the Warlord himself. And the Overseers began to feel that they, too, needed an agent out among the worlds.

Then came the horror of Moros. The Legions, whose planet's

only natural resource had been the martial skills of its people, had always made those skills professionally available to others. But it was well known that they would not fight on the side of aggressors or exploiters or anyone who was launching an unjust war. More often they hired out their services to those defending against such attacks.

Clearly these ethics would have posed a threat to the Warlord. So he had destroyed the Legions, in a pre-emptive strike, before they could learn of his existence and perhaps move against him.

But Keill Randor had survived that destruction, and in him, the last legionary, the Overseers had seen an ideal agent for their purposes. So they had gathered him up and healed him. And so, in turn, Keill had agreed to work with them. With life and hope restored, he had resumed his search for the murderer of Moros, knowing now just how much more was at stake than his own vengeance.

In his quest he was accompanied by Glr, the alien wanderer who had, much earlier, met and befriended Talis and the Overseers, and who had readily joined in Keill's search. Since then they had had several encounters with agents of the Warlord, and had learned much.

They had learned that some of those agents formed an elite group that called itself the Deathwing. The leader of the Deathwing, known as The One, was the only person with direct contact with the Warlord. And eventually, inevitably, the time came when Keill Randor met and faced The One.

He had barely escaped with his life – but The One had also escaped. And since then the Overseers had turned all their efforts to the more particular task of locating The One, hoping that through him they might learn the whereabouts of the Warlord.

During that time Keill had come as close as he ever had to impatience. The Overseers' monitoring devices were concentrated on looking for clues to the location of one person among many billions. And while the Overseers laboured to gather, sift, collate and study the information from the monitors, Keill and Glr remained idle.

So Keill had devised his plan. If he could not go and find The One, he would let The One find him. He was certain that his enemy would not pass up a chance to take revenge for the way Keill had defeated him and thwarted one of the Warlord's central plans. So Keill had gone – with some sense of shame, since it went against the Legions' preference for keeping out of the limelight – to compete in the much-publicized Battle Rites.

As Keill had anticipated, the Deathwing became aware of his presence on Banthei. As he had also predicted, The One did not send men to kill him, but to capture him. It would be the Deathwing way, to seek a more prolonged and satisfying revenge.

The bait had been taken. Now, Keill thought wryly, we have to make sure the bait survives.

chapter three

Keill had begun a series of basic Legion exercises, adapted for the cramped space, both to keep himself occupied and to rid his body of the last effects of the gas. So he was upside down, balanced on the splayed fingertips of one hand, when he sensed a change in the light within the room that was his prison.

He came effortlessly to his feet, and found to his astonishment that one wall of the room had become entirely transparent. Beyond it, five men were watching him.

They were all dressed like the rifleman on Banthei, in long belted tunics of bright green, high-collared and reaching nearly to their boot tops. Four of the men also wore bulky protective helmets – and those four seemed to be of the same race. They were all unnaturally tall and thin, with a greyish cast to their skin. Their features were clustered together in the middle of their faces – small puffy mouths, narrow eyes, noses not much more than slits in the grey flesh.

Keill smiled grimly to himself. He had seen a face like that before.

But his outward expression did not change, nor did he move. The four men were carrying energy rifles of very advanced design, aimed unwaveringly at Keill.

The fifth man wore a similar green tunic, but without the helmet, and with an energy handgun strapped at his waist. He was of a different race, closer to the human norm – about Keill's height, though even leaner, with grey hair clipped short and wide-set eyes that seemed to glow with a light of their own. The eyes of a fanatic, Keill thought – or a madman.

And it was the fifth man who broke the silence, his cold voice coming to Keill through the air-vents in the now transparent wall.

'The first thing you must understand, Randor,' he said, 'is that you are entirely helpless. I am required to keep you alive, but my orders say nothing about you being intact, or uninjured.'

Keill digested the information silently. That was final confirmation that the gunman on Banthei had not been shooting to kill. It was even very likely that the man who had fired that gun into the arena was now standing before him.

'You have already discovered the properties of your cage,' the other man was saying. 'The planet Golvic is renowned for its imaginative genius in technology. I strongly doubt if you could ever find a way through these walls. Should you do so, however, these men will be waiting.' One narrow hand gestured to the four riflemen. 'They are all excellent shots.'

He paused, as if expecting a reply. But Keill waited, silent and watchful. The man's eyes flared brighter for an instant, and his lipless mouth twisted in what might have been a smile.

'I am Festinn,' the man said. 'You may freely ask me questions – I wish you to have no doubts or illusions about your position.'

'Is that,' Keill said with studied insolence, 'the standard uniform of the Deathwing these days?'

Again the twisted grin. 'It is the uniform of the militia on Golvic. Some of the Deathwing—' he made Keill a mocking little bow— 'wear it out of courtesy while we are there. As we soon will be, all of us.'

'Where I'll no doubt meet some old friends,' Keill said sardonically.

Festinn laughed, an ugly sound. 'You will find many surprises awaiting you, Randor. And you will have plenty of time to savour them.' The light in his eyes blazed up again. 'Because you will never leave Golvic alive.'

The planet Golvic, Glr informed Keill, *has come up on the viewscreens. I will be in a landing orbit shortly.*

'*Maybe you should stay out there*,' Keill replied. He did not doubt that Golvic, like most worlds, would have orbital detectors scanning the planet's territorial space.

What use am I going to be to you, Glr asked, *sitting in deep space?*

'*More use than if the Golvicians spot you and blast you out of the sky*,' Keill said.

Perhaps. But you are certainly not going to free yourself without my aid.

Keill smiled. Glr seldom missed a chance to inform him how much he needed her. '*I'm not sure I want to make a break yet. I may be able to learn more as a prisoner than as a fugitive.*'

What more is there to learn, other than the Deathwing plans to kill you? Glr said chidingly. Keill had told her, as soon as she had emerged from Overlight, about his encounter with Festinn.

'*Not yet*,' Keill reassured her. '*They'll have other ideas for me, first. It'll be interesting to find out what they are.*'

Interesting? Glr's repetition of the word came as close as possible to a telepathic snort. *Then while you sit there being interested, I shall land on Golvic.*

According to the ship's detectors, she informed him, much of the land surface of Golvic was bleak, rolling desert. She intended to come down at high speed, and seek a suitable hiding place among the dunes, where the ship should be able to escape discovery.

Once I have landed, she went on, *I will wait for night and make my way to wherever you are. Even if the ship is spotted, the Golvicians will not be looking up in the air for its occupant.*

'*I suppose that's true*,' Keill said reluctantly. '*And I may well need some of your valuable aid.*'

Without any doubt, Glr said triumphantly, and withdrew her mind.

Keill lay back on the narrow bed, smiling. Let's hope that nothing too exciting happens before she gets here, he thought idly.

He passed the time that followed with more of the muscle-tuning exercises, alternating with periods of deep relaxation when he sought to tune his mind as fully as his body. Hours later he was still calm, relaxed and alert when he felt the heavy vibration of the ship's descent to a planet's surface. And soon after the landing was completed, the wall of his cage shifted again into full transparency.

Outside, as before, Festinn stood with his four riflemen. Keill began to rise from the bunk.

'There is no need to disturb yourself.' Festinn grinned mockingly. 'A transport is waiting that will take your entire cage. You will remain within it until we reach Golv City, the capital of this world. Also, my men and I will be watching you. I expect the journey to be without incident.'

In a short while, Keill was sitting quietly in his cage within the broad interior of a heavy transport flyer, sweeping across the strange landscape of Golvic. Festinn had not been exaggerating, Keill realized, about the level of Golvician technology. There was the cage itself, with the unique material of its walls which also contained the polarizing effect that allowed transparency. There was the silent, invisible tractor beam that had efficiently plucked the cage out of the spaceship and loaded it on the flyer. And there was the appearance of the planet itself.

As far as Keill could tell from glimpses through the transport's forward windows – for Festinn had left the cage wall transparent, to keep a watch on Keill – the capital, Golv City, must have contained most of the population of the planet. The city seemed to stretch to the far horizon – a gigantic, sprawling monster of a metropolis. The buildings were widely spaced at the fringes, especially near the spaceport, but they soon grew more dense, so that kilometre upon kilometre of Golvician architecture stretched below the flyer.

The transport moved unhurriedly, a robot mechanism apparently guided by an invisible power beam. And the air was thronged with other traffic, flyers of every shape and size, weaving intricate patterns among the upper levels of the taller buildings. Below, a minimal amount of ground traffic moved in similarly controlled lines.

Golvicians seem to like their roadways straight, Keill mused. And their buildings, mostly made from what looked like a metallic stone, were as orderly and disciplined. Their heights and breadths varied extensively, with vast skyscraping towers especially prominent, but always the edges were tidy, the corners square, the surfaces smooth and nearly featureless. After a while, the eye might cry out for a curve, a roundness, or any pleasing effect within the vast regimented march of architecture – made even less appealing by the chill, wintry grey of the Golvician climate.

Keill was still studying the cityscape, interested in what it revealed of the technological Golvician mind, when Glr spoke to him.

The ship is safely down, and I have found a place to wait until nightfall. Where are they taking you?

'*I'm not sure,*' Keill told her, briefly describing what had been happening.

Wherever you are, I will find you. Glr's voice grew serious. *Do nothing rash until I come.*

Right now, Keill thought sourly to himself, looking at the walls of his cage, I can't think of anything to do at all.

The sky was beginning to darken with approaching dusk by the time the transport swept in to land, on a broad plasticrete apron in front of an enormous building that dominated the far side of Golv City. It was many levels high but even more immense in breadth, sprouting many extensions, wings, annexes, and other additions that were all as bleakly tidy and uniform as the central structure.

Festinn stood up as the flyer came to rest. 'This can be called the nerve centre of Golvic.' He grinned as if at some private joke. 'Some day soon, it may serve as the centre of the entire galaxy. You will find it . . . interesting.'

Keill looked at him expressionlessly, but his mind was racing.

What did that mean? Was this building Deathwing headquarters? Or could it be a command centre of . . . even greater importance?

But there was no time to consider the mystery, for Festinn and his four men were approaching the cage, and one of the Golvicians was carrying an oddly shaped object.

As Keill rose to his feet, Festinn's hand seemed only to twitch, and the energy pistol appeared in it.

'Stay as you are,' he snapped.

Keill relaxed, impressed in spite of himself at the other man's dangerous speed.

'This man,' Festinn continued, indicating the soldier with the odd object, 'will enter the cage. You can of course overpower him, but it will serve no purpose. You will still be in the cage, and the man is expendable.'

The Golvician, unaffected by this cold statement, marched towards the cage's door. It slid aside to admit him, then slid back as tightly sealed as before.

'The object he is carrying,' Festinn said, 'is a body-shackle of Golvician design. It carries its own power source – and it is designed to tighten its clasp, if you struggle against it. Should you try to break free, Randor, at the very least it will crush your ribs. It might even kill you.'

Keill remained silent, but smiled within himself. The unbreakable skeleton given him by the Overseers was going to prove its value yet again.

The Golvician did his job indifferently and efficiently. The body-shackle, made from some heavy but flexible metal, fitted like a strait-jacket around Keill's upper body, clamping his arms tightly to his sides. And when the Golvician brought the two edges of its front opening together, they seemed to flow into one another, sealing the body-shackle almost seamlessly.

'You see what care we take with you, Randor,' Festinn said mockingly. 'The Deathwing knows that you can be dangerous. And remember that I have seen you in action, on Banthei.' His eyes glowed hotly. 'Though you might not have succeeded so well, had *I* been in the arena with you.'

Keill gazed coldly at him. 'Perhaps not – if you'd got me in a body-shackle first.'

The mad eyes blazed. 'I am the Deathwing second in command, and its premier executioner! I need no advantage . . .' Festinn broke off, calming himself with an effort. 'But you seek to anger me, hoping that *you* will gain an advantage. You will not.'

He turned to the stolid Golvician soldiers.

'Bring him. And keep your guns on him at all times.'

They marched into the mighty building, the soldiers fanning out behind Keill, Festinn leading the way. As they entered, Keill tested the shackle gently, with an imperceptible outward push of his arms. At once he felt its response as it tightened around him. He relaxed the pressure, and turned his attention to his surroundings.

Within the building, they passed through a vast, high-ceilinged entrance hall, thronged with people who halted and stared as Festinn and the riflemen conducted Keill towards a broad moving ramp that led up from the entrance hall to the higher levels.

Keill noted every detail – the many doors leading from the entrance hall, the positions of militiamen who seemed to be on guard duty, the hectic activity of the place. He glanced with interest at the Golvician civilians, tall and spindly like the rest of their race, garbed in long, flowing robes.

Many of them, he saw, wore thin, colourless cords around their heads – possibly a badge of rank.

Then they were on the moving ramp, ascending without haste. On a higher level they entered a corridor where the floor itself was a moving walkway. At its end stood a pair of impressive doors that led into a broad, equally impressive room.

Keill had been in such a room before. Its walls were lined with complex banks of communicators, data storage consoles, and other high-technology equipment. And the central area was dominated by a huge, heavy table, its surface covered with vid-screens, more computer equipment, sheaves of thin plastic printouts, all the detritus of an operational command centre.

But Keill had spared all that the briefest of glances. His attention had been fixed on the person who had been seated at the table, and who had loomed hugely to his feet as Keill and his guards entered.

A giant figure who seemed to have been shaped almost entirely of golden metal, like a perfect sculpture of the human form carved by some forgotten master.

But, in ugly contrast to the superb metal body, the golden giant had a face of flesh – the grey, puffy, small-featured face of a Golvician. It was made even uglier by the livid scar that puckered the grey flesh at the junction of the face and its golden metal hood.

Festinn's cold voice held a note of savage enjoyment. 'You have met the lord Altern before, Randor, have you not?'

Though Keill had half-expected this encounter, he felt a chill along his spine as the golden giant's small eyes fixed on him with a gaze of pure hatred.

Altern. Leader of the Deathwing. The One.

chapter four

For a prolonged moment, Keill and The One stood in silence, their gazes locked. Keill was remembering how he had last seen his enemy – when he had discovered that The One's golden body was not permanently united with his flesh, as a cyborg's body would be. It was an exo-skeleton, a covering of high-technology armour linked by servo-mechanisms to The One's real body. On their previous encounter Keill had wrecked the metal body, and had seen The One as he truly was.

Whatever mutating effect the planet Golvic had had on its human population – and Keill had no doubt that it was one of the Altered Worlds – it had wreaked terrible havoc on the being who was The One. His face and head were normal, for a Golvician, but his true body was horribly misshapen, tiny and twisted, with spindly withered arms and useless legs that were little more than tentacles. Without the golden armour he was nearly helpless, barely able to wriggle along the ground.

Now he had been supplied, by Golvician technology, with a new metal body. Once again he was a golden giant, as fearsome as before, and perhaps for Keill even more dangerous.

The One broke the silence, still without taking his hate-filled gaze from Keill.

'Festinn, you have done exceedingly well.' The voice was hollow and flat, lacking all life and resonance, as Keill remembered it. 'You shall be rewarded.'

'My thanks, lord.' Festinn's cold tones were tinged with respect.

'But I am preoccupied with many matters,' The One went on,

'and have no time for Randor now. Take him to the guardroom, until I summon you.'

'As you wish, lord.'

The One resumed his seat at the table, still with his eyes fixed on Keill.

'You are a fool, legionary,' the hollow voice said. 'You have been fortunate in the past, and have cost me many good men. But you have been opposing something of whose power you have not the slightest conception. And your time of good fortune is at an end.'

Keill remained silent, and his gaze remained steady – but he smiled slightly, derisively.

The One's puffy lips tightened, and one golden hand unconsciously reached up to touch the scar at the edge of his face. The small eyes shifted towards Festinn.

'Take him away,' The One ordered. 'And, Festinn – *watch him*!'

The guardroom lay deep in the bowels of one of the building's distant wings. Again Keill moved under the guns of the Golvician escort, with Festinn preceding, through a series of broad corridors. The passageways were as straight as the roads of Golv City, and their floors were all moving walkways as before, divided in two, to carry people in opposite directions.

Keill stood impassively throughout their progress, but his mind was busily memorizing their route through the labyrinth of the vast structure, noticing that the corridors were almost deserted as they moved farther from the great hall.

And his body was occupied too – exerting unseen pressure against the body-shackle. By the time they had reached the guardroom, the shackle was painfully tight.

The room was bare, windowless and bleak, but it did not seem to have the special features of the cage on the spaceship. As if to underline its lower level of security, Festinn ordered Keill to stretch out on the floor, and positioned the guards within the room, spread out against the walls several paces from Keill, their rifles ready.

Then Festinn left the room, with a final reminder to the guards of the need for total watchfulness. Keill was glad to see him go, knowing how much more dangerous he was than any Golvician soldier. No one became the Deathwing's principal assassin, he knew, without prodigious skills – and an equal capacity for evil.

Ignoring the silent guards, Keill turned his attention back to the body-shackle.

By then the shackle felt like an oversized vice, cramping and squeezing his flesh painfully. But Keill blocked the pain from his mind, and continued to exert pressure. The process was so gradual that the watchful guards could have seen no movement. Yet steadily, the shackle's painful grip was tightening.

I'll put you into overdrive, Keill told it grimly, and see which of us breaks down first.

Time drifted past. All of Keill's steely concentration was turned inwards, to control his movements, to resist the increasing pain of the shackle's constriction. Within a short while he could feel a patch of heat against his upper back, and guessed with satisfaction that the shackle's inner power source was heating up with the strain. Soon it grew red-hot, adding that pain to the growing torment of the constriction.

But it was only his flesh that was being hurt. His bones, he knew, could withstand more force than the shackle could exert. He continued his outward push, as imperceptibly as before. And the shackle continued to compress him more and more tightly.

At last, one of the guards leaned slightly forward, and gave a small start of surprise.

As the guard stepped forward, Keill closed his eyes to slits, let his mouth sag open, and gave a low, strangled moan. The guard leaned over, and his eyes widened as he looked at the small dials on the side of the body-shackle. Instantly he turned, with a muffled aside to the others, and hurried from the room.

377

Keill lay still, while the twin agonies gained in strength – the cruel compression of his flesh, the searing heat at his back. The body-shackle's now white-hot power source was only minutes from burning out, balked finally by Keill's uncrushable bones.

But the door was flung open and Festinn entered, followed by the nervous guard.

'. . . must be a malfunction,' the guard was saying. 'He has not moved, yet the shackle is crushing him, and seems to be overheating.'

Festinn bent close to Keill, who was lying as if half-dead, his controlled breathing almost undetectable. 'He may be attempting suicide,' Festinn snapped. 'Death before dishonour – just what a legionary might do. But he will not escape The One so easily. Raise him.'

Hands grasped Keill, lifting him roughly from the floor, and Festinn reached to open the invisible seam of the shackle. At once the agony receded from Keill's body. The relief to his bruised flesh was almost overpowering, but Keill ignored it as he had ignored the pain. He saw, through his slitted eyes, that Festinn was examining the shackle closely, with the guard who had gone to fetch him. Two of the other guards were supporting Keill on his feet, while he let his body sag as a dead weight. And the fourth guard stood by uneasily, his rifle barrel drooping.

The bruising of the flesh on his chest and arms did not slow Keill down. Without warning the two guards holding him were flung savagely, effortlessly aside, and Keill was leaping at Festinn.

The assassin's own speed was exceptional. He dropped the shackle, and one hand flashed to the gun at his belt. But he had no chance to fire it. Keill grasped and spun him, in a painful, one-handed restraining hold, while his other hand clamped on to Festinn's gun and wrenched it away. Using Festinn as a shield, Keill backed towards the door.

'How expendable do your men think *you* are, Festinn?' he snarled.

The answer came at once, as the two guards still standing swung their rifles up. But they had no chance to use them. The lethal beam of Keill's gun scythed across their chests.

As they collapsed, their tunics ablaze, Keill caught a movement on the edge of his vision. One of the guards he had hurled aside lay motionless, but the other had recovered his senses, and his rifle. In the instant before it fired, Keill flung Festinn towards it.

The beam bit deep into the assassin's shoulder. And then the two bodies collided, tumbling to the floor in a painful heap, as Keill sprang for the door.

His route lay clearly mapped in his mind, as he sprinted along the moving walkways in the corridors, Festinn's gun ready in his hand. Ahead of him the walkways were still deserted, and so he could spare part of his attention when Glr's voice spoke to him.

Keill, I do not wish to distract you. But you are in grave danger.

'*You don't have to tell me,*' Keill said, and began a quick outline of what had been happening.

There is a greater danger than The One, Glr interrupted, her voice sombre. *From the centre of that building I have sensed emanations that are more frightening than anything I have encountered in this galaxy.*

Keill slowed his headlong rush, puzzled. '*Some kind of telepath?*'

Not precisely, Glr said. *If it is a mind, I cannot penetrate it. Nor do I wish to. It is extremely powerful, and extremely evil.*

Keill was disturbed by her tone as much as her words. It was unlike Glr to be so troubled – there was no lack of courage within that small being.

'*I'll go and have a look—*' he began.

No! The word was almost a scream. *Stay away from it! Get out of that building!*

'*I will, soon,*' Keill said soothingly. '*But I didn't come here to hide from things.*'

Glr might have continued to argue. But she sensed, in the same instant that Keill did, that he had something else to occupy his attention.

From a door along the passage ahead, an armed Golvician soldier was emerging.

chapter five

The soldier made the mistake of freezing with shock, as he saw Keill hurtling towards him. Before he could begin to reach for his weapon, the rigid fingers of Keill's left hand had sunk deep into the soldier's belly – and as he doubled over with an explosive grunt of pain, a hard fist thudded into the bone behind his ear.

Warily Keill peered into the room the soldier had come from, and gratefully saw that it was empty. He dragged the soldier in, swiftly stripped the long green tunic and heavy helmet from the limp form and pulled them on over his own uniform, indifferent to the poor fit. At least the belt had a clip for the energy handgun, so that he could ignore the more unwieldy rifle that the soldier had carried.

He paused for a moment, studying the inert form of the soldier. This one, like some of the other Golvicians he had seen, wore one of the thin, pale cords around his head. If it is a badge of rank, Keill thought, should I take it? He tugged at it briefly, but it was tightly fastened – yet with no visible clip or opening.

In the end, knowing he had no time to waste, he abandoned it. He turned to the door and walked calmly, unhurriedly away along the still-deserted corridor. Until someone looks closely at my face, he thought, I might get away with this.

In fact he was confident that the disguise could have taken him safely out of the building. But instead he changed course. Despite the seriousness of Glr's warning, he needed to know what it was that could stir such fear in his little companion.

There were a few other people in the corridors now, as he approached the building's centre, and he readied himslf for instant action if it was needed. But the others moved past indifferently, preoccupied with their own business. Once a full squad of soldiers charged past him, in the opposite direction, but Keill had turned away slightly so that they saw only a green-uniformed back. They rushed on, ignoring him.

On their way to the guardroom, Keill guessed. The alarm must be out by now.

Even so, he continued to move on, rising several levels on the broad ramps. Soon his unerring sense of direction told him that he had reached the central area of the huge rambling complex. And there he began to find that many of the corridors seemed to be leading inwards, towards one section, like the radiating spokes of a wheel. At the ends of all of these corridors there were solid doors, guarded by at least two soldiers.

When he had been balked in this way for the fourth time, he made up his mind. The risk was no greater than if he remained at large in the corridors, where every Golvician soldier would soon be searching for him. Calmly he moved along one of the corridors, towards the heavy doors.

The two guards had obviously not yet heard that an escaped prisoner was at large. They seemed bored and indifferent, barely sparing him a glance as he drew near. But when he did not pause, when his hand reached out towards the doors, their rifles snapped up.

'You know you're not allowed—' one of them began.

He did not finish the sentence – partly because the shock of seeing Keill's non-Golvician face had only just reached his awareness, and partly because in the same moment all his awareness was cut off. Keill chopped down with measured power at the sides of both guards' necks, just at the junction of helmet and high collar. The guards folded as if their legs had suddenly developed extra joints, and Keill pushed at once through the heavy doors.

Beyond them there was a small, deserted space that led to

another set of doors. And these were of thick, multi-layered metal, immensely strong, and tightly locked.

Keill drew his gun. No point now in going backwards, he thought.

The beam from his gun bit hungrily into the narrow seam between the doors. Metal flared and melted under the onslaught, and in a few moments the blazing energy had done its work. The doors sagged open, and Keill slipped through, gun ready.

He found himself on a metal gantry, a narrow platform with a low railing on one side. The gantry ran round the outer perimeter of a broad, deep space – like an enormous open shaft, extending downwards at least two levels, and upwards the same distance.

But Keill was barely aware of those details, nor of the glittering incomprehensible machinery that jutted here and there from the shaft's gleaming metal walls.

His stunned gaze was fixed instead on what the shaft contained.

It floated below the gantry where he stood, near the base of the shaft, supported by an almost invisible force field. It was ovoid in shape, about three times the size of a human body. And it was multi-coloured, its hue changing constantly with the dazzling, luminous flow of energy that bathed its surface.

And from that surface, reaching upwards almost the full height of the shaft, seeming to fill all of its breadth, was a myriad of slender, almost colourless tendrils – hundreds of them, perhaps thousands, the thickness of light cords. They were in ceaseless motion, writhing, coiling, flailing, entwining, as if blindly groping through the air for some unseen prey.

Automatically Keill drew back from the edge of the gantry as some of the pale tendrils swept in his direction. And the unexpectedness of the sight, the mystery and alienness of it, had their effect even on his honed alertness.

So he had no warning when a giant golden arm closed around his throat in a crushing grip, and a golden metal hand clamped immovably on to his gun, jerking it from his grasp.

At once Keill searched for leverage for a throw that would break the grip. And he might have succeeded, despite the frightening strength of the huge metal body. But the golden giant flung him away, towards the edge of the gantry, raising the energy gun.

'Be still, Randor,' the hollow voice of The One said. 'You have trespassed where only I may enter, but I will make you welcome. You have achieved the final goal of your long search. Relish the achievement while you may.'

The words resounded within Keill's mind. *Achieved my goal? Can that mean what it seems to mean?*

Again a twisting cluster of tendrils swung towards him from the thing in the shaft. As he moved aside, the giant's hollow laughter rang out.

'Do not draw away, Randor. Here is what you wished to find. Here is the object of your quest. Step forward, Randor – and meet the Master.'

Keill felt as if his heart had stopped, as if his body had turned to frozen stone. 'This . . . this *thing* . . . is the Warlord?'

'No, legionary.'

The reply came not from The One but from above Keill's head. He looked up, and saw that into the wall of the shaft a deep, spacious alcove had been constructed. He could not see who or what was within the alcove, but the voice had sounded like many people speaking in uncannily perfect unison.

'No, Keill Randor,' the unseen voice repeated. 'That is not the Warlord. *I* am.'

His mind whirling with shock, Keill climbed a spiral metal staircase, urged on by The One's gun. When he emerged, within the wide chamber contained in the alcove, shock piled upon shock.

He was facing twenty-four Golvicians, of both sexes and various ages, wearing plain robes. They sat in heavy, mechanized chairs, their bodies thin, huddled, withered. And Keill saw that the chairs were life-support extensions, attached to a bulky console at the centre of a circle formed by the chairs, to keep the wasted bodies alive.

But also from the console rose twenty-four thick, smooth cables, like heavy power leads.

Which in a way they were, Keill guessed with sudden horror. Despite their greater thickness, the cables bore a clear resemblance to the tendrils that rose from the thing in the shaft.

And the cables reached out from the console to twine their ends round the heads of the twenty-four seated people.

'What . . .' Keill fought the sickness that rose in his throat. 'What are you? What is *it*?'

'Tell him, Altern.' The twenty-four mouths moved perfectly, eerily together, as if their owners were mechanical dolls all working on the same circuit. The single voice that emerged was soft, even mild. 'It will be interesting to assess his reaction.'

The One inclined his golden head. 'Master.' And with an evil pleasure, he replied to Keill's question.

The thing in the shaft, he said, had been named Arachnis. It was the ultimate achievement of Golvician technology. It was partly organic, but also partly pure energy – supplied by the luminous flow of power that washed over it from the energized walls of the shaft. Arachnis was not truly alive, nor did it have a mind. In a way it was like a huge, complex, artificial version of the ganglia in the human brain.

But its function was to *unite* human minds – and, in some cases, to enlarge their capability.

The Twenty-four, continued The One, were its creators, the greatest geniuses of Golvic. At first, Arachnis had been much smaller. But even then, at the beginning, when the Twenty-four had placed the heavier tendrils on their heads, it had done what it had been created for. It had united the Twenty-four into a single supermind.

And that supermind had been growing more powerful as

Arachnis, fed by the energies of the shaft, had grown larger. Now the Twenty-four formed the supreme intelligence of the galaxy, said The One. And they had recognized their destiny – to rule over all the Inhabited Worlds.

So they had devised their plan, which meant spreading the destruction of war through a host of carefully selected planets. The plan had also meant the erasure of enemies, The One added with a gloating laugh – including the Legions of Moros.

'And Arachnis serves the Master in another way,' The One went on. 'It provides him with a mental link, through which he can now reach across vast distances, even into space, to control his servants.'

'Servants?' Keill asked hoarsely, hardly able to believe the appalling tale he was hearing.

'Slaves, if you prefer,' The One replied blandly.

The terrible account went on. Some served the Twenty-four willingly, Keill heard, like The One and all the Deathwing. So they were merely guided by their Master's orders, relayed through The One. But others needed to be coerced and controlled. And so they had their minds overcome by the Arachnis link – a fragment of tendril, round their heads.

'Once the initial link is made,' The One said, 'the rest of the tendril can be withdrawn. Yet the connection remains – over almost any distance. And those in the link are powerless, no longer able to control their own being. They can perform no actions, think no thoughts, other than as the Master directs.'

The grey lips twisted in a brutal smile. 'And if the tendril fragment is removed from their heads, their minds seldom survive. They become no more than empty, mindless shells.'

Keill's fists clenched. Even his control could barely hold back the storming rage and hatred that had begun to seethe within him in the face of the madness, the cruelty, the sheer stark evil, that had been spawned by the twenty-four seated figures before him.

The One continued, picturing the day to come when the reach of the Arachnis link would extend the Master's power across the galaxy. By then the Master's plan would be nearing its climax, in the final holocaust of galactic war. But Keill scarcely heard the words. He was concentrating on regaining his control, building his combat readiness.

He seemed to be standing half-slumped, as if overcome by what he had learned. The One, arrogantly confident as ever, was not even looking directly at him, as he concluded his blood-chilling story.

And Keill exploded into a hurtling leap.

The leap ended with the hammering impact of his boot into The One's golden midriff. As the metal giant staggered back, Keill found his balance and swung round to the Twenty-four.

Inexplicably, they were smiling. Inexplicably, as he regained his feet, The One was laughing.

And Keill, about to leap again, felt as if he had stepped into the clinging, gossamer strands of a giant spiderweb.

He tried to fling himself away in frantic desperation. But the web-like tendrils of Arachnis clung, entangling him as he fought. And then, besides the hundred-fold grip on his body, he felt a feather-light touch on his brow.

As black despair swept over him like a tidal wave he heard in his mind, remote and fading, Glr's wild scream of terror.

Then silence and darkness descended. And that which had been Keill Randor had ceased to be.

Slave of Arachnis
chapter six

It was awareness, but without comprehension.

It was perception, but without reaction.

Sight, hearing, all the senses were unimpaired, so that information poured as it always had into the brain. But the mind that inhabited the brain was unable to assess, understand or use the flow of data. The flow by-passed the mind, funnelling directly to those who controlled the brain.

In the same way, messages flowed *from* the brain, along the nervous system, and the body responded as smoothly and efficiently as ever. But the messages originated from a different source, also by-passing the mind that lived within the brain.

The human mind may always remain something of a mystery. It is said that mind cannot perceive itself entirely, and so can never study itself properly. But human minds are *aware* of themselves. It is that self-awareness which sets humans apart from beasts, for a beast is said to have no sense of 'I'.

What, though, if barriers are erected within the mind, by some outside force? What if the input of information, the output of governing messages, are rechannelled? What if the inner self, the sense of 'I', is walled off, in a terrible void of isolation that does not seem to differ from the depths of total insanity?

The self, the 'I', will struggle feebly for a while. But, in most cases, it lacks the resources to function in a void. It has been cut off from too many of its necessary connections with the mind – its own 'life support' system.

Somewhere in the brain the memory will still be working, storing information. But the inner self has no access to the data, and so cannot even confirm its own identity.

Somewhere the reason, the imagination, the intelligence will still be working, waiting for some stimulus to spur them into assessing, deciding, responding. But they too are cut off from the isolated self. Neither stimulus nor response reaches past the barriers.

Somewhere even the emotions and instincts are still alive – the capacity to feel anger or fear, to laugh or weep. But their normal channels have also been blocked, and they cannot touch or activate the self.

So after a while, in most cases, the sense of self at the core of the mind will begin to fade, shrivel, dissolve. Slowly, behind the barriers that imprison it, it will die.

Then the brain and body that the self had once inhabited become fully those of a puppet, a robot. And if the outer controls should be removed, the brain and body would be as helpless, as useless, as a puppet without strings, a robot without a power source.

When the tendril of Arachnis wrapped round Keill Randor's head, the barriers were instantly slammed shut in his mind. The tendril broke away, closing upon itself to form a tight cord encircling the skull, but the link remained, even though the brain was no longer directly connected to Arachnis.

And through that link, at the unimaginable speed of thought, the supermind of the Twenty-four *reprogrammed* Keill's mind, to make him their puppet, their robot.

If the isolated inner centre of Keill's being had been able to make a noise, it would have been an endless scream.

But it could not. Curled in the void at the core of his mind, Keill's sense of self merely floated – in an endless deprivation, forgetful of the past, unmindful of the future, unaffected by events.

For a while the robot that had been Keill Randor was left mostly alone, in a narrow, bleak room in one of the extensions of the vast Deathwing building. There he waited passively, sitting on the edge of a hard bunk and staring emptily at the wall. He was unaware of the activity that was going on within the mind that was no longer his own.

The Arachnis link did not only wall off Keill's control over his own being. It also gave the Twenty-four full access to all of his knowledge and memories. In no time they had extracted every scrap of information about the Overseers, their hidden asteroid, and their far-flung monitoring devices. They had studied every detail of Keill's life since the destruction of Moros – including the fact of his remade skeleton. And they had dug out all that Keill knew about Glr.

They did not learn where the Overseers' base was located, nor where Glr was hiding on Golvic, for Keill did not know. But every other secret contained in Keill's mind had been uncovered and opened like a book.

In his narrow room, passive as a disconnected machine, Keill knew nothing of what had been revealed. He merely waited, while at the core of what had been his mind his inner self curled more tightly, not even aware of how close it was to its final dissolution.

Yet there was a unique quality within that isolated inner self of Keill Randor. Something that retained a spark of strength, that fought to resist its destruction.

The legendary self-discipline and control of the Legions of Moros did not grow solely from the ceaseless, rigorous training imposed on every legionary from earliest infancy. The training merely reinforced something that was bred into the Legions, implanted in their very genes, over the centuries of their life on Moros. So deeply was it embedded, so unyielding was its strength, that it might have been a mutation in its own right.

It was the resolute, indomitable, diamond-hard *will* of a legionary.

And at the deepest core of the robot-being that Keill Randor had become, his will endured.

It was blind, wordless, cut off from all sense of identity, purpose or control. But it was intact – for it simply fell back on its last, defiant, defensive position, its ultimate resource. The pure determination to survive.

Steadfastly, unconquerably, the will of a legionary kept what remained of the real Keill Randor, the essence of his true self, intact and alive. And waiting.

Days passed, though the robot Keill did not measure their passing. But at last green-tunicked Golvicians came to take Keill from his silent room, through the corridors of the huge building, into the presence of a golden giant, whose grey puffy lips wore an evil smile of triumph. As did the narrow face of another man, waiting with the giant – a man whose eyes glowed oddly, and whose right shoulder was heavily bandaged.

The robot Keill was indifferent to their expressions. He stared straight ahead, empty-eyed.

'His functions, his skills, will be quite unimpaired, Festinn, I assure you,' The One said.

Festinn nodded, gazing thoughtfully at Keill. Without warning he lashed out his left fist, a blindingly swift blow at Keill's face.

But reflexes are automatic, not needing the conscious control of a mind. Keill's reflexes, and all his power and speed, had not been damaged by the Arachnis link. Festinn's fist struck empty air as Keill swayed aside – and then Keill's own hand was chopping down in a counter-blow that might have broken Festinn's one good arm.

But the chop was not completed. Keill froze like a statue, as the controlling supermind of the Twenty-four clamped on its restraints. Then he relaxed, and resumed his former stance, staring blankly into nothingness.

'Excellent,' Festinn said. He stepped closer to Keill, grinning into the empty eyes. 'You are to be honoured, Randor,' he said mockingly. 'The very cream of the Deathwing has assembled, to receive the benefit of your guidance.'

The gloating laughter that followed meant as little to Keill as the words.

Festinn took him then to another room – broad, bare, with a few items of gymnasium equipment scattered at one end. Clustered idly at that end was an assortment of humans – a dozen of them. Some of them seemed wholly normal, almost ordinary, save for a trace of cruelty in the set of their mouths, a flinty coldness in their eyes.

But among them were several whose appearance was weirdly different from the human norm.

Two might have seemed to be Golvicians, at first glance. But the livid green of their covering was not that of Golvician tunics. They were naked to the waist, and the green was the colour of their ridged, reptilian skin.

Another of the group was a skeletally thin woman, her skin a bleached white, looking even more deathlike by contrast with her shock of black hair and her bright scarlet jumpsuit, which had heavy metal bracelets at the wrists.

Another was a misshapen figure that seemed more beast than man – short bowed legs and immensely long arms, dangling almost to the floor, extended even more by multi-jointed fingers three times longer than a normal human's.

Yet another was an unnaturally broad and bulky dwarf – his face almost hidden in a massive black beard, his body covered with segmented, glittering armour like a mosaic made with mirrors – holding in one fist a short, heavy baton of black metal.

Once Keill might have studied them with interest, as examples of the Altered Worlds. But the robot Keill remained empty-eyed, indifferent, as he was led towards them.

'Here comes our teacher,' a sneering voice from the group called out.

The woman in scarlet rose to her feet, bloodless lips set in a thin line. 'Festinn, this is an outrage!' she said sharply.

A chorus of angry mutterings arose in agreement from the group around her.

. 'Silence!' Festinn shouted, eyes blazing. As the group quietened, he swept the fury of his gaze across them.

'This is by direct order of The One,' he snapped. 'We are well aware of your abilities, your successes, your skill with your own chosen weapons. But now we wish you to extend yourselves!'

His voice took on a conspiratorial tone. 'It is only just. Randor was responsible for destroying The One's earlier plan for a special strike force. So now he can put the final touches on the new one!'

Cold smiles appeared on the faces of some of the group, and there was a rumble of cruel laughter.

'Each of you,' Festinn went on, 'will be responsible for a section of The One's special task force. Each unit must be as formidable, as invincible, as a command group of the Legions of Moros themselves.' He grinned viciously. 'So we will use our tame legionary, to polish your skills with other weapons, besides your favourites. To perfect your ability to kill without weapons. To advance your knowledge of many techniques – infiltration, ambush, high-speed raiding, much more.

'When this course of instruction is over, each unit of the Deathwing will be the equal of an army, on any planet of the galaxy!'

He had won them over. The hard faces now wore coldly eager smiles – except for the woman in scarlet, who stood apart from the others, scowling angrily.

The entire scene meant nothing to the robot Keill. Nor did the intense activity of the days that followed, as the inner programming of Keill's enslaved mind directed his efforts.

Much time was spent in practice with the most advanced weapon of the Inhabited Worlds, the energy gun. There the armoured dwarf proved most adept, for his preferred weapon was the heat-wand, the metal baton that fired a controlled ray of heat, almost as powerful as the energy beam.

With other hand-weapons, the green-skinned reptilian pair came into their own. They were experts with a lethal weapon formed from razor-edged blades, fanning out into a disc-like circle, like the petals of a flower – which gave the weapon its name, the blood-rose.

They adapted readily to a variety of other bladed weapons, and weapons to be thrown, that Keill demonstrated.

In unarmed combat, the long-armed monkey-man was outstanding, with his immense agility and wiry strength. His skill was that of the stealthy assassin – those unnaturally long fingers had crushed many a throat. He followed avidly Keill's instructions about the holds and blows, to pressure points and nerve centres, that would instantly disable or kill.

So long, wearying days went by. Soon some of the Deathwing group were detailed to continue the special training of the others, while Keill worked with the less adept. Increasingly, each of them grew more skilled, more deadly. And all of them were being welded into a tight and murderously effective combat unit.

All except the woman in scarlet, who did no more than go grudgingly through the motions, whose angry scowl remained in place whenever she looked at Festinn, or at Keill.

At last what patience Festinn possessed came to an end. The group were in the gymnasium again, where Keill was tirelessly demonstrating a complex counter move, in unarmed combat, designed to leave an attacker with shattered vertebrae. The woman in scarlet was pointedly paying scant attention, and Festinn's eyes were flaring with anger.

'We can't be expected to learn all a legionary's tricks in two or three weeks,' the woman spat.

'You know very well what is expected,' Festinn snapped. 'Now continue at once!'

'Why should I bother?' the woman shouted. She tapped her heavy bracelets meaningfully. 'There's no one alive who can get near enough to use that hold on me!'

'Marska,' Festinn said, his voice dangerously cold, 'you will do so because I order it. Or I may instruct Randor not to hold back, so that you will learn how easily your back can truly be broken.'

'Can it?' the woman raged. 'Let's see how easily he can counter *this*!'

She wheeled, and her right arm snapped forward. And from the bracelet flamed a burst of pure energy – not a beam, but a controlled, shaped bolt, like a fireball.

Keill had been standing several paces away, robot-patient, not even looking at the quarrelling pair. But his reflexes were intact still. He moved almost casually, and the fireball flashed harmlessly past him, to explode against the far wall, blasting a gaping hole in its smooth metal.

The rest of the Deathwing turned to look at Marska – and went very still. There was even a trace of fear in some of their eyes. For Marska's bone-thin body was suspended high in the air, by the crushing grip of two huge golden hands on her wrists. The One had come unannounced among them, and he was angry.

'You will be punished, Marska,' the hollow voice was saying, 'until you understand. I intend the Deathwing to be the supreme fighting force in the galaxy. You will give all your effort to it, fully and willingly, or I will put an end to you.'

The golden hands opened, and Marska fell to the floor in a huddled, terrified heap.

'As for Randor,' The One went on, 'should a time come when he is to be killed, it is I – and only I – who shall have that pleasure.'

He turned to Festinn. 'This period of instruction will shortly end. The spacecraft are now being assembled, and the Master is preparing for transfer.'

Festinn's eyes glittered. 'Then the base has been located, and is suitable?'

'Entirely,' The One said. 'It was not difficult for our technology to locate some of the monitoring devices, and eventually to trace their messages back to their origin.'

He glanced at Keill with a small evil smile. 'How unfortunate that Randor cannot appreciate the irony – that he and his Overseers have provided the ideal command centre, from which the Master can complete his conquest of the galaxy.'

chapter seven

The One's ominous words meant no more to Keill than all the others that were spoken to him in those days. And he was just as unaffected by the change in his routine. Soon after that day, he no longer met and worked with the Deathwing. Now he was assigned more simple duties as an instructor for Golvician soldiers.

'These troops will form the special units led by the members of the Deathwing,' Festinn told him, still taking a perverse pleasure in speaking to Keill as if he could understand. 'They will strike the final, disruptive hammer blows that will complete the Master's victory, once the final galactic war is ended. Won't you be proud to know how you have contributed to that victory?'

And he laughed viciously into Keill's empty robot face.

In the days that followed, squad after squad of soldiers assembled with Keill for hours of unceasing instruction. Within the Deathwing building they acquired some of the basic skills of unarmed combat – moves and defences that the children of Moros would have mastered by the age of eight. Out in the empty desert beyond Golv City, Keill directed the soldiers' practice with handgun and rifle. He led them through basic assault patterns, and defensive regrouping. He demonstrated the close-combat use of military flyers. He improved their speed, mobility, discipline and tactical awareness.

Through all those days his body moved with all of its former flowing power. He gave orders and instructions with crisp efficiency. Yet the movements, the words, were not his. All his supreme military skills were at the command now of another mind. The blankness of his eyes did not alter for a moment.

But eventually those days, too, came to an end. Keill travelled with the soldiers, and several flyers full of Golvician technicians, to the Golv City spaceport. There he waited passively as the soldiers and some of the technicians filed on to a vast spacecraft, a troop carrier, that finally lumbered with thunderous power up from the port to vanish into the chill grey sky of Golvic.

And Festinn came again to gloat.

'You should know that the Deathwing assault on the new base was successful, almost comically easy,' he said. 'Now those men will prepare the way for the Master. And you, Randor, are to lend your services to the transfer.'

He stepped closer, peering hopefully into Keill's eyes. 'Is there not some part of you left,' he murmured, half to himself, 'to feel anguish over what has been done?'

But there was not. The robot Keill went as blankly as ever about his new duties. They concerned another giant spaceship, the largest type of transport freighter that could be landed on a planet. A small army of technicians laboured in and around it, and Keill laboured among them.

The whole interior of the ship was ripped out, and in the shell a new structure began to take shape. It took the form of a deep well, or shaft, constructed from an unusual metal that arrived at the space-port in pre-formed sections, to be assembled. Within the shaft a complex array of delicate, high-technology equipment was fitted, all sheathed in the same unique metal, and then tested and re-tested, while more alterations went on in the other sections of the freighter.

Keill did what he had to do, without curiosity or comprehension. In the same way, he dutifully followed Festinn, many days later, into one of the sleek flyers, which carried them swiftly back to the Deathwing building in Golv City.

'The transfer will go smoothly,' Festinn said. 'But you need not be troubled by the Master's departure. His power is immense. He will be able to reach you, even from the new base. Nothing will change.'

As always, the mocking laughter had no more effect on Keill than the words.

But it was true. Even after the great freighter also lifted off with its burden, Keill's days remained the same. The training of new squads of soldiers continued, and so did the constant jibes and mockery from Festinn.

And there were other experiences that continued – things that had been happening throughout all the days and weeks of his robot existence. But these seemed to have their origin from *within* the empty regions of his enslaved mind – though they meant no more to him than outer events.

One of the inner experiences took the form of a frequent, fragmentary image of a large ovoid shape, glowing with the changing flow of the energies that bathed it, sprouting countless long tendrils that writhed in unending motion, like some giant, alien, undersea plant.

With it came another recurring image, of twenty-four serenely smiling people, wearing what looked like thick coronets around their heads. They seemed always to be whispering, murmuring, tugging, urging, within Keill's brain.

The robot Keill did not understand these images, nor was he troubled by them.

Equally, he was untroubled by another awareness, within his robot-mind. It appeared less often than the others, and mostly at night, while Keill lay on his narrow bunk and stared obliviously at the bare ceiling, waiting for the greater oblivion of sleep.

This further awareness was of some unknown presence, roaming through the reshaped channels and passages of his mind. There it seemed to be searching, probing, testing the strengths of the barriers that had been imposed by the Arachnis link.

The presence did not ever remain for long. Nor did it have any effect on the barriers, or on Keill. It might have been a dream – if it is possible for robots, or puppets, to have dreams.

❊

Once again, a time came when Keill was taken away from a morning of instruction with the new Golvician squads, and marched through the corridors of the building to the huge room that had been the Deathwing command centre. Now a good deal of the equipment had been removed, though several computer units and communication devices remained. So did the broad, heavy table at the room's centre – and behind it sat Festinn, his shoulder now healed and no longer bandaged, his eyes glowing as mercilessly as ever.

'You may be pleased to know,' he smiled mockingly, 'that you are to suspend your duties as instructor for a while. There is another task for you.'

He rose and moved forward, watching Keill's eyes, still hoping for some glimmer of response, some hint of pain and despair.

'We have been receiving many reports,' he went on, 'of disruptive activity, minor sabotage, in Golv City. It seems some kind of winged alien creature is on the rampage. And you know all about that creature, don't you, Randor?'

The robot Keill replied, directed by the power that owned his mind, in a voice as bleak as a polar wind. 'I know about her.'

'*Her*?' Festinn leered, arching his eyebrows. 'Yes, of course, it is female, isn't it? You must tell me more about that relationship, one day.' The ugly smile faded. 'But for now, it will be your task to put an end to the relationship. The creature has eluded the militia for weeks. But it will not elude you, Randor, since you know it so well.'

Festinn leaned closer, eyes ablaze, almost spitting the words into Keill's face.

'You will go out into the city, in the company of myself and a squad of riflemen. You will lead our search for this creature. And when we locate it, wherever it may be hiding – then *you*, Randor, you personally, will kill it.'

chapter eight

The chill climate of Golvic had produced a biting wind, with frequent scudding bursts of rain that felt like particles of solid ice. It was enough to make Festinn duck his head and wince with discomfort, while the six Golvicians following him huddled as deeply as they could into their tunics' collars and plodded sullenly on.

Keill moved at the head of the file of men, efficient and single-minded. He felt no discomfort from the knife-edged wind; he felt no concern over the reason for the expedition. His robot-mind had been given its directive. Without hesitation he was going about his duty.

Under Festinn's command they had been touring Golv City for some time, sweeping above the wintry streets in a sleek, fast flyer. At intervals they had landed, to look closely at places where signs remained of the winged creature that Festinn had said was at large in the city.

At one spot, in a seedy backwater of the giant city, with low, crumbling buildings and ill-dressed residents, they had studied damage to a foodstore, from which packets of food concentrates had been stolen. The thief could not have been a Golvician, because the access had been through a nearly inaccessible upper-storey window, and there had been no sign of the use of a ladder or other climbing equipment.

At another spot, a building worker had chanced to look out of a window and had seen the wrappings of some food-concentrate packets on a ledge. He had been amazed, and had reported it, for the ledge was high on one of the more lofty towers of the city. And the windows, in deference to Golvician weather, were not designed to open.

At still another place, in a sector of the city containing the huge, solid structures of heavy industry, a maintenance worker had actually caught a glimpse of the winged creature, swooping towards him within the shadowy expanses of a giant power station. But it had only been a glimpse, for a blow on the head had sent him toppling into darkness.

Moments later, nearly a third of Golv City had been plunged into darkness, when a major feed line into the power grid had been skilfully disrupted.

Now Keill and the other searchers were returning to the flyer after examining the scene of the latest, and perhaps most serious, event. A Golvician militiaman, returning to barracks the previous night, had been attacked. He had not seen his attacker, but had heard an odd sound, as if someone had been flapping a sheet of cloth above him.

When he awoke, with a bruised and aching head, his energy gun had been missing.

Back in the flyer, relaxing with the Golvicians in its heated interior, Festinn turned inquiringly to Keill.

He knew that by then the Twenty-four would have reviewed the data. And that small portion of their supermind which controlled Keill Randor would have access to everything that Keill's mind contained about the winged alien, to form their conclusions. Those conclusions would be communicated to Festinn through Keill himself, speaking under their guidance, as if he was merely a mechanism, a walking communicator.

'The creature called Glr,' Keill said, 'is engaging in random activity.' His voice was as empty as his facial expression, showing no awareness of the words' meaning. 'There is no visible pattern. It is doubtful whether she has any fixed base, or any logical, predictable plan of action.'

'Then, with respect,' Festinn replied, 'how are we to find it?'

'She is clearly seeking to attract attention, perhaps hoping to draw me out from the Deathwing headquarters. She may believe that she can release me from Arachnis.'

The dead voice of Keill, speaking so flatly of his own enslavement, might have caused an ordinary man to shudder. Festinn merely raised a curious eyebrow.

'Can it do so? It is telepathic . . .'

'She cannot do so with mental powers alone,' Keill's empty voice replied. 'She can make only superficial contact with human minds. And even if she could reach deeply enough into my mind, she could not overcome the controls of Arachnis.'

'Surely it cannot hope to get close enough to remove the link physically,' Festinn mused. 'Which in any case would destroy what is left of Randor's mind.'

'She may not be aware of that,' the dull voice replied.

'Indeed,' Festinn said with a twisted smile. 'Clearly, then, we must continue the search – with you, Randor, as bait. The creature will undoubtedly show itself at some point.'

'No doubt,' Keill said. 'She is a telepath. She knows precisely where I am at any moment.'

Festinn laughed coldly. 'And that, Randor, will be its undoing.'

For the next few hours they continued their search more or less at random, sweeping the flyer over the entire area around the scene of Glr's attack on the militiaman. Frequently they landed on the roofs of the taller buildings in the area, emerging to search more carefully. And when they did so, Festinn and the men under his command no longer huddled so deeply into their tunics. They were watchful and cautious, knowing that they were now hunting not just a winged enemy, but a winged enemy armed with an energy gun.

But the search proved fruitless. And by the time that the first tinges of dusk had begun to darken the overcast sky, Festinn was feeling thoroughly disgruntled, as well as half-frozen. He was even beginning to doubt the conclusion of the Twenty-four, that Glr would sooner or later show herself if Keill was out in the city.

And so he was on the threshold of calling off the search, for the day, when the communicator in the flyer crackled into life.

'Sir!' The Golvician voice held a note of urgency. 'The winged creature has been located – on the main route to the spaceport! It has fired on two military flyers, and disabled them!'

Festinn gestured abruptly to the soldier at the controls of the flyer. 'Get us to the spaceport – top speed. And stop at nothing!' The vehicle leaped forward with a throaty roar of power, and Festinn leaned forward to the communicator. 'Did anyone return the fire? Was the creature hit?'

'No, sir. It showed itself for an instant, crippled the flyers, and was gone before anyone could shoot. But the pilots brought the flyers down safely, sir.'

'Then they are as lucky as they are stupid,' Festinn snapped. 'See that the spaceport guards are more alert.' He switched off and turned to Keill. 'The spaceport . . . Do you think your friend is planning to desert you?'

'I do not know what she is planning,' Keill said tonelessly.

'Of course not.' Festinn smiled. 'But you can tell me one thing. How fast can the creature fly?'

Keill looked out of the flyer's window. The buildings on either side seemed to be blurred and smeared, such was the speed of the vehicle's hurtling flight. And across the gulf of space, through the Arachnis link, the Twenty-four assessed his perceptions, compared them with data from his memory, and framed his reply.

'Not as fast as this, even in a short burst. Much less fast, over a distance.'

'Excellent.' Festinn settled back with satisfaction. 'Then we shall overtake it. Are you looking forward to seeing your friend again, Randor?' The cold laugh rang out. 'Once you have killed it, I may also let you have a last look at your own spaceship. For old times' sake.'

He laughed again. But Keill merely stared woodenly ahead at the darkening sky around them.

Full night had begun to gather by the time the flyer came within sight of the lights on the spaceport perimeter. There was a brighter area of light within the perimeter, as well – which, as they swooped down near ground level, defined itself as a merrily blazing fire.

Festinn did not need the breathless report over the communicator to know that Glr had reached the spaceport only moments before. And she had managed, without being spotted, to fire at and explode a power unit in a storage area.

'Let it burn!' Festinn was raging into the communicator. 'Put every man to the task of finding that creature! Let me know the instant it is located!'

But in fact it was Festinn himself who first had precise knowledge of Glr's location.

As the flyer dropped even lower, skimming the ground in a sweeping curve towards the spaceport entrance, an energy beam stabbed towards it from the night sky. It struck with blazing accuracy at the front of the vehicle, melting and burning its way through the housing of the engine.

With power cut off, the flyer plunged to the ground. Bouncing, skidding and slewing over the rain-wet surface, it finally struck some unseen obstacle and rolled crashingly – once, twice, a third time – before finally coming to rest.

Almost immediately, Keill was squeezing out of a shattered window and coming to his feet. His reflexes and balance had as always operated automatically, curling him into a tight protective ball, so that he suffered only minor bruises in the crash. He was already moving away before Festinn and the others, groaning and dazed, had begun to disentangle themselves painfully from the shattered machinery.

'Randor!' Festinn shouted. 'Stop – wait there!'

But if Keill heard, he did not obey. He took his primary orders through his programming, via the Arachnis link. And he had been programmed to seek a winged alien, and kill it. When he had first emerged from the wrecked flyer, he had caught a glimpse of broad, membranous wings, soaring into the darkness towards the central area of the spaceport.

And like the obedient robot that he was, he had leaped in pursuit, freeing his energy gun from his belt as he ran.

Elsewhere on the broad plasticrete expanse of the spaceport, he could hear the cries of many men, the sound of running feet and clattering machinery. Some men were hurrying towards the wrecked flyer; others were still milling around the scene of the fire, some distance to Keill's left. But the noises held no meaning for him, and he ran on, ignoring them.

The icy wind moaned around him, dashing a flurry of bitter rain into his eyes. He blinked – and as his vision cleared, he saw again the ghostly suggestion of wide wings in the air ahead.

His hand became a blur as he snapped up the gun and fired.

But Glr had swerved, telepathically sensing the shot before it was fired, and the deadly beam missed. Keill ran on, peering into the darkness, all his automatic alertness poised, ready to kill.

The strange pursuit continued, towards a dark cluster of unlit buildings that loomed on the far edge of the spaceport. Keill sprinted round the scarred expanse of a landing pad, caught another glimpse of the shadowy wings, fired again. But again Glr had swung aside in time, and again the shot missed its target as she once more vanished into the darkness.

Keill slowed his pace as he neared the buildings. On one of them, wide doors yawned open, a patch of deeper blackness. It was a compact spaceport hangar, which might be used to house one of the smaller, individualized types of spacecraft. So its doors should not have been open, at night, unguarded.

Unless someone, or something, had just opened them.

It was not Keill's reasoning, for he could no longer reason, but that of the controlling power he obeyed. It sent him moving forward, with caution, to slip silently in through the gaping doors.

Darkness swallowed him. He was aware, near him, of the shape of a spaceship, but it meant nothing to him. His hearing was tuned to catch a whisper of movement, a sweep of wings through the air.

The small portion of the supermind that was attending to Keill plucked from his memory the fact that his alien companion's round eyes had exceptional night vision. A flicker of concern became a command, sent out on the Arachnis link. Slowly Keill began to back out of the hangar.

But . . . was that a rustle of wings, just on the threshold of hearing, high above him?

In the instant that the sound reached him, Keill fired towards it. The blazing beam of energy lit up the darkness for a fractional moment, illuminating the hull of a blunt, wedge-shaped spaceship, with a sky-blue circlet glinting on its side.

The sight was meaningless to Keill. His shot had struck only the wall of the hangar, had revealed no sign of a winged creature. He continued to back away, almost blind for an instant in the after-effects of the beam.

The rush of wings came, unexpectedly, from behind him. A small, firm body struck powerfully against the back of his head, and broad membranes of wings folded down over his upper body.

Reflexively, Keill had maintained his balance under the impact, and had without pause struck upwards and back with the deadly chopping edge of his hand. But the folds of a wing blocked and impeded the blow, tangling Keill's hand for a brief instant.

The instant was long enough. Keill felt sharp talons on the ends of small fingers rake painfully up the side of his head, leaving bloody furrows on his scalp.

Then the talons hooked over the thin cord that formed the Arachnis link – and ripped it away.

chapter nine

An impossible, unbelievable agony that was beyond agony exploded inside Keill's head. Every cell of his brain, every nerve fibre, felt as if it had burst into livid flame.

All the normal connections and patterns that had been blocked, bypassed or diverted by the Arachnis control had snapped simultaneously back into their regular formations. And, like limbs that have been unused for a long time, and are suddenly called upon to function at top output, they shrieked their protest in the form of excruciating, unbearable pain.

Keill staggered and reeled forward – unaware that he was screaming, unaware of the strong little hands that grasped his tunic and kept him upright, on his feet, while great wings beat above his head. Before he could fall, Glr half-dragged him back into the impenetrable darkness of the hangar where his ship lay. She propelled him around the ship, as far away from the hangar's yawning doors as possible. And only then – among an array of machine parts and tools, the usual clutter of a spaceport hangar's maintenance area – she let him collapse to the hangar floor.

Keill knew nothing of that. For him there was nothing but pain, the overwhelming shock of his brain's abrupt reassembling of its own functions. And more – even beyond that agony there was the growth of a greater torment.

In that explosive moment of his mind's restoration, he had regained his self-awareness, his knowledge of who and what he was. And he had regained access to his memory. In one overwhelming blast of realization, he remembered everything that had happened to him – what he had been under the Arachnis control, what he had done, what had been done to him.

A tidal wave of revulsion, guilt, horror and hatred swept over him in that single convulsive moment. And with that moral torment heaped on top of the psychic agony of his restored mental functions, his mind tottered upon the brink of oblivion. Not the merciful release of mere unconsciousness, but the oblivion of total insanity, of mind-death. His mind cried out for the peace of forgetfulness, of blank non-awareness. It swayed upon the threshold of its own destruction, and reached yearningly towards it . . .

But it did not cross the threshold. Two forces went into action within the storming, boiling confines of his agonized mind, and rescued it.

Freed from the barriers that had left it suspended in disconnected darkness, his unyielding will asserted itself. Before, it had known only that it had to survive. Now, reconnected with reality, it knew *why*. And it reached out through all the areas of his mind, and fought the desire for oblivion. It confronted the crippling agony, and fought to make it bearable. It confronted the sweeping waves of remorse and revulsion, and fought to quell their power.

It snatched Keill's mind back from the black edge of madness – and it summoned up all the resources of a legionary's self-discipline, and flung them into the struggle for mastery.

And as Keill's will went into battle, it was aided by the second force. Another presence entered into Keill's tortured mind – the healing, gentle presence of Glr, wrapping invisible wings comfortingly around Keill like a mother holding an injured child. Surely, carefully, her mind touched the flashpoints of Keill's mental anguish and sought to calm them, to bring the healing balm of understanding, reassurance and love.

The slow stumbling retreat of Keill's mind from the edge of the abyss, the slow restoration of self-control, seemed to be timeless – to extend over eons of suffering. But when at last he opened his

409

eyes, it was to find that only moments had passed since Glr had lowered him to the cluttered floor of the hangar.

He was unbelievably weak, feeling half-paralysed as his nervous system re-learned how to accept messages from his own brain. The agony within his head remained as fiery and blinding as before.

But he was Keill Randor again, legionary of Moros, no longer slave, puppet, or robot. And a fierce joy rose in him, to aid the task of restoration.

Glr was perched beside him, among the clutter on the floor, with an energy gun nearby. Keill looked into the round, bright eyes – and though he was too weak, too mentally shaky, to form a thought clearly enough, he had no doubt that she would sense the fullness within him, the flooding of gratitude that he wanted to express.

In turn, he sensed Glr's voice softly, carefully within his mind, echoing with relief and thankfulness – and with something that, if the two words had been spoken aloud, might have been a sob.

Welcome back.

Then, despite the pain-wracked exhaustion of his mind, Keill wanted to frame some of the swarm of questions that needed answers. But he could not – for their time had run out.

Without warning, the lights of the hangar blazed on, obviously controlled from some outside source. Beyond the doors of the building, Keill heard the clatter of many boots on the plasticrete.

And Glr snatched up her gun and flung herself into the air, as the Golvician militia burst into the hangar.

Raging at his own weakness, Keill fought to rise. But his body moved sluggishly, painfully, still unwilling to respond to the dictates of his brain. It seemed to take him forever merely to roll partway over, and to force his upper body into a sitting position.

And while he struggled, Glr plunged into furious battle.

Six armed Golvicians had come through the door. But they had come with too much clumsy incaution, and Glr's gun had cut down two of them before the remaining four were able to take cover at the sides of the hangar.

From there they began a furious fire fight, their guns blazing and crackling almost without pause. Yet Glr remained miraculously unhit, as she wheeled and swooped, darting into cover behind the bulk of the spaceship which also sheltered Keill, bursting out again to return the Golvicians' fire.

In a moment another Golvician screamed and fell, his green tunic a smoking ruin. A second tried a sudden rush towards the ship, but before he could reach the safety of its shadow Glr's energy beam had slashed across his legs to send him tumbling in a screaming, bleeding heap.

Keill heard within his mind the high-pitched whoop of Glr's battle-cry. And it galvanized him to greater efforts in his grim struggle to make his body obey him. His hands swept out to find leverage, and brushed across the ice-smooth length of a slim metal rod. He clutched at it, recognising it as an extension rod for the electro-probes used to reach deep into the mechanisms of a spaceship. It was just what Keill needed.

Bracing himself on it, as an old and crippled man might lean his weight on a stick, Keill lurched to his knees. But there he halted, frozen by a movement he had glimpsed at the edge of his vision.

A previously unseen access hatch at the side of the hangar had slid open. And framed in it, Keill saw the stealthy figure of Festinn, gun in hand.

The Deathwing assassin took in the scene at once. Keill, unarmed and on his knees, looking half-paralysed and helpless. And Glr, still engaged in combat with the two remaining Golvicians, but entirely exposed to Festinn's position.

The mad eyes blazed like twin beacons of murderous joy, as Festinn raised his gun.

Keill did not call to Glr. For one thing, he dared not distract her from her own fight. For another, the appearance of Festinn had acted upon him like a jolt of electricity, bringing with it a renewed surge of the revulsion and hatred that had so nearly swamped his mind, moments before.

But now the force of those emotions was channelled into a gigantic burst of vengeful rage, which called up reserves of strength from the deepest areas of his being.

As the assassin's gun steadied, its deadly muzzle tracking Glr's rapid swooping flight, Keill hefted the slender metal rod in one hand, drew it back, and flung it.

The smooth end of the rod struck precisely between the glittering eyes. And such was the power of the fury behind the throw that the metal smashed onwards through flesh and bone, to bury itself in the depths of Festinn's brain.

Less than an hour later, Keill and Glr were seated, or perched, at the controls of his ship, in deep space, and locked in determined argument.

Glr had managed to flush out and finish off the last Golvician attackers in almost the same moment as Festinn's body had crumpled to the floor. Then she had urged and half-supported Keill as he staggered into the ship – his own ship. From her special sling-perch, she had taken the controls, lifting them off in a crashing escape straight through the roof of the hangar, just as a larger force of militia had poured in through its doors.

Once safely out of Golvic territorial space, Glr had begun to answer the swarm of questions in Keill's mind. It was a sombre and fearsome story.

From her hiding place, after she had landed Keill's ship, she had been telepathically aware of the unbearable moment of Keill's capture by the Arachnis tendril. What happened then to Keill's mind had very nearly done serious damage to her own mind, Glr said. But she had recovered herself quickly, and had quelled her terror and rage enough to reach out with her mind across the stars to Talis, the leader of the Overseers.

The old man had also been almost overwhelmed by despair and sorrow when he heard Glr's news. But he too had rallied quickly. He and Glr realized that every corner of Keill's mind would now be open to the Twenty-four – the Warlord. And that supreme, evil intelligence would do everything it could to locate the Overseers.

So Talis decided to send the Overseers to safety, though he himself made up his mind to remain on the asteroid, and would not be budged by Glr's desperate urgings.

Meanwhile, Glr had kept watch on events on Golvic. She had watched with glum misery as flyers searched the wilderness for Keill's ship, and found it, once the Twenty-four had learned from Keill's mind where it might be hidden. She had then made her way unseen to the city, and had even spied on some of Keill's own robot activities.

And she had filled her days with many other things – including the grimly enjoyable game of disrupting what she could in Golv City, while eluding the men sent out to hunt her. By doing so she hoped that one day the Deathwing would send Keill after her – so that she could try to lure him to some safe place, on his own, and perhaps release him from his evil bondage.

At that point in her narrative, Keill's eyes had darkened. 'I came very close to killing you,' he said.

Since they were alone, he could speak aloud, knowing that she would pick up the thought behind the words. And his voice shook with the memory of that deadly pursuit at the spaceport.

Glr laughed quietly. *I was beginning to fear you would. Otherwise I would not have risked removing the tendril so drastically – which came close to killing you.*

'No matter,' Keill said. 'We're both alive. The Warlord will find out just how alive we are.'

You are aware, Glr said forlornly, *that the Twenty-four and the Deathwing have the asteroid.*

Keill's eyes clouded with pain. 'I know. They traced it through the monitors. I even helped them prepare the assault.'

You are not to blame, Glr replied soothingly. *But certainly they succeeded. I lost contact with Talis's mind many days ago. In the same way, Keill, as I lost contact with yours.*

Keill slumped back into his sling-seat, wrapped in numbed horror as he contemplated the kindly old man who had created the Overseers, who had saved Keill's life, who had been concerned above all for the safety of the galaxy, and not at all for his own.

And now that old man was a prisoner of the Warlord, a puppet-slave of Arachnis.

'Somehow, then,' Keill said through clenched teeth, 'we're also going to have to locate the asteroid.'

I know its location, Glr said. *Talis gave me the co-ordinates.*

Keill stared at her. He remembered, at the beginning of their travels together, how Glr had explained that while she could reach across interstellar distances to touch Talis's mind, she had willingly submitted to a hypnotic block implanted by Talis, as part of his obsessive secrecy. The block had prevented her from pinpointing the position of the asteroid base. But now, Talis had clearly lifted the block – when the need for secrecy no longer existed.

'Then if you know,' Keill said fiercely, 'let's go!'

And that was when the argument broke out.

Glr insisted that Keill was in no condition to dash off into what would be a fearful battle, against terrible odds. Keill was determined not to delay a moment more than necessary before launching an assault on the asteroid. Glr urged him to rest, promising that with her healing telepathic aid he would have recovered full control of his mind and body in no more than a day or two. He insisted that there was not a day or two to spare. She grew annoyed, and scolded. He grew more determined, and resisted.

In the process he tried to raise himself from his slingseat. But the burst of strength that had come to him in time to destroy Festinn had been temporary. His legs trembled; his arms seemed to be made of lead.

He sagged back into the slingseat, sweating, and turned with a shaky smile to Glr.

'Your point has been made,' he said. 'But whatever it takes to get me back to normal – can we make it happen quickly?'

It will be quick, Glr promised him. *I know your resilience, your powers of recovery. After a day's rest, and some special treatment from me, we can set out. By the time we reach the asteroid, you will be ready.*

A muted shadow of her bubbling laughter sounded in her mental voice. *After all, my friend – you will need to be at your best, when you go to save the galaxy!*

Asteroid apocalypse
chapter ten

Glr was proved right about Keill's condition. After he had resigned himself to a period of rest, he slept for the span of nearly a full day. It was a deep and healing sleep, made more so by Glr's gently soothing presence that he vaguely sensed, like a lingering, peaceful dream, within his mind.

As carefully as before, but now more thoroughly, her mind moved among the still pain-racked centres and channels of his mental being, the after-effects of shock and disruption. She was like warm sun-light, like the soft breath of a summer breeze – and where she passed storms were quelled, menacing clouds were driven away, tranquillity began to gather.

When Keill at last awoke, he found himself refreshed, alert, free of pain. Even his head-wound, from Glr's claws, had been treated and was healing well. His mind was clear, his self-control restored. His body responded readily to his every command. And he retained, like the fleeting shadow-memory of a dream, a sense of the healing presence that had floated through his mind as he had slept.

He stared at Glr wonderingly. 'I didn't know you could do such things. I thought nearly all of a human mind was closed to you.'

Not closed, Glr said. *Just mostly very alien.* Her laughter was still muted. *I have been with you a long time, Keill. I can reach depths in your mind that I could reach in no other. And while I may not understand all the human strangeness that I find there, I can recognize pain and turmoil.*

'Then perhaps,' Keill said softly, 'you can also see just how huge a debt of gratitude I feel I owe you.'

Glr's round eyes gleamed. *You repaid a good part of the debt*, she laughed, *with that makeshift spear back in the hangar. Not a bad throw, for an invalid!*

Keill laughed, but there was ferocity as well as humour in his voice – a fierce gladness that he had been able to deal with Festinn as he had, and that he was now able to deal with the rest of his enemies.

Glr caught his mood at once. Her wings half-flared as she shifted her position, her small hands reaching for the controls.

I will take us into Overlight, she announced. *You may continue preparing yourself for what we must face, a few hours from now.*

As the formless void of Overlight blotted out the stars on the viewscreens, Keill rose from the slingseat, marvelling at how easily his body moved, and began his preparations. He selected weapons and equipment, and checked them with a legionary's thoroughness. He ate hugely, a refuelling meal of food concentrates, while Glr nibbled at a portion, complaining as always about the intolerable food on humans' spacecraft. He even had time to put himself through a series of limbering exercises, testing his strength, speed, reactions and stamina – and feeling pleased that he seemed to be wholly himself again, unimpaired.

When the speedy preparations were done, he returned to the slingseat, to wait patiently for the emergence from Overlight. As he waited and watched the viewscreens, he saw not the grey void, but a crowding host of memories.

One memory in particular stood out – the image of his world, Moros, as he had last seen it, enveloped in the radiant haze that had ended all life upon the planet. And he heard again the dying words of his then closest friend, Oni Wolda, who had dragged her ship away from the dead planet to warn Keill, and to launch him on his mission.

Avenge us, Keill, Oni had said. *Avenge the murder of Moros.*

There's more to it than that, Oni, he told the ghostly memory.

There's an evil that we never guessed at, threatening all the galaxy, certain that it can't be stopped. But it can be – and will be. And Moros will be avenged.

Only moments later the cells of his body felt that eerie, disorientating shift, and the greyness on the viewscreens gave way to the star-dappled blackness of space.

Keill reached for the controls, sending the ship forward on normal planetary drive, operating its long-range detectors. Soon they produced the information he sought.

A small spherical body, moving slowly through the incalculable emptiness among the stars. Not an orbiting body, for there were no suns or planets near enough. It was certainly the asteroid, its path following the co-ordinates that Glr had put into the ship's computer.

And it was not moving alone on that path. Close to it, in its wake, the detectors showed a collection of even smaller bodies – minor asteroids and rocky chunks of space rubble.

Keill pointed them out to Glr. 'I didn't know the Overseers' asteroid had company.'

I was only told of them once, while I was with the Overseers, Glr replied, *and did not think them important.*

Keill shrugged. 'Maybe they aren't, except to show that the asteroid was once part of a larger planetoid, a few million million years ago. But on the other hand . . .'

His fingers flicked over the controls, sweeping the ship sideways on to a new course. 'It's likely that the Deathwing have their own detectors, watching space around them. So we'll come at them through all that rubble.'

You will wreck the ship, Glr warned.

'Don't worry,' Keill said. 'We'll get through. It's just the cover we need, to get close before they spot us.'

Setting the computer guidance system, he rose from the slingseat and moved swiftly to the neat stack of equipment that he had set out earlier. Much of the stack was formed by the sections of a

Legion spacesuit. Fully protective, but remarkably light and flexible, it allowed the unhampered mobility that a legionary needed in combat.

When he had donned the spacesuit and carefully checked it, he gathered up his weapons. Two energy-guns that clipped to a belt on the suit. Two extra energy charges, which he felt sure would be enough. And four small, flat plastic objects – the special grenades of the Legions – that also fastened to the belt.

Keill's battle plan was blatantly simple. He knew that he had little chance of reaching the surface of the asteroid undetected, once he had emerged from the cluster of space rubble. So he intended to go in at top speed, his ship's guns blazing, and blast his way through the asteroid hull – relying on Glr's telepathic reach to guide him to an area where he would not be putting Talis at risk.

He was not concerned about who else might be at risk when his ship smashed through the hull and brought with it, into that area, the vacuum and absolute zero of space.

Once inside, he would leave his ship, protected by his spacesuit – and then he would take things as they came.

I know there is no suit for me, Glr said. *But am I to wait quietly while you go out to fight alone?*

'Not for long,' Keill reassured her. The hull of the asteroid, he told her, would be like the exterior skin of any human space station. It would contain a self-sealing substance, that would swiftly flow into the gap made by Keill's ship, sealing the hull so that atmosphere could be restored.

Then I can come out and join you, Glr said with satisfaction, flaring her wings.

'Then you come out,' Keill corrected her, 'and locate Talis, to see what you can do for him.'

Keill, from what you told me there must be forty Golvician soldiers in the asteroid, Glr protested. *And there are twelve Deathwing killers, besides The One. You will need me.*

Keill shrugged. 'Even counting the Twenty-four, that makes less opposition than I had when I last tackled The One.'

You do not have the Starwind to help you now, Glr pointed out.

'The Starwind nearly killed me,' Keill reminded her. 'Anyway – I'm going to be raising up a storm of my own.'

He poured on the power, and the ship surged forward in a great glittering arc through the emptiness.

Within minutes, their goal had appeared on the view-screens – the cluster of space rubble, and on its far side the larger bulk of the asteroid. Within a few seconds more they were near enough to see greater detail.

'Look at it,' Keill breathed.

Once the asteroid might have presented a normal, undistinguished surface of flat rock and shallow craters, like any number of similar wandering bodies in space. That had been the Overseers' camouflage. But now the surface showed deep scars, great rents and gashes, through which the glint of metal showed from the exposed hull that was the artificial skin of the Overseers' base.

Nor was it damage that could have been caused by meteor showers, or minor collisions with space debris. This damage came from a savage attack by human weapons of great power.

'Talis must have put up quite a fight,' Keill said.

Glr agreed. *Let us hope that the Deathwing is not manning the defences so thoroughly . . . Keill!*

Her shriek had been caused by the sudden arrival of the first fragment of the space rubble – a huge, sharp-cornered boulder looming in the forward viewscreens.

But Keill's reflexes were untroubled. The ship veered away, its drive howling, then twisted again to avoid another rocky lump. 'Try to be calm,' he advised Glr absently, his hands a blur over the controls.

Calm? Glr flared, as the ship flashed among a scattering of smaller rocks, none larger than a man's head, all capable of disabling most spacecraft if struck at that velocity.

Then she fell silent, knowing that Keill needed no distractions. The space rubble, which had looked so small at a distance, contained some chunks of rock considerably larger than the ship. And there were countless more of the smaller lumps lying in wait among the spaces between.

There was a faint jolt, then another, as the ship spiralled up and around one of the larger bodies. But they had been only glancing blows, grazes, that did not harm the ship's tough hull.

Again the ship's drive bellowed in protest as Keill dragged it back upon itself, like a living creature trying to bite its own tail, to force it through a gap between two giant fangs of rock. Then it was swerving sideways again, weaving and fishtailing, before suddenly bursting out into open space, with the curving bulk of the asteroid appearing to rush towards it at a terrifying speed.

Glr flung her mind across the rapidly narrowing gap.

Keill, Talis is safely on the other side of the asteroid. And look . . . there!

Keill had seen it too. A fearsomely broad, jagged scar on the surface of the asteroid, showing a sheen of smooth brown at its centre.

'That's the sealant!' Keill shouted. 'They've already made a hole for me – what's on the other side, can you tell?'

Swiftly Glr's mind reached out again, sensed the presence of human minds, caught a mental glimpse of a cavernous chamber, a high domed roof . . .

I think it is the large chamber where your ship was kept, she said urgently, *when you were with the Overseers!*

'Perfect!' Keill yelled. 'Anyway, if it isn't, we're about to find out!'

As he spoke, he cut the ship's drive, fired his retro rockets at full power, and slammed a hand on the firing studs of his forward energy guns.

The retros thundered, the guns blazed. A dark redness swam across Keill's eyes for a brief moment, as the terrible deceleration took effect. As his vision cleared, he saw the enormous gash in the asteroid's skin, filling the viewscreen, being blasted open again by the furious impact of the guns.

Then his ship smashed into the centre of the smoking, widening gap. Again the redness blurred Keill's vision as the ship's forward plunge was checked – by the impact as well as by the retros – and then was halted completely by a grinding, splintering collision with some object within the asteroid.

Keill could not see what it was, for the forward screens had blanked out, wrecked by the destructive plunge. But in any case he was not looking.

The ship had scarcely come to rest, a portion of its stern still jutting out into space from the hull of the asteroid, when Keill had sprung to the airlock, and through it, both guns leaping into his hands.

One swift glance told him that Glr had been right – it was the high-domed chamber where the Overseers had kept his ship. And the object that his ship had finally struck had been a huge curved section of metal, clearly designed to be put in place as a permanent repair to the yawning gap in the hull.

There had been a few technicians working on the repairs. But they had worn spacesuits, and so some had survived the explosive entry of his ship.

Charred bodies huddled among the wreckage showed that they had not all survived the blast of his retros and ship guns. But at least two were still standing.

They were green-tunicked Golvicians, and they were resilient enough to recover from their shock in time to reach for their weapons. But they got no further. As Keill sprang from his ship his own guns flamed, and cut the two men down with their guns only half-raised.

Keill spared an instant to check his ship. Its blunt nose seemed even blunter now, somewhat crumpled, and there was a good deal of damage to the exterior, including some of the viewscreen scanners. But none of the damage looked serious from where he stood.

The fact that he had come through the material of the hull's sealant, and not through the much tougher metal of the hull itself, had been a piece of luck. He could probably fly his ship out – if he lived to do so.

He glanced at the rear of the ship. The self-sealant in the asteroid's hull was flowing round the new gap, and would soon hold the ship in a solid grip to allow atmosphere to flow back into the chamber. Then Glr could get on with her part of the job.

'See you soon!' He flung the thought at Glr as he turned and ran towards the nearest door out of the chamber.

But he had taken only a stride when the door was flung open.

Ten space-helmeted Golvicians burst into the chamber, guns ready. And as Keill dived towards the skimpy cover of nearby wreckage, scattered by his ship's entry, another door clanged open on the far side of the chamber.

Ten more armed soldiers advanced – positioned to pin him down in a deadly crossfire.

chapter eleven

Energy beams crackled around Keill as he flattened himself behind the inadequate cover. Only an instant remained before one of the beams would find its mark, but he was not going down easily. In that instant, while the first group was still bunched within the door, he flung one of his four grenades towards them in a high arc, and then rolled quickly away to turn his guns against the second group.

It proved unnecessary. Just as the grenade exploded, in a flat crash of sound, a huge burst of energy lanced through the air from behind Keill. It swept in a broad swathe of destruction along the wall of the chamber – and the second group of Golvicians, reacting a split-second too late, were scythed down as they tried, panicking, to turn and run.

Keill rose to one knee. The floor of the chamber at each doorway was littered with unmoving, Golvician bodies. The grenade had flattened the first group – and Glr had fired the powerful portside guns of Keill's ship at the second group.

'*How did you do that?*' he asked wonderingly. '*The viewscreens are out.*'

I looked through your eyes, Glr replied simply. *Not too accurately, at first, but effectively.*

'*That's cut the odds a bit*,' Keill said with gratitude. As he spoke he was resuming his rush to the door of the chamber, hurdling the dead soldiers in his path.

Outside the chamber, a broad corridor led towards the heart of the asteroid – and there were no soldiers in sight. He sprinted along the corridor, remembering another time when he had fled through the interconnecting passages that honeycombed the asteroid's interior. He had then been seeking escape from what he had wrongly assumed to be captivity, by the Overseers. That was before old Talis, his face hidden in the dark cowl of his robe, had revealed to Keill the monstrous truth about the Warlord. It all seemed a long time ago – but now it had brought him full circle, back at last to the asteroid where his quest had begun.

And where it would be finished, Keill promised. A silent vow – to the dead Legions, to Glr and the Overseers, to himself.

He swung into a narrower side passage, slowing his pace, moving with wary care. His concentration and alertness were tuned to their highest pitch. All his speed, his power, his uncanny combat skills were poised and ready.

And more. Because he was launching into the final desperate battle – because he was one against so many – something else arose within Keill, fuelling and focusing his skills.

The awesome, irresistible battle fury of a legionary.

It was never the blind, foaming fury of a berserker. It was cold, defined, controlled. And within Keill, it was composed mostly of a pure and towering vengefulness. For the murder of Moros, for the pain and horror that Keill himself had suffered – but also for all the death and destruction, all the terror and cruelty, that the Warlord and his minions had spread through the galaxy.

It was as if Keill had released a ravening beast within himself. Yet the beast that was his battle rage was kept on a tight rein, disciplined and directed, a formidable extra source of power during his plunge into the last battle.

There could be no quarter, no mercy, no prisoners. And certainly no surrender. A legionary in his battle fury, facing monstrous odds, fought on until he died, or until no more enemies remained.

So for a while Keill Randor ceased to be a man. As he moved through the corridors of the asteroid he was a predator, a killing machine, a relentless force of terrible, inescapable retribution.

The narrower passage that he had entered was intersected by a steep gangway, rising to the next level. From above he heard movement, and he sprang up the gangway, his soft-soled boots silent on the smooth metal floor. He emerged in front of a group of three green-uniformed soldiers, obviously hurrying to get behind him and cut him off.

Compared to Keill's supreme combat readiness, everyone else was moving in slow motion. He had slid sideways into a compact crouch and fired three times before the soldiers' eyes had finished widening in shock. The three men spun and crumpled, their hoarse cries of fear cut sharply off. Before they had hit the floor Keill was leaping past them towards another gangway.

He knew, with fierce satisfaction, that by now the entire asteroid would be close to panic. The psychological effect of his ship's unexpected, destructive entry would have been strong enough. But the fact that they would surely now know who it was – Keill Randor, impossibly escaped from the living death of the Arachnis slavery – would be badly affecting the nerves of his enemies.

So would the fact that he would now seem to have vanished into the mazy depths of the asteroid – to have become a will o' the wisp, eluding those sent to destroy him, appearing out of nowhere with unsettling suddenness to destroy the destroyers.

He expected that The One would eventually gather the Deathwing and make a stand, preferring to let the soldiers risk the open fighting in the corridors, knowing that Keill would have to come and face them. But there would be time to think about that in a while. First, he intended to whittle the odds down further. He wanted no Golvicians coming at his back when he went to confront the Deathwing.

Up the next gangway, into a deserted corridor. Two metres away he saw one of the smooth doors, like the interior hatchway of a spaceship, swing open a crack. Without breaking stride, Keill leaped, slamming a boot in a ferocious flying kick against the door.

It burst open, half-ripped from its hinges, and the soldier who was waiting behind it to ambush Keill was flung crushingly against the far wall of the narrow room beyond the door. The angle of his neck, as he slid to the floor, showed that he would not be getting up again.

Keill had already rushed on, not sparing a backward glance. Glr had calculated about forty Golvicians on the asteroid – and more than half of those had been put out of action in the first devastating assault that followed the entry of Keill's ship. Now he was cutting down the rest of them, a few at a time.

The surviving Golvicians, hunting in small groups, began to be more wary. But it did them little good, as Keill weaved his deadly way through the network of passages.

One moment he was ghosting through a series of connecting rooms to emerge suddenly behind a nervously watchful trio of soldiers – disappearing abruptly as their corpses toppled.

Another moment he materialized in front of six soldiers who were rushing to the lower levels to guard the asteroid's life support systems and artificial gravity unit. Their panicky shots went wildly astray – and then Keill led them away from the life support area, led them into one of the stout-walled outer rooms where part of the asteroid's defensive system was located. As they charged in after him, Keill slipped out through a separate hatch, leaving another of his grenades behind, primed and ready. No one in that room escaped the carnage.

Nor did the back-up troop, also sent hurriedly to protect the vital life support area. Among the solid, bulky shapes of the machinery Keill played a lethal game of hide-and-seek, luring them into traps, cutting them down one at a time, finally closing with the last man and finishing him with a savage chop that crushed his throat.

In the brief lull that followed, Keill took a moment to fit new charges into his energy guns. No other soldiers seemed to be threatening his position – but then there were probably few, if any, left. And the Deathwing was not likely to risk the life support system by coming in after him with any heavy weapons. In that pause Glr reached her mind to him.

I have left the ship, she reported. *Atmosphere was restored quite soon. The Deathwing has moved Talis, and I am making my way to him.*

'Where?' Keill asked crisply.

If you remember the large recreation room, Glr replied, *where Talis first explained everything to you* . . .

'I remember. Near the centre, on the next to topmost level.'

Exactly. They are moving towards that room, with Talis. Next to it lies a deep vertical shaft that has been cut into the heart of the asteroid, to contain the Arachnis thing.

Keill nodded grimly to himself. The Deathwing was, as expected, gathering in their defensive position.

'Give me time to get there first,' Keill told Glr. 'And be careful.'

Why? The word held a hint of Glr's laughter. *There are only a few Golvicians left – and they are searching for you in areas where they fervently hope you will not be found.* The inner voice became grave. *It is you who must take care. There are twelve of the Deathwing, and The One, awaiting you. And what I can sense from their minds is . . . disturbing.*

As her mind withdrew, Keill clipped his recharged guns on to his belt and moved towards the passage that would take him most quickly to the section of the asteroid that Glr had specified. The corridors were empty – so Glr was right, that there would be little more resistance from the Golvician soldiers. Only the Deathwing remained.

And he did not need Glr's reminder. Any Deathwing agent was dangerous – that was why The One chose them. And he knew exactly how much more dangerous this group was, especially the mutants. He could remember all too clearly the hours and days of combat training that he himself had given them, to improve and extend their skills.

But he was not troubled. The woman in scarlet, Marska, had

been right. It took more than a week or two for anyone, even a Deathwing mutant, to achieve the combat level of a legionary. It would not be easy to oppose the thirteen of them, well-armed and highly skilled as they were. But it would not be impossible.

Then the thought struck him, with a flash of grim humour. Thirteen of them, including The One. It'll be just like the Battle Rites of Banthei.

Except nobody's cheering – and there's no rule against killing.

There was a ghost of a smile on his lips as he raced through the corridors unhesitatingly, even eagerly, towards the final confrontation.

chapter twelve

Keill came to an abrupt stop as he entered the wide passageway that led, at its far end, to the door into the asteroid's recreation room. The corridor was empty and silent, the door firmly closed.

His mind worked at computer speed, seeking a possible battle plan. He knew the Deathwing would be waiting for him inside, expecting him. Somehow he had to go through that door and into some kind of cover without thirteen weapons cutting him to pieces.

A faint scuffling sound at his back interrupted his thoughts. He was already whirling and leaping before the green-tunicked Golvician, who had entered the corridor behind him, realized that the scrape of boots had betrayed him. The man went down, under the axe-blade edge of Keill's hand, with a faint look of puzzlement on his face.

Keill looked down at the body, toying with a thought. It had worked for him once before, and though he wouldn't fool the Deathwing for more than a second or two, that might be all the time he needed.

It was worth a try. Swiftly he tore off the spacesuit that he still wore, and wrenched the tunic from the soldier crumpled at his feet. The tunic was bulky and loose, even when worn over Keill's own uniform. He transferred his guns and his two remaining grenades to his belt, inside the tunic, and closed only one of the tunic's fastenings, so that he could reach the weapons easily. Then he placed the heavy helmet on his head, and was about to move away when his eye was caught by a small detail of the Golvician uniform.

The seams of the trousers carried a kind of trimming, or piping – a stiff, tight roll of fabric, formed into a stout cord, very light in colour. It looked a little like another kind of pale-coloured cord in his recent experience . . .

Steely fingers ripped away a length of the piping from the fallen man's uniform. Then Keill removed the helmet and twined the cord round his head, knotting it firmly at the back, before replacing the helmet. The cord was clearly visible, tight across his brow.

Ready at last, he strode calmly down the corridor towards the door to the recreation room. As he moved, he forced all expression out of his face, made his eyes blank and empty.

He knew that he was relying on illusion, but he also knew that he did not need to maintain it for long. He was counting on the fact that people did not always look at the faces of men in familiar uniforms – not at once, anyway. The Deathwing eyes would be drawn to the green Golvician tunic and helmet – and to the cord, the imitation of the Arachnis tendril.

By the time any of them had seen past these superficialities, it might well be too late for them.

His expression as dead as that of the robot Keill had been, he reached up and knocked with metallic resonance on the door.

There was a pause. Then the door slid slightly open, and to one side of the opening Keill saw a flash of scarlet. So Marska had come to answer the knock – and was sensibly staying out of any line of fire.

But she had in turn glimpsed the green uniform, perhaps had even noted the cord showing beneath the helmet.

'A soldier, alone,' she snapped, obviously speaking to others in the room behind her. She moved slightly more into Keill's view. 'What do you want?'

Wordlessly, Keill stepped into the room.

It was low-ceilinged and spacious, as he remembered. When he had seen it, it had been furnished with several heavy, comfortably cushioned bench seats, along with a scattering of small tables, free-standing light fixtures and a few vid-screens and tape-viewers. Now some of the furniture had been pulled back, clustered together to form something of a barricade, leaving a broad open space between it and the door.

All that Keill noted during his first step into the room.

'What do you *want*?' Marska repeated, her voice showing both puzzlement and irritation.

Another stride forward. The woman in scarlet began to step away from the door as well, beside him, reaching out to grasp his arm. By then, though his eyes seemed wholly blank and motionless, Keill had scanned the Deathwing and their defences.

Some of them were grouped behind their makeshift barricade on the far side of the room. Four or five of them there, he estimated, though others might be hidden from his view. The rest were scattered more widely, though just as well protected. Near the corner farthest from Keill, he glimpsed the lustre of gold, and knew where The One was.

Predictable, he thought wryly. That corner held the only other exit from the room.

Another stride forward.

The woman in scarlet had grasped his arm by then, and tried to halt him, but he resisted the tug of her skeletal hand. One or two of the others were half-rising, peering towards him. He saw the bulky figure of the black-bearded dwarf, with his mirror armour, and next to him the ugly pair with the reptilian green hide. There too was the man with the long monkey arms, crouched half out of sight.

Very like the Battle Rites, a part of Keill's mind said, remembering the odd collection of mutants in the arena in Banthei.

The rest of his mind was concentrating hard. Only a fractional second remained, he knew, before the illusion broke. But his three paces into the room had brought him close to one of the heavy bench seats that had not been taken into the Deathwing barricade. Its bulk of metal and plastic might protect him, too, for a while. If he could just make one more step . . .

But his time had run out.

Marska had continued to advance with him, black eyes peering suspiciously from the stark white face. Suddenly the expression on that face changed, and her harsh voice rang out.

'It's you! *Randor!*'

She started to fling herself back, started to snap her arm up, to release the blazing death of a fireball from the heavy bracelet at her wrist. But Keill had begun to react before her first word was fully spoken. He grasped Marska and swung her around in front of him, just as the fireball erupted. It blazed towards the far corner, sending three of the Deathwing diving for cover as it exploded against the wall. Then, lifting Marska's skinny body, he flung himself forward, holding her like a shield, towards the bench seat.

Some of the Deathwing were quicker than others, and almost as quick as Keill. Three energy beams blasted towards him as he leaped. Two missed entirely – but the third stabbed into the narrow body of Marska.

As she screamed in her death-pain, Keill hurled her aside and dived headlong into the welcome shelter of the bench. Even as he struck the floor, one of his two remaining grenades was sailing towards the barricade.

The floor trembled with the shock of the explosion. Then the air of the room seemed to be filled with the crackling blaze of energy guns, the crash and flame of other weapons, and the pain-filled cries of those whom the grenade had left alive.

Odds cut down a bit more, Keill thought grimly. But I can't stay here forever.

He shrugged swiftly out of the heavy green tunic, and flung the helmet and cord off his head. His guns seemed to spring into his hands. Already the cushions were aflame on the bench sheltering him, and the metal and plastic were beginning to melt under the withering onslaught of the Deathwing weapons.

But suddenly the firing halted. And the silence was filled with the hollow shout of The One.

'You are going to die, *now*, Randor! Look – see the form your death will take!'

Letting no more than an eye show past the edge of the half-destroyed bench, Keill looked. And sickness welled up within him.

Advancing openly towards him across the room came an aged man, with a deeply lined face and a straggle of white hair, his tall but stooped body draped in the folds of a long, plain robe.

Talis.

The heavy cowled hood of the robe was thrown back. So Keill could not only see the old face for the first time, but could also see with revulsion the thin, pale cord wrapped around the wrinkled brow.

Talis, enslaved by the Arachnis link, controlled by the Twenty-four – advancing on Keill with an energy gun clutched in both of the long, thin hands.

The gun blazed. The beam bit deeply into the floor, a few centimetres from where Keill lay.

The Deathwing will be enjoying this, Keill thought bleakly. Sending Talis to be my executioner, knowing that I'm not likely to shoot him.

But while they're enjoying themselves, he thought, they'll relax a little. Maybe just enough.

Talis's gun fired again, the beam burning deeply into what was left of the bench protecting Keill. As it did so, Keill replaced his left-hand gun at his belt, and slid the fingers of that hand under the heavy metal base of the bench. It was free-standing, he was relieved to find, not fixed to the floor. He gathered his strength, sought the leverage he needed.

Then in one smooth surge of power he came up off the floor, bringing the bench with him, upended. And in the same movement he flung it into the path of the advancing Talis.

The old man tumbled reflexively backwards, losing his balance as he tried to avoid the toppling bulk of the bench. And Keill dived – one hand slapping on to the floor, the arm forming a rigid pivot as he swung his body around horizontally, and swept Talis's feet from under him.

Talis crashed down, the gun spinning from his hand, the white head cracking painfully on the floor, stunning him.

Sorry, old friend, Keill thought. There was no other way.

But the speed of his movement left the thought behind. He had let the sweep of his body continue so that he came, crouched and ready, to his feet. His left-hand gun leaped again into his hand, and both weapons blazed out their fiery death. The battle fury surged within him as he hurled himself forward against the Deathwing.

He was a shadow, a whirlwind, a blur of non-stop motion at the utmost limits of his almost inhuman speed. As he moved he was spinning, swivelling, dodging – he was half-falling, rolling, springing up again – he was leaping, whirling, twisting . . . The room was criss-crossed with the flaming beams of Deathwing guns – yet they slashed through empty air, for somehow, miraculously, Keill was never there.

And yet also, somehow, within the dizzying, blinding speed of his rush, his own guns were finding their marks. Two more of the Deathwing fell with charred and gaping wounds in their bodies, in the first micro-seconds of that storming charge.

The others were leaping away from the barricade, striving to regroup themselves in the face of that awesome attack, when Keill came among them.

If he had been a whirlwind before, now he was a tornado. Still at the eye-baffling upper limit of his spinning, twisting, hurtling motion, the computer-swift mind of a fighting legionary wove a smooth pattern of destruction among the Deathwing group. Yet the Deathwing too were fighting for their lives.

Out of the wild mêlée a hand struck at Keill wielding the white-hot blade of a therm-knife. But the edge of Keill's hand blocked the blow and broke the wrist that struck it, while as part of the same motion one of his guns sliced another attacker nearly in half.

The long-armed monkey-man sprang on to Keill's back, un-natural fingers clutching for his throat. But Keill reached back to

436

grasp one wiry wrist, and smoothly flung the man over his head, hearing bones crack as the man struck the far wall.

Out of the midst of the furious battle Keill saw the flashing movement of the reptilian mutants, saw the glitter of the two blood-roses leaving their hands, razor-sharp circular blades spinning with deadly speed. But Keill was already flowing into a perfect back somersault, and firing to both sides at once, so that the green-skinned killers were falling, their scaly chests half-incinerated, before the blades passed through the spot where Keill had been.

The whole onslaught, from the beginning of Keill's charge, lasted only a few seconds. And then Keill was alone, leaping away from a heap of twisted, bloody corpses, towards the door at the far end of the room.

His computer mind had already done its sums. Three Deathwing agents out of action at the first, from the grenade; Marska making four; and now seven more overwhelmed in that terrible close-quarters slaughter.

That left two – who had discovered the better part of valour, and were making a dash for the far door. One of them was the bearded, armoured dwarf.

And the other, well in the lead, was the towering golden figure of The One.

Keill went after them in a headlong rush.

The dwarf wheeled, raising the short baton that was his preferred weapon – the heat-wand. Keill's body arrowed forward in a smooth, flat dive, one hand taking the impact, as the wand flared. The narrow ray of unbearable heat hissed harmlessly over his head, and Keill's gun fired at once in reply.

But when his beam struck, he realized the nature of the dwarf's shiny armour. The mirror-bright substance deflected the energy beam, harmlessly, to one side.

Surprise might have delayed some men for a fatal instant, as the heat-ray blazed once more. But the reactions of a legionary are not slowed by surprise. Even as he rolled smoothly aside from the ray,

Keill fired again – into the centre of the dwarf's unprotected face.

As face and beard vanished in a bloom of flame, Keill was up and running, slamming out through the door that had allowed The One to escape.

An empty corridor.

He flung himself along it, towards the end that formed a T with two branching passages. Both empty.

But one of the side passages led to a dead end, and another bulky metal door. And was there a hint of some sound beyond the door? An eerie sound, like the whisper of a distant wind, just on the threshold of hearing?

He was at the door and through it in an instant. And then he stopped, rooted, his blood seeming to congeal into ice.

It was as if he had stepped back in time. He found himself on a narrow metal gantry, stretching across one side of a broad, deep, metal-lined shaft, where strange energies glowed and radiated.

From the depths of the shaft, yet reaching high above the gantry where Keill stood frozen, rose the thousands of writhing, flailing, seeking tendrils of Arachnis.

But there was something else – something immeasurably worse.

In the air above the shaft, the air that was sickeningly alive with the threshing tendrils, he saw Glr – with a hundred or more of the tendrils coiled and tangled round her.

One wing was still partly free, but was beating only feebly, as the monstrous tangle drew her down.

Down towards the blazing luminescence of pure, lethal energy that surrounded the body of Arachnis.

chapter thirteen

Keill's frozen pause ended as soon as it began. He sprang forward to the gantry railing, his guns blazing. The withering beam swept like a scythe through the tangled cluster of tendrils that held Glr, slashing at them again and again.

As the severed ends fell away, Glr's wings came free. They thrust down with thunderous power, lifting her up as Keill swung the searing blaze of his guns across other tendrils that groped up towards her.

At the same time, he was weaving and dodging at the gantry's edge, for more of the tendrils had writhed their way in his direction. He needed all his self-control to keep from flinching back, as he remembered how those filaments had found a grip on him once before – and what had then followed . . .

Yet his primary concern was for Glr. If her mind had been trapped by the Arachnis link, if only for a moment, she would now be in the grip of that shattering agony of sudden release.

But as she wheeled towards the gantry, wings booming, her voice came into his mind, seeming unaffected.

Get back, Keill, while you can!

But Keill stood his ground. Wielding one gun in scythe-sweeps across the tendrils that lashed in his direction, he leaned over and fired the other beam in a steady burst down into the well of the shaft. As he did so, he saw with a jolt of surprise that the Arachnis monster, glowing in all the shifting colours of the luminous energy around it, had grown immensely. The ovoid shape now filled the entire breadth of the shaft, and bulged upwards almost to the height of the gantry.

Surprise also jolted him when the furious beam of his energy-gun had no effect, except to create a small patch of extra brightness where it struck the rippling blaze of the energized surface.

No use! Glr cried as she wheeled above him, evading the clutching grasp of more tendrils. *It lives on energy!*

Keill nodded to himself. The energies that bathed Arachnis did not extend upwards to protect the tendrils, but would certainly absorb the blast of his gun when aimed at the body of the matter. At once he shifted the crackling beam of his gun to the wall of the shaft itself, which held the complex mechanisms and power sources that were the monster's life support. But the energized metal showed no more effect than had Arachnis itself.

Keill's left-hand gun was still sweeping its beam back and forth through the air, to keep the grasping tendrils at bay from himself and Glr. It seemed that for every dozen that he cut down, several dozens more flailed up to take their place. There must have been hundreds upon hundreds of thousands, now, of the tendril extensions from the vastly enlarged body of Arachnis.

And if neither the body nor the shaft that supported it could be harmed . . . how could it be destroyed?

Below him he saw the ends of the tendrils he had severed, drifting down to the upper surface of the monster. They vanished at once, vaporized in a flare of radiance by those swirling luminous energies.

Come away! Glr's voice entered his mind like a whip. *Guns are no use against it – but it is helpless without the Twenty-four!*

Her broad wings swept her towards the door that had led Keill on to the gantry, and he followed her at once. Of course she was right. Even though Arachnis could not be harmed by a hand-gun – and maybe not even by my ship's guns, he thought bleakly – it was not the true enemy.

If he could find the Twenty-four and deal with them, Arachnis would no longer be guided by a superintelligence, and would be rendered nearly harmless.

If . . .

Outside the door they paused. Glr wheeled down to settle on his shoulder, small fingers clutching him in a fierce clasp.

I feared that the massed force of the Deathwing might be too much even for you, she said.

Keill smiled fiercely. 'They may have thought the same. Shows the danger of over-confidence.' Then his expression grew serious. 'But how did you get tangled with Arachnis?'

I was coming by another route, Glr replied, annoyance in her voice, *to see if I could aid you. But before I reached you, The One burst out of the room – and when he began firing at me, I fled. The door I chose led to Arachnis, and it caught me before I could escape.*

'And your mind . . ?' Keill asked worriedly.

The Arachnis link is made to enslave human minds, Glr laughed. *I shielded against it with no difficulty. That is why the Twenty-four were using it to drag me down and kill me with its energies – until you came along.*

'That's more of my debt repaid,' Keill said. His mouth tightened. 'And there are still some debts to pay here, before we're done.'

Glr agreed. *The One has joined the Twenty-four,* she announced. *I can sense their minds, though I cannot look into them.*

'Where are they?' Keill asked urgently. He had seen no sign of a spacious alcove in the wall of the Arachnis shaft, as there had been on Golvic.

On the other side of the shaft wall, Glr told him. *The heavier tendrils that link them to Arachnis now pass through the base of the wall.*

Into his mind she projected a picture, a diagrammatic map of the asteroid's interior. A glowing spot of light indicated a spacious room – close by, and on the same level where Keill was standing.

'Right,' Keill said quietly. 'I'll go and visit them.'

Keill, we must be careful . . . Glr began.

'Not *we*,' Keill interrupted. He gestured towards the door to the recreation room, down the corridor, where smoke was drifting out, a hint of the carnage that had occurred within it. 'Talis is in there – probably still unconscious, but alive. He's an Arachnis slave, like you said. You must help him.'

Glr was quiet for a moment. *I would like to come with you*, she said at last, *but you are right. Talis needs me.*

'You *can* free him, safely?' Keill asked.

I believe so. He is old, but his mind is strong and clear. And he has not been under their control as long as you were. He should survive.

'Good.' Keill grinned tautly. 'I'll try to do the same.'

Keill. Glr's voice was heavy with concern. *The Twenty-four will be much more powerful, now that Arachnis has enlarged so greatly. I can sense terrible strengths within their united mind. And they and The One will be waiting for you.*

'I know,' Keill said harshly. 'I'm counting on it.'

Once again, Keill plunged into the network of corridors. But this time his route was more direct – and he met no opposition on his way to the room that Glr's mental map had indicated.

Its door was tightly shut. And Keill was well aware that ruses or disguises would be no use, this time. There was only one way in – just as there had been only one way for his ship, into the asteroid. A flat-out, frontal assault.

He plucked his fourth and last grenade from his belt, and readied his energy guns. Not a great deal of firepower left, he knew – but he would probably be facing only whatever weapon The One was carrying. It was unlikely that the Twenty-four would join a fire-fight. They were generals, not soldiers.

In any case, he would tackle The One bare-handed, if necessary. He had done so before.

With a snap of the wrist he sent the grenade spinning towards the metal door, and dodged back from the bludgeoning force of the explosion.

Then, as billowing smoke and flame clogged the opening where the door had been, he sprang through.

At once he swerved to his right, letting himself fall to the side, his gun seeking a target through the dark clouds of smoke.

There, directly ahead . . . A huge, looming figure of golden metal.

He was firing in the instant that he saw it. And despite his swift sideways motion, his balance and accuracy sent his beam directly at the heart of the golden giant.

At it – and through it, harmlessly, as if it was not there.

And in the next instant, it no longer *was* there. The golden figure faded and vanished, leaving Keill staring at empty air.

Then cruel, hollow laughter sounded from beyond the smoke cloud.

And from it an energy beam crackled – and blazed agonizingly into the flesh of Keill's left shoulder.

He spun, half-falling, one gun dropping from suddenly nerveless fingers. And the hollow voice sounded again.

'Throw the other gun behind you, Randor, out of the room, or my next shot will remove your head!'

Slowly, cold anger rising within him, Keill tossed his other gun away, and turned in the direction of the voice. As he did so, Glr's worried voice came to him.

Keill . . .?

'*I'm all right,*' he said grimly. '*They used some kind of illusion.*'

An image, projected by the Twenty-four, Glr said. *Keill, the growth of Arachnis has awakened a huge telepathic power in their mind. I sense it clearly – and there is no way of telling what it can do!*

'*All right,*' Keill said. '*It's my problem now. You get Talis to the ship.*'

He stood still, balanced and ready, forcing himself to ignore the livid pain of his seared arm, as the last of the smoke cleared.

He saw a broad, sparsely furnished room, with one wall that was entirely transparent – through which he could see the loathsome, flailing tendrils of Arachnis, and the upper bulge of its glowing body.

He saw, near the opposite wall, the seated figures of the Twenty-four, in their chairs round the bulky console of their life-support, from which the twenty-four cable-like tendrils reached out to entwine round their heads.

And he saw The One stalking towards him, puffy lips parted in a vicious grin, great hands cradling an energy rifle that was trained on the centre of Keill's torso.

chapter fourteen

'Come forward,' The One said, his hollow voice gloating. 'Very slowly and carefully.'

Keill stepped farther into the room. His arm felt as if it was still on fire, but he moved it imperceptibly and found that, despite the pain, he still had some use of it. He glanced around the room again, seeking something that he might turn to his advantage.

The transparent wall panel? Clearly it was part of the shaft wall, which had looked so solid from the other side. So Golvician technology was able to polarize that metal, to make it transparent from one side, just like the wall of the cage that had carried him to Golvic.

The One followed his gaze, and his smile widened. 'Do not develop false hopes, Randor. The metal is as impervious from this side as from the other. In any case you would not enjoy making renewed contact with Arachnis.'

Keill remained silent, watchful, as he continued to move forward, poising himself.

'Stop.' The One gestured with the rifle, and Keill halted. Still too far away, he thought sourly, to try to beat that rifle.

The One looked inquiringly towards his master, and Keill looked as well. The Twenty-four were frowning slightly, exactly the same expression on the face of every one of them.

'I am displeased, Altern.' Again the unsettling sound of twenty-four soft voices speaking in perfect chorus – and again the reference to themselves as one person. 'He is far more resourceful and dangerous than you had led me to believe.'

A shadow flickered across The One's small eyes, and Keill

recognised it as fear. 'He has been fortunate, Master,' The One said defensively.

'He has escaped Arachnis, and survived,' the soft voice said. 'He has come here, fought his way through an entire detachment of militia, and wiped out the elite of the Deathwing. That is not merely good fortune. It is as well that I decided to destroy the rest of his people, if this is what one legionary can do.'

'But he has done only superficial harm,' The One insisted. 'The asteroid can be repaired, the militia are replaceable, and I can rebuild the Deathwing in no time.' The gloating smile reappeared. 'Whereas we have finished off the old fool who employed Randor, and will soon finish him off.'

'Not soon. Immediately.' A whiplash of command had entered the soft chorus of voices. 'Kill him now, where he stands.'

Keill did not seem to move, but he was gathering himself, ready for a last desperate rush.

'Master . . .' There was a pleading note in The One's voice that made Keill's skin crawl. 'You know how long this man has opposed me. Let me have my revenge more sweetly, more slowly. You may even find the process . . . amusing.'

The Twenty-four were silent for a moment. 'I understand your feeling, Altern,' they said at last. 'But you have faced him alone before, and failed to kill him.'

'True,' The One said, glowering at Keill. 'But now he has no weapon, and he is injured. And my new body is stronger and more invulnerable than the last one.'

Keill considered those words gloomily. When he had fought The One before, hand to hand, the golden armour had resisted his fiercest assaults, for a considerable time. If this replacement was even tougher . . .

But the thought broke off, as the Twenty-four came to a decision. The frown cleared from all their foreheads, at once, and twenty-four simultaneous smiles curved their lips. 'Very well. Deal with him as you wish. And if you get into difficulty, I can perform a

446

further test on the newest gift conferred on me by Arachnis.'

That would mean the telepathic power, Keill knew. Glr might know what to do about it – but there was no time to contact her. The One was lowering the energy rifle, his cruel smile broadening.

'Be grateful, Randor,' he said. 'You will have some extra moments of life after all.'

Keill watched him, expressionlessly. Here it is again, he thought – the Deathwing arrogance, the total belief in the superiority of those who follow the Warlord. That supreme over-confidence had been the undoing of the Deathwing before, in encounters with Keill. Perhaps it would be so again.

The golden giant was fumbling with the rifle, and Keill saw with surprise that he was removing the energy charge. Casually The One flung the charge into the far corner of the room – and then gripped the empty rifle and effortlessly bent it into a twisted, useless shape.

'No weapons, Randor,' he grinned savagely. 'Just our bare hands – to the death.'

But the grin on the grey face faded at once, for Keill had already begun to move. One running stride and he was launched into the air like a projectile, boots hammering forward in a ferocious drop kick. One boot slammed with crushing force into the centre of the great golden chest, where Keill knew the almost invisible seam of the armour lay. The other boot struck upward, towards the mottled flesh of the face.

But The One was protecting his face, the one exposed area of his true body. A vast golden hand had flashed upwards, to block that blow. And the battering impact of Keill's other boot, against the chest, had only staggered him.

Keill came to his feet lithely, circling away, thinking hard. The One moved much more quickly now than he had in his previous armour. And he had spoken the simple truth about the strength of his new body. That kick, Keill knew, would have damaged a plate of niconium steel. But the broad golden chest showed not a scratch.

The One raised a hand, unconsciously, to the jagged scar at the edge of his grey face – a legacy of his earlier encounter with Keill. 'You will not catch me that way again,' he snarled.

He leaped forward, hands clutching. Keill spun away out of danger, but was again surprised at how much more speed The One had acquired, as well as strength. One of the hands had grasped an edge of his tunic, and had torn the fabric as if it were paper.

Again Keill twisted and dodged away from a hurtling attack. And as he evaded the deadly grasp, his right hand chopped savagely up at the puffy face.

But The One was swift enough, turning his head so that the edge of Keill's hand struck the metal of the golden hood, and rebounded harmlessly. And Keill was barely able to fling himself backwards in time to avoid a brutal counter from one massive golden fist.

So the pattern of the battle was maintained. The One advanced, swinging swift, clubbing blows, or reaching out to clutch Keill in the terrible grip of his hands. And Keill retreated, dodging and evading, striving to find a way to make his counterattacks effective against that impervious armour.

And as the battle went on, Keill grew uneasily aware that the injury to his arm, and the huge output of energy in his earlier assault on the Deathwing, had taken a toll even on his supreme resilience. He was soon breathing heavily, and there was the faintest of sensations in the muscles of his legs that warned of the approach of exhaustion.

Time to change tactics, he thought grimly.

He had retreated most of the way across the room, and now there was a wall close to his back. As The One charged once more, Keill feinted a slash at the eyes, feinted once more as if to dodge to his right, then with blurring speed moved in towards the golden body. The One's murderous blow swept millimetres past his face – and then Keill had grasped the metal arm, adjusted his stance, and used the giant's own impetus to fling the metal bulk up in the air and over, crashing into the wall.

The One bounced up as if he had been made of rubber rather than metal. But by then Keill had turned, and was running.

Not towards the door, to escape. But towards the far corner of the room, where The One had casually flung the energy charge from his rifle.

He knew exactly how to alter the mechanism, so that the energy flow would be disrupted. The resulting explosion could kill everyone in the room. He intended to use that threat to hold The One at bay, until Glr could get there with a gun. It was his only chance . . .

His hand was just reaching down to scoop up the energy charge, when the inside of his head seemed to erupt in an explosion of enormous, intolerable pain.

It lasted for only a microsecond, before it was cut off as suddenly as if a switch had been thrown. But the brutal agony, no less overpowering than the pain when Glr had torn away the Arachnis link, had driven him to his knees, and left him momentarily dazed and shaken.

He remained where he was, trying to regather his strength, as The One stepped forward and kicked the energy charge out of reach.

'Most effective,' said the chorus of the Twenty-four. 'I had wondered if he had some special resistance, when he escaped from Arachnis. It seems not.'

The One replied, but Keill did not hear the words. He was listening to another voice – inside his head.

Keill, that was a psychic blast, Glr said rapidly. *Part of the Twenty-four's new mental power. I shielded you at once, as I did on Veynaa.*

'Can you keep it up?'

It is immensely powerful, in human terms, Glr said. *But I can withstand it. Shall I come to your aid?*

'See to Talis first,' Keill said. 'I'll try to hold out. And if I don't . . .'

The image in his mind showed Glr what he wanted. If he lost this final battle, she was to take his ship out, and use every particle of its firepower to destroy the asteroid and its occupants.

If you wish, Glr said bleakly. *But you must survive!*

'There's no law that says so,' Keill told her. 'But I won't go down easily.'

The entire exchange, at the speed of thought, had taken the briefest of moments. In that time Keill had come to his feet, fighting off the last effects of the psychic blast, as The One advanced once more.

The battle resumed. Again Keill began a blow that smoothly became a lifting hold, swinging The One off his feet and hurling him halfway across the room.

That might shake some of those mechanisms loose, inside the armour, he thought.

But as before The One came at once to his feet, unharmed, and charged back to the attack. Again Keill dodged, and gripped, and threw. Again the giant form hurtled to the floor. But first, the lunging blow of The One had found a target. Not the side of Keill's head, where it had been aimed – but the muscles of his left shoulder, only centimetres from the gaping wound in his arm.

The pain of the arm blazed up overpoweringly, and Keill staggered slightly as he fought for control. In that moment The One was upon him, swinging a terrifying kick that smashed against Keill's side.

Ordinary ribs would have been pulped, but the unbreakable alloy of Keill's bones survived the impact. Yet the immense power of it flung him back, vision blurring, half-falling at the feet of the nearest member of the Twenty-four.

He fought to clear his head. The One was advancing again,

unhurriedly, certain now that Keill was on the edge of defeat. And at the same time, the smiles widened on the faces of the Twenty-four, and they leaned slightly forward, their eyes narrowing slightly. Keill realized that they were hurling another psychic blast at him, to ensure the victory of The One.

He felt nothing, for Glr's sturdy mind-shield had operated at once. But he contorted his face as if in agony, let his body tense and convulse, then sagged limply to the floor.

The Twenty-four sat back, nodding with satisfaction. The One's advance slowed, deferring to his master. And that momentary pause was just long enough for Keill to overcome the effects of the punishing kick, and gather himself.

Without warning, he launched himself from the floor. Not towards the golden giant – but into the midst of the circle of the Twenty-four.

Simultaneous expression of shock appeared on their faces. 'Altern!' they shrieked. '*Stop him*!'

Panic-stricken, yet still moving as one, the Twenty-four struggled out of their chairs, flinging their wasted bodies towards Keill. The great tentacles of Arachnis attached to their heads twisted and tangled as they moved, impeding The One's lunging rush.

And Keill reached to the console with his right hand to clutch a handful of the thick tendrils.

They were smooth, clammy, writhing slightly in his grasp. He struggled to get a firmer grip, while sweeping his injured left arm backwards to free himself from the clawing, flailing, shrieking mass that was the Twenty-four.

The renewed pain from the movement threatened to weaken his hold on the tendrils. And then The One was plunging through the tangle of bodies, swinging a fist like a huge golden club down on to the wrist of Keill's hand, where it clutched the Arachnis tentacles.

Again Keill's vision blurred as the new pain of the bruised flesh lanced up his arm. But neither his wrist nor his grip had been broken – and still he fought to find the leverage he needed.

'Kill him, fool!' screamed the frantic Twenty-four.

The giant lunged forward again. The grey face was contorted with fury, and there was a fleck of foam at the corner of the puffy lips. The sudden, unexpected turn of events had thrown The One almost into a frenzy – and though his speed and strength remained, all caution had been flung aside.

With a heave of his shoulders Keill sent several of the Twenty-four sprawling. And in a movement too swift for any of their eyes to follow, he swung himself up and around, using his grip on the Arachnis tentacles as a pivot, and met The One's charge with a crippling smash of both boots into the giant's unguarded face.

The One fell back, crashing to the floor in a sliding, threshing clatter of metal limbs. And Keill swept the remaining members of the Twenty-four aside, and reached both hands to the tentacles of Arachnis.

But one of the Twenty-four, finding strength in terror, regained his feet. Before Keill could stop him, he had slapped his hand on to a small lever at the side of the console.

Behind Keill, the great glass panel that was one wall of the room slid smoothly open.

And a hundred, a thousand, of the writhing tendrils of Arachnis whipped in through the opening, ready to enclose Keill in their web-like trap.

He had no hope of preventing one of the tendrils from finding a grip round his brow. There was only an instant before he would again be a slave-robot of Arachnis, at the total mercy of the Twenty-four.

In that instant he wrapped both his arms round the clammy bulk of all the tentacles rising from the console, and jerked backwards, in an irresistible, balanced explosion of power.

The thick tentacles writhed, stretched – and gave way.

Their coiled ends ripped free of their grasp on the twenty-four heads.

And the Twenty-four went insane.

The screams that filled the room were no longer in chorus, but a shrill and ragged discord. The twenty-four bodies no longer moved in unison, but twisted and shuddered and convulsed in separate, agonized contortions. Some clutched their heads and curled tightly upon themselves, squealing in anguish. Some fell threshing and foaming to the floor. Some toppled silently, and lay motionless, struck instantly dead by the unbearable disruption of their union with Arachnis.

And the tendrils of the Arachnis monster, no longer directed by the united supermind of the Twenty-four, waved quietly in the air, brushing harmlessly past Keill as he watched the grisly death agonies of the Warlord.

But beyond that horror, there was a different movement. The giant golden body of The One was clambering slowly to its feet. The grey face was now a mask of red, from Keill's ferocious kick. But the metal body was intact.

Bellowing with the wordless fury of a monster run amok, The One charged.

And Keill sprang, his own battle fury rising to a crescendo, to meet the charge head-on.

He slid easily below the huge, clutching hands. He swayed away from the battering impact of the mighty body. But as he evaded, he also gripped, and held, and pivoted.

The One's charge provided the momentum, and Keill provided the strength and leverage. He came smoothly up from his crouch – and The One came up with him.

For a fragmentary second, like the isolated single frame of a film that freezes an action for the blink of an eye, the golden giant hung suspended in the air, supported by the steely rigidity of Keill's extended arms.

And then the throw was completed, and The One flew in a smooth arc through the air – hurtling out through the open panel in the wall, into the blazing, luminous embrace of Arachnis.

When Keill reached the window, a second later, he saw the huge body lying on the bulging upper surface of the monster. The arms and legs were struggling weakly, as the furious energies that bathed Arachnis bit deep into the golden armour.

In another instant the metal began to melt and run. Keill saw the central seam of the armour gape open – and inside, he glimpsed the deformed limbs of The One's true body, writhing in agony. Then they were gone, and only crisped and blackened fragments remained.

And almost at once the whole ghastly sight ceased to exist, as the energies of Arachnis reached the power source within the golden armour, and what was left of The One vanished in an eruption of light and flame and vaporized metal.

Aftermath
chapter fifteen

Below the sculptured sweep of a broad patio, shaped from glistening translucent stone, the ocean extended to the distant haze of the horizon – a calm, turquoise ocean, the precise mirror image of the calm, turquoise sky of the planet Arkadie. The patio was bathed in the sun's warmth, the unique spicy fragrance of the ocean, and the unbroken silent tranquillity for which Arkadie was famous over half the galaxy.

Keill Randor lay at the patio's edge, on a body-contoured recliner, letting the sun put the finishing touches on the task of healing his injuries. High above the patio, Glr soared in leisurely circles, relishing the gentle currents of air beneath her wide wings.

But part of her attention was focused, worriedly, on Keill. During the weeks of their stay on Arkadie he had been growing more and more silent, withdrawn. Glr was increasingly disturbed by his seeming inability to wrench himself out of a gloom that she did not fully understand.

At the moment, her telepathic perception told her, he was once again reliving those last climactic moments on the asteroid . . .

He drew back from the volcanic blast of energy that signalled the death of The One. Around him, the bodies of the Twenty-four had stilled – some dead, the rest with minds shattered beyond repair. As he moved to the door of the chamber, sparing them only a glance, weariness and pain nearly made him stagger. But even so he did not make his way directly to his ship.

Instead he went again into the bowels of the asteroid, to the life-support area. There he found tools, and worked for several moments among the complex machinery. Only then did he retrace his steps towards his ship.

Entering, he brushed aside Glr's mixture of concern over his wounds and delight at his victory, and went to kneel by an improvised sleep-pad that she had placed behind the slingseats, for old Talis. There was no pale cord now around the white head – and though the aged face bore deeper lines, etched by the agonizing removal of the Arachnis link, Talis's eyes were open. And they were focused on Keill.

'Thank . . . you . . .' The whisper was barely audible.

Keill nodded, and clasped the thin old shoulder. '*Will he live?*' he asked Glr silently.

With my help, she assured him. *Which you need as well.*

'*Shortly*,' Keill said. '*When the job is done.*'

He sank into his slingseat, reaching for the controls. Thunder erupted from the retros, and the ship's hull creaked ominously as Keill poured on power. But the sealing substance, gripping the ship within the gap in the asteroid's skin, gave way first. And the ship blasted out of the gap, arrowing away into space.

Glr had only begun to ask her question when Keill gestured to the rear viewscreens, the only screens still operating. 'Watch,' he said aloud. 'I rigged a feedback loop in the power energizer . . .'

No further explanation was needed.

In the screens the asteroid seemed to tremble. Orange flame gouted from the gap where Keill's ship had been.

And then the entire substance of the asteroid was swallowed up in a gigantic, convulsive detonation. It filled the screens like a mini-nova – and the shock wave swept the ship even farther away, in a titanic blast of force.

When the aftershocks died away, the screens were nearly empty. Even the cluster of space rubble that had been trailing the asteroid had been scattered over millions of kilometres by the blast. And the asteroid itself, with all its contents – including the Arachnis monster – had been wholly destroyed, disintegrated, in that final cataclysm. Only a ghostly cloud of space dust now drifted, silent, amid the emptiness.

And then at last Keill closed his eyes, and let his body sag into the slingseat . . .

Afterwards Glr had been very busy. Much of the time she was reaching into the mind of old Talis, as she had done with Keill, sending her soothing, healing telepathic presence to repair the damage done by the breaking of the Arachnis link. At the same time, outwardly, she was using all the resources of the ship's medikit on Keill's injuries, especially the terrible charred gouge in his left shoulder.

And meanwhile she had set the ship's computer guidance and sent it into Overlight, towards a planet that Keill had once told her of. Arkadie, planet of the endless summer, where the environment and the people created a haven of peace and tranquillity that was deemed priceless by its galactic visitors.

There time and proper medical care had completed the healing that Glr had begun. Talis himself recovered enough to use his own supreme medical knowledge to patch Keill's arm wound, grafting muscle fibre and skin, so that the arm would be restored as good as new. And since then the three of them had simply enjoyed Arkadie – the rest, the peace, the ease of undemanding days.

Except . . . there was the darkness within Keill, growing more worrisome for Glr as each balmy day progressed.

Now, from her soaring height, she saw Talis striding on to the patio towards Keill. She curved her wings and swooped down, settling on the patio's balustrade as Talis came up.

'I have good news,' the old man was saying. 'It may even brighten your mood.'

I trust something will, Glr said tartly. Because of their proximity, she could project into both minds at once.

Keill glanced at her with a crooked smile. 'Am I being as glum as all that?'

457

The stones of this patio, Glr replied, *have been brighter company.*

Talis smiled, then turned his amiable gaze on Keill. 'If you could tell us what is troubling you, we might be able to help.'

'If I knew,' Keill said with a shrug, 'I'd help myself.'

'Perhaps it is nothing,' Talis said thoughtfully.

Keill and Glr both looked at him, surprised and puzzled.

'I mean it literally. Perhaps the trouble is that there is no trouble.'

Keill shook his head tiredly. 'I don't understand that.'

'It seems obvious,' Talis said. 'Since the death of your world you have lived with danger. You have searched the galaxy for the murderer of the Legions. You have fought terrible battles. And finally you have confronted the Warlord and his minions, and destroyed them. Now it is over. You have nothing left to search for, nothing to fight.'

'You may be right.' Keill's voice was low and bleak. 'I've been thinking about Moros lately – more than for a long time. And I've been feeling a little . . . lost.'

'Vengeance is very single-minded,' Talis said gravely. 'It can spur a man to great deeds – but when it is done, it leaves an emptiness behind, a vacuum.'

'That's me,' Keill said.

'Just so,' Talis went on. 'You are a warrior, and you have won your war. Now you feel you have no purpose – and you cannot even go home, for you have no home. Nowhere to go, nothing to do.'

And so, Glr put in acidly, *you sink so far into depression and self-pity that even I cannot drag you out.*

Keill swung round sharply – but the glare in his eyes died away, replaced by a rueful smile.

'All right, I suppose I deserve that. But now you've identified the disease, what's the cure?'

Keill, there is an entire galaxy out there, filled with peculiar and fascinating things. We can go and look at them!

Again Keill shook his head. 'I've had enough planet-hopping for a while. Anyway, I can't just go wandering. I have to pay my way. But the only way I know is the Legion way – and I've had enough fighting, too, to last me a while.'

'But that is my good news!' Talis interrupted. 'You know that I have been in touch with the other Overseers. And we have been making certain . . . inquiries.' A smile lit up the wrinkled face. 'Keill, there were many sizeable fees still owed to the Legions, for their services, when Moros was destroyed. We have traced them, and I am arranging to collect them – for you, the sole surviving legionary. You will be a very wealthy young man.'

Keill stared at him for a long moment. 'I . . . I don't know what to say . . .'

While you grope through the mud in your head for words of gratitude, Glr said, *I have an idea for you.* Her round eyes gleamed. *If you have had enough of this galaxy, we can leave it. We can go to mine, and meet my people, the Ehrlil. You will find the experience improving.*

Keill turned his dazed stare towards her. 'What are you talking about? You know I'd never make it.'

Talis nodded in agreement, well aware that the empty grey void of Overlight had a dire effect on the human mind, over a long period of time. And the incalculable distance between galaxies required a ship to be in Overlight for months. Even a legionary's disciplined mind would crumple, during such a voyage.

Glr sighed. *I know how weak humans are. But remember that I have grown very familiar with what passes for your mind, Keill. I could place you in a temporary coma, and you would sleep peacefully between the galaxies.*

Keill's eyes widened. 'Suspended animation? You could do that?'
Easily. I might even manage Talis as well, if he would join us.

Talis raised a long hand with a laugh. 'I am too old, and have been hidden away for too long. I wish nothing more than to go back to a normal life, in this galaxy.'

But Keill scarcely heard him. He was sitting up, gazing unseeing into the distance, excitement flooding through him. If the barrier of distance could be lifted . . . The thought of it! Another galaxy . . . meeting the Ehrlil . . . seeing alien worlds that no human eye had ever rested on before . . .

And while we are there, Glr broke in, *I could ask my people to design a ship – suitable for <u>both</u> of us. With an Ehrlil drive that can cross between galaxies in weeks, not months.* Her wings flared excitedly. *Think of that, Keill – other galaxies, a whole universe of wonders and adventures!*

Keill seemed stunned. Slowly he turned to Talis, who smiled and nodded with encouragement. Then he looked back at Glr – and a wide grin spread across his face.

'That's it,' he said at last. 'That's what we'll do. We'll go and look at the universe!'

Older Piccolo fiction you will enjoy

○ **Deenie**		£1.25p
○ **It's Not the End of the World**	Judy Blume	£1.25p
○ **Tiger Eyes**		£1.25p
○ **Scottish Hauntings**	Grant Campbell	£1.25p
○ **The Gruesome Book**	Ramsey Campbell	£1.00p
○ **Blue Baccy**		£1.25p
○ **Go Tell it to Mrs Golightly**		£1.25p
○ **Matty Doolin**	Catherine Cookson	£1.25p
○ **Mrs Flannagan's Trumpet**		£1.25p
○ **Our John Willie**		£1.25p
○ **The Animals of Farthing Wood**	Colin Dann	£1.75p
○ **The Borribles**	Michael de Larrabeiti	£1.50p
○ **Goodnight Stories**	Meryl Doney	£1.25p
○ **The Vikings**	Mikael Esping	£1.00p
○ **This School is Driving Me Crazy**	Nat Hentoff	£1.25p
○ **Alien Worlds**		£1.25p
○ **Day of the Starwind**		£1.25p
○ **Deathwing over Veynaa**		£1.25p
○ **Galactic Warlord**	Douglas Hill	£1.25p
○ **The Huntsman**		£1.25p
○ **Planet of the Warlord**		£1.25p
○ **The Young Legionary**		£1.25p
○ **Coyote the Trickster**	Douglas Hill and Gail Robinson	95p
○ **Haunted Houseful**	Alfred Hitchcock	£1.10p

○	**A Pistol in Greenyards**	} Mollie Hunter	£1.50p
○	**The Stronghold**		£1.25p
○	**Which Witch?**	Eva Ibbotson	£1.25p
○	**Astercote**	Penelope Lively	£1.25p
○	**The Children's Book of Comic Verse**	Christopher Logue	£1.25p
○	**Gangsters, Ghosts and Dragonflies**	Brian Patten	£1.50p
○	**The Cats**	Joan Phipson	£1.25p
○	**The Yearling**	M. K. Rawlings	£1.50p
○	**The Red Pony**	John Steinbeck	£1.25p
○	**The Story Spirits**	A. Williams-Ellis	£1.00p

All these books are available at your local bookshop or newsagent, or can be ordered direct from the publisher. Indicate the number of copies required and fill in the form below   12

....

Name_____
(Block letters please)

Address_____

_____

Send to CS Department, Pan Books Ltd,
PO Box 40, Basingstoke, Hants
Please enclose remittance to the value of the cover price plus:
35p for the first book plus 15p per copy for each additional book
ordered to a maximum charge of £1.25 to cover postage and
packing
Applicable only in the UK

While every effort is made to keep prices low, it is sometimes
necessary to increase prices at short notice. Pan Books reserve the
right to show on covers and charge new retail prices which may
differ from those advertised in the text or elsewhere